She Whom I Love

Tess Bowery

This is a work of fiction. Similarities to real people, places, or events are entirely coincidental.

SHE WHOM I LOVE

First Edition, 2018.

ISBN: 978-1-7753003-1-1

Written by Tess Bowery.

http://tessbowery.com

Dedication

To EB, NF, MA, RS, RM and VR, for always pushing me to do better. Your initials don't spell anything cool.

Contents

But why should I begg more Love,
when as thou
Dost wooe my soule for hers;
offring all thine

John Donne, "Holy Sonnet #17"

Chapter One

Emmeline: Tell me now, for you must! As Viscountess I order you, and that you must obey. [stamps her foot] ~~Diclose~~ Disclose your name and purpose here, or I'll call for the guards.

Cynthia: I would not except that you have ordered me direct; ~~I throw myself upon your mercy~~ you find me here in dire straits. Until a fortnight ago, when he did discharge me most cruelly, your husband's mistress have I been ~~for six months time~~ this whole past year—

"Miss Armand!"

The call echoed through the garret, the burst of sound cutting through the silence previously broken only by the scratching of Sarah's quill. She sat up, startled, knocking the inkbottle with her elbow. It teetered but didn't spill, only a slashed line in the middle of Cynthia's long-winded explanation left as evidence of Sarah's surprise.

A hurried knock followed the rush of footsteps down the hall. Ellen, the newest housemaid, peeked around the door, her mouse-brown hair mostly hidden beneath her cap.

"Miss Armand, Lady Horlock is back, and she requests that you attend at once!"

Sarah sanded the pages, shook the dust off and crammed the probably still-damp script into the small box alongside her battered, nicked and ancient pen, dull nibs and watered ink. The box went under her bed, her hands flew to her head to make sure that her linen cap was on straight and tidy and she dashed out of the tiny garret room as though the hounds of hell themselves were behind her.

It wasn't entirely metaphor.

"They're back early?" she hissed, and Ellen fell in step beside her. "What happened?"

The Earl and Countess of Horlock shouldn't have been back from their outing for another hour, at the very least. That should have been plenty of time to prepare her ladyship's clothes for dinner, do a handful of minor repairs to buttons and sock heels and still have a quarter of an hour or so to steal for herself. Those moments of leisure were coming fewer and further between these days, as the spring days grew longer and preparations to move down to London for the Season were moving into full swing. Cynthia and Emmeline's budding alliance would have to wait.

"His lordship turned his ankle in a rabbit hole." Ellen was young and green enough that she made a show of rolling her eyes, even though they were on the back stairs where anyone on the staff could run across them. "He's in the drawing room with his leg up now; Jack's gone to call for Dr. Woodrow, and I'm to get Mrs. Colby to make up a poultice."

Sarah sighed inside. "Watch you don't make faces around anyone else," she warned Ellen, both out of altruism and a vague but distant fondness for girls new to service. "One tale told and you'll be out on that aproned rump of yours." Ellen groaned at the reminder and Sarah ignored her. She hurried down the stairs, fixing her cap at her hairline and her foreign accent in her mind.

A step out into the main rooms, and she was no longer Sarah-from-Cheapside, but Sophie, a lady's maid born to service for the elite, and *very* fashionably French.

And God help me if the style ever changes to having German maids.

Groans and muffled conversation from downstairs proved that Horlock had indeed taken to the settee in a huff, Brookes—his tall, ancient, disapproving scarecrow of a valet—in attendance. The doors to Lady Horlock's rooms on the second floor stood open, the redoubtable mistress of the house sitting at her dressing table. Her gray hair was still up in the coils that Sarah had so painstakingly pinned in place that morning, and her pinched face displayed her general level of disappointment with the world.

Oh, this is going to be bloody fantastic, this is.

"Armand." Lady Horlock looked her up and down. "It took you long enough. Help me off with these ridiculous riding clothes." She made no move to be useful, sitting at her dressing table and drumming her fingers on the surface in irritation while Sarah unpinned her hat and set it aside. "Horlock's gone and made a mess of the day. I suppose it was only to be expected, those great oafs jumping about like they were bucks in their prime. But at the very least, it's not a permanent injury." She mitigated her own complaint, the lines around her eyes and between her brow smoothing out somewhat.

Lady Horlock stood, just as Sarah's fingers were fussing with the buttons beneath her chin, so naturally the moment most likely to cause discomfort and further annoyance. She looked down at Sarah's hands, disapproval twisting her lip into a scowl.

"Is that ink on your fingers? Good heavens, Armand, I expect better from you," the countess scolded. "What on earth have you been doing?"

Writing a play all about the upper crust, your ladyship, and the bloody foolishness you lot get up to on the regular.

"Washing bills, m'lady," she lied instead, curling the offending fingers into her palms. "And a list for the new maid. She can read better than she can remember things."

Lady Horlock didn't seem particularly fussed about Ellen's memory. "Well, for God's sake, next time use pencil. I don't know what the world is coming to, when we waste good ink on maids and washing bills!" She lifted her arms and let Sarah tug the dark green riding habit from her shoulders, the velvet deliciously soft against Sarah's palms. She resisted the urge to stroke it, setting the gown aside. The mud splatters around the hem would need to dry before they could be beaten off. "Come, get me out of this nonsense; a dressing gown next. Master Tibbert will be coming over this afternoon to do the fittings for my new pairs of stays, and I dread the notion of getting dressed and undressed a half-dozen times in one afternoon. It's not as though we were in Town."

"New pairs, *madame*?" In the plural?

"Indeed so. One cannot approach a Season in old underpinnings, regardless of whether one is eligible or otherwise engaged. It simply isn't done."

The question of who, besides Sarah, Horlock and the master staymaker himself, would ever see the countess' underpinnings was left thankfully unbroached.

She had the countess ready, her dressing gown tied about her waist over her older stays and her hair redressed, by the time a bell jangled at the front door. "That will be Tibbert now." Lady Horlock glanced out the window, setting down her embroidery.

Sarah, her arms filled with the endless yardage of velvet riding habit, paused at the door. "Shall I go or stay, *madame*?"

"Stay," came the order. "I shan't be alone with Master Tibbert and his journeyman; it wouldn't be proper. Who knows what kind of gossip could be spread about!" Sarah eyed Lady Horlock with skepticism. She was old, true, but still pretty enough, if one liked the older, regal-looking sort. She could use another ten pounds on her to flesh out the pinched lines of her face, but since half of that came from her semi-perpetual scowl anyway, maybe eating more jellies wouldn't help.

"Of course, *madame*." She curtsied, then moved to set the riding habit down out of the way—

"What are you doing? Take that dirty thing away," Lady Horlock scolded. "Then show the staymakers in."

Sarah picked up the habit again, the folds of velvet warm and suffocating in their luxurious weight. She reached for the door handle.

"And make sure you come back with some handwork; you know how I hate idleness."

"Yes, *madame*." *You self-righteous pain in my*—

"What on earth are you lingering for? Go to, girl!"

Sarah smiled and curtseyed, keeping sweet. Inside her head, however, she managed to run through every cursed foul word she had ever learned. She had only just finished the list by the time she had set the gown down in Lady Horlock's dressing room, found her mending and torn off down the hallway again to find the craftsmen who had come calling.

It was more than time to move on. Who stayed at a Great House longer than a few years, at her age? She was hardly some old drudge, bent double by the demands of hard labor and with nothing more to recommend her than a lifetime of service to ungrateful, spoiled-rotten, miserly, demanding—

"Miss Armand! I had hoped it would be you come to guide us."

And there was another option, standing right before her. Mr. Glover bowed deeply, sweeping his arm down with the motion of his trim, muscled body, as though she were proper and not a serving girl dressed up as a fancy lady's maid. He stood beside his employer, an older, shorter, slim-shouldered man with graying hair and more wrinkles in his face than in his shirt. Tibbert had been making stays for the ladies of the *bon ton* since they had been whalebone bodies with tabs splayed out across ample hips, before the styles had changed and confining bones replaced by cords that curved with the figure and raised the bosom high. He was the undisputed master of his craft, those gnarled and arthritic fingers turning out works of sumptuous beauty that rivaled those of the *modistes* on Bond Street—and his were intended to be hidden away from the eye. How could he stand it, having such a talent and knowing that the utmost expression of it would nevertheless stay entirely invisible?

Mr. Glover had been Tibbert's apprentice in his younger days, his junior partner now, and poised, one presumed, to take over the business and Tibbert's client list once the old man retired. Or passed to his eternal reward, since he was well past the age now that most men, if they were able, retreated to hearth and grandchildren. Tibbert had none of those. Perhaps that was why he kept on working, with no wife or family to maintain but for himself and his shop. He was certainly not of an age now to begin again.

Mr. Glover, on the other hand—he was young, no more than twenty-and-four, surely, and in form and countenance beyond pleasing to the eye. He had the sort of blue eyes that Sarah most adored, with just a touch of gray for mystery. His hair looked like it had been blond once, when he was little, but had darkened into a honey-brown shaded with gold that gleamed in the light. His shoulders were broad, his hips slim—utterly not the fashion these days. But Sarah wasn't likely to be looked at by fashionable men anyway.

"Mr. Glover." She curtsied, a ridiculous gesture aimed at a junior staymaker, but it was all part of the game. Living in these ivory- and watercolor-decorated walls, surrounded by the trappings of domestic wealth, for a moment, they could pretend to be something more than what they were.

His gaze stayed on her as she dipped and rose, as though they were alone in the hallway for a moment's time. He carried a parcel and a bag under his arm, full of fabric samples and tools of his trade. Those brilliant eyes lingered on her after she'd straightened. "I trust you're well, m'sieurs," she continued, the lilt in her voice fake, but also so much a part of her now that the pretense was automatic. "Please, come this way."

Master Tibbert nodded and tilted his head, looking through her as though she were nothing. To him, of course, she was—just one more lady's maid, an obstacle between himself and the execution of his craft.

But Mr. Glover smiled, his eyes crinkling at the corners. "All the better now," he flirted gently, a dimple appearing in his cheek.

"Lady Horlock is through here, I presume?" Master Tibbert moved ahead of them, surprisingly quickly for a man with a stoop to his shoulder, and he vanished through the open door.

"You're looking very well." Mr. Glover's dimple never wavered, his eyes gleaming in a way that Sarah wished she could allow herself to believe was because of her. "It's been too long since we've kept company. Dare I hope that you will be attending Lady Horlock in Town this summer?"

Sarah kept her head high, but she could feel the treacherous warmth creeping into her cheeks. "Milady wouldn't trust anyone else with the task, thankfully; I expect I'll be in Town for the full four months." The light in his eyes there couldn't be feigned, and her self-consciousness fell away, if only for a moment. "Mrs. Colby passed on the news about your parents," Sarah said impulsively, laying her hand on his arm. He was warm beneath her touch, the muscle beneath his coat solid and firm. Her fingers tingled at the contact, a *frisson* of excitement that sped up her arm and vanished just as quickly. "Will you accept my deepest condolences?"

She could have kicked herself for the way his smile lessened, then; she'd reminded him of painful things. Hardly the way to ensure that he sought her out again! But he didn't frown at her, or call her out for rudeness, which was better than nothing.

"I will, and gladly," he replied. "And thank you for your kindness. It means a great deal to know that we've been in your thoughts." Something fierce and wonderful passed in their locked gazes that she couldn't even begin to name, lodging deep inside and pulsing there.

"But that goes to show," he added with cheer that only sounded a tiny bit forced, breaking the spell, "that it has indeed been far too long since we've spoken, as my sister and I have been out of mourning since New Year's." Those piercing blue eyes never left hers, and his expressive lips quirked up at one corner. "I don't suppose, Miss Armand, that you could convince Lady Horlock to bring out another niece or cousin? Surely she has some country girl in her family who could use a Season sponsor…"

"For which, of course, she would also need new underpinnings?" Sarah asked, following his conversational lead automatically, not knowing where it would take them. "Is business so bad, Mr. Glover, that you have to drum it up through the maidservants?"

"Not at all, and I'd never ask another—but the more times we're summoned to Bracknell, the more precious minutes I have to spend in your company." They had passed the moment of connection, then, and it was back to the easy flirtation that usually colored their stolen snatches of

15

conversation. It had never signified anything before. Why should that change now?

He flicked open the old and scratched watch hanging in his waistcoat pocket, the gold plating worn off in patches and the monogram on the cover half-gone from rubbing. "I mark this another three to add to my tally," he announced, clicking the watch closed with a gleam in his eye.

She laughed, couldn't help it, the mirth bubbling up inside at his audacity, and at thinking it could ever be directed at her. "You're terrible, m'sieur—a flirt and a troublemaker." He beamed at her reaction, his back drawing straighter. "If you think that your charm is enough to entice me, you should return to your lessons and books." She wanted to step closer, be drawn into his arms and kiss him as a reward, to feel the supple response in his lips as he kissed her back—

And that would never happen. She was in proper service, not some doxy to be bedded and abandoned. Merchants and tradesmen with money and clients married other tradesmen's daughters—not maids.

He didn't seem to notice the things running through her mind, for he was still smiling at her warmly when she pulled her attention back. "Aha, you admit it—you do find me charming!" he said gleefully. His smile seemed so brilliant and genuine, she almost melted.

She put a hand on her hip to show him her annoyance with his games and cocked her head. It took almost all her strength to keep the smile off her face, but it tugged at the corners of her mouth regardless. "That is not precisely what I said, which you well know."

His warm, soft laugh suggested that he didn't believe her act. "Someday I'll convince you to go walking out with me, Miss Armand. We'll spend a whole half hour in each other's company, perhaps more. I will shower you with compliments, each more passionate than the last, and I'll beg a lock of your glorious chestnut hair to keep within my watch. What man could ask for more?"

The image was too tempting, and yet he'd never once said the magic words "marriage" or even "understanding". If she allowed herself to believe it was possible, even for an instant, the fall in the end would be too painful to survive.

Joshua had managed it. Her oldest and dearest friend in the Horlocks' household was now living in his tiny cottage somewhere in Belgium, his true love in his arms, far away from the trials and tribulations of life under some patron's or master's thumb.

Lucky wretch.

Someday, it would be her turn to fly. But not today.

"Don't make promises you're not intending to keep, m'sieur," Sarah chided him, a brittleness to her voice that she, at least, could hear. He frowned at her, seemed about to say more, when Tibbert called to him from Lady Horlock's chambers.

"Glover!"

"Glover? Master Tibbert, I thought I had hired a staymaker!" Lady Horlock retorted cheerfully.

They chortled together. Mr. Glover closed his eyes, his face taking on that blank look Sophie knew so well: the *I can't mock you because you're paying my wages, but*

17

honestly! expression of pained resignation that she herself saw in the mirror from time to time.

"Another palsy attack and he'll drop," Mr. Glover muttered under his breath, and traded rueful looks with Sarah. Then he closed his mouth and said no more on the subject. "Shall we, Miss Armand?" he asked, gesturing with his less-burdened hand for her to lead the way.

"Indeed," she said quietly, and walked beside him toward the open chamber door. She had a shirt to mend tucked in the crook of her arm, but Mr. Glover handed her a packet of sketches and fabric swatches to arrange on the table, his fingertips brushing against her knuckles with the gentlest of attempted caresses. She met his eyes and arched a single dark eyebrow, boldly. He had the conceit to flash a grin and his dimple at her one more time before he turned back to his own work.

Apprenticing to Master Tibbert had turned out rather differently than the way James had pictured it when his father had originally made the arrangements. Even now, as a supposedly full partner, albeit a junior one, he was still stuck at the old pander's beck and call.

The money was good, there was no denying it, but the constant state of panic that preparations for the London Season engendered, the endless trips in a rickety carriage out to the estates of the wealthy and fashionable, the endless cups of tea in identical lifeless drawing rooms while Tibbert cosseted and flattered the dowagers and maiden aunts—

It was foolishness, that was what it was. James sipped at the tea in the fine china cup balanced in his broad and rough-worn hands. They had been smooth enough once, for the son of a businessman, but more than a dozen years of leather thimbles and iron needles, steaming cauldrons and sinuous curves of whalebone had left their mark. No gentleman ever bore this many scars and cuts on his knuckles or calluses on his fingertips.

And all that work would come to nothing, eventually, if Tibbert did not permit him to properly court the younger set for their custom. For once the older whaleboned women met their maker, who would be left to patronize the staymaker who catered only to them? The rising jewels of the *ton* and the constant changing needs of the stage—that was where money was to be made.

The girl sitting in the chair by the window was the perfect model for that new fashion. Miss Armand, Lady Horlock's personal maid, had the sort of glorious figure that whalebone would only conceal. Chestnut hair coiled up around Miss Armand's head, and her pale skin was colored cream and peach by the golden glow of the late afternoon sun. She sat primly, perched on the edge of her chair, her round, pert breasts raised high in the unmistakable soft and curving shape of the new rope-stiffened stays. She kept half an eye on the proceedings as her needle darted up and down in the pile of linen stuff in her lap. There was little, he reckoned, that would escape that one's notice.

As though she felt his eyes on her, Miss Armand lifted her head and met his gaze with her own unflinching, questioning stare. She arched a single dark eyebrow, her clear gray eyes unreadable.

He tipped his cup at her, just enough for the movement to be deliberate but not remarkable, and he smiled. She cast her eyes heavenward, as if in exasperation, but there was a small smile on her lips when she looked down at her handwork once more.

There were some benefits to the endless rounds of traveling the countryside. Miss Armand and her pretty wit was one of them. And as long as Master Tibbert and Lady Horlock sat twittering over jam tarts and tea, the longer he could watch the swift and sure movements of her fingers, trail his eyes along the delicate point of her chin and full pink swells of her lips, imagine what sorts of things he would say to her if she would consent to let him court her for real. He had already wasted too much time dithering. Now—his father's death leaving him the sole master of his house—things had changed.

A day and a half in a carriage with Tibbert's constant complaining about the state of the roads was a small fee in order to be near her. If he was fortunate again, he could claim some more small moments of her time before they left, and make more of a case for himself. And then—oh then!—she would be in London with her employers for the entirety of the Season. With a little finagling, he could steal hours here and there to be near her, court her, perhaps get better acquainted with those glorious, full, round—

Tibbert stood and gestured imperiously; James set his cup down and rose to begin the actual work they had been summoned for, rather than the gossip that lubricated the fittings so well. Once again he was relegated to the role of an assistant—despite his skills and years of training— setting up with the measurement book while Tibbert encircled Lady Horlock's waist and chest with his knotted string. His crooked and bent fingers tied and untied the marks along the length to make his measurements and adjustments, until finally he handed it to James, apparently satisfied.

"You are as trim and lovely as ever, Lady Horlock," Tibbert complimented her. The countess inclined her head to accept the compliment, while Miss Armand helped her draw on her wrapper and petticoats. "Your figure will be most perfectly enhanced by this new design from London—" and they were off again, Lady Horlock's attention entirely caught by the swatches he set out before her.

Miss Armand lingered, her fingers tracing wistfully over some of the vividly colored fashion plates laid out on the table.

James took the chance and murmured in Miss Armand's ear. "And yours would be as well." Her hair had been faintly scented, with something flowery, and her pulse thrummed in the pale exposed skin beneath her ear. It screamed out to be kissed, but that was an impossibility here. She stopped moving, her head turning slightly in his direction, and he pressed his luck once more. "I can see you now in a candlelit ballroom, pearls in your hair and a gown of pink silk to bring out the roses in your cheeks."

Those delicate cheeks flushed pink just as he'd envisioned, and she shook her head at him in admonition. "You are, I think—" she murmured in return, half-turning to look him in the eye. Her own gleamed with shrewd mischief. "—the only man I know who attempts his seductions through the mental *dressing* of his prey."

He pressed his hand to his heart, pretended to object. But Tibbert was rattling off notes about fabric choices and styles, and James had to take a moment and scribble them down in the book before he forgot. By the time he looked up once more, she had moved back to the security of her chair and her mending, and out of his reach.

One of the blank pages at the back of the book sliced away cleanly, leaving only a small edge within the spine to hold everything else in place. He wrote his note in a clear and careful hand, folded it small and tucked it into the cuff of his shirtsleeve.

It was not until they were ready to leave that Miss Armand stood up once more, ready at the door to hand them off to the responsibility of the footman. "When can I expect the delivery?" Lady Horlock asked, and Tibbert shrugged.

"The closer it comes to the Season, of course, the busier we get, and three days of travel, while I do not regret an instant of the effort for your company, milady, becomes more difficult to arrange. Let us say the next fitting will be the day after your arrival in Town? And then the stays themselves will be finished within the day following."

She made a thoughtful noise in her throat, and James took the moment of their distraction to brush his hand lightly against Miss Armand's. Her eyes flew open wide when she felt the folded paper in his hand, but she took it— first hurdle, jumped cleanly!—and secreted it away somewhere about her person.

"A pleasure, Lady Horlock, as ever." James shifted his attention to the lady of the house, bowing respectfully.

"Mr. Glover," she acknowledged him.

"Come along, Glover." Tibbert sighed dramatically. "And do stop flirting with the countess. She's much too beautiful for the likes of you, you know."

Lady Horlock sighed and laughed indulgently, and James could feel the tips of his ears start to go warm with indignation. But Miss Armand's gentle smile was one of understanding and commiseration, and warmth flooded through him at that simple gesture.

He forced a chuckle, made a more dramatic bow than was strictly necessary and bit his tongue. One day, he would be his own master, take on only those clients he chose, and be free of the entire bloody charade.

One day.

Hours later, the Horlocks at dinner and the spring sun setting, Sarah set aside the stack of mending in the fading afternoon light. She'd need a candle to keep going and have the fallen hem resewn for the next day, so taking a moment to read the note—surely she couldn't be begrudged that. She pulled her feet up underneath her on her small cot, the lumps in her straw tick mattress familiar now and so much better than other lodgings she had once known.

I'd be a fool to walk away from security on a fanciful whim. I'll not go out to the streets.

Unfolding the small scrap of paper , revealed Glover's fine and elegant handwriting, looping in curls across the creamy space. The message itself was short.

Not prey, but a prize.

Yours ever, JG

Her heart fluttered alarmingly, the frantic wing-beats in her breast impossible to quell. Perhaps her treasured little fantasies had not been foolish after all. She could sew and manage a household, after all. She knew the great families and no one could speak against her character—at least, no one who knew her as Sophie Armand. Who better to make a wife for a staymaker? She could keep his house well enough, he would have money to support them both and more besides. He was no lord, but what would she even *do* with an aristocrat if she caught one?

She could be very happy leaving service to the Horlocks, if she could swap this life for that one.

And yet. She was not really "Sophie" at all, and he had made no promises. Men were full of pretty words. Unless they came with an offer of marriage and the bans read at the church, they meant nothing.

She folded the note back up again and tucked it away beneath her pillow. A short trip out to get and light a candle, and she was back, her sewing untouched beside her on the bed. She got down on her knees beside the low-framed bed and tugged the small box out of its hiding place. Her pages were undisturbed and, thankfully, still legible despite a minor smudge or two across the bottom of the page. She dipped her pen.

Emmeline: His mistress! Do not tell me such things, I cannot bear it! Tell me you are lying! But no, I see in your eyes that you are not. Oh, how may we women survive the horrendous duplicity of men?

Mr. Glover's note was promptly forgotten in the chaos of packing the Horlock household up for the trip down to London for the Season. Tibbert would have the stays ready for a fitting by the time they arrived and settled, and so there was no point at all in having either master or journeyman make the trek out to Bracknell one more time.

Mrs. Colby had sent her undercook down a day before to make sure the London house was well stocked and that food would be prepared for the family's arrival. Sarah and Ellen had packed all of Lady Horlock's gowns and trinkets into the trunks. All that remained was for Sarah to gather up her own small collection of belongings, the handful of skirts and dresses that she owned, her aprons and caps—and a single small box, only slightly larger than a sheet of paper for writing letters, that could also serve as a writing-desk.

A piece of folded paper fell out from under the pillow when Sarah stripped her sheets to change them, landing on her tidy floor without a sound. She was halfway through unfolding it before she remembered what it was, her brow sweaty from the work of packing and escaped wisps of hair tickling the back of her neck.

Men.

She could have just tossed it in the fire downstairs or set the edge in her candle to burn it. Lady Horlock wouldn't look too kindly on her personal maid receiving flirtatious notes from men, invited or not!

And yet.

A prize—no one had ever called her that before, nor called the flush in her cheeks anything close to "roses". It unsettled her as much as it flattered. She was certainly no prize to be won in a game, for who, in that case, was the master of ceremonies who would be giving her hand away? She didn't belong to a father or even a father figure. She'd had Joshua, once, the closest thing she'd ever had to a brother. But she'd taken care of him more than the other way around, and now he was gone on his own adventure. She had no one but her own self, and she was managing just fine.

But it was very nice, even if it was only a game, to feel wanted. Just once, to have been *seen.*

For heaven's sake, you're worse than your own characters.

Rolling her eyes at herself and her own foolishness, Sarah tucked the note away inside her writing box, wrapped the box in a piece of old, soft, linen, and hid it at the bottom of her own small trunk.

To London, then, and another Season of carefree days filled with pleasures not meant for the likes of her.

The gossip networks in London really shouldn't have surprised Sarah at all with their efficiency and speed. Someone must have seen the house being opened or noticed life coming back to the Horlock townhouse at Bruton Place, because they'd barely been there a handful of hours before one of the scullery girls flagged Sarah down in the hallway with a note.

"Begging your pardon, Miss Armand, ma'am." The terrified little thing popped into a curtsey that would have been ludicrous if it wasn't so earnest. She was young and certainly hadn't been around the last time the family had descended on Town. "A boy brought this 'round to the kitchen door for ye." Sarah tucked her sewing box under her arm and took the folded note.

That fluttering picked up inside her chest again, more brilliantly nerve-racking than the last time. Was it Mr. Glover? Did he know what day they'd planned to arrive? Perhaps he was sending a note to arrange an assignation, or to ask her to "walk out" with him, or—

Her false name—*Sophie Armand*—was inscribed on the letter, but not in Mr. Glover's firm, angular hand. Those loops and swirls were Meg's.

The girl lingered, glancing at the paper inquisitively, and Sarah shooed her away.

"Off with you," she scolded, sliding into the accent here in the townhouse the way she never bothered to do downstairs back at Bracknell. Other than the handful who had come with them from the country house, the staff here were new—and word traveled.

It wouldn't do at all to spoil the healthy fiction of Lady Horlock's French abigail, even though she'd happily wager that nine out of ten of the so-called "French maids" working for the good families were as thoroughly English as she was. Such was the fashion these days—French servants for everyone, even when there weren't enough real *emigrés* to go around.

She sped along the corridor until she reached the servants' hall, thankfully, momentarily, empty. Sliding her thumb under the unmarked wax seal popped the letter open. She unfolded the page with a grin at the unholy mess of the calligraphy inside. Meg had been hopeless at writing neatly when they had been young, and she had hardly improved

27

since. The spelling was better, mind, but the wide looping scrawl more resembled letters formed by the eleven-year-olds they had been than the old ladies of twenty and twenty-one they had become.

Belov'd Soph, the letter began, *the chimes of St-Paul's whisper on the wind; you've come back to me! Tell me that this Message is true, or I swear I shall die Right Here upon my cot for loneliness and want of you. I'm playing at the Olympic Pavilion for four more nights and have lodgings in Charing Cross. Come find me, darling, I pine for you!*

Ever Your Meg

Becoming an actress certainly, and perhaps entirely predictably, had not made Meg any less dramatic. "Pine" was even underlined four times, an affectation surely more appropriate for a love letter to some young swain than to her girlhood confidante. Nevertheless, the letter itself seemed to exude a glowing warmth that sank deep into Sarah's bones. She folded it back up and tucked it into her bodice, in beside her left breast.

It wouldn't take long to send a note back, and then, tonight, when the house was at peace, she would find some excuse to leave.

Darling Meg,

Worry not, dearest, I am here. I will find you tonight, after your show.

Ever yours,

Sarah

Chapter Two

"I will never be your bride!" Marguerite Ceniza's final, triumphant rejection echoed with all the force her body was capable of producing. The count reeled back a step in shock and disbelief, fending off her gleaming silver dagger. One step, two—then, with a flourish and with tears streaming down her face, she plunged it home.

Meg collapsed to her knees, the floorboards rough through the fine linen of her flowing white nightgown. Her black hair tumbled down around her as she fell, fell into oblivion, tears streaking down her face all the while.

There was a pause, a silence that creaked on a moment too long.

Then William remembered his lines and carried on the scene, exclaiming over "Matilda's fallen corpse" with a reading so stilted that she would swear he had only received the script yesterday. She dared not move, despite the pressure of the blunted prop dagger shoved into her armpit, the sticky false blood from the bladder secreted within her stays spreading over the stage—and her shift, and her hair. She'd need another bath tonight, a basin for hair washing *and* another visit to the laundress. Heaven forbid.

How much longer now?

"And now with this unholy end I see my wrongs all too clearly—"

Marvelous.

"If I must burn in hell for my crimes, then I say let it *all burn!*"

Meg braced on the cue and the stage rumbled, the audience shrieked and light flashed red and yellow beyond her closed eyelids, followed by the heat of air and flames. That would be the machinists setting off the castle explosion. God help them if they lit the curtains again.

The audience exploded in an entirely different way. Hoots and hollers and wild applause came from the direction of the pit, more restrained cheering from the galleries, and by the time William (no longer Lord Ruthven, The Monster of Munich) took her hand to help her to her feet, the Olympic Pavilion was alive with ecstatic shouts of praise.

The applause was more than just noise—it was a wind that lifted her to her bare toes, carried her up in soaring ecstasy, so that she had to close her eyes when she raised her arms for the bows and curtseys to follow. Their approval and their cheers washed her clean, scoured her skin and left her fresh and newborn, loved and adored. One of the ballet girls pressed flowers into her arms, collected from the posies flung toward the stage by her admirers, and she lifted the gloriously colored armful to her nose to smell them. The crowd roared for her, for her alone.

She floated offstage on that same wind, past the errand boys who were busy stamping out a small fire from a pile of paint rags, and up to her dressing room.

Technically not *her* dressing room, she supposed, since it was shared among all the eight of the actresses, but she was undoubtedly the star. After all, she had more scenes than anyone except William, and he could barely remember his lines when he was sober, never mind half in his cups.

And it was hardly *his* heaving bosom that the lords and bucks came to see.

Said bosom was stained now with sweat and stage blood, and Meg flounced to her seat with a sigh of distaste and not a little exhaustion. But a note sat at her place along the wall, along with a single flower. The paper crinkled in her hand when she popped the seal, and Sarah—no, she was called Sophie now and Meg must remember that—*Sophie's* handwriting in the reply was as clear and neat as it had ever been. She would come! Her darling Sophie would be there, in her rooms, tonight!

That buoyed her spirits so much that she barely even noticed the name on the card beside the rose before she opened it.

For a magnificent performance, it said, in James's tidy hand, with nothing further. She turned over the card, half hoping for some further sign, a declaration of eternal devotion and a promise of an apartment of her own, perhaps. Nothing. Meg sighed again and set it aside, disappointment lingering longer than it should.

She really should be more grateful that things were moving along well in that direction—she needed a patron again if she were ever to find better living arrangements.

Charing Cross was certainly not a fashionable address! And James was wonderfully handsome, his broad shoulders and muscled arms bearing promises of erotic strength and stamina. He was clever to boot and very pleasant company, along with having money...and no wife.

That, following the whole debacle with Montpress and his new bride, was a mark in James's favor that utterly outweighed his lack of title. Titled men bought themselves entitled wives, and *they* spent entirely too much energy on making a mistress's life miserable.

Never you mind that if Meg had been born with half the family or connections of the wives of the *bon ton,* she'd hardly be forced to support herself by whatever means remained. Allowing women to engage themselves as lawyers and bookkeepers for a reasonable wage would go a lot further toward eliminating kept girls than any number of fits of temper about secret apartments in the city.

Forget him, though, and wayward men in general. *Sarah* was in London again.

Meg finished changing and washing the stage paint from her face and chest, dressed quickly and hurried out the stage door, tying her bonnet on as she went.

Home—at least for the moment—required stepping down through an alley and over the body of a drunkard who hadn't made it farther than a few steps from the doorway of the tavern on the corner. Meg picked up her skirts to avoid dragging the hem through heaven knew what in the gutter, but she was so busy making sure that her nice boots didn't touch the muck that the man in the shadows caught her entirely off guard.

His hand caught her elbow, and Meg bit back a scream. *Don't show fear.* She lifted her chin instead, turning to see him beyond the curved brim of her bonnet and the way it cut off her vision on the sides. *Like a blinder for a horse.* He made no other move in the meantime, and Meg glared defiantly.

"Where are you off to in such a hurry, Miss Ceniza?" "Baron" John Thomas asked, her name sounding like some filthy proposition in his mouth. He was handsome, in that sharp-edged, dangerous way that predators carried around with them like a case of swords. His dark red coat fit him in a manner that no decent mamma would allow her daughters to stare at for too long, cleaving to his narrow shoulders and sinewy arms like dampened petticoats to a strumpet's legs. Brown hair swept low across his forehead, cut short behind, and when he smiled she expected to see pointed teeth. They were neat and straight, though, gleaming white in the gas-lit dark.

"Nowhere that concerns you, Baron," Meg replied smartly, and the Baron—for so this man, worst among the local procurers, insisted he be called—pressed a wounded hand to his heart. His other hand lingered on her elbow, fingers curling around her sleeve. "I'll thank you to leave me be."

"One of these days, my sweet Marguerite," he oozed slick charm and false sincerity, "you'll walk out with me, and I'll show you riches beyond your dreams. Why waste your precious few years of youth and beauty prancing about on a stage when you could spend your nights in a silk boudoir?"

Her skin crawled, and she jerked her arm away. She regretted the impulsive move the moment she'd made it—his eyes lit up and amusement curled the corner of his lips at the proof that he'd gotten beneath her skin.

"The only boudoir I'll grace is my own, *your lordship*, so be off with you. Collect your flock of silly geese and go pester someone else." She made a shooing gesture, and he tipped his hat, that mocking smile never fading.

Meg walked carefully up the narrow stairs to the door. He didn't follow, thankfully—she'd have been ill-pressed to defend herself right now if he tried to do something stupid. She glanced behind her as she opened the door. In the darkness it was impossible to tell entirely, but the street—for the moment—was empty once more, the drunk snoring away undisturbed in his gutter. Good. Her honor could easily survive being impugned by a bull-headed cock-bawd, but the less she had to deal with the likes of him, the happier she would be.

Small and in a poor area though it might be, Meg's lodgings were a riot of color and draped-fabric luxury inside. She tossed her pelisse over a chair already mostly hidden by petticoats and pillows, the blue velvet settling down overtop to create a mountain of plush and pile. She left a trail behind herself of discarded clothing and fripperies, her bonnet landing on the end table, her dress across her bed, and finally her stays and shift in a crumpled pile on the floor to be sorted out later. A hot bath wasn't happening, but a long and luxurious wash in the lukewarm water from the basin by the fire, followed by clean linen sliding over her still-damp body as she redressed, made all the difference in the world. The rest of the day sluiced away, along with the kinks in her shoulders and the traces of leftover cosmetics from her brow.

A rapid knock at the door interrupted her ablutions as she buttoned the last few buttons on her dress, and Meg flew toward the door, her heart pounding. Lifting the latch, she peered out the door, spotted clear gray eyes beneath curls of mahogany brown.

Meg flung the door wide, the rush of excitement and bliss utterly taking over the control of her limbs. "Sarah darling!"

"Meg?" Sarah stepped inside, and the world brightened up as though someone had lit another candle inside Meg's mind. She looked just the same as ever, her masses of deep, dark red-brown hair braided and neatly coiled about her head, her gray eyes light and dancing, her slim figure closely held in a simple blue dress, a cape and bonnet covering her against the spring night's chill.

"Come in and close the door!" Meg took Sarah's hand, slim and rough from her years of working in service, and tugged her past the threshold and into the small room. A closed door and a thrown latch later, Sarah was setting her bonnet aside, and Meg flung herself into her friend's arms. "Oh, dearest, it's been so long!"

It had, too—months and months and *years*, almost! Sarah hugged her back, her arms about Meg's waist and the faint scent of lilacs in her hair. That press of bodies together, curving and firm, so real, finished the job of warming Meg through that the small fire had only been able to half accomplish. Here—here was safety and affection without complications, the friend who knew everything about Meg and loved her anyway.

Meg lifted her chin imperiously, her hair wet on her shoulders. "You are never allowed to go away again," she declared imperiously. "I simply won't have it."

Sarah laughed, pressing a soft, closed-lip kiss to Meg's cheek. Something sultry and tight coiled deep within Meg's belly, and she laced her fingers through Sarah's possessively. "When you're enough of a success to hire me on as your maid, sweetheart, I'll come gladly."

"Oh poo." Meg waved off the pragmatic complaint, letting Sarah's hand go. She crossed the tiny room in a matter of three steps, and rescued a bottle of brandy she had secreted in the trunk at the end of her narrow bed. "Employment," she drawled out with disdain. "Who are we to be bound by such things?" Two glasses, then, and by the time she turned around, Sarah was curled up, catlike, in the ancient armchair that had come with the room. "Throw off the bounds of convention, darling," Meg entreated, and Sarah's smile turned into a throaty chuckle. "Let us be free!"

Sarah took the offered glass and cupped it between her hands. Her dress was a lovely fabric, no patches, letting-outs or stains to be seen. Whatever else about Sarah's current employers, at least they treated her well. "When food and rooms to let are also free, then I'll consider it."

"Pragmatist."

"Romantic child."

"*Actress*," Meg pointed out, then set her own glass down and draped herself across the side of her bed, her elbow propped up on the pillow.

"A fair point, fairly made." Sarah drank, both slim hands curled around her glass, the tip of her tongue curling out to touch her bottom lip and catch a drop that nestled there. "I received your letter," she said unnecessarily, because of course she had! "What is the emergency, dear heart?"

The cut crystal sat heavy in her hand and cool against Meg's lips. The glasses had been a gift from Lord Whitton-Ffaulkes, her last patron but one. Gifts she could carry with her were the best sorts. "Why, the two of us being in the same city again, of course!" She tossed her head, ignoring the swelling feelings of satiety, calm and a softly pulsing, warm sensation somewhere between her navel and her groin.

"The Horlocks have kept you locked away in the country for so long, I was beginning to think they'd never come back to London again! You should run away and come live with me," she blurted out unexpectedly, then clamped her mouth firmly shut. The brandy chased the impulsive words away, burning a clear path down her throat to heat in her belly.

"It's not that bad." Sarah shrugged, but there was a lack of light in her eyes that suggested otherwise. Meg burned to say it, the words on the tip of her tongue, but Sarah kept talking. "The house is nice enough, even if the grounds are quiet, and the money is good compared to what some girls get. Lady Horlock's a dragon and a bear together in one, but she doesn't cheat my pay packet."

It was impossible not to pout at the horrid unfairness of it all. "Small consolation if you never go anywhere you can spend it."

"I'm here now, aren't I? And for the next four months, at least. So don't be cross with me, dear heart." Sarah reached out and squeezed two of Meg's toes, all that she could reach from where she was sitting, and flashed a bright smile. "Tell me of your adventures instead of arguing— what has been happening here this winter?"

Fine, she could change topics, but let it not be said that this was the end of it! Meg shrugged languidly. "Not a terrible amount. The rain has been dreadful, as ever." Another sip of brandy, and Meg wrinkled her nose. "Sir Toby Montpress got married."

Sarah's dark eyebrow arched and concern flickered across her face. "And?"

"And the new Lady Montpress apparently disliked the whole idea of sharing him." That wasn't exactly how things had gone, of course, but the baronet and his bride were still too irritating to dwell upon. "So I am here, as you see me." She gestured around the small room, currently festooned with crumpled gowns and small untidy piles of books and scripts. "Alone and unloved." She pressed her hand to her forehead and sagged back amongst her pillows.

Silence fell.

Meg cracked one eye open.

Sarah had her knuckle in her mouth and was biting down on it, the better to suppress the laughter that made her shoulders shake. A snort finally escaped, and she let go, giggling. "And you're on the hunt again, I suspect?" There was an edge to her question that Meg didn't entirely like.

"Indeed I am, and I have made up my mind," Meg decided on the spur of the moment. "You must meet him. There is a party in two days' time, once we've struck the show. He has promised he'll attend. We shall go on each other's arms, you and I, and you, oh pragmatic one, may evaluate his prospects for me."

From her twisting frown and the way she looked into her glass, Sarah did not share her enthusiasm for the plot. "Meg, it's not that I don't relish the notion of attending a party with you—"

"But you will not come."

"I haven't been invited," she pointed out quickly, and then, before Meg could protest further—"I cannot answer that I'll have that evening off, not unless the Horlocks are also out. And you know how I feel about you and your patrons."

"I'm no lightskirt," Meg interrupted, before Sarah could continue on along that train of thought. "Nor a Covent Garden Nun, so remove those considerations from your mind right now, Sarah Harlow. I want only one man at a time for company."

"Company?" Sarah laughed softly. "Is that what we call it now?"

"Hush, you. There is nothing wrong with enjoying the pleasures of the flesh on occasion. In return, a lover may provide me with the luxuries of life. The only difference between myself and those doting wives of theirs is that I've no dowry to pay my way to a wedding ring." Meg toyed with the ribbon of her shift, where it poked out from the neckline of her dress. She lifted her chin, pride and stubbornness battling it out inside. "But if I'm a whore for batting my eyelashes at men with deep pockets, then so is every girl in the *bon ton* who ever chased a ducal coronet."

In an instant, Sarah had set her drink down and was on the bed, her arms curling tightly around Meg's shoulders. "Oh, darling," Sarah sighed, disappointment and perhaps some guilt weighing heavily in her voice. "I never said it, never thought it! We do what we must to survive, we all do. This is not a kind world, especially to fatherless women."

Sarah's arms around her, their thighs pressed close together, the strong shoulder on which Meg could rest her head—it all settled the aching grief in her chest and restored her mood to some of what it had been before. Meg turned, curled into Sarah's embrace. Sarah didn't flinch, nor did she sit up or leave, merely set her arms snug around Meg and held her close, one hand rubbing slow and gentle circles on Meg's back.

"If you wish me to," Sarah said after a while, time immaterial and her hip warm and round beneath Meg's hand, "I'll come to the party. I'll meet your newest beau. And if he's no good for you, darling—"

"I'll listen," Meg vowed. And in the bliss of the moment, she meant it.

Sarah snorted kindly, the swell of her bosom rising with her breath to press against Meg's cheek for but a moment. "That'll be the day." And all was forgiven in the world.

It should have been odd, Sarah mused, lying there on Meg's bed, her oldest and dearest friend curled up in her arms. Their conversation, such as it had been, had died away after her latest vain attempt at guiding Meg to better choices. And yet here they lay, curled up against each other as they had when they were children.

But they were neither of them children any longer.

Meg had blossomed first of the pair of them, drawing eyes and compliments in the street from the moment her bosom had begun to grow. No girl in the world loved the attention more; taking to the stage to be the center of everyone's regard had been the only natural choice. And she was only more beautiful now as an adult, her long legs curving into plump thighs, her waist so little that she seemed half drowned by the high-bodiced dresses that were all the rage, a creamy golden hue to her skin that, while not fashionable white and pink, turned her coal-black hair and coral lips into splashes of dramatic contrast.

Dramatic contrast indeed. Everything about *Meg is a dramatic contrast, never mind her pretty breasts and—*

Sarah banished the thought with a flash of guilt. Dalliances with some of the giddy *demimondaines* she knew were one thing, but this was Meg. For the honor of their friendship, she could think no such heady things. Remember Liliane's long legs, rather, Jeremiah's broad hands, or Katerina's biting kisses instead.

Meg sighed softly, half asleep, and curled her hand against Sarah's hip. Her bottom lip jutted out, a perfect plump promise, and something untoward burned hot in the middle of Sarah's chest.

Sarah was no retiring virgin—she knew full well what it meant to desire and be desired. And there were always men and women whose desires tended towards the lesser-trodden paths. She had found bliss in a woman's kiss before; it was safer by far than the powerful, terrifyingly thrilling love of men. But this?

Meg felt wondrously *right* in her arms, a delicious swell of firm curves. Her slow, deep breaths made her chest rise, so that if she tilted her head at the right angle Sarah could see the dark pink edge of her nipple pressed against the soft linen and lace of her shift—

No.

To look, to think about such things, when Meg had no earthly idea—it was a betrayal, and one Sarah would never forgive herself for if she took advantage.

If she knew, Meg would never feel safe with her again.

If she knew what? What, precisely, am I contemplating doing?

Kissing Meg was out of the question. She had always behaved toward Sarah more as a sister than a lover, and so Sarah should do the same—not betray their friendship by trying to make it become something more. Lying here, on the crumpled bedclothes illuminated only by the dim light of a single flickering candle end, the soft scent of orange blossoms and soap lingering in the air, with Meg warm and lithe, their legs intertwined and breasts pressed against one another's…it was all too much, all at once.

The hour was late; Sarah had to be home. She wanted nothing more in the world than to slide back in beside Meg, press kisses against her eyelids until she awakened.

She could suckle at Meg's pert nipples, caress and tease them to hardness with her tongue and the edges of her teeth. Meg's small and perfect breasts would fit in the palms of Sarah's hands, her golden skin and the roundness of her belly crying out for Sarah's lips, her teeth. She would suck pink weals into Meg's skin, bite at the curve of her hipbone, then spread Meg's cunny lips and slide her tongue along the sweet pink folds of skin. Meg would writhe under her, buck and cry out, clench tight around Sarah's fingers deep inside.

All this bounty, here in Sarah's arms, delicious and warm and sweet. All she had to do was declare herself.

And then what? Even if she could possibly love me in return, if we are caught, we will be turned in to Bedlam. Or worse, to the stocks, like those poor men last year.

Sarah tipped her head, pressing a single (soft, tender, chaste) kiss to the top of Meg's head, and she slipped her arm out from beneath Meg's shoulders. The cool air struck her like a blow when she sat up, and Sarah shivered, despite the heat pooling low in her belly. She tied on her bonnet and her cape, turning only when she heard a small noise. Meg had rolled over, now entirely asleep, sprawling loose-limbed and vital across the plain white sheets. Sarah stepped quietly to the bedside and drew the coverlet up over Meg, to keep her warm.

"Good night, dearest," Sarah whispered softly. She wanted to kiss her.

She turned and left instead, being sure to latch the door.

Midafternoon the next day found Meg dashing up to the stone pillars of the King's Theatre in the Haymarket, holding a newssheet over her head to protect her bonnet and curls from the misty, drizzling rain. The main doors would be latched and barred at this time of day—there was nothing playing until the evening. The artists' entrance around the side of the vast Doric-style building was a much more modest single wooden door, and it was this one Meg opened cheerfully, holding up her skirts in her other hand so they wouldn't drag through the growing puddles.

Backstage hadn't been papered up. There was hardly any point to covering the walls with pretty paper when it was half-dark most of the time and pitch-black the rest. So they stayed bare, rough-hewn brown wood and darker struts, rising high into the blackness that encompassed the theatre loft. Up there were the flies where all the backdrops, pulleys and inner machinery of the stage had their secret, unseen homes. How much of the magic of the stage would be lost if the clapping masses were to have a look at the grunting, sweating mechanics behind all of the deeply cherished illusions?

The disappointed letdown would be as bad as a man discovering his bride was no virgin.

The machinists were in the middle of moving vast pieces of scenery back and forth, apprentice boys no taller than Meg wheeling giant wooden periactoids twice or three times their heights over to the wings. The audiences would never see them like this, the bits of different scenes painted on each side of the tall prism-shaped set pieces jumbled up all out of order. They crammed together so the back half of a cow from the farm scene butted flat up against the apple-green wallpaper of a duchess's boudoir.

"'Scuse me, miss." A stagehand ran past and Meg dodged, narrowly missing being splashed by the water sloshing out of the buckets he had in each hand.

He vanished around the corner, followed by the shriek of aggrieved metal, and a string of inventive cursing. A low rumbling started and a series of small cannonballs came crashing down the long wooden channel of the thunder run, piling up into one another at the end in a brilliant cacophony. A couple of the balls bounced out the end from the concussive pressure and kept rolling across the floor and out of the stage door, one of the boys running frantically to capture them before they tumbled down the ramp into the orchestra pit.

"Son of a goat-loving fussock—" Three-fingered Ned shut his mouth tight on whatever words he had been about to swear when he caught Meg's eye. She winked at him and his startlement dissolved into a wide grin, deepening some of the multitude of wrinkles across his wizened face. The propsmaster leaned on his walking stick and waited for her to approach, nodding at her all the while. "Good to see you, Miss Ceniza. Come for a look-around?"

"Come to see Mr. Langston. Is he about?"

Langston's voice echoed through the backstage space. "If you ass-backwards boat-lickers don't get this disaster sorted immediately, I'll plant my boot so hard in your nethers that you'll have to turn yourselves right-side out before you can crawl to the poorhouse!"

Ned stuck out his thumb and jutted it in the direction of the stage from where the curses could be heard, rolling out like the cannonballs' uncued thunder. "Thar he be," Ned added unnecessarily. "This may not be the best of times, girl."

"I'll take my chances." Meg patted her curls and brushed her gloved hands down the front of her muslin, as much her battle-dress as any centurion's armor. "Tally-ho, Ned."

"Tally-ho, Miss C," he replied, leaning back against the pillar, his walking stick propped up between his hands.

Someone whistled, a high tone and two low notes. She paused at the warning, stopping in the wings by the wide light reflectors and their unlit argand lamps. A few feet away, two burly men, in only their shirtsleeves and trousers, hauled on winches to send the richly painted backdrops flying up into the air on their ropes. The scene on stage changed from a pastoral view to a rolling storm at sea, and Mr. Langston, director of the King's Theatre, stormed off the stage, his hair in wild disarray.

Langston brushed right past her, made it four more steps, then spun around and cocked his head. He'd grown gray streaks in his dark brown hair somewhere in the past few years, similar speckles in his sideburns only adding to his look of distinction. The look was broken at the moment by the half-buttoned mess of his waistcoat and his shirtsleeves rolled up to his elbows, but he could be forgiven. He was working.

"Miss Ceniza?" he asked, head still cocked. "Did we have an engagement?"

"No, not exactly." Meg followed him as he shrugged and moved away from her out into the scene shop behind the stage. "Only I needed to speak with you. About a role in a play."

Langston removed a book from a false shelf that was part of a library set and opened it up to the middle. He pulled out a small flask, uncorked the top, drank deeply, then offered it to Meg—which she refused—before closing it once more and tucking the book back amongst the others on the shelf. The back door to the props room stood open, a ribbon holding the latch to the door in lieu of a nail, and a gentle breeze stirred the air. "That's what we do here."

He was going to be like that, was he? Meg laughed. "Don't play coy, Mr. Langston, you know what I mean. You're going to be preparing for the Season soon, and you'll be in need of actresses."

"True enough." He sat on a gold-leafed throne, crossing a leg over his other knee, and tapped his lip with a long forefinger. His eyes slowly traveled up and down her body, his expression cool and calculating when he looked her in the eyes once more. "We're doing an Inchbald next. *Animal Magnetism.*"

"I should think the title alone will sell seats." Meg giggled. Langston only smirked. "You're not doing *Lover's Vows?*" Miss Inchbald's most popular play by far, and one that had some delicious speaking parts for girls—

Langston seemed unimpressed. "It's been done."

Animal Magnetism it would be, then. Well enough—at least it was a play she knew. "Oh, Mr. Langston," Meg emoted deliberately. "Do consider me, won't you? I'd play Constance brilliantly, you know I would."

He frowned, a crease nestling between his bristling brows. "Aren't you at the Olympic?"

"We close tonight, and I know you've seen my reviews. I'm free as a bird from tomorrow on, Langston, and dying to play for you." Begging was unseemly at best, but she had managed to keep clear of that mark. Most likely. It wasn't begging, it was...*requesting* something that would be mutually advantageous.

A crash rang out from somewhere back by the stage, and Langston pushed himself up out of King Richard's gilded throne, unfolding like an awkward cricket. "We've not done the casting yet, Miss Ceniza, but rest assured that your name will be placed on the list for proper consideration."

"Mr. Langston!" Three-fingered Ned appeared in the hallway, tapping his walking stick impatiently on the floor. "You are requested, sir."

Meg pouted. "Mr. Langston!"

Langston headed for the door. He paused half a moment, turned and nodded at Meg with a distant, uninterested sort of grimness. "I will be certain to let you know."

The only two in the Pavilion's dressing room this far before the show, Grace and Meg had taken over the best seats, in front of the looking glasses with the fewest chips, blotches or distortions. Grace dipped her brush in the pot of black, stared at herself in her glass and carefully swept the line across her upper eyelid.

"What are you doing after this run closes?" Meg asked idly, twisting a curl around her finger and setting it to her head with pins.

"I've a role promised me at the Surrey." Black-eyed, brown-skinned Grace, who wore breeches and frocks over her stays as though it were the most normal thing in the world; who had danced across half the stages of Europe, once upon a time…though she was *miles* too old for that now. Why, she was *ancient*—almost twenty-nine!

And she would still be drawing eyes on the stage when she was bent double with cronehood and had to be wheeled onto downstage left in a Bath chair. It wasn't fair.

"Not another melodrama?" Meg recoiled in exaggerated horror, and Grace made a face. "Don't tell me you're going to be murdered again." She wrinkled her nose in distaste, then snuck a glance at it in the mirror. *Acceptable expression—keep that one to be used later. Remember how it feels.* "One does get so *tired* of being killed off on the regular."

"A show is a show," Grace replied in her usual commonsense way. She tipped her head and turned her face into the light, then carefully lined her other eyelid with her steady brush. "At least it will be a proper death at the Surrey. None of this waving a piece of red crepe about and calling it a murder scene."

"That stuff don't half itch when it's crammed down into your crannies, either," Meg drawled, her laugh sparking with mischief. "But goat's blood stains. I lost three good shifts and almost lost my laundress the last time I played anything there."

"It's a good thing I do my own washing, then," said Grace, ever pragmatic. "There will come a time, my dear, sweet Meglet, when you will not have the options you have now. The ingénue stays the same age, but her players...we cannot stop our own marches of time."

"Don't be so dreary." Meg frowned at herself in the glass once more. Dark-limned eyes stared back at her, bright enough to catch the light from the candles. Her red lips and cheeks would never pass for natural on the street, but against her skin in the firelight of the stage, she glowed like Aphrodite risen from the waves. Montpress had told her so enough times, anyway. "Just you wait. I'll be at Drury Lane playing Viola and Portia, while you have long given up on advancing yourself."

Grace laughed aloud, her head thrown back and cheekbones catching the light. "Meglet, you shall be of an age to play Queen Gertrude by the time either of us sees stardom on a patent stage. In the meantime, we shall be dying every day, festooned with red crepe."

"Gertrude was poisoned," Meg grumped. "And she's not such a bad role. At least a patent theatre means having the licenses for Shakespeare, and tragedies with lines! I should play Lear, if the court ever permits it to be mounted again." She curled the last of her hair up and slid the jeweled pins home. "Is there a Queen Lear? There should be. She would have some lovely speeches."

"Husband, halt, for thou art an enormous twit and thy plan is as one conceived by a knob with cheese for brains." Grace placed one hand on her chest and the other reached out, fingers crooked just so. "The whole play would end when it had only just begun."

Grace was, Meg supposed, her second great passion. Another girl she had never kissed. She was so unlike Sarah in so many ways, except the one that really mattered. Grace and Sarah both showed about as much interest in kissing another woman as they had in kissing goats.

Grace finished with her makeup and slid off the dressing table to land on her booted feet with nary a sound. "There now—done, and with time enough to dress before Sheridan starts cursing about the half hour."

"Are you planning to attend the party tomorrow night?" Meg started the question as a courtesy only, but the image of Grace and Sarah meeting, perhaps finding each other amiable, Sarah's fierce cleverness and Grace's contained poise in the same place at the same time—yes, that was a delightful thought!

"No." Grace shook her head and tugged her man's shirt off over her head. "I think not. I don't enjoy crowds." She stepped out of her breeches, the fabric puddling on the floor. "Are you?" she asked back over her shoulder.

Meg pursed her lips at herself and fussed in the looking glass. "Indeed I am! I have a gentleman's favor to secure, after all." And if it sounded a little brittle this time, so be it.

"Careful, Meglet, careful."

"Whyever for?"

Grace simply shook her head, and Meg sighed inside. "Taking presents from admirers is one thing; dangling after men for their pennies and pounds is another. The law sees all theatre folk as thieves, vagabonds and whores as it is. Don't give them a chance to prove their suspicions right."

Chapter Three

The mirror steadfastly refused to show James the taller, more handsome, professional man he wished to see. The blasted thing must be broken.

He made a face at himself in it instead, at the dark straw-colored hair that oil refused to tame, at the fair eyes that steadfastly refused to smolder and the strong chin that said more "rough laborer" than "refined gentleman". His reflection made the same face back, and James ignored the rudeness to untie his cravat and try it again. He could, if one were to be pedantic about it, afford to hire a valet purely for the tying of his ties in the mornings. But money did not a gentleman make, and for a tradesman to hire a body servant to go with Mrs. Lambert, Cook and the maid who puttered around when he wasn't home—well, it seemed a bit ridiculous, really.

It was only a party for the theatre folks, after all. They were hardly likely to care if their favored staymaker arrived in a properly tied cravat—or a ball gown, or not clothed at all, frankly. They were remarkably accepting that way. It was what made them so receptive to his newer designs, the patterns for more modern clothing and silhouettes than

Tibbert would ever consider displaying in his shop windows. They weren't afraid of novelty the way the wealthy shied away from anything not somehow picked up *en masse* by the Right People.

Having seen all the performers in their underclothes at one time or another also helped immensely with the comfort between them. There was little mystery left in the shape of a woman. His mind kept going to seams, patterns and bones, what cut would elevate a particular bosom to its finest, or color to tone down the ruddiness in a cheek.

The less tangible things caught his attention far more now: the sparkle in a woman's eyes, the curve of a smile meant just for him, a ready wit without cruelty.

Gray eyes, ice covering pools of thought so deep that he could never find the bottom.

Red lips, barely parted, tipped upward and yearning to be touched, kissed, nibbled—

"James?"

Startled, he jumped, his elbow almost knocking over the vase of flowers sitting on the little table in the hallway. Cecily caught it and righted it before the vase could hit the floor, and she laughed at him. "Honestly, how can you make a living with pins and shears when you're a bull in a perfume shop the rest of the time?"

"It wouldn't be an issue," he replied smartly, "if you weren't filling all corners of the house with knickknacks and little breakable things."

His sister put her hands to her hips and made the same kind of face at him as he'd been making at himself before, her nose crinkled and her tongue out. "And if Mrs. Lambert and I didn't make the effort, the whole place would be filled top to bottom with fabric scraps and lost needles, so you should count yourself lucky that you even have women to look after you." She crossed her arms in front of her and scowled.

It took him a moment to notice what was different about her this evening—Cecily had changed from the simple dress she'd worn to dinner. She had a muslin on now, a pretty one that had been a hand-me-down from a cousin some years ago, only now it seemed to fit her properly. It had bagged on the floor only last summer, but Cecily was almost sixteen now and had gained the last inch or so of her adult height. It brought her almost up to his nose, but her wide, luminous blue eyes—still glaring at him, though for what sin now he could hardly imagine—and the fresh peaches of her cheeks kept her looking like the child she still was.

Boys will come courting soon.

And that would be a new fresh hell for James to somehow manage on his own.

She'd put her hair up in curls, a jeweled pin left to her by their mother sitting amid the tumbled sunshine-yellow mass. She'd borrowed gloves, from God alone knew where, and they came up to her elbows. Somewhere under there, he was sure, would be fancy dancing shoes, just to round out the entire business.

"And where, precisely, do you plan to go dressed like that?" James asked archly, one eyebrow coming up.

"With you, of course." Cecily tossed her head, curls bouncing on her shoulders. "You're going to the theatre, aren't you? And then to a party. I heard you speaking to

Sally about having your suit pressed. You haven't taken me out *once*, James, and you promised you would. I'm longing to go, and Miss Ceniza's play *closes* at the Olympic tonight!"

He was the worst brother in the world. And yet, tonight was not negotiable. "No, my dear, you most certainly are not," he replied, and her hopeful expression fell. "This is related to work for me, Cece, and growing our list of clients. Tibbert has no interest in anything except the wealthy *grande dames*, and so I am left with the younger set to charm." He had to be firm, put his foot down. What would their father have done, if he were here? Banish her to her room for a week, most likely, for the sin of impertinence.

But Father was dead, and James was all there was. "It's a late show," he advised, trying a different tack. "There will be far too many young dandies blundering around, half in their cups, and you're not yet seventeen. You should still be in the schoolroom, if it weren't for—"

"If it weren't for me taking on the job that you should be having a wife do," she said snidely. "Whose fault is it that I came back to London to keep house for you? Certainly not mine!"

"That's not the point. You're too young, Cecily. This is not the right night, or the right show, for you. There's a concert next week at the Haymarket," he offered instead, inspiration blooming late, "with pieces of an opera. I'll take you there, and we'll have a lovely dinner beforehand."

"Uch," Cecily groaned, and rolled her eyes in a gesture of adolescent disdain so palpable that he could almost feel it striking his skin. "*Opera.*"

"'*Opera*,'" he teased her in return, mimicking her voice. She stomped on his toe, and thank goodness for crepe dancing slippers, because her little foot didn't make a mark. "See?" he pointed out, grinning. She leaned back against the wall and rubbed her toes, shooting daggers at him with her eyes when he chuckled at her plight. "Definitely too young to be allowed out in public."

He kissed her on the top of her ridiculously done-up head as the clock chimed nine. "I have to go. Have Mrs. Lambert leave some of Cook's scotch eggs out for me. I shall be back around midnight. I promise we'll have a day next week, Cece." He put a hand over his heart as he headed down the stairs toward the front door of their little townhouse. "You and I, and all the excitements that Town has to offer."

"I despise you," she called down over the stairs, though he suspected that she didn't entirely mean it. "I want ices!" she called louder, as he shrugged into his coat and tapped his hat onto his head. "A trip to Decker's bookstore, *and* to see the elephant at the Exchange!"

"A promise!" he called back, made a sloppy salute and closed the door behind him.

The street, darkly amusing though that was, gave him a quieter space to think than his own home. Chelsea buzzed like a hive with activity in the early evening, carriages and riders in the streets and light spilling from the windows of taverns and houses. Artists flourished here, in the bend of the river, their studios becoming salons of their own filled with noisy debaters and revelries.

It was hardly the worst of all options, but Cecily did not belong here. She should have had a quiet country home, a governess to teach her music and art. And a proper springtime in town, even if it would not have been a Season of her own, their mother introducing her around to all the best people in their set. Instead, they had buried both parents within six weeks of each other, and his trade required him—and therefore her—to remain in London all year round.

He should find teachers for her. It wasn't right that her education should be interrupted as much as the rest of her life. Between his inheritance and his profession he could afford to hire some decently skilled tutors. As for who...well. Miss Ceniza would be able to give him the name of a decent dancing-master, at least, if not a music teacher as well.

And there was the crux of his other troubles. James skirted the gutter at the corner, overflowing with water from the day's cleansing rains, and turned down the next street. A couple strolled past, the lady's arm tucked securely in the crook of her gentleman's elbow, and something wistful struck a sad chord deep inside James's chest.

Miss Ceniza, indeed.

The ingénue with Spanish looks, walnut-brown eyes and black hair long enough to caress the small of her back when she let it loose. She hid nothing about her carnal desire for him. She moved, catlike, on stage or off it, prowling and glorious, promising things in the tilt of her head and purse of her red, red lips that braver men than he would kill—or die—for.

And on the other hand, the flip side of the coin, his Madonna. Miss Armand, whose lilting accent curled her words into music. She was a mystery to unwrap, self-contained and wry, with secrets in her wide gray eyes and purpose in every motion, and with the sort of uncompromising fierceness that made a man bold. What was her story? Had her parents fled the ravages of the Terror and come to England's welcoming shores? Or had she fled France herself, scared and alone, cast upon the kindness of strangers to make her own way in the world?

Miss Armand would be good for him, and to him. He would be a better man if she were the one he could come home to every night.

Miss Ceniza would light his nights on fire.

If only he could decide.

Marguerite Ceniza's body, her pink-tipped breasts firm and high, her thighs gripping him as he sank into her, discovering paradise.

Sophie Armand's walls crumbling, looking at him with the kind of affection and vulnerability he had to believe she carried beneath her brisk efficiency, pressing sweet kisses to her lips.

He could hardly court both with any seriousness, not and call himself a good and honest man, and two flirtations would cause him trouble even if neither returned his affections. But how to choose?

On the one hand, there was the sure and certain return of mutual desire, for a short period of time. Miss Ceniza had never hidden her disdain for the sacrament of marriage.

On the other, he could commit his attentions fully to Miss Armand, propose to her and forge a brand-new life...and take the risk that she could never love him in return. Many married for convenience or for money; he would not have that be his fate if he could avoid it.

He pushed open the gate, creaky on its hinges, and jogged down the steps toward Westminster Bridge, and the crossing over the Thames. It was the sort of problem that he usually sneered at when seen in a play—the choices always seemed so clear when faced by someone else. Now that he was embroiled in it himself, what was *he* going to do?

Sarah pulled the comb through Meg's hair, the silken curls rolling over her fingers and through the teeth, the motion itself as reassuring and comforting as any caress ever could be. Meg sat on a cushion at Sarah's feet clad in a silk-and-lace dressing gown, a gift from that irritating baronet, her former patron. She lolled her head back against Sarah's knees, toying with the hem of Sarah's skirt between her fingers. The Horlocks had an invitation to a dinner party that night, followed by some card party that was expected to drag on into the early hours of the morning. Sarah had let herself in to Meg's lodgings less than an hour after they'd departed in their carriage, and now sat in her working clothes, a frothy yellow confection of a gown tossed on the chair beside her.

"You don't sit with Lady Horlock like this, I'll wager."

"Perish the thought!" Sarah shuddered dramatically. "When I do her ladyship's hair, it's an entirely unsentimental matter, mark my words. '"Pull it tighter, Armand,'" she mimicked harshly. "'Not so tight, girl. Use these clasps, no these ones, no *those*.' Lady Horlock is a shriveled, bitter old bat. I don't imagine even Horlock himself has seen her tender side. Not in years, at any rate."

"I suppose they must have been in love, once." Meg was in a mood tonight, her usually cheerful, exhilarating energy faded and wan.

"The better folks aren't like regular folks, Meg. They marry for names and money, not affection. If affection's there, that's a lovely thing, but—well." Sarah shrugged, though Meg wasn't at an angle to see her movement. "You know how bad it can be for a girl, not to have a man about to provide. Imagine how much worse it would be if you had no man *and* no profession—and no hope of ever having one?"

"How dull their days must be." Meg wrinkled her nose in an affected way she'd begun to put on. Her face smoothed and lost its artifice, and she curled a delicate hand around Sarah's ankle. Her fingertips played up and down the tender skin along the inside of Sarah's ankle, the instep of her foot, the line where the curve of her shoe kissed her heel. Tingles, faint and telling, raced along Sarah's skin and up toward the join of her thighs.

"Stop that, it tickles." That wasn't quite true, but her touch was unsettling nevertheless.

"Sometimes I think I must be broken," Meg announced, apropos of entirely nothing. She rested her cheek on Sarah's thigh, her skin warm through the layers of cotton of Sarah's day dress. She glanced up, sidelong, her hazel eyes as devastating and rawly honest as anything Sarah had ever seen. There was no actress here, only a girl of twenty, lost and lonely and often confused.

Sarah rolled one of Meg's black curls between her fingers, softer than any velvet. "Why do you say that?"

"I've never felt it for a man, you know."

Meg stood abruptly, and the loss of her weight and warmth from between Sarah's knees felt like the arrival of winter. She shivered, unaccountably. Meg stood, fingers on the top of her dressing table, and cast a look back over her shoulder. Her curls tumbled to her waist, unbound and glorious, the pale blue silk of her dressing gown clinging to the shape of her stays and rising bosom beneath.

An image, heretical and entirely forbidden, flashed into Sarah's mind: stroking the edge of the silk (*it would be soft, yet still not as soft as Meg's hair*), letting it crumple to the ground in a shining pool of frippery, caressing the round swells of Meg's bosom where it rose above her stays, simply to know what those curves would feel like beneath her fingers.

The faint ache between her legs grew to a distant throb, heat spreading up across her tight lower stomach.

"This wild explosion of love, or whatever it's supposed to be." Meg kept talking, though Sarah's mouth had gone dry. Surely she could hear it, the pounding of Sarah's heart? It betrayed her wild and improper fantasies as surely as a flashing sign above her head.

"Perhaps you haven't met one worthy enough?" Sarah shrugged it off, gathered the brush and comb sitting in her lap and set them aside, waiting for that unaccountable burst of *something* to dissipate. *This is Meg. She is pursued by others for her beauty every day; she doesn't need it from you now.* "You hardly meet the right sort, given the quality of those who approach you at the stage door."

"But what is so *appealing*?" Meg blurted out, her nose wrinkling again. This time it didn't look like affectation.

"Some of them know enough about lovemaking, I'll grant you that—"

"Meg!" Sarah laughed in surprise.

"But aside from a skilled tongue and prick, what on earth is there to recommend them? They're big, brutish, hairy and entirely too loud," Meg complained. "And not a single one has any patience for a woman except for the parts of her within her stays or between her legs. I'll tell you frankly, Sarah, my perfect life would be one lived with a darling friend by my side, a heart-sister who knew the unfolding of my soul, a woman soft, round and warm beneath the sheets at night." Her voice trembled unaccountably, and she looked back over her shoulder, her hair falling across her cheek.

Their eyes locked, hazel to gray, and a question that Sarah didn't dare trust lay bare in Meg's expression.

A breath, and then another.

Meg tossed her head, and the moment was gone. "And perhaps a fancy man in a back cottage we pull out now and again for the abusing of his privy parts," she added outrageously. "Will you choose one for us with a large and skillful prick? I swear that's the only part of them that's of any use to me."

Sarah burst into laughter, for lack of any other way to reply without exposing too much. How much of any of it did Meg mean, and how much was purely to see if Sarah could still be taken aback? Sarah's heart pulsed rapidly within her, so loud that surely Meg must hear it.

Meg joined her after a minute, giggling at her own ridiculous comments. "You're terrible," Sarah scolded, her laughter dying away. "I swear, you come up with these things just to try and shock me. I'll have you know," she continued, drawing herself up tall, "there's little that can do that." She picked up the yellow gown that Meg had tried to insist she borrow, shaking out the length of silk.

"I think I just uncovered one thing," Meg teased, and picked up her combs and pins. "You need a tumble, Sarah darling—you're becoming a prudish miss in your dotage."

"Dotage? I'm all of five months your elder, *child*." Sarah pinched Meg's arm lightly as vengeance.

Meg came close and perched on the arm of Sarah's chair, so close again that Sarah's brain buzzed with it. She had come near so that Sarah could put up her hair, nothing more. But then why was she curling her stocking feet beneath Sarah's thigh, her firm calf pressing against Sarah's arm? "I note you don't deny your encroaching prudishness."

"I could tell you stories of last summer that would curl your hair even tighter, my fine young trollop," Sarah teased, struggling to slow the pounding of her heart and stop her face from flushing hot. "Besides, where would I find a lover? Not to mention I have no interest in risking the sort of unhappy accident that apothecaries are hard-pressed to cure. Lady Horlock would have me out on my ear in an instant."

Meg reached out and wrapped a lock of Sarah's hair around her finger. She tugged on it gently, and sparks ignited along Sarah's spine, settling in her lower back.

Sarah held herself still, Meg so warm against her side, and—bewilderingly, distractingly—watching her intently. Could she tell? Sarah's gut clenched. Did she know that her touch, her red pouting lips, the sight of the golden swells of her breasts above the edge of her stays, were lighting curling licks of fire deep inside Sarah's body?

The night they had lain down together, Meg had smelled like orange blossoms. Sarah had come close to pressing her lips to Meg's in sweet benediction, before she'd come to her senses.

Meg bit her bottom lip, teeth white against the soft pink flesh. She reached out to Sarah, traced her fingertips down Sarah's cheek. The touch, tentative and feather-light, stirred something wonderful inside. *This is Meg*, her mind screamed at her. *This is your closest friend, the only one who knows the self you keep hidden from the world, your most particular and dearest companion.*

Who better, then, to give in to?

Who safer?

If Meg wanted her as well, why deny it?

Sarah tilted her head up and moistened her dry lips with the tip of her tongue.

Meg leaned in, cupped Sarah's cheek with her hand and pressed a closed-mouth kiss against Sarah's waiting lips.

Yes.

Some part of her had expected Meg's kiss to be gentle—softer, more delicate, a fevered flutter of butterfly wings or angel's eyelashes.

Twaddle. All of it.

The kiss began tentatively, true, but when Sarah pushed back, laying her hand on Meg's thigh and parting her lips to return the press, the place where their mouths joined—lord! Meg's mouth was hotter than any fire, slick and fierce, her tongue dancing along the space between Sarah's lips, her fingers burying themselves in Sarah's hair.

A gasp ripped itself free from Sarah's lungs, the distant throb expanding and rolling across her entire body. She ran her hand up Meg's thigh, clutching at the soft silk of her dressing gown, so much softer than Sarah had imagined, warm through from Meg's skin. Sarah yearned up into the kiss, tasted Meg's mouth with a tentative sweep of her tongue.

Meg moaned, low in her throat, and she turned, sliding across Sarah's lap until she was straddling her, cupping her face in both hands. Hairpins clattered to the floor around them, and Sarah couldn't find it within herself to care. She tipped back until the chair caught her, cradled her, and her throat was bared and open. Meg pressed soft kisses down her jaw, her neck, then a single solemn brush of her lips against the hollow of Sarah's collarbone, uncovered by the bodice of her dress.

How could she not have known? She had loved Meg since they had been girls, burgeoning women, and not for a moment had Sarah ever suspected that kissing her would feel like *this*. She had never once pictured what it could be like to have this hot bundle of round and fulsome girl straddling her lap, tasting her mouth, returning every moan of pleasure with another of her own.

This, *Meg,* was that indefinable thing she had been missing this entire time.

Sarah laid tentative hands on Meg's hips, and the tremors of nerves and something else exciting and heart-pounding and indefinable made her entire body shiver. The world was orange blossoms and the taste of brandy, the rise and fall of Meg's body as she rocked up against Sarah's hands, pressed her pelvis toward Sarah's chest, the pull and tangle of her fingers through Sarah's hair, the tinny clatter of Sarah's hairpins on the floor.

It would be glorious to feel Meg's breast in her hand, wouldn't it? She could cup it in one palm, kiss the rounded swell—she—

Could she? Sarah slipped her tongue in between Meg's lips, sucked tentatively at Meg's bottom lip. Meg groaned, her voice cracking partway through with a new and desperate sort of longing.

She had Sarah's bodice partway open, enough to expose the tops of her breasts, the coarse gray fabric of her simple stays, the linen of her shift and the ribbon that tied it closed. Sarah closed her eyes, tried to breathe, shivers running across her skin where Meg's fingertips trailed.

Meg's fingers brushed against the taut point of Sarah's nipple, down inside the top of her stays, and Sarah's body convulsed. Her eyes flew open, saw Meg's laughter in her eyes and smile. She felt the lightning that arced down through her and down to that small nub of fire aching in her groin. Meg pinched her, rolled Sarah's nipple lightly between her fingers, the sudden, firm pressure-pain making Sarah gasp. She needed—needed more of this, more of Meg's hands on her, better yet, Meg's mouth on her, and then—then—

And then do what? Meg bit along the top of Sarah's breast in little sharp nips, her own breath coming in soft, fast pants, though Sarah's hands had selfishly never moved from Meg's hips.

She should—what? Dive between her legs? Run her fingers through the folds of Meg's cunt, no doubt slick and wet by now, as Sarah's were?

Slide a finger up into the most secret of places inside her body and make her writhe, humid and tight? Sarah had dreamt this, brought herself to climax with fingers and thumb, imagined Meg in the most feverish of fever dreams. But had Meg? Had she dreamed of Sarah too?

Sarah's confusion swirled around her mind, tainting and muddling everything. Meg didn't seem so afflicted, working her hand in the buttons at the top of Sarah's bodice. She pressed dry lips to the corners of Sarah's mouth, her eyelids, then slid her mouth over Sarah's once more.

"Meg—" Sarah broke the kiss, curled her hands in the cotton of Meg's dress, tried to catch her breath and her runaway mind all at once. "Stop," she begged, and Meg sat up. "I need—" *A moment to breathe, just one.* A wounded, hunted look flashed in Meg's eyes, all fear and panicked self-loathing. "No, darling," Sarah tried again, clasping her hands. "It's not…" She trailed off, words failing her.

"I don't know what you like," Sarah confessed, her face flushing hot with embarrassment the way it hadn't quite managed with lust. "Or what you want."

Shoulders uncurling, hands coming back up to cup and stroke Sarah's face, Meg shook her head. "Whatever you want," she promised. "I'm yours, if you want me."

And what could be said to that? "I do."

It was easier, after that, Meg's delight suffusing both of them and bringing laughter back to Sarah's lips. Meg tugged at the lacing of her short stays and let them fall open.

The pink silk brushed away beneath Sarah's questing hand, then the white linen beneath, exposing Meg's breasts. They were perfection, small, round and firm, her pink nipples riding high and tight, pebbling under Sarah's caress.

Sarah cupped one in her palm, rolled her hand across the fullness, and Meg gasped when Sarah's palm smoothed over the hard pink of her nipple. Sarah bent her head and tasted it, gently, with the tip of her tongue, circling and flicking, laving and growing bolder with every whimper and gasp Meg made. Each sound spurred her on, made the heat in Sarah's privy parts burn and her center throb. Meg's skin was sweet, a faint trace of powder lingering against the warmth of musk.

Meg's breasts begged to be bitten, her hips starting to rise and fall with the press and pull of Sarah's mouth. She ran her hands up Meg's thighs, still braced on either side of Sarah's knees, and tugged at the fabric enveloping her legs.

Sarah's own body burned, her breath coming in short pants, her heart pulsing loud in her ears. Her cunt ached, empty and untouched. If Meg slid her thigh between Sarah's, then she could find the pressure she needed so desperately.

"Come here." Sarah cupped Meg's bottom in her hands, rising up on her own knees to maneuver them into a better position. Meg didn't seem to understand, until she did, pressing one leg between Sarah's and riding high on Sarah's thigh. Meg's pantalets were a ridiculous affectation, just one more place for her to pin lace. But they were split at the seat, and the contrast between the rough edges of the linen and the silken heat of Meg's skin, the divot of her inner thigh, the damp curls of hair, oh! That had to be why she wore them.

Sarah rose up and pressed herself against Meg's thigh, the pressure sending coils of fire snaking around her cunt, sliding up along her limbs, making her push her tongue into Meg's willing mouth. Heat, Meg was all heat, and her cunt so slick with desire that Sarah could slide her fingers inside just…like…that!

Meg arched, *tight hot wet* inside, closed around Sarah's fingers, rubbed frantically against the pad of Sarah's thumb placed just at the apex. And her breasts—her round little breasts that Sarah had imagined cupping, that she had imagined biting, now bare and bouncing. Sarah, desperate, bit at the swells. She rubbed circles with her thumb and sucked Meg's nipple into her mouth, crooked her fingers inside Meg and made her writhe.

"Please, please, please, oh yes, *please*," Meg begged, her head tipped back and her golden-hued skin gleaming with sweat. Sarah rutted up against her thigh, impeded by the linen, rough and damp now, Meg riding Sarah's fingers and closing tight, tight, tighter—"*Yes!*"

Meg shook, she shook and she curled forward, her sharp nails digging into Sarah's hair. She arched and when her nipple brushed Sarah's lips, Sarah sucked at it obligingly. Sweet, hard, it fit perfectly against her lips. And there were those sounds again, little gasps of air—could she make Meg cry out again? Sarah suckled one, then the other. Meg shuddered again, still rocking against Sarah's hand, even as her breathing slowed. It picked up one last time, one last tremor, and then she was falling, sliding forward with her arms about Sarah's neck and her body trembling, sweat-prickled and limp.

Sarah still burned, the hunger in her groin insatiable and desperate, her clitoris throbbing. She needed; she needed. *Fill me, taste me, take me to pieces and let me die in your arms.* But she could let Meg have this moment, revel in the pleasure she had taken.

Meg seemed to think differently. She raised her head, the gleam in her eyes the same sort seen in the eyes of a cat pouncing upon a songbird or a wolf on a lamb. She licked her lips, cupped Sarah's breasts in her hands and pressed tight, hot kisses all around her nipples.

"Lie back," she ordered, slapping Sarah lightly on the thigh when she did not move fast enough. The sharp tingles shot through Sarah like lightning, setting fire to the fuel in her belly. She squeaked despite herself. "Lie back, I said," Meg threatened, her grin wide, and slapped Sarah again.

"Enough," Sarah half-laughed, her stinging skin growing hot under Meg's hand. "All right. What do you plan to—"

She couldn't finish her sentence before her head was on the floor, and Meg was stuffing a pillow beneath it. Meg's arms went beneath Sarah's knees, pushed Sarah's dress up around her waist, the fabric rasping against her stinging, pink-bitten skin. Sarah's knee-high stockings, plain ribbon garters and her bare thighs and cunt lay exposed, open and—no, not vulnerable, but powerful. Because the burning look in Meg's intoxicating, caramel-brown eyes was aimed at her alone.

Meg's fingers gripped tight on Sarah's thighs, and she bent her head to kiss Sarah's lower stomach. She kissed the bare skin, kissed and bit at it, ran her tongue down, down over Sarah's hipbone, along the crease at the very top of her thigh. Meg's tongue left a damp streak behind, one that grew cool and warm in turn when Meg breathed across it.

There was a pause, a pause that seemed to drag on for so much longer than the couple of seconds it must have been in reality, then Meg adjusted her grip. Her thumbs stroked along the tender skin of Sarah's folds, stroked up and down and never once touched her clitoris. Sarah arched, strained her back to lift her hips higher, Meg's hand falling away the moment she came close. Meg brushed her touch over the hood that covered Sarah's pleasure, never enough pressure to give her what she needed. Sarah cursed, she dug her nails into the pillow behind her head, she bucked and rocked her hips, and still Meg would not show her mercy.

Then, oh then, when the burning throb of desire was too much, all her thoughts incoherent and every fiber of her body screaming for release—Meg licked a broad stripe up along Sarah's cunt, from entrance to apex, and her thumbs pressed Sarah's folds open. The cool air, the pressure, the heat of Meg's tongue—it blended and swirled in Sarah's brain. There was only this, Meg's mouth closing over her and sucking; hot-hot-wet and strong. Meg's thumb pressing into Sarah's entrance, up and in; her tongue drawing clever circles and figure eights, ripples of pleasure and desire so strong that details faded into a rolling sea of sensation. Meg's fingers slipped inside, filling her and stretching her wide. Sarah rose on the wave and crested it.

She shook, shuddered, jammed her fist into her mouth and gripped the pillow so tightly with the other that she heard stitches popping. Her feet slammed into the floor on either side of Meg and she pushed up into Meg's mouth, up, and Meg's hands came under her buttocks to support her. Meg sucked, licked and tasted her, rode her through convulsion after convulsion, heat and pure, radiant joy crashing over Sarah again, and again, and again.

Finally, her body shaken apart from head to toe, Sarah collapsed, her hips landing gently on the wooden floor. She ached gloriously, satiation flooding every inch of her skin, muscles, poor confused brain. Meg curled into her arms, pressed kisses to Sarah's lips. She tasted like Sarah must, all musk and sour-sweet fruit, her lips plumped up from the pressure and her voice breathless from laughter.

"Meg, Meg, my Meg," Sarah murmured, flattening her hands on Meg's back, her hips, running her touch up Meg's thighs once more to cup her beneath her pantalets and stroke her once more.

Meg shuddered and pulled back from Sarah's hand, but kissed Sarah again, which took away any sting. "Too sensitive," she murmured soft against Sarah's lips. "But give me an hour, my darling, and I can be yours again however you want me."

"You never said," Sarah began, words still floating away and difficult, if not impossible, to catch.

"You never asked," came the equally faint reply. Her earlobes had no rings in them, and Sarah scraped her teeth across one, plump, warm and rounded.

This was glorious, though they would have to move eventually—the wood floor was no good for sleeping on, and the euphoria of lovemaking would ebb soon enough. But for the moment, yes, she would enjoy this.

What of Mr. Glover?

The thought came unbidden, and with a new flash of guilt.

He has yet to declare himself, and there's no man alive who comes to his wedding day a virgin. If Mr. Glover ever marries. Which he may not intend to do.

No, she would admit no fault for this. Meg would never leave her with a bastard to raise, after all, nor would any man consider her ruined by their adventures, though the pleasure she'd had from it was greater by far than anything she'd experienced with fumbling boys. Let them admire their pricks and concentrate on ruination and women's folly—she would keep Meg as her lover for as long as she could, and enjoy all the benefits thereof.

"What will this change?" Sarah asked, unable through the whirling of her thoughts to leave well enough alone.

Meg lifted her head from where she had it cushioned on Sarah's shoulder, and brushed a kiss to Sarah's lips. Sarah chased it as much as she could without sitting up, catching Meg's lower lip between her teeth. "Nothing, if we do not allow it," Meg said firmly. "You are still my dearest darling, and I am still your particular friend. Men will come and go, my love, as they must. But you are the one I give myself to."

Sweet promises, made the sweeter by admission of their reality. Sarah stole more kisses, Meg still pressed against her, so gloriously curved. She cupped Meg's breast, for the sheer novelty of being allowed to do it. It sat heavy and warm in her palm. Then she frowned. "But what if one of us receives a proposal, Meg—"

A clatter and a crash outside broke the moment, the sharp noise of splintering wood followed immediately by a string of loud and inventive curses. The fog around Sarah's mind shattered like frozen ice on a pond. She was more dressed than Meg—she would have to go look. Smoothing her dress back down as she rose, Sarah moved to the window. A cart lay in the road, overturned and one axel broken, a stocky man in workman's clothes stomping around and loudly listing off all the problems of someone's ancestry.

"It's only an overturned cart," Sarah reported, and Meg made a rude noise from the floor. Chickens tumbled out of a crate that lay beside the wagon and fled, squawking, across the road, feathers dropping in a haphazard trail behind them.

The driver stopped, and he looked up, right at her through the dark of evening. He couldn't see her face; most likely all he saw was a silhouette, a form of a woman in the window looking down at him. That cold, blank regard speared through her nonetheless, skin crawling on the back of her neck.

Sarah closed the shutters and shut him off from view.

A clock chimed somewhere in the distance.

"Sarah?" Meg had stood while Sarah had been woolgathering, and she laid a tentative hand against Sarah's cheek.

"It's late," Sarah realized with real alarm. "I need to go." She coiled her hair and pinned it back up loosely, so that it would sit under her hat and not be in the way. "You need to get to the theatre before it's too late, or the show will start without you," she teased gently.

"They can't start without me—I play the lead," Meg retorted, tossing her hair imperiously. It didn't distract completely from the flash of hurt and confusion in her golden-brown eyes. "And you're supposed to come to the party with me after the show."

Sarah shook her head slowly. "I don't think I can," she confessed quietly. "We've just changed things, Meg, into something new and brilliant. I need to think things out, put it all right in my head. This is only good night and I will see you on the morrow," she promised, her head back together now and her thoughts starting to fall in order again.

Ducking her head, Meg appeared to be considering it. "There's nothing happening that wasn't meant to happen," she ventured after a beat. "When bodies are in turmoil and there are no other ways to quench the fires burning within, why not turn to a beloved friend to seek solace?"

"Is that what this is?" Sarah asked, her lips tugging into a curve despite herself.

"Absolutely." Emboldened again, Meg stepped in close, cocking her head to one side. "I love you, Sarah darling, though one day you will marry and leave me all alone to pine and die of grief."

Ah. She's feeling better.

"I shall do no such thing," Sarah promised recklessly. "I shall live and die an old maid, still in service to the Horlocks, and we will make love whenever we can find our time alone. Then I'll have no need of a man to complicate matters."

Meg leaned in, brushed her lips tentatively against Sarah's as though testing for something. Sarah slid her hands along Meg's arms, pulling her closer for another attempt at a kiss. They lingered on each other's lips, Meg's eyelashes sweeping dark shadows across her cheeks.

"Don't go," Meg murmured against her mouth, sweet as could be.

Sarah closed her eyes. "I have to. You'll be magnificent tonight, dearest. I know you will."

"Not without you!" Meg objected, hands dropping to become fists against her hips.

It was all Sarah could do not to laugh, partly out of habit, partly out of nervous energy bubbling up inside. It wouldn't do. Not now with things changing more rapidly than she could keep up. "Don't be dramatic, darling. What about your manhunt? I would only be in your way. I'll see if I can get away again tomorrow, and you can tell me all about it. I expect to see you set up in your new apartment by Sunday, you know, looking down from Mayfair on all of the peons in the street below."

Meg stalked away, dropping down into the lone, worn-out armchair in a flounce of ruffled silk and a pout meant for the stage. "Don't mock me, Sarah—you're unkind."

"And you're utterly ridiculous," Sarah replied fondly. She knelt down before Meg, sprawled upon her chair like a drunken knight upon the queen's throne. Her pantalets spread apart a little, giving Sarah flash glimpses of thigh, dark curls, sweet pink flesh that begged to be kissed. She settled for laying her hands upon Meg's thighs and squeezing. "I will see you tomorrow. I love you, even as we change the meaning of it."

Meg blinked up at her, her lip still jutting out but her eyes merry. "I suppose I shall have to believe you, then."

"Yes, of course you must," Sarah insisted, pressing a kiss to Meg's lips. The urge was mounting, to squirrel herself away in a dark corner, turn over everything that had just happened and examine it for motives, implications, import— She stood. "I will never lie to you."

Meg took a breath, as though to say something, but then she closed it quickly and reclined in her chair. She gestured imperiously, an unmistakable dismissal, and Sarah laughed, then slipped away into the night.

The cool evening air battered harsh against her skin, opening her eyes and driving away the last curling fog of lust from her addled brain.

What had that been? Was it only a symptom of their bodies in turmoil, as Meg had suggested? Or a more natural occurrence, taking them from soul-deep friendship to something more in the blink of an eye?

Her body throbbed with sensations that she had not felt in years, pleasure still making her limbs leaden and thick. Something momentous had just taken place. All she knew, at this moment, was that she wanted to do it again, and as often as possible.

James had made up his mind by the time he arrived at the Olympic Pavilion. The walk in the crisp evening air had done wonders to clear his mind, and with it, reevaluate his priorities. What he wanted—what he needed in his life— was stability.

To be loved with someone's whole heart, and to love her eternally in return; a marriage like his parents had enjoyed; a home, filled with joy, music and laughter. A partner to share his triumphs and sorrows.

Cecily tried her best, but the two of them could not fill up the rooms enough, replace his father's booming laugh enough. It had been a little less than a year, and he still felt…unsteady. Unsure of his decisions.

For his sister's sake, as well as his own, he had to keep up the pretense that he knew what he was doing. Let her, at least, be confident in her future.

Fine. A home, then; someone to build one with him and keep him strong when he felt most alone. What else?

He wanted children, God willing—maybe even a son who would carry on his trade in turn. Tibbert didn't have that, after all—he'd devoted himself to his labors. And look what that had won him. A friend's son as a partner, and no one but James and a cluster of rich old women to mourn him when he was gone.

Miss Armand responded to his flirting, but never pushed him further. She was in service, had been for all the time he'd known her. She would have no dowry of any sort to bring with her, but he didn't need her money. And who better to run a household with finesse? She was clever, very pretty, and every so often he caught a look in her eye that suggested she liked him as well.

Miss Ceniza had given no indication that she wanted any of those things. She teased and tormented, a darling, willing succubus. He'd be hard-pressed to imagine her keeping house or with a baby at her breast.

But oh, she was exquisitely beautiful.

James settled into his seat in the first gallery, leaning forward over the railing to take everything in: the pit below, the backless benches covered over in blue fabric, the boxes for the slightly more moneyed running around the edges of the pit and the gallery above that faced the stage. On the final night all were full, the heavy velvet draperies closing them in to the artificial world of the stage. He'd seen this show before, of course. He'd sent Miss Ceniza a flower to wish her luck. The buzz and hollering of the crowd was as wild and excited tonight as it had been then, and he couldn't help but be caught up in the familiar rush of anticipation.

A pack of young bucks lounged at the back of the pit, a strikingly dark-haired man—vaguely familiar in the face, though James knew they'd never been introduced—in the center of the throng. He watched the stage with as much avarice as James had been doing a moment ago, seemingly unaffected by the pressing and jostling of the other audience members around him.

Was he also waiting for Miss Ceniza to appear?

The musicians struck up the overture and the theatre grew quieter—never quiet, not in this section of town—the immense oil lamp above the proscenium shedding a golden glow over the proceedings. The scenery showed a castle in the back, stone walls running hither and yon to divide the space like a maze.

Miss Ceniza made her entrance, a raven-haired angel in a flowing blue dress, running pell-mell through the painted-canvas thickets. Enraptured, James no longer remembered what he had been thinking about before.

Intermission saw the audience taking over the lobby of the small theatre for drinks and conversation, but the true celebration of a struck show took place after the fact, in the stage manager's apartments behind the theatre itself. Sheridan wasn't a wealthy man—one never was, working on the stage, unless one began that way—but his lodgings were larger by far than anyone else's in the cast or crew, and his landlady had something of a fixation on actors. She was more than willing to allow them the use of her best parlor, as long as some of the leading men promised to attend.

Someone had taken James's hat and coat from him when he came inside, and now he stood by the fireplace in his nice suit, a glass of wine in his hand, smiling and making petty conversation with one of the stagehands who had only just arrived.

"Mr. Glover!" A vision in lavender and cream burst into the room and made a line directly toward him. Miss Ceniza had made a brilliant recovery from her on-stage death, all traces of stage blood and madness washed away, the artifice replaced with shining eyes and coral lips, black hair pinned up with pearls and pale purple ribbons. "You did come tonight! I'm so glad."

"I never break a promise," he replied, her exuberance and joyful reception melting away the hesitation and turmoil in his heart. She extended her gloved hand and he took it, pressing a playful kiss to the back. She curled her fingers around his and laughed, a stream trickling down a mountainside. "You were marvelous tonight."

That was true enough, though she had seemed oddly distracted.

"I thought I was marvelous *every* night," she replied coquettishly.

Think fast. "You are, but it is ever more bittersweet when you finish a show," he suggested. "Because when you play I am guaranteed a chance to see you every night. And now your other admirers will have you so thoroughly ensnared with invitations and entertainments that a poor young staymaker could never compete."

"Never!" she pouted, and took his wine from his hand. She sipped at it, dark lashes veiling her eyes. "You're neither poor nor terribly young. And I daresay that a man who has made his life's study of women's forms would be hard-pressed to find competition anywhere." She gestured in the air. "So many don't even bother to try understanding us, and yet you've made our beauty your life's work."

"When you phrase it like that, how can a man argue? The more fool other men, who cannot see the wonder that is before them." He chuckled softly, but the lump in his throat remained.

She took another drink, and her throat bobbed as she swallowed. She'd inclined her head just so, in order for him to see it, and the faintest trace of red wine lingered on her lower lip. The tip of her tongue darted out to taste it. His body reacted with stirrings of desire so immediate that he was hard-pressed not to seize her by the arms and kiss her immediately.

"Miss Ceniza," he breathed out, and she laughed. "You need no assistance from me."

She colored prettily, casting her eyes down. The shadows cast by her long, dark lashes stroked gently against her cheekbones. He could imagine stroking the pad of his thumb across those same lines, smooth and fresh.

His rough fingers would scratch her, this sun-golden angel. He should leave her to be the pampered prize of nobler, softer-touched men.

"Prettily said, Mr. Glover," she teased, apparently unaware of his train of thought. "Have you ever considered taking the stage?"

"No, never," he insisted immediately. "I shall leave that role to those better suited for public presentation. I toil behind the scenes, my work—when done right—invisible, in happy service to you."

Miss Ceniza laughed prettily and handed him back his glass. "And we are happier for it."

He put his lips to the place hers had been and drank, and now there was definitely color in her cheeks as well. "Where do you go from here?" he asked, double meaning in his words. *What show, what theatre, do you have someone else waiting in the wings?*

"Tonight?" she asked, her voice deepening to a purr. But even at that moment there was something hesitant and sad in the back of her eyes. A surge of protectiveness welled up inside him, the overwhelming desire to take her in his arms and promise to keep the pressures of the world at bay.

Would you want me to save you, if I could? Give you a home and a life beyond this noise and chaos?

Not a question he could ask here.

"Miss Ceniza!" One of the dancers called from across the room and she turned with a bright smile and a ready wave. "Come here for a moment and let me make an introduction!"

"You're heavily in demand tonight." James searched her face for some sign of an answer and found nothing but a vague sense of distance that had not been there the week before.

"Do you mind terribly?" she asked, biting her lip in a calculated gesture.

He shook his head. "No, not at all. This is your night, after all," he added for good measure, to show just how much he really was fine with the interruption. Honestly. "You must enjoy yourself to the fullest."

"Keep that thought present in your mind," she replied, her eyes lingering on him a moment longer before she let herself be drawn into the crowd and away. She moved with a sway to her hips that was almost certainly intended for him, and the yearning coiling low in his body wouldn't allow him to look away.

"You're deep in thought tonight, Mr. Glover!" Sheridan's voice cut in to his distraction. The Pavilion's stage manager, tall, barrel-round and dark-skinned, approached and handed James another drink. His large hands all but dwarfed the small flagon. Even in his forties, or near to, and long past his days of hard labor, Sheridan had managed to keep the muscle he'd put on at the dockyards. He'd only been managing the Pavilion for a short while, since an accident had ensured he'd never do heavy work again, but under his management the small theatre was thriving.

James had become terribly fond of the Backstage Behemoth over the past few months. Having been commissioned to do new bodices for all the ballet girls at the beginning of the fall season had played no small part in that. "Sheridan! Thank you kindly for the invitation tonight." He took the drink and set his now-empty wine glass down on the mantel of the fireplace, saluting as he did so.

"What else?" Sheridan's deep voice boomed. "It's always good to see you enjoying a show, rather than working your arse off behind the scenes. Though I suppose your job's not so arduous, then, getting to see all your clients in their altogethers. Not a hard life at all." And he winked.

He was only teasing, James knew it, but couldn't help grinning and taking the bait. "I'm a gentleman through and through, believe me. I'd never have repeat clients otherwise!"

"Too right. Speaking of which, I'll arrange a time to have you come by and see the missus. She's been mumbling about her underpinnings since the last baby came, and heaven knows she could use a few nice things to 'erself," Sheridan said tenderly.

James chuckled softly. "You're a good man, Sheridan." He took a healthy swallow of the drink in his cup—not wine, as he'd anticipated, but some incendiary concoction that burned and seized in his chest all the way down. He coughed, and Sheridan politely pretended not to notice.

"Don't tell anyone else that, or me reputation's ruined," he pointed out instead.

James couldn't speak to Tibbert about love—the old man had never felt it, of that James was sure. It would be utterly inappropriate to disclose any of his thoughts to his sister, and what sort of advice could she have for him anyway? Sheridan, on the other hand, had been happily married for years. He had three—no, four—children now, and by all signs, his had been a love match that had stayed loving.

Perhaps...

"Tell me," James said, swirling the drink in his cup before taking another stinging gulp. The liquor settled in his stomach and burned through him like a star, casting its heated rays out through all his limbs. It loosened his tongue as well, and the question came easier. "What would you do, if you had to make a choice?"

Sheridan curled one thick, dark eyebrow up, skeptical. "What sort of choice?"

"Let us say," James began, "that a friend of mine—" Sheridan snorted with laughter, and James stopped talking. Sheridan waved him off with a swing of his hand.

"No, no, pray, continue."

"A *friend of mine* is caught in a bind," James said pointedly, but the men shared a grin. "Between a fine, lovely woman he longs to take to wife, and a tempestuous, unmarriageable angel who haunts his dreams."

Sheridan dropped his chin and chortled, shaking his head with the easy way of a man who has seen too much. "First things first, that friend of yours better hope that even one of 'em will want him. Assuming he's no fool."

"Oh, he's a fool, all right," James said ruefully.

"So let him be foolish," came Sheridan's unexpected reply. "Marry the one and keep the other, in whatever manner he can afford. The wife for bed and board, and the mistress for play. It's the done thing among fashionable men. I could never manage it, meself."

"Too expensive?"

"Too fond of keeping my bollocks attached to my body."

"Ah."

"But Kemp's wife is a sweet, biddable sort of thing, and he's got a girl in apartments over on St. James," Sheridan said, not helping James's moral quandary in the slightest. His dark eyes twinkled with amusement and he leaned in to finish speaking, dropping his voice to a murmur. "And I've heard that young Ramsbury—the poet—spends more time burying his ram in a strapping butcher boy than in his own new bride."

Miss Ceniza's laughter rang out across the room, and when James turned, she was looking back at him. She winked, utterly outrageously, and James's skin felt too tight and too hot everywhere. He wanted to take her to bed, to lie her down and press kisses along her skin, to suck her nipples into his mouth and toy with them, bite and lick her perfumed skin until her blood ran as hot as his and she begged for sweet release.

Marry the one, and keep the other.

Would it be possible? If so, if he were never found out, then everyone could be happy.

Chapter Four

Emmeline: How could fate be so unkind? I, who must by rights ~~bare~~ *bear my husband's heir and in so doing assure my own security, am as barren as the* ~~salty sea fields in winter~~ *Arabian sands.*

Cynthia: While I, who cannot raise a child, have his lordship's ~~bastard~~ *heir growing beneath my heart.*

Emmeline: Dear Cynthia, my only ^honest friend, would that I could take your burden and your shame from you, and in so doing, relieve me of mine own.

~~Cynthia: If you spent less time moping and more time thinking, you silly cow~~

Cynthia: If you will trust me one more time, my lady, sit here a moment longer while I unfold my ~~plans~~ *thoughts. I have a plan that may yet save us both.*

The door to the stillroom opened, and Sarah slid her pages beneath the washing bills spread out upon the small, cluttered table in front of her.

"Another letter for you, Miss Armand." Jack, one of the London footmen, passed her the square-folded note with its dollop of wax. The handwriting was Mr. Glover's, and Sarah turned away rather than let Jack see the flare of interest in her eyes. He laughed at her anyway, not unkindly. "And this came with it." He grinned, brown eyes laughing, and brought out a sprig of flowers from behind his back. "Will you be leaving us for holy matrimony sometime soon?"

"Hush your mouth," Sarah scolded him immediately. "Don't let anyone hear you make such foolish speculations, or I'll be in for a beating." She slid the note into the bodice of her dress, something to be opened and read later on, when she had some privacy. Jack looked momentarily put out. But he shrugged and set his finger to his lips in a promise of his own silence as he left the hall, the door closing quietly behind him.

That was it for the letter, then. She had work to finish before she could take herself a moment to open and read it. The flowers, on the other hand—the supple branch bent low with its tumult of blooms, a brilliant splash of pink and white with a sunshine perfume that filled the room. Apple blossoms, some of the first of the year.

Why on earth?

A flash of memory, a conversation they'd had the previous spring, when making Lady Horlock's preparations for summer parties. Tibbert and Glover had come to Bracknell then as well, that time staying for two days to prepare Lady Horlock's fittings before retiring back to their workshops in London. Mr. Glover had come upon her in the garden, that time, cutting rose buds for Lady Horlock's dressing table. Presumptuous as ever, he had made a comment.

"No," she had said then. *"Roses are my least-favored flower, all overblown and frowzy. They try too hard,"* she had complained, in a fit of ridiculousness, and he had thrown back his head and laughed so openly and so honestly that she had decided to like him better immediately. *"I much prefer apple blossoms. They are simple and sweet. Rather than give up and die when their luster fades, they become something even more useful in the end."*

He had remembered. That, or he was the luckiest man alive to have stumbled upon it later.

No, she liked that first idea better. He had remembered and gone out of his way to give her that thing she liked the best. Sarah buried her nose in the blossoms, breathed in the sweet scent of springtime and sunlight, and promises of new beginnings. The pounding sound in her ears had to be the rush of her pulse; the ocean was too far away to be heard.

Forget waiting. She opened his letter, the two thin pages crisscrossed with words to use up all available space.

Miss Armand,

I pray this letter finds you well. I hope I am correct in assuming (or more fool I!) that the things I should like to say to you will not come as a complete shock, nor that they will fall on deaf or closed ears. In the short few times we have been in each other's company, I find that—

No, let me begin anew.

I am not, in my heart, a wordsmith. I pray you will forgive my stumbling and imperfect words, as unworthy as they are. I only mean to tell you that I am entranced by you, captured and <u>enthralled</u> by you, and so pleased by the *happy accident of our friendship that I am quite in a confusion.*

Part of my self aches to know you better, to sit with you and hear your life's accomplishments, to know all your desires and dreams, your pains and sorrows—to unfold my own bosom to you in similar manner and discover together whether we might be as well suited one to the each as I imagine.

The rest of me swears "no, no," for I feel already the possibility of a deeper connection between us, and with it the sure and certain knowledge that we are suited—as well suited as any man and woman could be...

On and on it went, the angles of his handwriting sharper than usual, as though the writer were clutching his quill particularly tightly or was in the grips of some fierce emotion.

Not a wordsmith, indeed.

His letter was a florid and ridiculous one, full of the kinds of sweet meaningless things that would sound better spoken by a character in a play rather than murmured in Sarah's ear. She checked the address quickly, in case it had somehow been delivered to the wrong house. No, there was her name, and his, and the unexpected flattery filling up the lines in between.

There was no mistaking his intent, not this time. He meant to court her, ideally to win her, and then what— matrimony? The marriage of true minds, and so on?

She came with a rather large impediment that would have to be clarified sooner rather than later—what if he imagined she was some kind of lost aristocrat? Oh, would he ever be in for a shock once she confessed the truth. But there was no method by which she could keep the farce up in private as well as in public. Especially if he knew how to speak French.

And then, oh! What was to be done about Meg? The drastic change in their friendship had been all Sarah could think about as she went about her daily tasks. Even her play had suffered—how could she be expected to concentrate on Emmeline's marital woes when she had her own conflicted bosom and loins to contemplate?

Mr. Glover's timing was really most inconvenient.

And below the practical litany, that measuring out of everything that could go wrong, would go wrong, pitfalls and dangerous grounds on which she was treading...a flutter of excitement and dreadful nervousness deep inside. More dangerous yet, a curling frisson of hope.

He'd remembered the apple blossoms.

"Be quick about it, Armand—the carriage is waiting." Lady Horlock stood impatiently in the hall, moving away and twitching in the wrong directions every time Sarah tried to help her on with her spencer and her hat. She had finally—*finally!*—managed to get the outer garments settled to her ladyship's satisfaction when Horlock himself strode through, patted Lady Horlock's bottom, took the hat from her head to press a kiss to her hair, then set it back down again...lopsided. "Armand!"

It would be bad form to jab the Earl of Horlock in the arse with a hatpin, no matter how much she might feel like it in the spur of the moment. "Yes, *madame*, hold still a moment, *madame*," Sarah urged, circling her employer until she finally got everything just *so* once more. "Will that do, your ladyship?"

Lady Horlock studied herself in the mirror for a moment, patted her once-blonde and now gray hair, and cast a steely-eyed glare over the rest of her sharp-edged countenance. "Yes, I suppose it will. Thank you, Armand."

Would wonders never cease?

"Enjoy your outing, *madame*." Sarah curtsied prettily, keeping her bland smile on until the door had finally shut tight behind them and the house could once again relax. She let out a puff of air from between her lips, and Jack, the young footman, chuckled softly.

"How long have we got?" he asked, glancing at the clock on the mantle.

"Until their high-mucketies return? It all depends." Sarah bit her tongue at the irreverence in Ellen's reply. It wasn't her job to make the younger servants guard their tongues—that was the housekeeper's problem. And it wasn't as though she hadn't muttered a few choice words herself, in the past.

Jack and Ellen kept talking as he arrived at Ellen's side, heading for the service stairs. "Depends?"

Ellen shrugged. "Aye. If his lordship finds himself a dice game and some drinking fellows..."

"They'll be out late?" he asked, the naïve boy.

"Just the opposite. She'll drag him home so fast that old elbow-shaker's head will spin."

Jack laughed along with Ellen's wry prediction. "Then let us pray for a temperate and dull afternoon for the pair of them."

The door closed behind them, cutting off whatever Ellen might have said in reply.

Right, then. Sarah had work enough to fill her hours, that was certainly not something of which she was in short supply. There was always plainwork and mending to be done, and Lady Horlock was running low on the lotion Sarah made for her face. If she was to mix more of that then she may as well turn her hand to blending the bleaching paste for the spots that had begun to show on her ladyship's hands as well—

The bell jangled and the door opened all at the same time. Sarah's head jerked up in surprise. She'd been lost in her own thoughts, slowly wandering back down the hallway, and now here was a fluttering bundle of ribbons and spotted muslin launching herself into Sarah's unready arms.

"Meg? What are you doing here?"

Meg tipped back her ridiculous bonnet and beamed a glorious, world-stopping smile at Sarah. "I've come to see you, silly creature. Won't you ask me in?"

"You're already in," Sarah felt utterly compelled to point out.

Frost, the butler, poked his graying head and beak-like nose around the corner, saw Meg in conversation with Sarah and peered down his pince-nez at the pair of them. "Guests, Miss Armand?"

"Only for a moment, Mr. Frost," Sarah replied firmly. "Miss Ceniza's only here to…" She stopped. "To…"

"Don't be tedious, Sa—Sophie," Meg complained, pulling off her gloves one finger at a time. "I know their lord and ladyship have gone off—I waited until the carriage pulled away. Can you not even offer your dearest friend a cup of tea for her troubles?"

Frost brought the rest of his elongated form to stand beneath his nose, all dark suit and disapproval.

"Come to the servants' hall," Sarah compromised quickly, more to get Meg out of the hallway before she said or did anything foolish. "We can chat while I work on Lady Horlock's *toilette*."

Meg beamed, and it was as though sunshine itself had burst into being in their front hall. Even dour Mr. Frost seemed to thaw momentarily. "Capital!" She sailed ahead of Sarah, knowing the way.

Not long later, the kettle on the boil and Sarah's little book of recipes propped up beside her mortar and pestle, Meg dug about in her ridiculous spiked knitted bag. She had always claimed that it was designed to resemble a pineapple, but Sarah could not quite picture the connection. No pineapple in life, surely, had ever been quite that shade of Pomona green.

The little book she pulled out of it was new, though. Not necessarily in and of itself, for the leather of the little cover was faded and looked as though it would be soft to the touch. It was one Sarah had never seen Meg carry before.

"Is this not the uttermost?" Meg set her reticule down beside her confection of a bonnet, her black hair gleaming in the late afternoon sun. "I was only just speaking about these poems to—well, you know—and what do you think he sent me yesterday?"

Her enthusiasm was as infectious as her eyes were bright, and Sarah stepped fiercely down on the confusion that swirled inside. Of course Meg would have to keep on pursuing a patron. Sarah could hardly pay her way, whatever else they might...end up doing.

And then guilt, deep and sour, for the letter from Mr. Glover was still sitting inside her stays, folded small and pressed against the side of her left breast, beside her heart.

"I cannot begin to guess," Sarah said dryly, buying herself some time.

"Oh, poo." Meg made a face. "It's the poems of John Donne, silly girl. The lewd ones, anyway. I can't abide the ones that are all about God. They make me feel like I'm a fidget in the pews at church." She passed the book over, the little cover dented and warm where her fingers had pressed. Sarah took it, flipped through the pages idly. "I do think he means to ask me to be his mistress soon. We had the most lovely conversation at the party the other night, even if he did end up having to leave early."

Used or not, the little book was still complete and well bound, a blank page at the front and back to protect the inner contents. And there, on the frontispiece—

Sarah's heart, only recently begin to swell with possibility and yearning once more, turned black and shattered into a million pieces within her chest.

On the frontispiece, in handwriting she had come to know very well, was a note.

And now good morrow to our waking souls, it read, in what was probably a quote. But what did Sarah know of proper literature? Her diet of novels and plays was nothing compared to Meg's explorations.

That was all it said, but it was signed with the initials *JG.*

Sarah traced them with her finger, the matching signature burning a hole into her breast.

Of course he desired Meg. Who could resist her? Sarah, despite her sex, was infatuated. How could a man refuse when Meg set her mind to have him?

He had seemed so genuine, when she'd stared into his eyes. He'd flattered and cosseted her, and she'd lapped up every false word like some house cat with a dish of milk. He had sent Sarah apple blossoms and Meg a book on the very same day.

What choices were left to her now?

She could say nothing, encourage his attentions, use all her wiles to secure the man she wanted, and Meg's plans be hanged! She had all but memorized his letter already, every compliment and description of his passionate longing.

What had he written to Meg, that she knew nothing of?

No, allowing herself to dream had been the prime mistake. Switching her loyalties would only compound her error.

"JG," she read aloud, and looked up. Meg had marked her uneasy silence, obviously enough. The brightness in her eyes had dimmed, and she watched Sarah with trepidation. "Is this…" Sarah hesitated, then forged onward. "…a gift from James Glover?"

Meg relaxed a little, but only a little. "It is! You know him? What a foolish question—of course you must. His father was a merchant to the Dutch, you know, exported clocks, I think, and other fancy wares. But James has gone into staymaking."

"He comes to take measurements for Lady Horlock," Sarah replied, her tongue thick and the words hard to form.

"You do know him! How exciting! Then you must have seen him. He's awfully good looking, for a man. But don't worry, darling." Meg leaned in across the table, hands pressed to the edge. "I still love you best of all."

Sarah pushed herself away from the table sharply, moving quickly to the hob to take up the boiling kettle and make the tea. "He has a pleasant face. And he's been very kind. But Meg—"

She had to be honest, marriage or not, future or not. Her loyalty lay first and foremost with Meg. "We may have a problem," she confessed, looking down at the teapot as she rinsed it with the boiling water. "Mr. Glover is courting me as well."

"What, to be his second mistress?" Meg gasped, and she didn't sound upset at all, rather, almost—amused? "I never imagined you'd indulge a man in such a thing. Nor that he might have the stamina to please two of us."

It stung more fiercely than she realized it might. "I've no intention of doing so, for anyone," Sarah replied, her words coming out more clipped and fierce than she'd intended. She bit back the rush of shame and humiliation and began again, setting the tea to steep before she sat. "Meg, he's been courting me to be his wife."

The letter tucked into her stays was all the proof she needed. The thin sheet crinkled when Sarah passed it over, the lines of careful script bleeding into one another until all she could see behind the prickles in her eyes were smudges.

Silence hung between them, but for the faint sound of birds screaming warnings to each other outside. She didn't dare look up from her hands.

Sarah had a roof over her head, after all—stable employment, clothes on her back and meals enough to fill her belly. Meg had only whatever contracts and work she could scare up, sometimes living week to week with no knowledge of what came next, and small plays paid small wages. Meg needed Mr. Glover more than Sarah did.

There. She had her answer after all. She would fade to the background, allow them to exercise their passions upon one another and find her own way to a better life. This was how it would end. Sarah had lost Joshua to his one true love; now she was going to have to give up both Mr. Glover and her Marguerite as well.

"Oh, darling," Meg breathed out, and a moment later her slim hand covered Sarah's. "That cad!" There was no recrimination in her voice, no hatred nor anger. Meg took her hand back and a moment later she sank to the floor at Sarah's knees, her skirts pooling around her in a narrow puddle of fine cotton.

"You liked him very much, didn't you? Oh! I see that you do," she began to prattle on. Sarah frowned, felt her brow pull together in a furrow, but Meg kept talking. "What a no-good flirt and a bounder! Oh, tell me he hasn't hurt you too badly, darling. Nor I—you know I would never had set my cap for anyone if I'd known you were the slightest bit intrigued, or even that you knew him in the first place! Promise me your heart isn't too badly wounded, and that you shall surely mend!"

What could one do in the face of such voluminous appeals? Sarah gripped Meg's hands and started laughing from the shock of the moment and Meg's sweet ridiculousness. *At least I shan't lose you.*

"But what about you?" Sarah asked; it was always easier to care for someone else's injuries than her own. "Are you not hurt as well? He's played us both falsely."

"Pish." Meg waved her hand in the air, but she didn't meet Sarah's eyes. "I'm impermeable." She cocked her head and her nose wrinkled. "Invulnerable? One of those in-im-words, anyway. What matters is that he thought he could have us both for fools, and that..." She trailed off, rising to her feet. Her fingers curled in under Sarah's, and a thoughtful grin spread slowly across her face. "No, that cannot stand."

"You mean to call him out? Meg, think it over," Sarah urged. "I can make myself scarce, reject his suit with finality and let the two of you be happy."

Meg gasped and placed her fingers to her breast, looking entirely too pleased with herself for Sarah's sense of security. "What, and let wicked deeds go unpunished? That doesn't sound like you, darling. What if you hadn't been my own particular friend? Then he might have been able to continue his games, the both of us entirely unaware. No. Mr. James Glover must be brought to heel, and I know just how best to do it."

"Meg..." Sarah said warningly, a thousand horrible images of what Meg might consider proper vengeance running through her mind.

"Be still, chuck," Meg purred, and the wicked, daring light in her eyes was enough to make Sarah long for the privacy of Meg's lodgings, where she could kiss those plump pink lips, mouth her sweet, round breasts and not be discovered. "I have just the plan. You write back to him and beg a few days' grace to think things over. I'll invite him to take tea with me on Tuesday." She bundled her shawl back on and tied her bonnet beneath her chin. "You will be there with me to surprise him, and together we shall see what this dishonest man of ours is all about."

"Meg, no," Sarah urged, rising out of her chair and folding her arms before her. "Or at least tell me what you mean to do. I won't play along if you leave me in the dark so."

Meg kissed her on the cheek, leaving a faint spot that burned with heat, and the scent of honey in her wake. She pushed Sarah gently on the breast until she fell back into her chair, leaned in so close that her hair curled against Sarah's cheek and her heartbeat throbbed against Sarah's lips. The whisper in Sarah's ear was a suggestion so audacious that Meg had to be teasing, or testing her, or maybe playing a joke, to take her mind off of employers, false promises and duplicitous men? Or did she honestly mean—

"You've lost your mind!"

"Don't think it for a moment, darling." Meg smiled, predatory and sharp. "Rather, I have found my steel at last. I will see *you* on Tuesday, four o'clock. Don't be late."

And she was gone, the tea steeped sharp and acrid, untouched, in the pot. She greeted Frost merrily in the hallway, the front door opened, then closed.

There was silence once more.

Sarah toppled forward until her forehead rested on the wood, her hand folding closed around the letter Meg had left behind on the table. "Oh, bloody *hell*."

The letter burning in James's pocket was the first of the two he had received. Were he the kind of man to try and read between lines, and were Miss Armand the sort to become all missish and coy he might have imagined—but no. She had been plain enough, asking him for a few days' grace to focus on her employment, and he had to be content with that.

He had not formally proposed, after all. He had only tried to make his intentions as clear as he could while at the same time tamping down the rising tide of guilt at his attempts at deceit. Miss Armand deserved better than a man already trying to split his attentions, no matter what Sheridan had suggested.

Unless, of course, she turned him down completely. Then at least he hadn't scuttled his chances with Miss Ceniza.

Cecily already thought he'd gone mad, shopping for books and scribbling out drafts of letters, only to crumple the unsatisfying pages and toss them in the fire.

Perhaps he had.

Because here he was, picking his way down the street in a veritable slum in one of the worst sections of London, his boots splattered with muck and his watch chain a golden draw to every would-be pickpocket and light-finger in the area. Miss Ceniza couldn't possibly be safe here. He would fix that, if there was any way he could manage it, whatever the end result.

Her letter had come at the right time, after the sharp disappointment from Miss Armand's hesitation had settled. He'd set aside his shears and the fine leather he'd been cutting for Lady Horlock's stays binding and popped the plain wax seal with nerves as shaky as a schoolboy trying for his first kiss.

Darling man, it had read. *How can I thank you enough? Do come and call for tea on Tuesday, if you can spare the time. Half past four would suit. I so long to see you!*

- M. Ceniza

"Pardon, guv." A slick and oily tough jostled him as he turned into the stairs to Miss Ceniza's lodgings, but a quick pat proved that James's money and watch were where they were supposed to be. James glanced up, ready to accept the apology, but stopped short. The man had stopped and was staring at him, looking him up and down as though carefully memorizing his face and form. Then, with a touch to the brim of his hat, he moved away.

What had that been about? Other than how much James stuck out in these surroundings—it was obvious that he did not belong here.

The wooden stairs creaked when he stepped up onto them, a faint hint of rot spreading on the end of the risers. A pack of screaming children ran down the street behind him after a rolling hoop, vanishing around a corner only to reappear a moment later, chased by a woman with a broom.

Enough lollygagging about—the anticipation built within him with every moment he spent standing at her door. Miss Ceniza would ask him in, take his hand, permit him a kiss? Perhaps more? He could bring her to such heights of pleasure that she would forget every one of her previous lovers. Her plump hips would yield to his mouth, her skin tasting of sugar and honey.

Those red lips of hers would part and she would breathe out his name in hushed abandon—

"Mr. Glover!" The door opened in front of him, his hand still poised to knock, and the warm rush to his groin threatening to become something immodest. Miss Ceniza stood there, the door half closed and blocking his view of the room beyond. She wore her hair loosely pinned, black curls tumbling down to brush her shoulders, and a delicate yellow dress that turned her lithe form into a beam of purest gold. When she smiled, her eyes flashed. "I thought that was you lingering on my stoop. Will you not come inside?"

"Miss Ceniza." James bowed and smiled. "You take my breath away, every time we meet. I swear you grow lovelier by the minute."

She stepped aside and held the door for him. He stood blinded for a moment in the dim light, following the bright afternoon sun. "You have a silver tongue, Mr. Glover," Miss Ceniza teased.

"Indeed he does," said another, equally familiar voice, one that should not have been there.

Oh. Oh, no. No, no, no.

Could one's blood actually turn to ice in one's veins? It seemed that it could.

James turned, blinking to let his eyes adjust.

Miss Armand sat on the settee, her hair bound up and her clothing plain, as though she had only just come from the townhouse.

"Miss Armand," he said unnecessarily, his brain stuttering to a halt and grasping for words. Her face was entirely closed off to him, more walls up between them now than even her usual barricades. Those unbearably compelling gray eyes were now walls of stone that his idiocy had built between them. "I didn't expect to see you here."

"Oh, we gathered that," she replied, tucking her feet up beneath her, a teacup balanced in her hands. "I take it you weren't aware that Miss Ceniza and I are well acquainted." She didn't leave room for it to be a question, and her accent, usually so lilting and charming, had a false note to it now.

"Fancy that, darling." Miss Ceniza laughed softly, pouring tea into a cup on the tray beside her chair and lacing it with a heavy slug of brandy from a bottle that sat on the sideboard. "He had no idea. We've been particular friends for simply ages." She addressed that last one to him, tossing her curls back over her shoulder. She didn't offer him tea.

He was a dead man. What were they planning to do? How could he explain himself in a way that would make them believe that his intentions were never to be cruel?

"You have." *Of course they have.*

Miss Armand drank deeply from her cup, her enigmatic eyes watching him over the rim of the china. Pale and drawn, she looked tired, as though sleep had recently eluded her. She had been wounded and by his own hand, not Cupid's treacherous arrows. Miss Ceniza's smile suggested that she was amused, but her eyes—they stayed on him, focused and unblinking, like a predator with her prey in her sights.

"I am so very sorry—"

No, there was no chance that he could charm his way out of this confrontation. Whatever they chose to dish out, he would face the executioner's axe like a man. With dignity.

James took a deep breath, clasped his hands behind his back and bowed deeply and thoroughly correctly, facing both the women that he desired. His stomach tangled into knots below his heart, the distant ache of regret sounding louder with every heartbeat

"All I have to offer are my apologies," he began, looking them in the eyes. "The only excuse I can deliver is that I am apparently hopeless at being a cad. I have done you both terribly wrong, and all I can do is beg your most humble forgiveness, though I do not deserve it."

"You should be on your knees to deliver a speech like that," Miss Ceniza replied.

"But *why?*" Miss Armand asked, shaking her head at him. "Why court both of us, even assuming we would not find you out? Can one woman not be enough to satisfy you?" And there was her well-deserved anger, thick and hot below her voice.

"That's not the case, I promise you. Perhaps...it seemed like a good idea at the time?" he hazarded.

Miss Ceniza gaped at him, before closing her mouth and breaking into laughter. That stung, humiliating and swift. "In heaven's name, how could it possibly have struck you thus?"

"He's a man," Miss Armand said, irritated. "They think with one part of themselves, and that part is not their brain."

"That's not the case," James said firmly, his hands still clasped behind his back. "I've courted you both at the same time, yes. You've caught me out at it. But I've never lied, nor made promises I cannot keep. I—"

Fine. Let me put it out there and earn your scorn in its fullest. So be it. I'm a doomed man either way—I'll not be damned for a liar too.

"I want a family. A wife, a home, a deep and abiding love that will sustain me into my dotage, all those things that I suspect Miss Armand craves as much as I." He held her eyes throughout his confession and—wonder of wonders—as much as her eyes blazed with righteous anger, she did not look away. Would Miss Ceniza take the rest so well?

If I emerge from this alive and with my manhood still attached, I will have succeeded beyond expectations.

"Miss Ceniza, you have told me often enough that marriage is not among your desires. You crave your freedom like a bird on the wing, and being caged would destroy everything about you that is so compelling."

And heaven alone knew that he would never try to capture a girl who did not wish to be caught.

"You do not want marriage, Miss Armand will not be a mistress, and I..." He faltered, the confession's rush out of him leaving him sagging and somehow empty.

Miss Armand had set her cup down in her lap. "Yes?" she prompted. There, was that the tiniest glimmer of a smile on Miss Armand's lips when she looked at him? It vanished almost as quickly as it had come, but there was some indication there that she might one day soften again.

"I admire and adore you both. Even now, when I am certain I'll never be in either of your good graces again, I cannot bring myself to declare for one over the other. Or even to say that I will stop adoring either of you, as long as I shall live." He hung his head, the weight of his idiocy dragging it down. Oh, how Cecily would mock him if she ever found out about this. "This day, my poor choices, will be my eternal regret."

Surely that had to be an honest enough grovel to earn him some measure of absolution in their eyes!

Silence fell, the women trading glances that spoke volumes. And how could he have missed it the moment he entered? They were in tune with one another, vibrating along the same universal string, something in their manners and gestures so alike, and yet so distinct, that he could have been watching lovers who had been married an entire lifetime.

But Miss Armand is French, and Miss Ceniza English-born, despite her Spanish name. How where and why could they have met, become close, bonded so?

"He's good," Miss Armand said acerbically, and in that moment she sounded as English as either James or Miss Ceniza herself.

"He knows his lines well," Miss Ceniza replied. She took up the brandy and filled both Miss Armand's cup and her own.

James protested sharply, commanding their attention for himself. "Not lines, I swear! Only a man at a loss for answers."

Miss Armand snorted delicately. "And it never once struck you that perhaps this would not turn out as you'd planned?"

"I never claimed to be smart," James admitted, and he smiled, with whatever charm and simple openness he could muster. "Only infatuated twice over. Can you ever forgive me?"

Chapter Five

Oooh, drat that man! He was as hard to resist as Sarah was, when he looked at them both with his big blue eyes and that curl to his bottom lip that made it look like he was pouting. Meg sipped her brandy, no tea left in the cup at all. It burned going down, not nearly as awfully as the first sip always did, and she felt her heart thaw in crinkles around the edges.

He could still be lying, of course, but his reaction had been one of such direct and immediate apology, accepting his correction and admitting to it—there had to be some reward given for that, however little it changed the facts.

For shoulders like his, though, broad and strong, the taper of his torso down to his narrow hips; for the way his honey-gold hair swept across his brow, the way it would likely feel to have those broad hands on her body—yes, his apology was adequate. She did like men for some things, after all, and he was one of the more perfect specimens she'd seen.

Montpress had never apologized, even when he had been undeniably in the wrong.

Now, how did Sarah feel? That was the main thing. She was the one who had been counting on him for marriage—that was a whole *lifetime*! How could Meg's little hurt compare to that?

They locked eyes, and Meg sent out her question to the universe. Sarah had reacted to Meg's plan with surprise and some indignation, at first, but then today responded with a kiss, gentle and sweet, and she had slowly nodded instead. "Let him feel our humiliation for himself," she had said, and Meg had laughed and kissed her again.

That had been all, barring the brandy in their cups for courage, until James had walked in the door.

Sarah tilted her head, a smile creeping over her lips. She nodded. *Time to make him pay.*

"Possibly," Sarah finally answered James's question, breaking eye contact to turn her attentions toward him. His shoulders pulled back as he straightened, his clear blue eyes filling with trepidation and concern. "Next time you send gifts," she continued, "*I* should like a book, if you please, and Meg deserves all of the prettiest words ever set to paper in a love letter of her very own."

That had caught him off guard. He gaped like a fish in a pond, and Meg burst into giggles both at the sight and the images that sprang to mind. "I—yes?" he replied, sounding so dumbfounded that Meg could have said anything next and he seemed like he would have accepted it as a natural follow-on.

"Good boy," Meg laughed, setting her cup aside on the end table and rising from her chair. "Fair is fair, after all, and there must be some *consequences* for trying to play us falsely."

"I never intended to cause hurt to either of you," James protested, unclasping his hands and following her with his eyes. "That I will swear until my dying day."

"Intention doesn't matter," Sarah pointed out, while Meg dug in her trunk for the item she needed to have on hand. "Not when it comes to hurting the people you claim to have such affection for."

"What will prove to you that I care?" James asked, glancing back over his shoulder at Meg, before crossing the floor in two long strides. He went down on one knee before Sarah, taking one of her hands in his. "Shall I serenade you? Woo you with flowers and books?"

"You will take your punishment like a man and not a boy," Meg replied, drawing the long ribbon from the clothing trunk and letting the lid fall closed. She stroked the length of amber silk between her fingers, twisting it and toying with it, and James's eyes went wide and uncertain.

"What do you intend to do with that?" he asked, standing and raising his hands before him in warning. "Tie me and leave me in the public square with a sign announcing my misdeeds?"

"Creative," Meg approved. Sarah snorted again, and James looked vaguely offended. "But no."

"You can leave now, if you wish," Sarah added, rising to the occasion and gulping down the last of her drink in one long swallow. She stood, resting one hand on the back of the simple wooden chair sitting by the fire. "But if you do, you won't have a chance with either of us again."

"And if I stay?"

"You won't be harmed," Meg reassured him, a sharp edge to her answer. She angered quickly and could forgive quickly, but even that only went so far. "Only you'll have a chance to learn what it feels like, to see the object of your desires betray you."

"I don't think I like this offer," he murmured, a vein working at the side of his jaw.

Sarah shook her head and, daringly, trailed her fingers across the lapel of his jacket only to poke him in the square chin. "Now imagine how we felt, who had no choice in the matter." The roughness in her voice betrayed more of her feelings than anything, and a lump formed, thick and heavy, in Meg's throat.

He paused, opened his mouth to speak, then shut it again. "I am duly chastened."

"In that case," Meg said, pretending to a certain amount of cheer, and gesturing to the chair, "sit yourself down, sir, and be corrected."

He sat, everything about him stiff and tense. Meg drew his hands behind the back of the chair, and with a few deft movements, bound his hands snugly in place, then his ankles to the chair legs.

"Is this painful?" she asked, tugging on her knot to make sure that it would hold.

He twisted his hands, his face set in what had to be a permanent state of shock and surprise by now, and coughed. "No. That is, I am well comfortable, thank you, albeit extremely confused. Tell me, ladies, please—what happens next?" he asked, his voice strained.

Sarah stood still, her arms folded across her slim waist, and Meg stalked across the floor toward her. "To you?" Meg cast a look back over her shoulder to smile wickedly at him. "Absolutely nothing."

"I'm afraid I don't foll—"

Sarah took Meg's hand, and her palm was so warm, though rough spots on her fingers betrayed the hard hours that she spent at work. James's hands were so similar, calluses from his needles and his shears, scars from slips with the whalebone and the knife. No wonder Meg was drawn to them both. Sarah's eyes flickered closed for a moment, and when she opened them, it was as though Meg were the only other person in the room.

"Look at her," Meg commanded, keeping her eyes on her beloved Sarah alone. "Look at how beautiful she is, and how precious. Think of how you intended to deceive her."

"Oh," James said. And "*oh*," again.

"Please," Meg murmured softly, this time to Sarah. Meg tipped her chin up, her hair falling down her back. She set her hands on Sarah's hips, the gentle slopes of her curves warm and solid beneath Meg's fingers. James stopped talking, and she heard a suck-in of air come from his side of the room.

Sarah kissed her. Nothing else mattered except this: the taste of brandy on her lips, the hot press of her mouth, Sarah's hands finding their way to Meg's waist and holding on as though she might fly away, or fly apart, at any moment. Meg kissed her back, tasted the seam of Sarah's lips with the tip of her tongue, coals igniting to fire in her groin.

The firm pressure of Sarah's hands fell from her waist as they broke the kiss, and Meg's heart thumped painfully in her chest. Had she said or done something to give offense? "We can stop," she murmured softly. "Only say the word and all will be as it was."

Sarah kissed the question from her mouth as she asked it, growing bolder and fiercer with each sigh and play of teeth against her inner lip. Her fingers worked at Meg's back, because of course she would know how to dress and undress another woman, even like this, distracted and sight unseen.

Meg turned a little to present their best side to their audience. From where he was tied he would be able to see their breasts above their stays. The firelight would soon be shining through their shifts, displaying everything he had wanted to keep only for himself.

Meg's lacings parted under Sarah's hands, her bodice then her short stays falling loose around her shoulders, her ribs, sliding down to circle her narrow waist. Sarah broke away, cupped the fullness of Meg's breasts in her hands, her palms so warm through the fine linen of Meg's shift.

"She's everything to me and would have given everything to you." Meg looked over her shoulder at James, his color up and his whole body tense, leaning toward them in his prison-chair. "And you would have broken her spirit with lies."

"Meg," Sarah warned, starting to shake her head. But Meg slipped her hand between Sarah's bodice and her skin, skating her thumb across the tight nub of Sarah's nipple.

A groan broke free from James, impassioned and needy. Meg stroked Sarah's cheek and turned her head to face him. He stared at them with amazement and barely parted lips, his chest rising and falling with his ragged breaths.

"Look how he watches you," Meg purred. Sarah was the beautiful one of the pair of them—Meg couldn't be the only one to see that. She cupped Sarah's breast in her hand, dropped her mouth to it and bit little kisses across Sarah's warm, supple skin. "He longs for you, and now he can't have you."

"Have mercy, ladies, please," James said, shaking his head as though to clear it. "I was lost, but now am found, was blind but now I see. Be my graces both and untie me?"

"If you still have the presence of mind to quote hymns, Mr. Glover," Sarah retorted, her eyebrow raised, "I think you haven't been punished nearly enough."

"God help me." His groan that time was a little more impassioned, a little more ragged around the edges. Good. He deserved that and so much more.

Sarah bent her head and kissed down Meg's throat, across the tops of her breasts, nipping and biting and leaving little damp marks across Meg's skin. She kissed and bit at the tops, the sides, her tongue darting out to circle the nipple, suck on it, hard and fierce. Her mouth was heat— red, wet heat encircling Meg's nipples, first one then the other, her thumbs stroking, caressing, rubbing the wetness from her mouth into Meg's skin so that her breath ran cool across the marks.

Meg pulled the pins from Sarah's hair and ran her fingers through it until it fell about her shoulders, a tumble of mahogany waves, dark with hints of red. It was harder to get Sarah's bodice unlaced than her own. She tugged at the knots until something gave way and the stomacher fell forward, exposing the laces crisscrossing down her front. Those loosened more easily and she slid the washed-soft cotton from Sarah's round, white shoulders. It bared her gray linen stays, the mounds of her breasts rising above them presented for Meg's desire.

"She's mine now," Meg gloated. "And you can't touch her. You can't feel how soft she is, how readily she responds to my fingers or my tongue." Sarah tried to cover Meg's mouth with her hand, laughing, but Meg traced circles on Sarah's palm with the tip of her tongue and was released.

"Please," James pleaded. One look showed that he was sinking into desperation, his trouser-front pushed out and full. She had the burning urge to take him there, even though that wasn't the plan; strip him and see his prick, ride it and bring Sarah on her lap, the three of them moving together, sweat-soaked and obscene.

Instead Meg pulled Sarah by the hand and she followed willingly, until they stood beside the low settee. Meg knelt there, the cushion sinking softly beneath her knees. "You don't deserve her," she told James, and he made a groan that sounded like a sob.

"You're being a little ridiculous, don't you think?" Sarah murmured against Meg's lips, but Meg only shook her head fiercely, her hair bouncing with the motion.

"Not at all. You deserve to be loved, darling, with all of someone's heart and soul." She rose up to bite at Sarah's breasts, scrape the edge of her teeth across the sweet fleshy curves. They sat just so, pressed up by the fabric and the cording until they were rounded like perfect peaches, held in check only by the drawstring of her shift. Meg tugged that down until she could see the pink circles of Sarah's nipples peeking out from the top of the stays. She bit at them lightly, slid her tongue down between Sarah's skin and the edge of the fabric to taste them, the hard nub tightening and the skin around it pebbling as she suckled and teased.

Sarah's breath came in gasps, her hands running up Meg's legs, pushing her skirts higher. Fumbling and her hands trembling, she gathered the cotton in swaths and pulled it up over Meg's thighs, her hips, exposing the white linen and ribbon edging of her drawers. Her mouth ran hot over Meg's throat, a slide with the flat of her tongue leaving a wet trail that she blew across, the cool air sending shivers down Meg's spine.

Now, she needed, *craved* more—Meg laced her fingers in Sarah's hair and pulled her face upward. The kiss that followed sank into her bones, settling deep and stoking the coals within her heart and soul. Sarah was hers, would always be hers, no matter what happened next, there would always be this—Sarah's tresses tangled in her fingers, their breasts pressed and riding against each other, skin sparking with sweat, Sarah's tongue sliding along hers, and—

And Sarah's nimble fingers, pushing aside the split in Meg's drawers. There, oh there... Meg rode high against the new pressure, fumbling at first and then in steady rhythm. Sarah rubbed firm circles around the center of Meg's need, the pearl that radiated lust, heat and joy throughout her body.

Her fingers slid down farther, firm and sold beneath Meg as she writhed and gasped. More, more, she needed—there! Sarah's fingers slipped inside, where she was so hollow and empty, filling her and curling inside her, Sarah's thumb riding high against Meg's clitoris, just like before.

The world was this, pressure inside, filled and thick, firm strokes outside, and Sarah's steady hand, soul-devouring kisses and trading breaths back and forth as she brought Meg to the very precipice—

Someone groaned in desperation, Meg cried out in return, "Oh glory, oh *love!*" and she was gone, nothing more than sparks, fireworks and flame, exploding in brilliant arcs across the sky.

The skin of Sarah's shoulder was hot and sweat-stung to the taste when Meg's breathing settled. The racing beat of Sarah's heart thrummed against Meg's lips. To glory, then, her own desperation slaked for the moment, and the endless bounty of Sarah's body begging, screaming to be explored with fingers, lips and tongue.

Sarah had no drawers on below her petticoats and Meg's hands found only the smoothest, firmest expanse of woman's thigh beneath her shift. Meg tugged Sarah's shift down, left her stays on, the gray linen thrusting her breasts up and her nipples peeking out at the top, rose-pink and hard.

"Beautiful," Meg murmured, pressing her lips first to one, then the other, in solemn benediction. Down her body then, pushing the linen out of the way, Sarah falling back upon the settee and settling her long, lean legs one on either side of Meg's hips.

There, oh there, the gateway to paradise! Meg nuzzled the damp curls that guarded it, and tasted her. Sarah's body rocked, jolted as though struck, her hips curling up to meet Meg's mouth. She laved with the flat of her tongue, long, wide strokes that encompassed the whole of Sarah's sex. Sarah's fingers curled tightly into hers, one hand sliding down to grab Meg's where it rested on her hip.

She squeezed and tugged in fair abandon; Meg traced circles with the tip of her tongue and Sarah writhed. She teased with a single finger at Sarah's entrance and Sarah begged. Meg fucked into her with three fingers, thick and curled, stroking up to that rough place inside where everything ignited—and Sarah pleaded, she arched and writhed and dug her nails into Meg's hand and clutched the cushion below her. Her back pulled into a bow and she shook apart under Meg's hands and wicked tongue.

"There, darling, there," Meg murmured, Sarah's taste warm and thick on her tongue. *Berry preserves, or some exotic tropical fruit, honey and lime. Let me never forget this.* She pressed kisses against Sarah's taut stomach, darted her tongue into the sweet hollow of her navel, stroked and petted her thighs until the quivering and shaking in her body settled, then stopped.

"Lord have mercy," Sarah groaned, releasing Meg's hand and brushing tendrils of damp hair out of her own eyes. She propped herself up on her elbows and stared down at Meg, still lying between her thighs.

Their eyes met and all the trepidation and uncertainty that had lingered in Sarah's expression last time they'd made love—it had fled, replaced with a dawning look of wonder and soft joy that sent a rush of delicious warmth down through Meg's chest.

Stay with me. Let us have the kind of love I play on stage and never see in life. Be mine, be mine, be—

Meg sat up, cupped Sarah's face between her hands and kissed her. Sarah kissed back, her lips slick, her hands curling around Meg's waist once more.

"You are a wicked woman," Sarah laughed softly, and Meg beamed.

"You're no better," Meg teased, delighted.

"You're both unspeakably cruel," a voice gasped from the far side of the room, one Meg had entirely forgotten was there. She burst into astonished giggles. Sarah's dumbfounded face betrayed her own surprise.

He was where they'd left him, of course, bound hand and foot to the old wooden chair. His cheeks and ears flushed red, his honey-blond hair sticking to his neck above his cravat and collar in little damp ringlets, as though he'd been sweating. He strained against his bonds as though he couldn't help himself, the muscles in his broad chest flexing and drawing his shirt taut across them, his knees fallen open. The evidence of their cruelty was obvious. His trousers tented obscenely, the turgid bulge in his groin impressive, assuming that it was all him—and all, she preened, because of *them*. One had to take one's praise from whatever direction it came.

"Oh." Meg affected a giggle, pressing a kiss to the center of Sarah's palm. "Look, S-Sophie darling. Do you think he understands his place now?" And she'd almost forgotten the name by which Glover knew Sarah to boot. Meg glanced back over her shoulder, a coquettish look that had served her well in the past, her shift and stays down about her waist and her drawers all askew.

Sarah turned pink, her cheeks and the tops of her breasts reddening at the same time. She adjusted her shift to cover her nipples and the sweet upper curves of her breasts once more. "So it appears," she said, lifting her head up proudly once she was partially covered again. "But how can we be sure he's learned his lesson?"

"I've learned," Mr. Glover said firmly, twisting his arms behind him once more. The knots held fast and he took a deep breath, his cheeks flushed red. "I will never be so foolish as to think that I could deceive either one of you, ever again."

"I'm not so sure," Sarah said slowly. She raised an eyebrow at Meg, as though Meg could understand exactly what she was proposing, and goodness! Where had confident, lusty Sarah sprung from? She who was so calculating and careful, choosing the safest paths while Meg danced across thin ice for the sheer joy of it all.

Sarah rose first of the two of them, her eyes dark pewter gray. Her dress finally fell completely from her hips, leaving her in her underthings alone. The firelight glowed through her linen shift in the semi-darkness of the shuttered room, outlining every luscious curve of her body. A speculative smile grew across her full, red-bitten lips, and she swung her hips as she walked.

Meg rose and followed, a moth to Sarah's striking, brilliant flame.

"I think," Sarah said, stopping in front of James. His eyes trailed, slowly, up the slim length of her body, over the half-laced plain gray stays, the rising curves of her breasts, lingered on her mouth. "I think that you still have some funny ideas in your head, Mr. Glover, about wives and lovers, men and women."

"Perhaps I do," he admitted softly. He stared at them both in turn, Sarah, then Meg, with wonder and with confusion, as though still trying to process the scene before him. He writhed his hands behind him, tugging against the silk, his hips rising slightly before he gave up and let himself fall back. "I am but a man, after all."

Sarah ran one finger down the hard length of the bulge in his groin. He stopped talking, squeezing his eyes firmly shut, his breath catching in his throat.

"That's no excuse for being a fool." Meg moved to stand behind him and slid her arms about his neck, warmth and desire roiling in a low simmer deep within. It was all still bandied over with a thick fog of satiation, her limbs loose and her mind, for once, entirely at ease. She nuzzled into his neck. He smelled of wax and soap, leather and oil, and the faintest hint of cedar.

"Shall we finish today's study?" Sarah asked, a knowing smile curving her lips. She was half dressed but covered, her hair hanging down her back in dark waves with the faintest hints of red.

She was beauty itself, radiant in the afternoon sun, a goddess risen from the parting waves.

James raised both his brows in amazement, gears turning behind his eyes as he gave something great thought. His tongue darted out to moisten his lips, and his hips jerked as Sarah stroked two fingers down the swollen center of his trousers.

"Hng," he said obligingly.

He really did have very nice arms, all muscled and firm against Meg's belly and breasts. She leaned against his back to soak in his warmth, ignoring the wooden planks of the open chair back, trailing her fingers down the buttoned front of his waistcoat.

Sarah unbuttoned his fall-front, let the fabric drop to reveal the lacings underneath. Another swift tug and they were undone as well, displaying his fine white shirt. James let out a shuddering sigh, his eyes fixed on Sarah. She pushed back the linen to expose his prick to view.

It *was* all him—one question answered. His prick was large and thick, well formed and, at the moment, standing against his stomach, red and purple with barely constrained desire. Moisture gleamed at the head, his shirt partly damp with it in spots, and more appeared under Meg's gaze. James groaned low under his breath, needy and desperate. Meg leaned over and seized his chin, turned his head to the side so that she could kiss him.

That meant James wasn't watching when Sarah wrapped her hand around his prick. He bit down on Meg's lower lip instead, the kiss changing from hesitant to desperate in the briefest of moments. He shifted, groaned, his body lifting up against the chair so that he could push himself farther into Sarah's clever hand.

Meg slid her tongue into his mouth. The rough set of his jaw was so unlike Sarah's honed edges. So different and so beautiful for that difference.

"Please," he begged them, his voice breaking in the middle. And "please!" again. Sarah stroked him, hard and fast, then let him go, watched his cock bob up to tap against his lower abdomen as he cried out.

Meg kissed him, then backed away a half step when he leaned up into her. Sarah knelt and licked the end of his prick with the barest tip of her tongue, and his whole body spasmed.

"Please," he begged again. "Anything you want, name it. Only end this torture!"

"We can end it," Meg offered, and she stepped back, releasing him.

He growled, low and fierce, a golden lion driven to his breaking point. "Not what I meant."

"Will you lie to us ever again?" Sarah asked, tracing the ridge around the tip of his prick with her little finger.

"Never."

"Are you courting anyone else?" Meg purred into his ear, her tongue trailing circles around his earlobe, along the outer curve, and lancing once into the hollow.

"No! Only you."

"Could you," Sarah began, then hesitated, the pause at odds with the persona she was wearing now. "Could you find affection for both of us, as deeply as we each thought we could care for you?"

It was blackmail, hardly fair to ask him that with his prick exposed and his limbs bound, his eyes dark with desire and the flush of need going down his neck as far as Meg could see.

"Yes," James said softly.

Meg seized his face and kissed him, Sarah sank her mouth down along the thick, desperately hard length of his incredible prick, and he convulsed as though he'd been hit by lightning in their arms.

He rocked and bucked as Sarah pulled her mouth off him, then his body went taut, his arms and legs straining against his bonds. His pleasure erupted, white over Sarah's encircling fist, his head thrown back and his tongue lancing deep into Meg's mouth in giddy abandon.

"I—" he stammered, and "oh," and "good God," as he slowly settled back into the chair.

Sarah found a cloth and began to clean herself with water from the washstand, and Meg loosened his bonds enough that he could slide free. He tucked his softening prick back into his pants and did up his buttons, casting Meg a beseeching look full of wonder, and awe, and a healthy dose of uncertainty.

She kissed him, because that was an easy way to fix a bad mood, and he smiled against her lips. Not a lion, then, but a tamed and docile predator, a dog who would bark at her command?

James shook his head, as though trying to clear away dust and cobwebs from inside. "I expected," he began, adjusting his clothes, "for this afternoon to have a much different sort of ending when I first walked in."

"By all rights, we should have thrown you out on your *derriere*," Sarah said archly, her carefully honed accent back in place. "But thankfully enough for you, it seems we both liked you too well."

"And have you two done…" He shook his head, stopped talking, seemed to be searching for words. "Is this sort of thing a common…"

"Don't ask those questions if you value your skin." Meg laughed softly.

"Suffice it to say that the greatest part of whatever this—*thisness*—is," Sarah added, "is as much new to us as it is to you. One presumes." She pulled her dress back on and fastened the lacings, re-pinning the stomacher at the sides. "I need to go." She addressed Meg most of all. "The Horlocks will be home soon, and I must be back before them."

"Wait?" James asked, and he stood, taking Sarah's hand. She hesitated, then curled her fingers cautiously into his. He turned, offered his other hand to Meg. She set her fingers against his palm, his steady grip solid and reassuring. "Before you leave," he said, "what is to happen from here? I had thought, in my foolishness"—he closed his eyes for a minute and shook his head again—"to court you separately and win you both—one to wed and one to bed, for lack of better terms."

"So much for his vaunted silver tongue," Sarah said dryly, but she did not pull away.

"And this, obviously, is a different thing." Meg pursed her lips. "Let it just be this," she suggested gently, Sarah's expression settling into something like restlessness and nerves. "For now, we three court together and in three pairs, and see what gifts *honesty* may bring."

The look Sarah gave her was one of faint and indistinct desperation, but she nodded, squeezed James's hand and leaned in to kiss Meg on the cheek. "So be it, then, for now. I must go, Meg. I honestly must."

"I'll see you soon," Meg promised, and James nodded, still seeming somewhat dumbfounded.

He took his leave not long after Sarah had departed, his suit resettled and as tidy as he and she could make it, and his hat in his hands.

Meg sighed, the empty room of her apartment cold suddenly, and utterly too quiet. She closed the window, the shutters clattering together as she latched them. She flung herself upon her simple bed with a drawn-out sigh.

"From no lovers at all to two at once," she said aloud, staring up at the wooden beams of her ceiling. A slow smile crossed her face, and she ran her hand down between her legs, memories of Sarah's fingers making the heat there rise and her cunny slick. "What an utterly delicious day."

Chapter Six

Running through the laneways to get back to the townhouse before her mistress's outing was over, her fingers damp from wash water and her own taste lingering on her lips from Meg's kisses—none of it was how Sarah had imagined the afternoon's appointment progressing. Oh, she had thought Meg's plan outrageous and funny at first, plainly hysterical after a generous lashing of brandy. A good part of her had never imagined that Meg would actually go through with it at all. But now in the aftermath, their hearts—among other things—bared to one another again and her whole body still tingling with the memory of lips and fingers and Mr. Glover's—*James's*—thick, hard cock in her hand, *well.*

Could anyone blame her for being a little bit distracted? Certainly if she had seen Ellen in the hallway when she slipped in the kitchen entrance, Sarah would have torn right up to her room. She certainly wouldn't have lingered by the mirror, taken off her bonnet with her hair all disheveled or allowed herself to touch the neckline of her dress, remembering the blazing passion in Meg's eyes when she'd dragged the fabric away from her.

"Have a good afternoon, *Armand*?" Ellen's voice came from behind her. The girl herself stood in the doorway to the scullery, a towel in her hands.

"Ellen!" She couldn't jump, even though her heart was racing. *I must be Sophie even below stairs here.* "I didn't see you there. In any case, yes, I ran all the errands I required." It would have been easier to give that lie had she actually remembered to pick up something in a parcel on her way home, but it was too late to worry about that now. "Has anything of note happened in the meantime?"

"In this house?" Ellen screwed up her face in a grimace, but her glance was sharp. "I imagine not."

"I'm going to change clothes now and do some mending for *madame*." Sarah pulled off her gloves with a brisk snap, tucking them away. "Please make sure there is adequate light and space for me in the servants' hall when I'm ready."

"Mm-hmm," Ellen answered, and when Sarah raised her eyes to the mirror, Ellen's gaze back at her was inquisitive and hard. Sarah touched her hair again, a reflexive, instinctive move, and Ellen turned away, back into the scullery.

Wonderful. More complications.

Nothing about this day was like anything she had ever experienced before, not in her entire life. It wasn't bad, necessarily, but it was definitely going to require a great deal of thought to wrap her head around. Writing would help, if she could find a few minutes later.

For the moment, however, she was back in the house, and there was a great deal of work to be done.

Contemplating the latest great turnabout in her existence was going to have to wait.

Taking half the measurement from bust to side, place the slash for the gusset there, the busk pocket narrowed and strap angled farther in to account for the slope of her shoulders—

"There you are, James!"

The front door of the shop had opened and closed without him noticing immediately. He stood up from where he was bent over the long wooden table, his back cracking and creaking alarmingly. It had gotten dark without his notice, which explained how he'd ended up with his nose almost down to the cotton, the sliver of soap so shrunken from use that he might as well have been drafting with his fingertips.

"Honestly, what are you doing in the dark like this?" Cecily prattled on, pulling off her gloves and lighting the candle stubs on the mirror with no regard for how much the spermaceti wax lights actually cost. "You'll give yourself forehead wrinkles from staring into the shadows, you know."

"Wrinkles lend a man some dignity. Perhaps then you'll show me some respect once in a while." He set his soap marker down and brushed off his hands. The stays draft for Lady Leighton would have to wait until morning.

Cecily tossed her hair impertinently and laughed. Where had she picked up that little maneuver? "Don't lie awake at night waiting for that moment to arrive."

"Impertinent wench."

"Horrible brute."

He laughed, then crossed the room to embrace her fondly and press a gentle kiss to the top of his sister's frothy confection of a bonnet. "Why are you here, Cece? You know I don't like you going about at night unescorted."

The huff he felt in her shoulders had undoubtedly been paired with an eye roll, but staring at the top of her head as he was, he could pretend he'd seen and felt nothing. "I'm not unescorted—Mrs. Lambert is with me. But *she* wanted to stop and look at the books in the window next door, and I said I'd come right on in. Honestly, you fret too much." Cecily took a step farther away and swatted him in the chest with one of her gloves. "And you work too much. It's late in the evening, you've left me all alone all day, missed *dinner* you hapless fool, and no one even came to *call*."

Guilt pricked at him at the plaintive sound in her voice. She needed friends, and ones closer to her own age than a brother eight years her elder and with a profession that kept him away at all hours. "I'm sorry, sweetheart," he started to say.

"And you promised you would take me out!" She folded her arms and jutted out her lip in a pout so deep that it looked false. "You're here all the time, and when you're home, it's as though you're off in your own dream world."

The worst of it was, she wasn't wrong. "I'm sorry," he said again, and poked her lip back in before she could curl it out so far that she'd be in danger of it freezing that way. "I've been busy. You know how it is with the families all arriving for the Season Everyone wants the newest styles, and they want them immediately. The rush will die down in a week or two, and then we'll have more time to spend together."

Her eyes flashed dangerously. "You seem to have plenty of time to spend with your own friends. Or was it work that kept you out Tuesday? Your shirt smelled all of brandy and perfume when you came home. Are you courting somebody, James Glover?"

Oh no.

"That's none of your business, *little sister.*" James waved it off, with a chuckle that rang false to his own ears. "Just hold on a little longer. When we are not so busy, then you and I will have plenty of time to spend together." Inspiration struck, and he cocked his head. "How would you like to meet Miss Ceniza?"

"Miss Ceniza?" Cecily's mood switched in an instant, her eyes lighting up. "Oh, how marvelous! Would you do that for me?"

James nodded. "I would and I shall." That would please Cecily enough to keep her from pestering him, at least for the next little while. Perhaps they would become friends? That would, most likely, be an unmitigated disaster. But he would enjoy the chance to see the two of them walking together. The two girls side by side in the sunshine, with Miss Armand on his arm—"Delightful," he murmured softly, and Cecily gave him a bewildered look. "Sunday," he said, louder. "I shall see if it can be arranged for Sunday. A picnic, perhaps, following church."

"You are the best brother in the entire world!" Cecily launched herself at him and flung her arms about his neck. He hugged her, conscious suddenly of the frail nature of her form, a chill running down his spine.

"Save that for once I've managed to arrange something," he replied, gathering his coat up and slipping his arms into the sleeves. "Come on now, sweetheart. Let's go home. Perhaps, if I'm very good, Mrs. Lambert will consent to re-warm some of that excellent dinner for me."

"Serve you right if she makes you eat it cold."

He blew out the candles, letting the small shop fall into darkness and silence once more, then closed the door and locked it fast. Their housekeeper joined them a moment later, and the three made their way along the road, on the long walk home.

Cynthia: It unfolds thusly. Tell thy lord husband you are with child. Rejoice, accept his blessings, fouled though they may be, and ~~within the month~~ banish him from your bedchamber. A contrivance of a fleece-filled cushion beneath your gown will finish your disguise.

Emmeline: It shall be done. My maid will keep my secrets, for she loves me well.

Cynthia: Be sure and tell none else. When the time comes for my confinement, ~~and thus for yours,~~ I will come to you. The child I bear upon your knee will be your lord's own heir, and both our lives will be preserved.

Emmeline: Take you now these clothes and coins. The ~~hermit's hut~~ ~~stables~~ cottage at the bottom of the garden shall be your undisturbed home until such time as plans, and more...

Sarah turned the page and dipped her pen.

...come to sweet fruition.

Was that terrible? It wasn't precisely terrible. At the least, Sarah had seen plenty worse be presented upon the minor stages. All anything needed in that regard was the chance for ample bosom on display, a murder or two to please the young men and true lovers either conquering all—or exploding into a ball of fire.

Both were unrealistic in the extreme.

How many times had Mother professed to be in love?

Not with the lustful men who paid her way, whose perfume lingered on her hair and hands when she would stoop to kiss Sarah goodnight. Sometimes she would come home with a new dress, *"only a little torn, see here at the hem, and easily mended!"* or a pretty ribbon to weave into Sarah's hair.

It was the others, the gruff-voiced toughs whose rough hands left her blue- and purple-blotched, weeping when she thought Sarah was asleep. The ones who took her coins and plied her with sickly sweet drinks and smoke that clung to her skin and left her eyes blank, for days or weeks at a time.

And Sarah, always Sarah, left to comb the filth from Mother's curls, bathe her skin with cold well water, search her mother's pockets and hoard the pennies found there in a box beneath the loose board in the floor. Scrawny and dirty, gnawed by hunger, the waif she had been then would not recognize the woman Sarah had become.

Mother Lilah—not willing to whore and too young and ornery to give up and die—had done what she could for the fatherless children in Charing Cross. She had offered Sarah a sanctuary while her mother lived—a few hours of peace here and there, a safe place to sleep when the men came banging at the door. And after sickness and the opium haze had ended Mother's pain for good, Lilah had opened her doors and given Sarah a home.

Perhaps she had fancied herself a future baud, training Sarah up from urchin to girl who could pass herself off in quality. Or maybe she had simply longed for a time long gone, when she had eaten from silver spoons and worn silk against her skin.

Meg had appeared when Sarah was nine, or possibly ten; another girl, this time of quick wit and some learning, just enough manners to show that she too had once had a home of her own. Lilah's wings were broad enough to cover two.

Lilah's motherly embraces had been gentle, her wrinkled mouth quick to smile, the tick mattress she laid herself upon to sleep large and warm enough to hide two wayward young girls amidst the piles of threadbare blankets.

And she had owned two books, from which she had taught Sarah to read, and maths to both. Two books, and a pen.

When they grew, when Sarah entered service and Meg went to the stage—they had transformed themselves in other ways as well. Plain little Sarah Harlow had become the fashionable French *émigré* Sophie Armand, all the better to find herself a placement in one of the better households. And Meg? Sneaking into the theatres through windows and backstage doors had taught her well. Marguerite Ceniza, British-born and of flamboyant and oddly untraceable Spanish looks, had become London's favorite new ingénue.

Those were the first loves Sarah had known: Mother, Lilah, Meg. No men at all, not that touched her heart, until Joshua's chaste and brotherly kindness. It had been safe with him—his desires had tended in other directions.

Until now. Now there was Sarah, and Meg, and Mr. Glover. *James.*

How did one begin to consider the possibilities of happiness between *three*? Two was complicated enough, never mind adding more!

The door to the stillroom swung open and Sarah tucked the papers beneath her book of recipes, exchanging pen for mixing spoon as Ellen came barging in. The lotion had come to no harm during the ten minutes she'd been woolgathering and scribbling, the faint scent of Lady Horlock's favored rosewater rising to perfume the air.

"Miss Armand," Ellen greeted her. "The staymaker's come asking for you. He's got her ladyship's underpinnings."

"The old one or the young one?" Sarah blurted out without thinking.

Ellen laughed knowingly. "The young and handsome one, thankfully."

Mr. Glover.

"*Merci*, Ellen." Sarah stood, smoothed her skirts, headed for the door, then hesitated. Could she see him? What would she say to him? Perhaps Ellen could take the new stays upstairs in her place, and Sarah wouldn't have to look him in the eye, only a day after having held his prick in her hands.

It had felt so delicious, his body melting beneath her touch.

But Ellen had already paused to bend her face over the mixing pot and breathe deeply. "Must be nice to be of the quality," she sighed, almost to herself. "Oh, I'll take care of finishing this off, Miss Armand," she said sweetly. "Don't you worry about a thing."

Rather than try to explain to a girl she barely knew why she didn't particularly feel like making casual conversation with Mr. Glover today, Sarah went to do just that. Which action would have made her a greater coward? She couldn't begin to guess.

It was some consolation that Mr. Glover looked about as awkward as she felt. He stood in the servants' entrance to the house, a packet wrapped in linen beneath his arm. He shifted his weight from one booted foot to another, watching the kitchen door rather than the hallway. His coat was a nicer one than any she had seen him in before, tidily pressed, and his cravat impeccably tied. *For me?*

An apple blossom, pink and white, peeped out of his watch pocket.

That, more than anything, thawed the crystals of ice that had begun to form tight around her heart. More so than the honey-golden hair that fell across his brow, or the tight set of his square jaw, or his thick, strong fingers, equally capable of stitches so delicate they could barely be seen and bending strips of steel and whalebone over steaming caldrons or hard-hammered anvils.

He was a tradesman, not a gentleman, but in the moment he looked the part.

"You asked for me, *monsieur*?" Sarah spoke up, stepping firmly on the urge to flush hot or look away. He was just as complicit in their misdeeds as she!

Mr. Glover's head jerked up and for an instant, only that, he looked hopeful, and vulnerable, and terribly young. Then the mirage vanished, an illusion cast by the light, and he smiled the same brilliant, cheeky grin with which he always favored her. "Miss Armand." He lingered on the name that wasn't really hers, infusing it with such warmth and yearning that she desperately wished that it were. "A good day to you, miss. I've come—" He glanced around, as though looking for something, or someone. "To deliver Lady Horlock's stays. They're quite complete, and if I may be so bold—"

"That's never stopped you before." Sarah's sharp tongue got ahead of her, but he barely blinked before grinning wider.

"Then without permission," he continued seamlessly, "let me say that they are fine pieces of work indeed."

That smirk. She had conflicting urges—to make a fist and poke him one in the nose, or kiss that curve from his mouth. Meg had kissed him yesterday—what had his lips felt like? "The most divine ever made by human hand, I'm sure," she said acerbically.

He seemed utterly unfazed, closing the last few paces between them. "Oh, indubitably. When I set my mind to something, I cannot rest until I've succeeded beyond my wildest dreams."

"You think a great deal of yourself, m'sieur, for someone who was only recently bested by a pair of girls."

"I think it was you, in the end, who were bested, considering the final result—"

It had started as an insult, meant to make him take offense, as all men did when compared unfavorably to those they considered the less deserving sex. Instead his ears flushed red at the tops, and he stared at her with such wonder and all-consuming interest that *she* almost blushed in return. And how would *that* have looked?

"I spoke out of turn—" he began, then, "No, never you mind that. I said what I meant to, and you may take it as you will. As in everything, I am your willing servant."

"Somehow I doubt that, very much," she snapped back, fear and uncertainty clutching at her heart. The hurt in his eyes could not possibly be feigned, but then how was she to begin to make sense of it all? The guilt sat thick in her throat and chest. "Now it is I who have spoken out of turn," Sarah replied softly, checking about them to make sure there were no prying ears around. Safe for the moment, she carried on. "I am afraid, m'sieur, and I am sure you can see why. Only a few days ago, we treated each other with respect. How can I believe that you will now look upon me with that same courtesy?"

He should have lied—that would have made everything easier. If he said that he cared nothing for her, then she could go her own way and trouble herself no more.

Instead he set down his package and clasped her hands in his, her fingers swallowed up entirely by the breadth of his wide, strong, callus-rough hands. He studied them for a moment, turned them over and scudded the pad of his thumb across her palm, an intimate caress that sent her whole body to tingle.

"Can you doubt me?" he asked, raising his eyes to meet hers. Warmth flooded through her, leaving giddy excitement in its wake. Her heart pounded so loudly that it seemed certain he would hear it, or that it should burst out of her ribs entirely.

"What you gave me was a gift." He kept talking, shattering more and more of her expectations with every word. "The honesty of your desire," he murmured low, his thumb pressing now against the hollow of her palm, warm and so, so firm. "Your trust, when I had done nothing to deserve it. I shall spend the rest of my days endeavoring to be worthy of it. And of you. I respect you more than I did before, if such a thing were possible."

"You make no sense, m'sieur," Sarah managed to get out, drawing her hand back more slowly than she ought. The sense-memory of his touch lingered on her skin. She should not want it as much as she did.

"Perhaps not." His grin was entirely too cheeky for someone she was still irritated with, and she thawed further despite herself. "But as long as you will approve my nonsense, we shall find ourselves most amiable friends."

"Friends, is it?" she asked, arching an eyebrow. "I see the nonsense begins already."

He chuckled. "You are free of her ladyship Sunday mornings, are you not? Will you permit me to walk you home from church? I should dearly like to have the opportunity to escort you. My sister will be with me, of course, to act as chaperone." He was teasing her dreadfully, ridiculous man!

"And I should warn you that I will have Meg with me to act as mine, though of course—" She flushed hot, but pressed on. "We both know what sort of deterrent she is like to be."

"Setting the wolf to guard the sheep springs to mind." He laughed, warm and roundly affectionate, and Sarah pressed her finger against her lip to hide her answering smile of delight.

"Mr. Glover—"

He brushed back the edge of her cap and tucked the apple blossom into her hair. "James, please," he murmured, the mood in the hallway changing in an instant to something thickly wrapped around them both. The world fell away, and it was only, ever, the two of them together.

"James," Sarah corrected herself, her tongue thick in her mouth and her breath catching in her chest. "I have work, I must get back. And you—"

"I will see you Sunday, Miss Armand."

And with that reminder of her duplicity, the moment shattered, the air thinned back to normal and the delightful compression and longing in her chest turned once more to self-loathing.

He leaned in as though to kiss her, and she turned her head so that his lips brushed, only barely, against her cheek. "I attend at Grosvenor Chapel, on the other side of the square. Until Sunday, m'sieur."

He bent and retrieved his parcel—giving her the opportunity to note that his backside was as beautifully formed as his front—and set it into her hands. She waited until the door closed behind him, then sagged back against the wall of the hallway, her mind in a turmoil worse than before.

Whatsoever he thought he admired about Miss Sophie Armand, poor old Sarah Harlow, whore's bastard, could never match it.

Back to the stillroom, then, up the long and shadowed corridor toward the small chamber with its fireplace and small, rough-hewn table, and the list of cosmetics she was to make for a mean-spirited old woman who was born to be her better.

The lotion had been scraped from the mixing bowl by the time she got back, the little glass jar for Lady Horlock's dressing table standing full and prettily sealed. Ellen was nowhere to be seen—she must have taken herself off to her own duties after completing Sarah's. Perhaps Sarah had misjudged her, mistaking honest interest and care for prying eyes and watchfulness.

Sarah's recipe book lay closed beside the jar of lotion. Her play sat beneath it, pages carefully stacked. *Oh no, oh no no no—careless! Careless, stupid girl!*

She had tucked them beneath the open book when called to the door, hidden from view but carelessly ordered and in no fit shape to read. The handful of sheets were all still there, still in the same order she had left them in.

Perhaps Ellen had simply swept them up and put them down again tidily, without looking through Sarah's cramped and crossed-out scribbles.

Yes, that was most likely, surely. She would not have had the time to read it all.

Could she?

Chapter Seven

Nothing was said about Sarah's play, either by Ellen or Jack the footman, who seemed to have become her new particular friend. Lady Horlock had only cared about her new stays, ordering Sarah to lace her into them immediately once she arrived home, turning and twisting about to look at her new sleeker shape in the mirror.

"Tibbert truly is a genius, is he not?" she'd asked, full of praises. But Sarah had seen the tiny stitched *JG* on the inside corner, in the same fine white linen thread that fixed the stiffened cords into place.

But "indeed, *madame,*" had been all Lady Horlock had wanted in reply.

The week passed without anything coming of the events of that afternoon. Meg sent a note begging Sarah to come visit, with her usual attention to melodrama. But Lady Horlock had decided to take a break from making calls, being "at home" for them instead, and so there was no conceivable way for Sarah to slip away. No response came to her letter of apology, but come Sunday, Meg slipped into the pew next to Sarah, a beaming smile on her face.

No harm done, obviously enough.

Meg was in high spirits, her bonnet bobbing as she looked up, down, peered at faces, at every which thing other than the service taking place at the altar. She curled her fingers around Sarah's down in the pew between their bodies, out of sight.

"Look there," Meg whispered, nodding ahead, her gaze fixed on something past the fat old man with straining suit buttons and the lady dowager with an unfortunate crease in the puff of her sleeve.

There, up toward the front, sat Mr. Glover, wearing the fine suit he'd worn on Wednesday last to deliver Lady Horlock's stays. A girl with his same golden hair sat beside him, tipping her head in to murmur in his ear every once in a while.

The Horlocks went further afield, to the much more fashionable St. George's parish, but the simple old chapel at Grosvenor suited Sarah well. It hadn't the prestige of the larger church, but had the benefit of not having to dance attendance at Lady Horlock's whims even in those times when she was supposed to be allowed her own hour or two for prayer and reflection. Though at the moment she was doing a great deal more watching the back of Mr. Glover's—*James's*—neck, than actively paying attention to the vicar droning on at the pulpit.

As though he felt the burn of her stare, he turned, looked over his shoulder, caught her eye. His countenance brightened like the sun, the smile spreading warm across his face. The girl beside him elbowed him and he returned his eyes to front, the smile visible for moments longer.

"There," Meg murmured. "He's seen us. Do you think that's his sister?" She gave one final squeeze, then slipped her fingers from Sarah's hand.

"I imagine it must be," Sarah whispered back, before the lady who needed a better maid turned to glare at them.

The service ended, the congregation all rising in their pews to make their greetings and trade the week's gossip. By the time Sarah managed to work her way free to the aisle, James and the girl had vanished in the throng. Meg tucked her hand securely in the crook of Sarah's arm and, pressing between the heavily scented bosoms of the matrons and the churning crowd of second-best suits, they ducked and wove their way to the front door.

The vicar stood on the porch, nodding and smiling in his absent, vacant way as his parishioners filed out past him. The Glovers caught up to them there, James nodding to the vicar and falling in step beside Sarah, his smile broad and his blue-gray eyes alight. The younger girl peeped out from behind his shoulder, leaning forward to smile shyly and excitedly at Meg and Sarah, honey-gold ringlets bouncing gaily beneath the brim of her bonnet.

"Miss Armand, Miss Ceniza," James said, breathless, once they had claimed a spot of lane for their own where they were less likely to be jostled. "May I present my sister, Miss Glover. Cecily, Miss Armand and Miss Ceniza. Cecily is a great admirer of your work, Miss Ceniza, and has been plaguing me incessantly for an introduction."

That was as catnip to a pampered pet, as he'd no doubt known it would be. Meg's eyes lit up and she positively beamed at Miss Glover. "How very kind, and how very perceptive," she laughed, fanning herself with her gloved hand. Miss Glover, on the other hand, looked halfway to keeling over.

"Breathe, Cecily," James murmured, and poked her in the side.

"Oh, James, don't tease so!" Miss Glover pinked in the cheeks. "He's a beast, honestly! I simply must put up with him because he's my brother, but I cannot for the life of me imagine why you might."

And *that* was a question best left unanswered.

"Might I induce you both to take a quick turn about the park with us before I walk you home? If you've the time, that is. The trees along the reservoir are full of new green leaves, and it's a delightful morning for a stroll." He glanced at the battered gold watch hanging from the chain on his waistcoat. "It's only eleven yet," he coaxed, his lips quirked up into a grin, "and the vicar at St. George's preaches until half-past, at the earliest."

"What do you think, darling?" Meg asked, breaking away from effusive commenting on Miss Glover's fashionably pale green dress. "He does beg so prettily."

And that brought an entirely different sort of thought to Sarah's mind. The red tinge to James's ears beneath the brim of his hat, and the way he suddenly locked his eyes to hers suggested that he was having similar recollections.

"Begging?" He laughed. "Never. I am the man here, after all—I command!" and he struck a dashing pose.

Miss Glover giggled. "Keep that thought in mind. You're unlike to hear it confirmed by us!"

Sarah pressed her finger to her lip to hide the smile. "Only as far as the reservoir, or I'll be late back," she cautioned.

Meg already had her arm linked in Miss Glover's and the two of them set off. "He really is a dreadful tease," Miss Glover was saying, tucking her hand into Meg's elbow like they had been chums for years.

"Shall we?" James offered her his arm.

Sarah shook her head ruefully. "If not, we risk being left entirely behind."

The sun shone down on the four of them as the street gave way to path beneath their feet, the grass and springtime flowers gleaming bright and cheerful in the midmorning light. James's arm lay strong and thick beneath Sarah's hand, the muscle in his forearm palpable even beneath the warm charcoal wool of his coat and, presumably, the linen of a shirt beneath.

"A beautiful day," James said.

"Indeed it is," Sarah replied.

A moment passed.

"I hope tomorrow will be as beautiful," he said.

"Perhaps it shall."

His lips were twitching and his eyes dancing with humor when Sarah glanced up at him, and yet he stared straight ahead, his arm crooked properly and his other hand slung easily behind his back.

"Do you often take such walks?" she asked, preempting whatever other inanity he was going to see fit to deliver.

They would make a pretty picture walking there, to anyone who didn't know them. James with his hat and coat, a proper figure of a fit young man, sloe-eyed and sensual Meg and the young Miss Glover in their delicate dresses and beribboned bonnets, collecting handfuls of posies from the sides of the path as they walked.

And Sarah: blue dress, woolen shawl to keep out the springtime chill and only one pair of handed-down gloves to call her own. And yet James's eyes seemed to linger on her the most.

"Oh yes," he replied cordially. "Very often, with beautiful ladies, boys, horses, cattle—" He couldn't hold it in any longer, the laughter bubbling up out of him as he teased her. "This is unbelievably foolish, you know."

She tossed her head, though her hair was all bound up and unable to flip coquettishly as Meg's might have done. "And you are an unbelievable fool. It's a wonder you remember everybody's name, if you have so many prospective partners."

"But none," he cocked his hat and grinned, "so utterly amiable."

Sarah chuckled. "Correct answer." And with that any tension that lingered there dissolved, floating away until, like the soul in one of Meg's books of plays, it turned to dew and then to mist, and then was gone.

Meg looked back over her shoulder at the sound of his laughter. A frown flickered across her face before Miss Glover demanded her attention again, and she turned away.

What was that about?

"So, Miss Armand," he began again, tugging her arm gently, so gently, until she was more closely pulled against his side. She'd wanted to mount him, there in that chair in Meg's apartments, wanted to slide across his lap and feel his thighs, thick and firm, beneath her buttocks. She'd fallen asleep with the image of his thick, proud cock in her mind's eye, imagining how snugly it might fit inside her body. *Hussy!*

"Yes, Mr. Glover?" she replied, trying not to let her distraction show. *Cursedly attractive man.*

"Other than talking Sunday promenades with craftsmen, how does a lady's lady spend her spare time?"

"You presume that I have any, for a start."

"Let us say that you do," he suggested. "You're certainly no scullery girl, up before dawn and to bed after midnight, nothing but scrubbing in between."

"There is that."

How much to say? Surely, given that he knew her most intimate secret—one that not even Meg had known until so recently—it was no more dangerous to tell him others. She had held the solid length of his prick, after all, felt the heat and blood rushing through it, his desire pulsing against her tongue. There were only a few greater intimacies in the world.

"Lady Horlock keeps my days full, but I find my solace in solitary work." Her heart ached for her own precious secret. *Please be kind.* "I have been working on a play."

"A play?" James sounded at once incredulous and delighted. "In English? Yes, of course, it would be, if you hope to have it produced here. How marvelous. Do you intend it for Miss Ceniza?"

"At the moment I only intend it for my own satisfaction," Sarah confessed. "To see if I were capable. There are things in it that I think would make my current position somewhat…untenable, were it to be produced now and my name attached. What I see most of is the way the *ton* treat each other and themselves." She tumbled over her words as they slipped out faster now than before. "And some of the things that have made it to my prose may be seen as less than flattering. If word were to get around— before I've moved on, if I'm ever to get a good recommendation, you see—"

James stopped walking and put his finger to her lips, pressed it gently there against the dimple below her nose. "Worry not. Your secrets—all of them—are safe with me." He stared down at her, his blue eyes gone so dark that they shone like Lady Horlock's sapphires. His lips parted ever so slightly, as though he were thinking about kissing her right there. The breeze plucked at her skirt, and the girls stopped walking, up ahead.

"Is everything all right, James?" Miss Glover called back, and the spell of the moment broke.

He looked away, waved up at the girls a few feet ahead of them on the path. "Yes, quite."

They fell in step once more.

"Might I read it?" The question came out of the blue, so unexpected was it, and Sarah, lost in her own thoughts, didn't register the import of it for a moment.

"It?"

He elbowed her gently. "Your play."

"I, oh." Sarah paused, considered. "Yes, I suppose. But only if you promise to tell me precisely what you think. No holding back for fear of hurting my feelings. I should much prefer to have the honest truth from a friend first, rather than critics after."

"I promise," James said readily. "Though I cannot imagine that I will have any trouble doing so. Your intelligence and wit are most devastating, dear Miss Armand. I cannot imagine your writing would be anything else."

"You are a contradiction, sir." She found the boldness to tease him, and his eyes lit up so encouragingly that she carried on. "With the arms and hands of a laborer, but the manners of a gentleman."

"Blame my parents and my trade for that." James curled his arm inward trapping her fingers in the crook of his elbow for a moment, before he released her again. Strange how such a simple gesture should send a shiver of guilty pleasure down her spine. "My father made good money in overseas trade, enough to provide both Cecily and I with good schooling and simple luxuries. But while I have a decent enough head for figures, and apparently selling-charm enough to convince two of the most delectable beauties in London to take a turn with me"—she swatted at him and he ducked out of the way, laughing—"I could not bring myself to care one whit about clock parts or manufacturing."

"And so instead you became a staymaker?" Sarah arched an eyebrow. It was growing more difficult to keep up the pretense of her accent, of the persona that propriety demanded she maintain in public as well as in the occupied parts of the Horlocks' London house. One slip, and James would know she was a liar; one slip in any facet of her life and she would be alone and without hope once more. *How desperately precarious a living is this.* "It seems a jump from one to the other."

"Not as much as you might think. The drive to create is still there, the need to design, to see things come together beneath your fingers in new ways. Except instead of lifeless clocks and dead gears, I breathe shape and form into canvas and cord, steam and bone."

Sarah rolled her eyes affectionately. "Why do I always seem to find myself consumed by romantic artists?" She meant Meg, she remembered Joshua, and now James, looking at her with amusement and affection in his eyes. "I am far too prosaic a person to countenance such goings-on."

"I find that hard to believe, you who surely document romance in your writings and show us frail human beings for the creatures of ridiculousness that we are." James paused, raised up on his toes and broke a small flowering branch from the apple tree arching its thin boughs over the path. "And with such a desperate history of your own?

"Come now." He clasped both her hands, suddenly, and pressed the flowers between her palms. "I want to hear your story. When did you come from France? Have you left anything or anyone behind? I cannot believe a sweetheart or you should have mentioned something." He faltered, looked at her shrewdly, then carried on. "But your parents? Did they come with you, or were they killed in the Terror? Is that how you came to know Miss Ceniza as well as you do?"

"Now I know I heard my name that time." Meg burst in between the pair of them, taking James's arm in one of hers and Sarah's in the other. Miss Glover fell in on the other side of James, laughing. "Look at them, Miss Glover," Meg continued, a sharp edge in her voice that Sarah barely recognized. "So besotted that they've entirely forgotten about the two of us."

"Let us be proper chaperones, then, and divert them," Miss Glover replied, taking it far less seriously than Meg's fingers digging into Sarah's forearm would suggest.

"Meg, what are you doing?" Sarah wiggled her arm, and Meg immediately released her hold.

"I'm sorry, Sarah darling," she replied, casting her eyes downward, immediately contrite. "I didn't mean to surprise you. But you looked so cozy there, how could I resist?"

Sarah smiled indulgently at the return of normal-Meg. "Don't be foolish, dearest—"

"Sarah?" James asked, his brow furrowed. He glanced from one girl to the other. "A nickname for Sophie?" he guessed, and the moment of Sarah's heart seizing, constricting into a tight ball of impending doom, passed unremarked. Meg's fingers digging into her arm this time were entirely borne from surprise, and she let go slowly.

Meg tossed her hair, and *her* curls bounced delightfully about her shoulders as she did. "Indeed. One can hardly expect formality between such close friends."

Sarah held her breath. Would he—?

James nodded. "Of course. Now I shan't be confused by the names."

And he let it go.

"Someday, Miss Armand," he murmured into Sarah's ear, when they had almost arrived back at the Horlock's townhouse on Bruton Street, "we shall all be 'Meg' and 'Sarah' and 'James' to each other, easy and simple as can be."

How could he believe it to be so? "Nothing in life is that simple," she cautioned him, amidst a wave of melancholy.

James only smiled, as irritatingly optimistic as Meg was capricious. "It could be." And when his sister took his arm and Meg took the other one, it almost, perhaps, seemed like he could be right.

Meg returned to her apartments alone. James had balked at bringing his baby sister to such a rough neighborhood, and so Meg had done the right thing and begged off, claiming to have errands to run on Bond Street that would keep her out of the house. What those errands might have been on a Sunday afternoon neither of the Glovers apparently thought fit to question. The relief and thanks on James's face at not having to go anywhere near Meg's address was enough to set her teeth on edge.

In the daylight it wasn't so bad. It looked like every other street in London, except the squares where the high-and-mighty lived. The city was dirtier and busier than the winding country lanes around her childhood home, but she liked it better for its honesty.

Though sometimes, there was such a thing as too honest. She saw the man in the long coat the same moment he saw her. He lurked in the entryway to the little side street leading to her lodgings, hands in his coat pockets and a hat pulled low down over his head. The coat was patched badly at the elbows, his hat shiny in spots, giving lie to the dashing figure he seemed to be trying to present. His waistcoat buttoned around his girth, but the coat strained at his bulky shoulders. No gloves could cover those ham-like fists, nor the scars upon his knuckles.

He approached, something vaguely familiar about his face, and sketched a mocking sort of bow, not taking his eyes off her bosom.

"Go away," Meg said to him, before he even opened his mouth. "I'm not company for the likes of you." The cut direct would have been simpler, of course, but far more challenging to pull off correctly when he stood between her and her stairs.

"P'rhaps not," he agreed amiably enough, but his smile had a hard edge, and his eyes were dead and cold. "But the Baron would have a word with you, Miss Ceniza, and he gets displeased when ladies keep him waiting."

Fear trickled through her veins, chill and foreboding. *He's always given up sooner than this before.*

"And I've told him what I'll tell you," she said instead, drawing on everything she had to keep her lip from trembling or her voice from squeaking. The curtain twitched in the ground-floor window, and Meg's courage returned. When the Baron's man followed her glance, she knew he had seen it too. Agatha was watching. "I'm nobody's doxy.

If he wants to see me, he can buy a ticket to my next play, like everyone else."

The Baron's bruiser shook his head slowly, but he stepped aside when she made to brush past him. "He'll have you in his flock, whether you will it or no!"

Meg ignored him, climbing the stairs and locking her door most firmly behind her. Two sealed letters blew past her into the room, caught by the quick rush of air. The first one had John Thomas's writing on the front and his blood-red wax seal on the back. That one she threw, unopened, onto the table. It would only be more of the same nonsense and deserved no response.

Damn Sarah, anyway, and her fashionable address. Even though it wasn't hers, James would certainly never have to be wary about being seen promenading about in *Mayfair,* of all places.

Let Sarah and James be cozy, and let John Thomas fuss and fume—what could it harm? Meg flung herself upon the bed in a flurry of skirts, though there was no one there to witness the glorious way they draped about her legs and hips when she finally settled on the bed, propped up on a perfectly plump elbow. She had wanted Sarah and James to meet, after all, and for them to find each other amiable. She had most certainly *not* intended for them to spend all their energy on each other and leave her to entertain his little sister!

Not that there was anything *wrong* with Miss Glover. She was as pert and happy as any girl with a loving older brother and a decent dowry could be. But she was not the one with whom Meg wanted to spend her time. Even though she was a perfectly adorable and adoring fan, which made up for quite a bit.

Meg turned onto her back and lay there for a moment, staring up at the ceiling. She tapped the edge of the folded letter against her lips, pursing them to make the gesture more dramatic.

James and Sarah adored each other, that much was obvious.

Meg had loved Sarah for at least half her life, and Sarah loved Meg in return. She knew that as surely as she knew her own name.

How did James feel? That was the key. Secure him for both of them, and the three of them could surely, somehow, live happily. She would *make* it be so.

And here—the letter from Langston and her Haymarket role. She could feel it now, the positive energy surging through the paper and the ink, all of it pointing her toward better and brighter things. No more scraping and scratching for patrons, for parts, for a decent living. She would be seen on the proper patent stages, she would have her name—*hers*—on the playbills at the top, and James would be proud of her.

He would look at her with the same shining devotion she had seen in his eyes for Sarah today.

She would make them both proud.

Meg opened the letter.

Miss Ceniza,

Thank you for your interest in playing our Constance. I thought it kindest to write you myself, seeing as you made your interest clear. I have made my casting choices, and offer you the role of Constance's serving girl. In a few years, once you have matured into your considerable promise, there will be opportunities for you in the more difficult roles. In the meantime, I require skilled actresses with intimate knowledge of the workings of comedy to play the lead roles, and a child best known for screaming at canvas monsters is not—

She crumpled the hateful, horrible letter into a tight ball and whipped it at the wall with all her strength. It bounced from the sconce and rolled into the cold fireplace, coming to a stop below the grate. Meg turned over as the tears began to flow, jamming her face into the pillow to block the ugly sounds of her sobs.

She *could* be a serious actress, but how could she prove it when no one would give her the chance? No, she was condemned now, to play fainting heiresses and maids, to wail her way through pantomimes and melodramas until she was too old to do even that anymore. She couldn't even get the lead in a *farce*!

Worse yet, James would fall madly in love with Sarah and carry her off to live a life of luxury, and Meg…she would die, alone, discarded, unremembered and unloved.

All was lost.

Chapter Eight

It could be that easy. What had he been thinking? The intoxication of the company he'd been keeping, perhaps. The easy way Miss Ceniza and Cecily had been drawn to each other, the ease of conversation with Sophie, the warmth of the sun and the glowing light of their smiles.

It had been too easy to imagine that it could always be that way.

Now, however, sitting in the shop on Bond street of an afternoon, carefully sanding down two identical pieces of whalebone until the surface was like satin under his fingertips…it all seemed far less simple. Better to concentrate on the work, on the gifts he was preparing, than on the women they were intended for. Or what could possibly become of them all.

He could hardly house both ladies in his home, could he? Not with Cecily living there, for servants talked. (Oh, the sting of disloyalty as he thought that! Would Sophie talk in such a circumstance? And how well did he even know his own servants?) To keep a wife and a mistress separately would work for himself, but would the girls be happy with such a separation? Would he be required to keep a daybook with appointments set aside to visit his own lovers?

What do Mohammedans do with their four wives?

Somehow he doubted very much that the Moroccan embassy would be at all amenable to such enquiries.

What would Father have done in such a situation?

Not be drawn into such a strange arrangement in the first place.

Sheridan would call him the luckiest man in existence and clap him so soundly on the shoulder that James would be sore for days.

Neither of those reactions was helpful.

He set the sanding block down, tapped the sharpened pencil against his chin and stared at the two busk blanks on the table in front of him. He might not be able to see a clear plan for his future, but at least, for the moment, he could make his ladies some beautiful things.

His ladies. How droll. His father would be disappointed in him. This was not how a gentleman should act. Father had married one woman and never, as far as James knew, taken a mistress or lover beyond her. He had loved exuberantly where Mother had been cautious; he had filled up the quiet spaces in her life with laughter and joy.

Much like Marguerite Ceniza did for him. She was bright where James was steady, lively when he would otherwise be still. She filled any room with laughter and left emptiness and wistful longing when she was gone.

For her, then, flowers in full bloom, exuberant and joyful, open and warm. Let her busk be carved with lilies and roses, circles progressing down the length as his lips yearned to press down the rounded curves of her belly. He sketched in the shapes with fine graphite lines, pressing the pencil against the just-sanded surface to map out the negative spaces that he would carve away.

And then the second, for Sophie, her careful protective shell opening for him, so slowly. Where Marguerite was exuberance, Sophie was calm resilience, strength and skill. She was curlicues and hidden mazes, flower buds worked into the abstract designs. Secrets hid behind her eyes, and he worked letters into the curling vines with his own hidden message.

Be mine.

He sat back and looked at his sketches with a critical eye.

What he needed to do was to stop overthinking and enjoy the gifts that they were willing to give him. The letter from Marguerite crinkled in his pocket, the two simple lines burned into his memory from the moment he first read them.

I long for you. Join us on Wednesday night.

Us, indeed. And now Wednesday it was, and the pleasures of Eden were rapidly approaching with the setting sun.

Not soon enough, however, for cursing and muttering erupted from the shop's back room. James braced himself on his stool, as Tibbert came storming out from behind the curtain, some of James's sketches in his hand. He clenched the papers so hard that they crumpled in his fist, flapping like leaves in a storm as he waved them through the air.

James set his pencil down and picked up his etching tool. "Does something ail you?"

The little man all but exploded at him, slamming the pages down before him. James's ponderings and design notions for long-line stays were creased through now, diagrams of gussets and seam details crumpled and smudged. "What is all this, young Glover? How much time have you wasted on this nonsense?"

James set his tools down and placed his elbows firmly on the table. Young Glover, indeed. He'd had it up to his neck and beyond with the insufferable condescension. "We are staymakers, sir. There in your hand are some sketches of stays."

"These are foolishness! They will never fit a figure, for one—the lines are all wrong."

Calm. What would Sophie want him to do? Stay calm, that was what. She never blinked in the face of such treatment. "Adding a split in the hem and setting in a gusset there will allow for a cleaner line over the hips and a smoother drape for the lightest modern dresses."

Tibbert rallied himself for a tirade, and all that came out was an agonized squeak. He took a breath that sent the top of his balding head bright red. "This is not how things are cut and not how they are meant to be! The fashion changes quickly enough—must you try and drive change further away from the things I have trained you for?" He sputtered. "You design for foolish young *Merveilleuses*, not the modest and noble ladies who will be your bread and butter when I am dead and gone." He drew himself up to his full height. "Stick to the drafts, Mr. Glover. Stick to the drafts and the pattern books, and you cannot go wrong."

James fixed him with a steely glare of his own. In the past, this would have been where he gave in, acquiesced solely to keep the peace. If he wanted to be his own man, the man that Sophie and Marguerite deserved, it was time to make a change.

He stood, splaying his fingers out on the worktable, rising a head or so higher than the little man who had taken him as an apprentice so long ago.

"There are no set patterns for the things I want to see in the world," he said, only realizing after the words were out of his mouth how true that was. "Think back on the days of *panniers* and *fontages*, and how far we've come in only thirty years' time. The next thirty will be full of change again, and I intend to be at the forefront."

There. Let him be fired if he must. He had said his piece.

Tibbert stared, opening and closing his mouth, and with no sound coming out. "You are in your cups," he snarled after a moment, casting about as though looking for a wine bottle that wasn't to be found.

"I am in my rights," James replied. He scooped together the busk blanks and his tools and rolled them into their canvas pocket. "And now I am off. To visit a client," he added, though that was only partially the truth. "I will return in the morning."

"Do so," Tibbert snarled, and there in the afternoon light, sputtering and fuming, he looked nothing at all like the tyrant who had so often struck young James across his knuckles until he bled. "And return tomorrow in a more conciliatory mood. I will not work with someone who challenges me in my own shop."

"Have a good evening, Tibbert." James tied his bundle and slipped it beneath his arm. First a stop at home, to freshen himself and change his clothes, then to Meg's lodgings and the evening of delights that awaited.

He was a man, after all, and not a confused and fumbling boy. Anticipation thrummed in his blood. Tonight, with their pleasure his goal, he would show both of his women the living proof.

Cecily was waiting for him at home, pelting him with a barrage of questions before he even got through the door. "You're home early," she exclaimed, trotting down the stairs. "Is everything all right? Are you ill? Are you meeting a client here and do I need to have the parlor tidied?"

James set his hat and coat aside and tousled her hair fondly, his mind entirely elsewhere. "Yes, no, no, in that order. I'm only here for a moment, to wash and change, then I have an appointment." He paused, then grabbed for her hand and swung her into an undignified spin. "I told off old Tibbert today," he confessed, giddy as a madman. "It was *glorious.*"

"You did?"

"I did!"

Cecily stumbled when he let go her hand and gaped up at him before shaking her head furiously. "What's gotten *into* you? You're not the same man these days, James."

"No," he replied, tugging his cravat loose as he mounted the stairs two at a time toward his bedroom. "No, I am not. And all the better for it!"

"Will you be home for dinner?" Cecily called up behind him. He paused on the first landing and looked down. She peered back up at him from the hall below, worrying her thumbnail between her teeth.

"I fancy not," he called back. "Go ahead and eat without me."

"Whatever will I tell Mrs. Lambert? Jaaaames!" Her voice betrayed her outrage, and he closed his door firmly behind him, cutting off her indignant squawk. Cecily would recover. This assignation tonight was one he had no intention of missing, bored little sister or no.

James arrived at Meg's apartments with fewer twists to his gut than the last time he'd approached. Anticipation made his blood bubble and sing instead, a glorious tingle running along his skin. There were too many people out in the street to give in and do what he wanted, which was run up the stairs full-speed and knock with all the exuberance he could muster. He had to be restrained, polite: a suitor and not a ravisher.

The door swung open almost before he had laid his knuckles to it, and Meg, clad in a lace wrapper and her glorious curls falling down around her hips, took his hand and pulled him inside.

"Took you long enough," she chided him, fists on her waist and her eyes laughing.

"I came with all haste! The streetlights aren't yet lit." James took off his hat and swept a bow to the room before looking up. Sophie stood by the window, the rays of the setting sun sweeping in and setting her cheeks and her bound hair aglow with red and gold. She wore a simple gown, her working clothes. He had only ever seen her in one other. Hadn't he? She'd worn something different for church, lighter and softer, that had turned her from a housemaid to a princess fair.

"Sophie," he greeted her, and oddly enough, she seemed to flinch. Only a trifle, so perhaps he had imagined her reaction, but she crossed the room with a smile so genuine that he forgot all about it.

"James." Her hand was so delicate in his, despite the calluses and hints of roughness from needles that picked at the skin. His were no better; decidedly worse, for what that was worth. But here, now, Meg's hand curled snugly on his arm and Sophie's skin was warm against his lips when he brought her hand up to kiss it. In that moment, they were all royals, all divine.

"Ladies," he added for good measure, rising out of his bow. "Your beauty takes my breath away, now as ever."

"And you're a flatterer." Sophie laughed as she said it, though, slipping her hand out of his and crossing the room to close and bar the shutters against the approaching night. Candles lit about the room and a small fire in the fireplace warmed the darkness, shadows flickering with their movements as they circled and watched each other. "Let me help you with your coat," she offered, starting to slide it from his shoulders.

James stepped back half a step and shook his head. "I'm not an employer, but a suitor," he said softly, the candlelight playing hide-and-seek with the shadows in among Sophie's braids. "I can do this work myself." He shrugged off his jacket and let it drape over the back of a chair. He stood there in his waistcoat and shirtsleeves, Meg pressing a drink into his hand.

The brandy burned like fire down his throat, his second compulsive swallow following hot on the heels of the first. There was no reason for his nerves. The apartment was as he'd seen it before, the girls as they always were, except that now…now their charms were not unattainable and baffling treasures to be desired from afar.

"Thank you," Sophie murmured, and sipped demurely from the glass that Meg had placed into her hands. She lapsed into silence again.

A log popped loudly in the fireplace and Meg jumped, squeaked, then sank into the only other empty chair in a fit of irrepressible giggles. "Oh, goodness, you know, I thought for a moment—"

"What, that someone had a pistol?" Sophie teased her. "Come to duel us for James's purity?"

"That's a prize long gone, in thought as well as deed," James admitted, and the ridiculousness of the entire situation started him chuckling.

"Is he laughing at us?"

"I think he must be," Sophie murmured in reply.

"No, only at the insanity of all of this," James gestured wide, the last of the brandy sloshing up the side of the glass as he waved his arm to encompass the room. In two swift strides he crossed the space and dropped himself down to sit at Meg's feet, his shoulder and hip warmed by the glowing coals in the fireplace. "Look at us, adults all, no strangers to each other and to carnal bliss, and yet—"

"And yet we sit about like children on the first day of lessons, barely able to speak to one another for fear of the schoolmaster's switch." Meg settled her chin in her hand.

Sophie gave Meg another one of those odd looks, one that he couldn't parse, but once again it passed without comment and once again he let it go.

"Switching? I hear there are some who enjoy that sort of thing," he joked lightly, throwing back the rest of his drink, the glorious warmth—even from the cheap brandy— burning up his throat and across each arm to the very tips of his fingers.

"You 'hear'?" Sophie asked, sliding down to sit on her knees beside Meg's chair, her head at the same level as James's. "Or you indulge? Tell me, Mr. Glover, how many lovers have you had? What is our number among your ladies of pleasure?"

If there was ever a moment to stop and assess his danger, this would be it.

"Tied for first, as God is my witness," he pledged, placing his hand over his heart. "Everyone else—and there have not been many, I promise you—pales in comparison to the pair of you. Sun and shadow, flame and coal, you hold equal places in my esteem, each surpassing all others entirely."

It was flowery, but he wasn't wrong.

"Good answer," Sophie laughed, a rippling, silvery sound he wouldn't ever tire of hearing. "Very good, indeed. You're a poet, Mr. Glover. James."

He shrugged. "I'm a fool, infatuated beyond belief."

Sophie looked at him solemnly, steady-faced and thoughtful.

"Come here," he coaxed gently, softly. She was a bird, skittish and watchful, but the memory of her fingers wrapped around his prick, the press of her lips, was seared forever into his memory. The familiar warmth spread through his groin at the thought, at the pictures that followed one after another in his mind's eye.

Sophie, her fist clenched tight around his cock, stroking him with fierce power. Spending himself all across her naked and willing body. Her red lips parted and gleaming as he slid his prick slowly between them—

She glanced up at Meg, as though asking permission, then slowly, carefully, laid her hand on James's upper thigh.

He held himself so still, unbreathing and close, that his lungs ached with the lack of air. She set her weight on her arm and down into his leg, then leaned forward and brushed her lips against his.

That was his cue to set his glass aside, bury his fingers in her hair, glorious and silken, and slide out the pins that held her braids to her head. Sophie's mouth was uncharted territory, new and strange, a hot, wet bed into which he eased his tongue. She moaned, low in her throat, and sucked on it, then let him go. Her hair tumbled down around her shoulders, the braids and twists slowly uncoiling.

"Let me make love to you," he urged, grazing his teeth against the fullness of her lower lip. He burned with the noises she made, the throbbing of her pulse beneath the pads of his thumbs. Every urge he could name called him to press her down, take and claim her. First her, then Meg, mark them both as forever his and only his. But first—first he had to hear it from those plump and sinful lips. "Say that we may."

He expected—what? Some kind of trembling sweet reply, more shyness and hesitation? He swept his hands gently down her sides, the lines of her short stays beneath her dress, the swells of her hips that would be so firm and solid in his hands.

He did not expect the hand flattening against his chest that began its own careful explorations, or the fierce way she pressed up into him, twisting beneath his hands and rising up on her knees to wind her arms around his neck. "Yes," Sophie breathed into his mouth, and the tip of her tongue traced the line of his lips in return.

"You two are like stage lovers, cooing and billing," Meg baited them, sliding from her chair to land lightly on her bare feet. She stroked Sophie's back, her hair, then curled her fingers beneath Sophie's chin and tipped her mouth up to receive Meg's kiss. Sophie kissed back, her arms still about James's neck, and he set his hand at the small of her back so that she wouldn't fall.

The sight of them like that, Meg's black curls falling down over Sophie's face and shoulders, their eyes closed and lips pressed together; it sent fire raging through James's body, brought his cock to full alert, pressing hard against the heavy wool of his breeches.

Sophie's breasts rose high as she breathed—he needed to see them, feel them, stroke his thumbs across her nipples while he teased and sucked at Meg's. James found the pins that held up the apron of her bodice and slid them free. He brushed down the soft cotton to expose the lacings that drew her bodice snug across her bountiful breasts, full and firm. Sophie sucked in air and let out a soft laugh.

Meg's fingers slid down between Sophie's breasts, pressed little circles into the swells. James dropped his head as though in prayer and pressed his mouth against her breasts.

Sophie's laugh turned to a breathy gasp, and her nails dug into James's neck. "That's lovely."

"Up, up," Meg urged, and tugged them both to standing. She slid between them, tugging at Sophie's lacing while Sophie drew Meg's wrapper down off her smooth, unblemished shoulders. James found himself tucked up against Meg's glorious behind, not a terrible position to take, considering.

He gripped her hips and pulled her tightly against him, rocked his hips so that she might feel the solid length of his prick. It was easier to be freer with her, with fewer worries about offending her, or scaring her away. Meg looked over her shoulder as she finished with Sophie's lacings, and pushed back against him in return. The pressure against his groin was barely enough to take the edge off of the ache, made so much better—and worse—by the sight of Sophie's breasts rising above her gray stays, Meg's shoulders and breasts equally uncovered, only her lacings now standing between his hands and her skin.

"Too many clothes," he urged, and Sophie flicked her hips like a dancing girl to send her dress sliding down her body to puddle on the floor. She bent forward and shook her shoulders again, to the rhythm of Meg's giddy laughter, her breasts jiggling and bouncing with every one of her movements.

Meg reached back and pinned James's hands. "Don't let him move," she teased, but this time—

"Oh no." James narrowed his eyes playfully, twisted his wrist gently and broke free of her hold. "Not this time, my loves." He ran his hands up the sides of Meg's body, her hips, the slim curve of her waist, the tender handfuls of her breasts still laced into her stays. Unlacing them was as much second nature as lacing a woman in had become, and he had them peeled from her within seconds. "You had your fun at my expense once," he purred, and Meg's eyes gleamed with anticipation. "Now it becomes my turn to show you what a man is capable of."

"Such big words." Sophie laughed, pressing boldly up in behind Meg and smoothing her hands over the sweet curves of Meg's body. "I wonder if you have the stamina to please us both."

"Aye, that's the question." Meg tossed her hair imperiously, despite being clad only in her shift. She had lost no dignity with the loss of her clothing, only gained in the single-mindedness of his driving need. There were her nipples, dark and round through the thin fabric of her shift, pressing through in tiny hard circles. He bent his head and sucked one into his mouth, wetting the linen and smoothing circles around the tight nub with his tongue. Meg gasped and arched up to give him better access, her body taut beneath his hands.

He stroked his palms up her plump thighs, met Sophie's hands coming on the same path down, and for a moment, interlinked their fingers over Meg's warm flesh and squeezed, tight.

Meg's other nipple, then, rolling over his tongue, the linen wet and sliding over her skin with the insistent pressure of his mouth. She cried out, rocked her hips back away from him and against Sophie who stood behind her. Sophie grasped the hem of Meg's shift and pulled it off over her head. Meg stood before them both, naked and bare, the dark thatch of curls between her legs inviting.

"Now you," Sophie urged, dropping Meg's shift on the chair and reaching out to slowly, carefully, trace her fingertips down the bulge at the front of his breeches. His hips jerked, desperate for more than that teasing caress could provide.

"You first," he countered, tucking his arm around Meg's waist and drawing her in close to one side, so that he could reach out to Sophie with the other. "Let me see you both entirely." His heart raced, his pulse pounding in his ears. She unlaced her stays, looking away.

No, no, that's not right—

He reached out, Meg's hands working at the buttons of his waistcoat. He brushed his fingertips along the side of Sophie's face, caressed her cheek, then gently, so gently, turned her head the way Meg had done, until her eyes locked with his. Could she be a virgin still? She had made lusty love to Meg before, but that was not the same as lying with a man.

Was it?

"You are so beautiful," he murmured, and Meg, mouth pressed against his breastbone, tongue tantalizing and deft, murmured her agreement. "Never be shy of this, of us."

"You ask quite a bit," Sophie replied, and her accent, for a moment, had vanished. He tugged at the bow and pulled the drawstring looser. The linen fell from her shoulders, caught for a moment on the fullness of her breasts, before she tugged it down impatiently.

Oh, God in heaven. Or he was in heaven, and they were— "You are angels of the Lord, sent to make my final days glorious," he breathed out, and reached for Sophie with his free arm.

"Final days?" Meg asked, confusion in her eyes when she looked up from the trail of red bite marks she was leaving down his collarbone.

"No man alive could survive this," he swore with all sincerity.

Sophie laughed, some of the last of her hesitation falling away. She pressed in against him as well, fingers curling in his shirt and her other hand resting low on Meg's buttock. "Are you calling us dangerous?"

"Are you saying that you're not?" He bent his head and kissed her again, her lips soft and welcoming. Hands worked at his buttons and then his cravat, pulling the strip of starched linen aside and casting it away.

He kissed Sophie and then Meg, cupped Sophie's full, round breasts in his hands and rolled her nipples between his spit-slicked fingers. He pressed his palm over Meg's smaller, teardrop-shaped breasts, sucked her nipples into his mouth again with no fabric barrier between them.

They stripped his shirt from him; who did what seemed so inconsequential as to be beyond notice. His breeches hit the floor and then he too was nude before them, his prick harder than it had ever been during other assignations. Harder, even, than during all the fevered solitary fantasies that followed the night he had first seen the women together.

Something wordless seemed to pass between the women, their eyes locking for a moment only, a small and indulgent smile passing briefly over Meg's lips. She dropped to her knees before him, and Sophie watched, biting her bottom lip so that her teeth made little white marks in the plush pink. He had only a moment to brace himself, to reach for Sophie and press his mouth desperately to hers, before the lightning shock raced through his system. Meg's mouth slid down over his prick, taking in the tip. Her tongue swirled around him, burning, molten heat and pressure. *God, a man could die from this.*

Sophie wrapped her arms around his neck. He slid his hands about her narrow waist, caressed the warm skin of her back, slid his hands up into her hair and stroked his thumb around the rims of Sophie's ears. Meg's hot mouth sucked him in and he held back, resisted the urge to push into her. He sank his tongue into Sophie's mouth instead, and she bit at his lips, nipped at the pulse point in his throat.

That was when Meg slipped away from him again, his hot, hard prick falling from her full red lips. Meg stood and bared her throat to Sophie, pressed her rear against him. He grabbed for Meg, filling his hands with her plush buttocks, as full and bountiful as Sophie's breasts. They all three twined around each other, hands and thighs and lips all yearning.

He backed up, hitting the wall behind him and leaning against it for support. James set his hands on Meg's hips, his fingers spanning their breadth. Sophie followed, Meg laughing and tugging her along, and the three crashed into each other in a pile against the whitewashed plaster.

"Here, now," Meg begged, and she reached behind her to slide her hand between his legs. Her clever fingers stroked his bollocks, cupped and tugged them, then she seized him by the root and gripped him tight to guide him home.

Wait, wait, wait—

He struggled for breath and for restraint, his muscles trembling with the effort of holding back. His hand splayed out against the soft swell of her stomach, holding her there, so desperately close. "Can we? I'll not risk your ruination, not for anything."

Meg moaned, grinding back against him until he was all but out of his mind. Her mouth, or between her breasts, those would do, but nothing would be as glorious as the riskiest of all options. "It's safe, as safe as anything can be. Especially if you don't spend within me. Women have our ways. I need you—both." Enough—it was all he needed. He took hold of his prick, her rear pressed against him promising a thousand different kinds of ecstasy. Stroking her lower back with his free hand got her writhing. Sophie slid her hand between Meg's thighs, and she gasped. James slipped his fingers down between Meg's buttocks, past the center of her pleasure, between the delicate folds of skin. She was wet, so wet and silken to the touch. She pushed back against his hand and then forward into Sophie's.

He pressed the tip of his cock against her cunny. Meg cried out for more. He thrust, one powerful stroke of his hips, her hips solid between his hands.

Tight, so tight and hot, far better than anything he could remember or imagine.

Encased in her, rocking with her—his mind took flight and his skin burned. Sophie pressed against Meg's front and kissed James over Meg's shoulder, his tongue inside her mouth mimicking the fierce and desperate efforts of their hips.

Sophie kissed him and she cupped Meg's breasts, fondled and stroked them. She slid a hand between Meg's thighs again, rubbing and tracing out shapes between their bodies. James, looking down, could see it all—Meg's small, dark nipples and the sweat beading down her skin, the wet trails left by Sophie's mouth. Sophie's full breasts swaying and her high, pink nipples tight, her auburn hair sticking to her throat and shoulders. The way her fingers appeared and then vanished again into that nest of dark curls, Meg's pleasured groans growing louder with every sweep, pass, thrust deep inside her body.

Meg gave way to him, his hands tight around her hips. "Sarah, Sarah my love—" Meg rested her arms on Sophie's shoulders and fell between them both, taking him deeper still until his bollocks struck her arse with every heated push inside.

"Gorgeous." He couldn't keep the words back, the compliments and adoration spilling out as he bent to cover her, and bit at the soft skin beneath her ear. "Glorious, beautiful, utter perfection."

"More," Meg ground out between her teeth. She buried her face in Sophie's neck, her cries muffled against their lover's skin. James sped up, his legs aching, snapping his hips to drive deep into Meg, claim her, mark her, take her so wildly that she would feel him, remember him with every step she took the next day, still have the sensation of him filling up the very core of her body.

"Come, darling," Sophie urged, and she kissed Meg, then James again, turning her head back and forth from one to the other as she moved her hand in circles between the women's bodies.

If he let himself go he could finish gloriously, just like this, Meg's back spread out before him. She cried out like a wild thing, driving back on to him. God, she was ferocious, demanding, taking everything from him, and he surged into her to give her more—more—anything she needed. He pushed into her and drew back, slower now, then faster, until she writhed and begged. She arched tight as a drawn bowstring, dug her nails so hard into Sophie's arms that she left marks from her nails and let out a muffled scream into the crook of her own arm.

"There, darling, there," Sophie soothed, stroking Meg's back in gentle circles as she shuddered, shook and then, finally, went limp. James gathered her up in his arms, held her close, Sophie on her other side to create a protective cocoon that surrounded Meg entirely.

7...8...9... James counted silently in his head, gripping himself at the base of his prick and slowly, agonizingly slowly, slid out of Meg, his own desire still raging hot. The cool air struck him like a blow, his prick red and wet from Meg's lust. She sagged back against him, drew her arms up to cradle his head, languid in the aftereffects of her pleasure. He had thought her beautiful before, but now she was exquisite, unbound and wild, and he—*they*—had brought her to that point.

"Now you," she instructed, an impossible smile blossoming across her face.

"As my lady commands," he murmured against the shell of her ear.

Sophie wound her fingers around his neck and Meg stayed between them long enough for three mouths to come together, slipping and sliding over one another in reckless desperation. Meg slipped aside but left her hands on Sophie, pressing kisses along her shoulder and then down her spine.

"Come with me." James drew Sophie close and held her in his arms, his cock hard and thick between their bodies. The pressure helped, the throbbing in his brain subsiding and easier to control, but not for long, not with this delicious girl in his arms, all her sweet hesitation gone. She followed and he guided her to the chair. She collapsed down into it when the backs of her knees bumped against the seat edge; he fell to his knees between her thighs.

This—this was something to focus on, to take his mind off the driving desperation in his body, the urge to *take* and *thrust* and *have* that he'd cut off midstream when Meg had reached her climax. No, this, here, between Sophie's legs, her auburn curls tickling his nose, his mouth pressed to the sweet, wet folds of her sex; this was good. And if she were a virgin still—

There would be time to find out, later. Not now.

Everything she was opened to him. He swirled his tongue up along the curves and edges and sucked her labia between his lips, traced circles around the nub at the top.

She shook, gripped his hair so tightly that he trembled with *her* ecstasy, sucked harder, harder, there, as she came apart around and over him, his tongue slick with sweet-salt musk and the tingling drops of her sweat.

Everything, everything was Sophie, and Meg's hands on her body. On the two pairs of hands lifting him up and stroking his prick. Sophie kissed him, Meg kissed *her*. Sleek, soft curves filled his hands and nipples brushed his back, his chest. Two hands wrapped around his cock and one beneath his balls—he couldn't tell whose and it didn't matter.

Pleasure, thick and full, raced through him, lightning coiling in his groin. His bollocks drew tight, he bit at someone's lip, fingers slid up his prick, dragging his foreskin up over the head and back down again, tight, tight, heat and friction, everything and everywhere all across his skin—

He cried out, the pressure building beyond unbearable. James arched and he cursed and he came, his head thrown back and eyes closed tight, body locked between the women he loved best in the world.

They didn't make it back to the bed for a while, the rug before the fire plenty comfortable enough to lie upon, as sweat dried and bodies succumbed to sleep.

Chapter Nine

Sarah had collapsed beside James, Meg sprawled on top of them both and her fingers laced through Sarah's. She dozed like that, before the fire, the soft rag rug cushioning her hips and shoulders, James's warmth soaking into her bones. She nuzzled into the crook of his elbow and he slid his arm beneath her head, curling her in close. His scent mingled with Meg's, her black curls spread upon the pale peach of James's skin.

If there was a better way to slip back into consciousness than this, she had never known it. Meg moved, as though she and Sarah had awoken at the same moment, on the same breath. She turned over and burrowed down between Sarah's breasts and James's chest, her back cool on one side and warm on the side that had been facing the fire. James's fingers tangled in Meg's hair, stroking down to run his palm across the supple skin of her back.

Sarah rose, ignoring Meg's soft complaint, to wash herself, her hair falling down her back. She found her way to the jug by the faint glow of the handful of small candles that lit the room. The water was cool when she smoothed the cloth over her skin, washing away the evidence of their passions.

Eyes bored into her and she turned, met James's heated gaze. He watched her, propping himself up on his elbow, Meg still curled in against him and her lips pressed to his chest. He smoothed his hand down over the curve of Meg's hip, and his smile was all for Sarah.

She felt wicked, all at once. More so now than in the hour that had come before, when they all three had tangled together, took and gave such an intensity of pleasure that she had never imagined possible. Holding James's gaze, Sarah brushed the cloth across her breasts, circled her nipples the way his tongue had done, slowly dragged the damp cloth down along her stomach, over the curls at her cunt. He swallowed compulsively, watching her hands, then her mouth, then her hands again as she moved the linen down, down along the length of her leg.

"Sophie," he said softly, his hand cupping Meg's buttock, his voice low and husky with desire. He drew up his knee and when she looked, his prick lay, thick and half hard, against the lean, firm muscle of his thigh.

Everything about him was firm, all but his lips. Those red-flushed lips rounded into a semblance of a pout, lush and swollen from kissing and from loving. Her body flushed hot at the lingering sensation, the sense-memory of his mouth and tongue on her skin, between her legs, the way he'd suckled at her clitoris and swiped his tongue across her entrance.

He stared at her again with that same intensity, his muscles rippling as he pushed himself up to sitting. Those wide, strong shoulders of his gleamed, the candlelight picking out the sparse blond hair scattered across his chest. That same golden hair got thicker beneath his navel, a divot in his flat stomach that cried out to be tasted, have her tongue traced around it, to drink Meg's favorite brandy from it and trace the curling drops across his hip. The line that curled over his hipbone and down toward his groin would catch the drink, channel the amber droplets down along that rippling vee, toward the tower of his prick, leaning now, even as it grew. He was impressive enough when quiescent, and now as his arousal resurged he became positively magnificent, red-crowned and thick, almost larger around than her slim fingers could span.

And that was something she had not yet tried. Not with him, at any rate. Meg's fingers and James's fevered kisses drew pleasure out of her, bringing her to heights of ecstasy that she still could not find words for, but she ached. She ached, empty and hollow, and her body throbbed in sympathy with her cunt.

She could do it, cross the room right now, leave the cloth with the jug, sit across his knees and slide down, sheathe his prick inside her body and take what she needed.

Was there any reason why she shouldn't?

Meg had her tricks. The carefully cut pieces of lemon rind sat inside them both, to be removed later once the loving was done. There would be no children born of this, only the freedom to find ecstasy.

Why not, indeed?

"Sophie—" he said again, a question in it this time. Meg rolled on to her back and watched, the edge of her thumb against her teeth and a greedy look in her eye. She

183

moistened her lips, her eyes taking in Sarah's nudity much as James'.

Meg's smile flashed bright with speculative delight, her hair coiling loose down her back and her small breasts riding high. "Take him, so I may watch. And then you can both focus entirely on me." She laughed at her own audacity, her hand already sliding down to circle the nub of her desire. She set her fingers apart and stroked herself like that, one finger on either side, her cunny still slick.

"With inducements like that…" Sarah found herself laughing, and she shook her head at Meg's ridiculousness. James reached out the moment she came near enough, though, seized her hand and pulled her down to him so swiftly that she lost her breath.

She found it in his lap, as he tugged her across his legs. Her feet tucked under his knees and his hands came around to seize her hips. His prick rose thick between them and she rubbed against him, shameless as a cat in heat. Pleasure flared in her lower belly, and that sensation of emptiness only grew.

"Are you sure you want to do this?" James asked, his brow furrowing with some thought she could not divine.

Sarah frowned right back at him. "Are you saying that you don't want me?"

"No, no, nothing of that sort! This puts proof to that." He took her hand and brought it to his prick, his arousal throbbing through the silk-soft skin. He gasped at the touch, his head dropping and his hair falling over his eyes. "But— are you still a maid?"

How had he come to that thought, after everything that they had done already? Would it change his opinion of her? How could it, unless he were the worst sort of man?

"No, I'm not." Then, his bright eyes locked on hers, his rock-hard prick pressed tight against her body, their legs and arms wrapped around one another and the heat from his body soaking into her sweat-tingling skin, Sarah smiled. "You won't ruin me."

He kissed her open mouth, diving deep. He bruised her lips with his, his tongue sweeping in and tasting her mouth. Sarah melted against him, let him take control. His broad, deft hands moved over her body, from her hips to trace lines across her stomach, then to cup her breasts and flick his thumbs across her nipples.

They grew hard and tight and he suckled at them, drew each one into his mouth, slowly pulled back and then released. He thrust up against her, his prick sliding hot and hard against every inch of skin between her legs, riding hard across her entrance and not once pushing inside. She rode him, rubbed against him, felt the head of his prick push at her clitoris, the rough contact sending shockwaves along her spine, her fingers and toes.

"Push him down." Meg's voice broke in to the sweaty motion and the rise of Sarah's pleasure. She could taste the edges of her second climax of the night, not there yet but a possibility dancing at the horizon.

"Do what?" James's voice was muffled, his teeth scraping hot against the tender skin of her throat. She put her hands at his shoulders and pushed, and he fell back to be cushioned on the rug. Sarah knelt up, rising off her heels, and James let out a low groan, his hands on her breasts again, kneading and supporting them, tracing her nipples until she burned.

She kissed his prick, licked the tip like Meg had done before, tasted the saltwater sea on his skin. "I need," Sarah said, and James gripped her hips.

"I know." He urged her forward, held her hips in place and drew his knees up behind to support her. Sarah slid down into his lap again, and he let go with only one hand, to grip his prick securely and drive himself home.

He thrust up inside her in one smooth movement, so thick and so deep that she would be split in half. Sarah arched with the sudden shock of it, arched and cried out, and he stopped moving. James held in place, his hips half off the ground, his hands seated on Sarah's hips, his fingertips denting her buttocks and thighs.

Too much, he was too big, she would die from this—and then hands circled her waist, Meg's lips covered hers, and her body, treacherous and afraid, relaxed and took James in.

She opened to him and he rose up to meet her. Meg kissed her, gentle and soft, then drew Sarah's nipples into her mouth. The spiral of sparks and fire coiled there, at her nipples, ran down in lines of fire to ignite in her groin, as James held her tight, held her safe.

Sarah rocked on him and he let her, his hands guiding her motions. Sarah braced herself with her hands behind her, arching up into Meg's mouth, her body awash with sensation, sparking lightning and desire.

James pushed up to meet her, his body pressing tight against that spot where her pleasure lived. He pushed inside, drew out, and she ached for emptiness until he pressed back inside, slow enough not to hurt, slow enough to draw every last needy sound from her lungs.

Four hands, three bodies; her own palms pressed flat against James's thighs; his prick filling up every hollow space inside; the taste of Meg's mouth, sweet as brandywine; her climax burning through her body like a firestorm.

"Now," she cried out, and "don't stop, just like that, don't stop." It came over her from the inside out, her body clutching tight around James's prick, her back flush against Meg's heaving chest. She died, white behind her eyes, and no words, nothing at all, in her mind.

Only blessed silence, silence and joy, and warmth like a summer day suffusing her limbs until they went heavy and limp.

Meg kissed the back of her neck. James shifted his grip on her thighs. Then in a move that they may as well have practiced, Meg was gone and James turned Sarah over, lifting her legs up to cross behind his back. His hair fell over his forehead, sweat-damp and darker gold, his eyes burning the deepest of all blues. His cheeks flushed, the redness extending down his chest, and his hands on either side of Sarah's head trembled.

He drove into her, over and again, the burning coals inside her stoked again to wakefulness by the pressure and the delicious, perfect friction. She arched, took him in. He buried his flesh deep inside her, under her skin, where he belonged.

Time held no meaning in this bliss, and yet it had to end. James pulled out of her, leaving her empty, sated and

187

exhausted. He rose to his knees above her, his body taut. She ran her hands up his thighs, his muscles tight, and wrapped her hand around his prick.

He closed his eyes and his head tipped back as he gasped. Sarah stroked him, her hand tight and sliding easily up, down, up again, her thumb catching the underside of the crown once, twice, again. James curled forward, a cry ripping harsh from his lips. His emissions burst from him, hot and white, landing on her stomach, one breast, her fingers.

He held himself still for a moment as she played her fingers along him one more time, drawing one last shudder and spurt of fluid from him. He fell forward slowly, carefully, and buried his face in Sarah's shoulder until his trembling slowed. He stroked into her hand slowly, then sighed as she let him go.

He lowered himself down to the rug again, stroked his hand up and over Sarah's soft belly, her thigh, her breast. Meg cried out and Sarah looked over, just in time to see Meg's fingers vanish into her body one last time, then the look of pleasure on her face as her body shook.

A moment later Meg curled into Sarah's open arms, spooning her rear end up against Sarah's belly. "Couldn't wait?" Sarah murmured into her ear, then grazed her teeth lazily across the nape of Meg's neck. Meg shivered as James wrapped his arms around Sarah, nuzzling into her hair and breathing deeply.

Their heat soaked into her on both sides, Meg and James, woman and man, lover and beloved, and Sarah was...

She was content. And nothing else in the world could ever matter more than this.

Except that eventually, a clock somewhere would chime the hour, and the duties of the world would come crawling back in to nag at Sarah's consciousness. She rose from the tangle of limbs for a second time, everything languid and dreamy. She washed, the cool water bringing back her senses one soft moment at a time, her defenses layering themselves up until she was herself again.

Meg sat up, pouted and folded her arms beneath her breasts. "You're not leaving, not now!" she exclaimed, the petulant edge that wanted to be in her voice softened by the lazy pleasure still lingering there.

"I must." Sarah searched about for her clothes, pulling a shift off the chair and drawing it over her head. "I've no excuse to be out of the house tonight, and I cannot afford to be caught sneaking in after the Horlocks return."

James pushed himself easily to his feet. "Let me walk you home. It's no time of night for a woman to be out alone."

"I don't need cosseting." Sarah pulled her stays on over her shift and tugged everything back into place before she relaced them. "I've been out at night before, you know, and nothing's happened yet."

"What, both of you going and leaving me?" Meg's pout grew deeper and more deliberate.

"You're safe here, dearest." James stood, his prick still half hard and resting now against his thigh. She couldn't help the look that he caught, nor the smile that curved the corner of her mouth at the endearment, so unusual. His

189

tenderness to both of them warmed her through, almost as much as their lovemaking had done. "And if something were to happen to Sophie when I could have been her protector tonight, I should never forgive myself."

"See, there's our problem," Sarah snorted. "We shall end up needing a man each, for evenings such as this. One to stay and make love again, and one to be an escort."

Meg flopped back to the rug and stretched alongside the fire, the light flickering along her breasts, her stomach, her full, round thighs. "Two men or one house."

"Either way, that is not the current circumstance." James washed and dressed quickly. "And I shan't be denied in this. I shall escort you home, Sophie, and see you safely to your door. Meg, promise me that you shall lock and bar your doors after we're gone. I dislike this street and the men abiding on it, for your sake."

"You speak as though I've not been looking out for myself for the past ten years," Meg complained. Sarah smacked her affectionately on the bottom as she passed by, and Meg jumped with an indignant squeak.

"*Who's* been looking after you? Get up and dress yourself, or you'll catch your death of cold." And Sarah bent over, kissing Meg on the end of her pert nose.

"Yes, *Mother*." Meg sighed but clambered to her feet nevertheless. She stood there for a moment, hands on her hips, Venus carved not from cold marble, but warm and yielding flesh. "But at least tell me, darlings both, when shall I see you next?"

James buttoned his breeches, shirt tucked into the waistband. "It's the third week of the month; Tibbert leaves early on Friday. He has a standing appointment to take dinner with the Dowager Marchioness of Plimpton. What do you say to a picnic in the park?" He held up Sarah's dress and helped her to slide into it.

"I may not be able to get away." Sarah pulled her hair out from beneath the dress and shook it so that it fell down her back again.

"Then it shall be James and I," Meg declared, pulling her wrapper around her body, nothing but her skin beneath. "For I have no plans, and a picnic shall be wonderful fun."

Them together without me?

But then, she and Meg often had plans without James in attendance. Why should this be different?

Sarah hesitated, then let it go without a word. Meg rose up on her toes to give James a gentle kiss. She slid his cravat around his shirt collar, tying it in a simple knot.

"Until Friday, then." James leaned down to kiss her, and she smiled against his lips.

"I'll send you a note if I cannot get away," Sarah promised, speaking to Meg and not to him. She tucked her shawl about her, and only then, once James's coat was on again, took his arm. "Otherwise, darling, until Friday."

Sarah looked up as they left, down the wooden stairs. Meg watched them from the window, the shutter cracked open and the light from behind her spilling out into the street. James stopped in the street, turned and gave her a low and sweeping bow, his hat in his hand. She lifted her hand in a half-hearted wave, closed the shutters and was gone.

Chapter Ten

Walking home to Bruton Street, arm in arm with James, came close to perfection. A faint mist hung in the air. It wasn't heavy enough to fall like rain, but just enough to turn the street lamps into shining stars and add an incandescent glow to the lanterns of the link boys guiding their clients along the city streets. It was almost enough to make her forget that she was still a servant, that these stolen moments were fragments of a life not honestly hers.

But oh, those moments when she'd had Meg in her arms, and James kissing her as though he could draw her soul out through her lips. When he'd put his mouth to her body the same way Meg had done before and sent her mind into the sweetest sort of oblivion.

Any amount of sneaking and lying was worth it, in order to find those moments of bliss in their arms.

That made her the worst kind of unrepentant sinner. But then, who was being hurt by it, if three people freely decided to make passionate love to each other? She'd seen far worse, once upon a time.

Even now, her shawl and bonnet growing damp from the evening air, far grander lords and ladies lining the walks as they passed from Covent Garden into Mayfair, that burst of pleasure faded. No, not faded, but changed by some alchemy, into contentment, deep and abiding. James stopped and pointed out funny things every moment or so— a very round man with a very thin wife, a small monkey on a lead, a group of laughing young men in fine black suits humming a chamber music piece, one playing conductor with a still-leafy broken twig.

It wasn't perfect, but it was wonderful. And perhaps her best chance still for something solid, something real. She glanced up at James, a full head and a half taller than she, his honey-gold hair curling beneath the brim of his hat. His beard was starting to grow in along his jaw, fine and light enough that only she could see it from this close. He must have caught her stare for he looked down and smiled at her again, that quirked-corner, wonder-filled look that seemed reserved for herself and for Meg alone.

If she had to share, at least it was with Meg, who loved her and whom she loved so deeply in return.

If anyone in the world could make such an arrangement work, why could it not be them?

Because you're a fraud, for one. How long do you think he'll stay by you once he learns the truth?

"Penny for your thoughts," James offered, his voice so rich and warm that she could let herself be wrapped up in it forever.

She looked away, unable to meet his eyes. "Nothing important."

"Liar."

He knows.

She stopped walking, whirled about and looked up at him, expecting scorn or hatred or—or—

James cocked his head and arched an eyebrow. "Your thoughts are important to you, so shall they be important to me. I want to know your mind, Miss Sophie Armand." He said her name liltingly, like the accent she had to remember to keep on like armor, but without mockery. "As much as you will allow me."

They approached New Bond Street. Only a few minutes from home now—she had to decide.

"What would you think," Sarah began, her hand still on James's arm and her eyes fixed steadfastly on the street ahead. Her heart pounded high in her chest, leaping toward her throat with every moment she wasted. "If you found out that someone you thought you knew had a secret?"

He didn't flinch, his arm beneath her hand as steady and sure as ever. "It would depend on what kind of secret it was." He leaned in, the brim of his hat knocking against her cap. "Have you killed a man?" he asked with a wide grin like this was all some big game, rather than a moment of such importance she could barely find the words.

"What? No! Not I. This is not that sort of secret." She glared hotly at him, and he left off murmuring in her ear.

James tapped his chin thoughtfully. "All right then, you're with child by the Prince Regent." He arched his eyebrow again. "Am I close?"

He was insufferable, utterly insufferable! "And still working in service? I rather imagine not." Sarah snorted.

There was no way not to be drawn into his infernal charm, damn him and his blue eyes.

He pursed his lips, those eyes still gleaming. "You're secretly a runaway princess of Bavaria?"

Sarah sighed a deep sigh of exasperation, and his grin only grew wider. "Now I know you're teasing me, dreadful man. Can you take nothing seriously at all?"

"You take things too seriously, I think. If there was ever a time and place for lighthearted smiling, it would be tonight."

Affection washed over her at the gleam in his eyes and the snug squeeze of his elbow around her fingers. "You and Meg truly are a matched pair, and I'm not sure which of you is more ridiculous."

James chuckled. "Myself, certainly. For she puts hers on and off as any role she plays—" He trailed off, then, looking into the middle distance as though something had only just occurred to him. He recovered before she could enquire, and kept talking. "And I am just as I was born, ridiculous to the core."

She could tell him, she should. He would forgive and understand, surely, and then they too could be easy as she was with Meg, as free to be their true selves. But they were at the corner and there was the house, and Jack the footman standing out by the kitchen door. The gentle red glow by his face meant his pipe, curse him! He'd be there for minutes yet.

"Damn!" She thought she'd cursed too low for James to hear it, but the startled swivel of his head proved otherwise. Sarah pushed him backward by the shoulders, forced him to fall a few steps behind and around the corner again. He backed up until he hit the wall, hands coming up to take her by the arms and stop her push. Sarah shook her head and broke free from his solid grip. "We cannot go farther together—we'll be seen and I'll be reported."

"So let them see." James brushed his gloved knuckles against the curve of her cheek, and she leaned into his sure touch as instinctively as a baby turned to a breast. "I have no desire to hide my affection for you."

"And yet I doubt my employers would see things the same way." Sarah stepped back, the words of her would-be confession still sharp-edged against her tongue. "Lady Horlock is particular about the manners and morals of her staff. If she ever knew—"

"She won't." James curled his fingers around hers regardless of the safety of the moment, and lifted her hand to his lips for a chaste press. It sent heat flooding down through her loins regardless, igniting that throbbing yearning deep inside. His cheek was faintly rough, his lips soft, even through the cotton of her gloves. "Not from me. Nor from Miss Ceniza, I am sure."

"Even so." The street still bustled with life, and any minute now someone who knew her, or him, would walk by and all would be lost. A rough-looking man in a dark suit stepped aside to allow a coach and four to drive by. Something in his silhouette seemed familiar, but once the carriage passed, he was gone. "I'll make my own way from here."

He opened his mouth to object and she leveled a glare at him. He paused, then chuckled softly and let go of her hand. "As you wish." But before she could turn and leave, he added, "And don't forget, you've promised me your play."

As if she could! Sarah's cheeks flushed hot at the thought of him reading it, but then, if she wanted to put it on stage one day, surely many people would have to have the reading of it before that. "Yes, of course. Only not tonight. I should make a cleaner copy of what I have so far, without all the scratching-outs and revisions."

"Oh, don't do that. I'd like to see your line of thought, how you move from one idea to another. If I have suggestions, they may be ones you've already tried and dismissed, after all, and I would never know."

"I don't think my inner thoughts are all that intriguing." Sarah frowned at him, but he never wavered, his lips curved up in a gentle smile, and his eyes—those damned blue eyes—so warm. "Fine," she sighed. "But not tonight. Once I'm in I'll not come out again. I'll send it by a boy tomorrow, if I cannot get away."

"I shall be waiting with bated breath and eager mind." James doffed his hat and bowed, deeply. "Until tomorrow, sweetheart."

Her heart jumped, leapt, burst into glittering shards at the easy endearment. She couldn't wipe the ridiculous and immediate smile off her face by the time he straightened up again.

"Until tomorrow," she promised, and her voice was much softer than she'd have liked.

"I'll wait here and watch until you're in the house safely."

"I don't need you to protect me, you know."

197

"I know. Perhaps I simply want to."

That earned him a huff and an eye roll, but he didn't move. She was left to cross the street, dodging horse leavings and rain in the gutters, knowing all the while he was watching her. She passed by Jack and closed the back door securely behind her.

"In the Master's bedroom, that's where, and—oh, Miss Armand, indeed." Mrs. Colby, the plump and sweet-faced cook, appeared in the kitchen door. "I thought I heard some'un comin' in."

Sarah bundled her shawl and bonnet, tucking her apron on over her dress. She could smell the faint perfume of Meg's hair oils on her hands, lavender and rose. Could Mrs. Colby see the flush on her skin? How much could that piercing gaze read in Sarah's guilty face? "No, only me. Are they returned?"

Mrs. Colby fussed, straightening Sarah's cap over her forehead and tucking her shift's drawstring back down inside her bodice. "No, no, you've plenty of time to get yourself put back together, duck. Good thing it was a nice night to be running errands. None of that mucking about in the rain and catching cold for you, now. I've enough to do without having to make soups and smuggling a warming pan up to the attic for you." And she poked Sarah gently in the chest with one thick finger.

There was something soothing about being fussed over, and Sarah submitted to Mrs. Colby's well-meaning muttering. "No, there's no rain, and I promise I shan't catch cold. We'll be coming into summer soon anyway."

"Not nearly soon enough, if you ask me." Something clattered in the kitchen and Mrs. Colby turned to go. "Off

198

with you now. I'll have Poppy run something up to you if you're peckish, out and about all this time. There's nobbut a few pieces of cold mutton, mind, and some cheese."

Sarah was already halfway up the first flight of the servant's stairs, but her stomach growled loud enough at the suggestion that she stopped in mid-stride. "That would be lovely, thank you!" And she darted up the rest of the way to the topmost floor and the little room set beneath the gables.

He wanted to read it, and not just the play itself, in a polished, finished state, but the notes and scrawling that had gone into it. Meg was the only one she'd ever shown her scribbling to, half-formed and raw as it was. And Meg had loved them, but then, she raved over everything that Sarah wrote, so how much of that could possibly be real, and how much simply because she loved *Sarah*?

She knelt on the rag rug that covered the cold wooden floor and tucked her hands beneath the bed to pull out her box. It slid out more easily than it should. Lighter, somehow.

The ribbon around the box was tied in a knot. She always tied a bow.

Sarah pulled at the ribbon ends with trembling hands, tugged and scratched at the knot with her fingernails until she could pull the loose ends free. The ribbon fell to each side, and she lifted off the top, her breath caught firm in her throat.

The box was empty, but for a broken pen nib and a half-full bottle of watery ink.

Her play was gone.

Sarah clattered down the back stairs, not caring how loud she was or who might hear her through the walls or the baize-covered doors to the main house. Poppy jumped back with a squeak, wide-eyed and startled, her stack of trays rattling in her hands.

"Has anyone been in my room?" Sarah demanded, her heart beating so rapidly that it was sure to burst, and terror lodged thick in her throat. "Tell me, girl. Has anyone been in my room today?"

The trays and dishes clinked together, the girl's hands trembling, and Sarah forced herself to reach for calm. She took Poppy by the shoulders and held her steady, staring her directly in the eyes. "You're not in trouble, girl, but think. I need to know."

"No one, Miss Armand," Poppy stammered out, and her voice was so very young. "No one at all, except Ellen, to do the dusting."

"Ellen?" Sarah stopped dead in her tracks, Poppy squirming under her gaze. But she was no longer thinking of the scullery girl, only the way her pages had been tucked back together in the stillroom, the gleam in Ellen's eye— "Damn and blast," she muttered aloud, forgetting herself entirely. Poppy squeaked in horror.

"Where is she now?" Sarah asked, then, "Oh, never you mind. I'll find her myself." Find her, stand her ground, make Ellen relinquish not only the pages but some idea of what her plans had been—

A distant thump meant the front door closing, and then the servants' bells started up a merry cacophony.

They're home.

And then, of course, there was no time for anything at all but to get back up to her room, splash water on her face and hands, tidy her dress and settle in a chair with her mending no more than the briefest moment before her own bell rang and she was called to service. She checked herself one last time in the small glass. Everything was in place and she was calm, as long as she didn't spend any time thinking about Ellen and the missing pages.

I can do this. Focus on what must be done, and worry about the rest later.

Down the stairs again, then, but only one flight this time. She came out onto the landing and ducked into Lady Horlock's dressing room. The countess was already sitting at her dressing table, frowning into it and running her gloved fingertips along the faint wrinkles that sunk around her lips and at the corners of her eyes. Deep blue sapphires sparkled at her throat and ears, glorious against the gray of her hair, but she wasn't admiring them.

For a moment, however fleeting, the dragon herself seemed almost...sad.

Sarah coughed, Lady Horlock's back straightened and her head came up again, and the moment was forever gone. "*Madame*, I am here." Sarah crossed the room when her ladyship beckoned, removing the sapphires and setting them in the ornate wooden jewel box before drawing Lady Horlock's gloves from her hands.

She'd imagined herself a fine lady once, dreamed of some handsome knight or baron finding her among the wretched and the poor, lifting her up into his carriage and driving her away to a life of safety and importance.

Some dreams deserved to die with childhood.

Meg had come closest of the two of them, playing the coquette with her string of wealthy patrons, receiving gifts of silk and lace, ribbons and jewels for her troubles. Was she better or worse off than Lady Horlock, who had been born to wealth, grown in wealth, married wealth, and seemed no happier for it than a shopgirl?

"Do focus, Armand. You're a million miles away tonight." Lady Horlock made a soft *hmph* as punctuation.

Sarah snapped her attention back to the task at hand, folded Lady Horlock's gloves neatly and set them aside. "Very sorry, *madame*; my apologies."

Sarah moved behind her and began unpinning the carefully set curls she had pinned up only this afternoon. Had it really been just a few short hours since she had dressed her mistress for the ball and then snuck out herself? It seemed like it should have taken longer.

"Was it a lovely event tonight, *madame*?" she asked, breaking the silence that seemed heavier than normal.

"Yes, it was," Lady Horlock replied, and then all was well with the world. She sat straighter, watching in the mirror as Sarah took down her hair. "Lady Stafford always throws excellent balls. Horlock even danced a set with me, if you can picture that! And him at his age, and with his foot still poorly."

The look Sarah received in the mirror was a piercing one, ice-gray and cool. It seemed for all the world as though Lady Horlock were examining her for some reaction, but there was no knowing what on earth it might be. She carried on with her task, and whatever question lingered in the countess's mind, she did not choose to ask it.

"I imagine he was quite swept away by your beauty tonight, *madame*," Sarah offered instead, and Lady Horlock arched an eyebrow, a small smile flickering on her tight lips for a moment only. "This gown is most exceptional on your figure, and for your coloring." It was true enough, though no one would ever mistake the countess for a young belle again.

"I shall take that compliment," Lady Horlock replied, and stood to let Sarah unlace her gown along the side. "In any case, Lady Stafford's guest lists are usually quite exclusive. None of this business with moneyed shopkeepers and country cousins you see at Almack's these days." She paused as Sarah continued about the task of readying her for bed. "Although there was one there whom you might recognize."

"Are you sure, *madame?* I am not well acquainted with the better families."

"Of course you aren't," Lady Horlock dismissed. "It was that dreadful Mr. Cade. From the Earl of Coventry's house party this summer just past."

Now him, Sarah remembered.

"Mr. Cade, the composer, *madame*? He was the handsome one who seduced the earl's daughter, *non?*" She was laying on the accent more thickly than she should, but tonight everything felt like she was moving through molasses.

What did Ellen do with my play?

"Indeed, that's the one. Mr. Cade may be trying to claw his way back to higher circles, but he'll never be anything more than a country vicar's son." The chill began in Sarah's

203

spine and moved up through her bones and blood. "Mark my words, Armand." Lady Horlock sat tall and serene in her judgment, giving voice to thoughts that anyone of quality would share. "Bad blood will show itself every time."

Closing the door of her own room behind her was an almost unbearable relief. Sarah sagged against the wall, the surface rough against the back of her neck. She slid down, slowly, to sit on the floor, wrapping her arms around her knees and pulling them snug against her chest.

Bad blood will show itself.

And whose "bad blood" was worse? Mr. Cade's fatal flaw had been coming from a family with neither rank nor wealth and trying for someone who had both. Sarah's parentage was darker by far.

I daren't let anyone know what my mother was. And I don't even know who my father is.

Never mind barons or knights—she wasn't even worthy of James. He was untitled, yes, but money had a way of disguising those sorts of faults. He came from a family with a good reputation and had a sister he would want to marry as well as she possibly could.

Sarah's scandalous background would be the end of all Miss Glover's hopes in that regard, if the truth were to come out.

And something more immediately important would be the end of all of *Sarah's*, if she didn't find an answer immediately. Sliding to the side of her bed, she reached under it, feeling for the box once more. Maybe the play had fallen out, earlier. Perhaps she hadn't put it away properly, in her rush to make ready to see Meg and James, and it was beside or beneath…

Nothing. Drat her luck!

Her bell rang while she was still under the bed. She sat up too quickly, banging the back of her skull against the hard wooden frame. "Ow!"

The bell rang again, jarring and insistent. Could a bell sound angry? Or was it simply her fear?

"I'm coming, keep yer shirt on," Sarah muttered darkly, pushing herself up to standing. Dust had accumulated on the hem of her skirt and she brushed it away, whipping her spare apron around her waist. She was still tying it on her way back down the stairs, narrowly missing colliding with Ellen on the landing.

"Watch yourself," Sarah scolded, not thinking, not looking, but—

"I'm not the one who needs to be watching out." Ellen smiled. She smiled, and didn't move, and her eyes were hard and cold.

A shout came from behind the partly ajar baize door through which Ellen had just come. "Where is that girl?"

"What have you done?" Sarah's whisper came out harsh and ragged, but doors slammed in the family side of the house, and there was no time to wait for an answer. Ellen lifted her hand and waggled her fingers in a parody of a farewell. A chill spun down Sarah's spine to lodge deep in the pit of her stomach.

Lady Horlock stood in the middle of her dressing room, where Sarah had left her, but her comportment could not have been more different. Her color was up, her throat and cheeks flushed red and her eyes snapped with fury. She held a packet of papers in her hand that she brandished at Sarah the moment she appeared in the doorway.

My play!

"Deceit!" Lady Horlock squawked, flourishing the pages in the air as though she were about to throw them. "Deceit, and lies, and a snake in my bosom."

"Your ladyship," Sarah begged, the click of the door shutting fast behind her the first note in her funeral march. "No. Never. Name me one of your confidences that I have ever betrayed, and I will put myself out the back door in an instant."

"What do you say to this, then?" Lady Horlock tossed the pages to the floor and they scattered, Sarah's handwriting, her crossed-out corrections and notes, all of them vivid against the cream of the paper and the pale wood floor. "Where the heroine is a maid who sleeps with the lord of her own house? He beds her and gets her with child—how much of this is based on life, deceitful girl?"

"None, your ladyship, I swear it." Sarah clasped her hands before her, the image of innocence. *Believe me, please. I have committed many sins, but this is not among them.* "Never have I darkened the door of Lord Horlock's bedchamber, nor have I ever taken him to mine. You are my lady and I your maid. Simple and poor as I am in learning, I am rich enough in morals and in my sense of duty for you to depend on that."

Should she fall to her knees? Meg would have by now, fallen to her knees and clutched tearfully at Lady Horlock's hem. But this was not that sort of finale. Sarah needed her wits about her.

Lady Horlock lifted her chin, her gray hair a cloud behind her that the lamplight caught in a glow. "Then where does he go? He no longer comes to mine." Then, oh then, she could almost feel pity for Lady Horlock then, her face drawn tight, her body burning not with rage, but with humiliation and the type of pain that killed the soul.

Sarah nodded, moistening her lips and choosing her words, just as she chose her voice next, thick and soft, laced with sympathy and forgiveness. "Men can be cruel, my lady."

They hung there in that moment, a tableau strung together by threads of emotion that ran too hot to last. Lady Horlock broke it first, stabbing a finger out in accusation once more. "You realize how ungrateful this makes you look. Such nonsense! Ladies, conniving to betray a master and husband who has no doubt given them everything they ever needed in life! What classless *tripe.* That such things could come from the pen of someone working in *my* house!"

Sarah dared to breathe once more, lead in her lungs even as she drew in air to clear it. "It is only a work of fiction, *madame*, and a poor one at that. I have never neglected my duties for my poor scribbles. Surely there can be no harm in writing stories for my own amusement!" That last she blurted out in frustration, standing tall amidst the pages that drifted about her ankles.

A beat of silence passed, the clock chiming downstairs marking the lateness of the hour.

If she were to be turned out now, it would be for that impertinence alone.

Her breath came thick and fast in her throat, her heart pounding and head spinning with flashes of thoughts and worries, notions she couldn't conceal or control—

This is how it ends.

That thought, alongside some distant understanding that her panic was unneeded, a moment of dramatics worthy of Meg—it helped, strangely enough.

Lady Horlock's shoulders curled and her chin came down. The Dragon was no more than a gray goose once more, settling her dressing gown around her like armor. "And *you* are not Horlock's mistress."

"Never, *madame*." That, Sarah could swear to in absolute truth. "He has never made overtures, nor would I consider them even for a moment if he had."

"Cease this foolishness. I should burn it and put an end to your infernal distraction." Lady Horlock pushed the pile of papers on the floor with one delicately shod toe. She gestured toward the fireplace with a grimace. "You've had your head in the clouds since before we came to London. You are a servant, *Miss Armand*, not a playwright."

Lady Horlock swept toward the door, pausing only to turn her head, exhaustion drawing her face cold and wan. From there, she delivered her final shot, words that slid between Sarah's ribs and into her heart as keenly as any blade. "Don't dream above your station."

And then she was gone.

The room echoed in its stillness once the mistress of the house had taken herself away. Sarah's chest heaved as she fought back the rush of...of *something*, she knew not what to call it. Picking up her pages helped, mindless and repetitive. She could do it without thinking, without letting the hurt sink into her bones.

Don't dream above your station.

Wise advice that she would be wise to take.

Chapter Eleven

The door to the stairwell closed firmly behind her once more, Sarah sagged back against it. She clutched her play to her chest, fingers curling tightly around the edges of the ragged, simple pages.

What had just transpired there?

She was not sleeping with the master. She had more than enough complications in her life to add *that* to her record of misdeeds. But wives always knew, didn't they? So if Lady Horlock was right, and it was someone in their household who made her a fool, who could it have been?

Mrs. Colby? Certainly not. She'd not be caught anywhere upstairs, and Sarah would be amazed if Lord Horlock could even pick her out in a crowd. Poppy? She was silly and foolish, but she was also so very young.

Not the footmen, surely, nor his lordship's valet, though such things did happen.

"Pondering what to do with yourself after your dismissal?" Ellen's voice echoed down the stairs before the girl herself appeared, leaning over the banister half a flight up. She smiled, coy and smug together, her dress impeccable and hair curled.

"You're entirely too sure of yourself," Sarah said firmly. Nip this now before it became household gossip! Drat that girl! "*Madame* has no intention of dismissing me over a trifle such as this." She tipped her chin up and stared Ellen in the eyes, gold-brown and venomous. "Whatever you're trying to do, it won't work. All you've done is upset her."

"And why should you care?" Ellen sashayed halfway down the stairs, moving with all the confidence of one born to power. "You despise her as much as I do."

"Despise?" Sarah surprised herself with the thought and answer that chased each other around in her mind. "No, I don't despise her. I pity her. I am not her dearest friend, but unlike you, she is honest."

"And unlike you, *Armand*." Ellen all but purred, undeterred. "I know you've been sneaking out at all hours, and it's not on family business. If you say word one about me, I'll tell all your secrets as well. And which one of us do you think Horlock will sack?"

Sarah struggled against the urge to tuck her pages into her apron pockets and take a swing. Ladies, even ones in service, did not engage in fisticuffs, no matter how dear the provocation. "*You.* You're the one he's bedding."

"I'd keep your mouth shut, if I were you." Ellen's eyes narrowed and a hiss entered her voice, but still she maintained her control.

"Lady Horlock spoke of a viper in her bosom. She has no idea how right she is."

Ellen descended the last few steps. She paused in front of Sarah only long enough to reach out with a finger and tuck a stand of Sarah's hair back beneath the band of her cap. Sarah curled her lip at Ellen's touch, jerking away. Her hands were full and she could do no more than that.

"And she won't. Not even when I have your position, Armand, and you are out and begging for coins on the street."

Oh really *now.*

Sarah took a step forward, curling her pages in her hands. "You will be a syphilitic Covent Garden whore, lying down for a dozen sailors at a time and *begging* for their coin, and I will still be here. One word to her ladyship, and you will be *gone*."

"Try it and see what happens," Ellen hissed, her eyes narrowed. "Who is in your corner? A shriveled old scarecrow who lost her husband's love a long time ago."

A door opened upstairs, the sound of the hallboys arguing echoing along the servants' stairwell. Ellen's grin flared in triumph. "I will be watching you, Armand. You had best behave yourself, unless you find yourself craving the touch of those pox-ridden sailors. They will be your only income sooner than you think." Her cruel, tight smile faded and was replaced with a sweet and open façade as the boys clattered past them with bobbed bows and hasty courtesies. Ellen swept off downstairs and Sarah, out of her eyesight, fled to the little room at the top of the stairs.

She had felt safe in here, once. Now the door closing behind her was the clicking sound of a key turning in the door of a prison cell. Ellen had been in here, rummaged through her secrets, gathered up everything she needed to destroy Sarah's life.

The ribbon went about the play once more, and she tied a tiny loop of thread around the knot. If it was broken again, she would know. She sat on the edge of her cot, the hard boards of the frame pressing into the palms of her hands. The cold air made her shiver, the shawl hanging over the back of her chair an impossible distance away.

Brave words aside, she was…she was *afraid*.

This was her punishment for becoming complacent, for believing that she deserved goodness and kindness in her life. She had let her guard down, and this was the result.

Paper. She needed paper and ink, a quill and a knife to sharpen it, just enough to scribble down a short note. There was no reason to say more.

Meg,

Friday has become impossible. I must focus on my work and on the needs of my employers, who are the reason I am here. Please do not let my absence spoil your enjoyment. I shall be in touch once more when my schedule permits. It may not be for some time. For now, take pleasure in your love, and in his tenderness for you.

Yours,

Sophie

A softer woman would have cried writing that last line; Sarah would not. She was strong. She had survived a long time without a lover's gentle touch. A life of honest work and moral moderation in her activities was by far the better choice. James and Meg would make each other very happy, possibly more easily without her interference.

213

Sarah sealed the letter, her hands most certainly *not* shaking or reluctant, and walked, ghostlike, down the stairs. A coin to a hallboy would see the letter sent. She could not write one for James—what could she begin to say? At least Meg would soften any blow that he might feel when she carried the news.

It was done.

Sarah slept fitfully, and her dreams were full of monsters.

The note from Sarah hadn't exactly been the passionate love letter Meg had been hoping for when she'd opened the letter, but what could she do? If Sarah was going to be dreary and thinking only of her employers, then it would be better for everyone for her to leave her alone and let her get it out of her system. She would come around again soon enough. And if she didn't, Meg had a whole long list of ways to convince Sarah around to her point of view.

In the meanwhile, she needed something to keep herself entertained. She wasn't needed at the King's for rehearsal until the week following next, and she already had a copy of the script. Looking about her flat showed her a handful of things that needed doing, of course, but folding gowns and washing stockings was hardly diverting.

Trailing her fingertips across the well-worn spines of her books—those that weren't the handy little chapbooks had been bought used with scrounged and saved pennies or gifts from patrons past. The mismatched row of folded-paper covers (and the occasional gilt-engraved edge) gave her an idea, better than actually *dusting* the shelf. Hatchard's bookshop had a little corner for plays. Not nice books of the sort elsewhere in the store, but the two-pence colored chapbooks were far more useful for their light weight and lighter price.

Better yet, the shop drew clientele from all over the city, rich and workers alike, and where there were people, there would be gossip. What better place to find out about the other stages? Even a hint at which plays were selling well could be enough to guess at which ones would be staged over the next few months, or even a year.

The day was fine, the streets busy, and Meg fit in with the swans and swains taking their ease along the high street. The bookshop was just down off Old Bond Street, after all, barely a ten-minute jaunt from there to Sarah's front door. It might be worth wandering over later, on the off chance that the Horlocks would be out and about during the fashionable hour, just to see if Sarah could be made to smile.

The windows held all sorts of wonderful things, Hatchard's windows best of all. She liked pretty fabrics and ribbons as much as the next girl, perhaps a little more than some, but the tall leather-bound books filled with stories were even more enticing.

Young Hatchard looked up from the ledger at the front counter and nodded to her as she entered, the heavy, swinging door setting the bell to ringing. She'd been there often enough that they knew her, but couldn't spend enough so that they'd put interesting things aside. *Someday.*

Plays and poems were kept on the third floor, up two sets of stairs that wound their way around shelves piled high with volumes of history and the new science for the men, glorious novels full of adventure and derring-do for the women. The corner was waiting for her when she arrived, the narrow shelf half-filled with plain, sewn folios, no taller than her hand from wrist to fingertip, and the other half with similar books in a rainbow's worth of different bright bindings, some of the fancier ones with the engravings painstakingly colored in.

A purring cat wound around her ankles and she reached down to scratch behind his ears. He rumbled low in his chest, a warm sound so delightful that Meg crouched down to encourage him to continue. She was stroking the fat gray-and-black tabby under his whiskered chin when the sound of chattering voices drifted up the stairs, someone coming up to join her.

Her head was down, the bonnet's brim obscuring her face enough that she saw them before they saw her. The two girls were dressed like fine noblewomen, in patterned muslins with delicate little clusters of embroidery dotted everywhere that a needle could reach. Meg brushed the shop dust from the hem of her simple printed calico dress with an inward sigh and shooed the cat away. She rose and caught sight of their faces, and that flash of self-consciousness turned into a tight knot of something unpleasant deep inside her stomach.

She'd only met the new Lady Montpress once, at a party that was better unremembered, but her face would linger in Meg's mind for a long time yet. In Meg's defense, had she known that her former lover would be attending the dinner, his bride on his arm, Meg would have made every excuse not to be present. It was Not Done to flaunt one's former position as a man's mistress, even if he had been unattached when you had first met.

And here she was again, this spring-like waif, her flaxen hair coiled and pinned in the latest fashion, silk ribbons on her dress, and her big blue eyes focused entirely on the equally well-turned-out girl beside her.

It was easy to see how Toby had found her appealing enough to drop Meg like she was poison. *Though the thirty thousand pounds that came with her couldn't have hurt her chances either.*

Meg should go. Forget that she hadn't found what she'd come for—she was the lover scorned (though she hardly wanted *Toby* anymore, not when she had James and Sarah!) and Lady Montpress was the victorious wife.

But then again, why should I?

On second regard, Lady Montpress walked with a lively step, she laughed merrily at something her friend said, and she was standing by the poetry shelves, scanning the titles with what seemed to be real interest. She was pretty, feisty and young, and it had been so long since the marriage—almost half a year!

We're not rivals anymore. Indeed, we hardly even were. There's no reason why we shouldn't be courteous, at the very least.

Standing, Meg brushed down her skirt again, settling it neatly. She may not be in muslins, but she looked well enough. Lady Montpress and her friend would be nearer to her end of the shelves in a minute. Time enough for Meg to look at the plays, time enough for her to calm her surprise completely and feel natural in the moment.

She took a book off the shelf, but couldn't concentrate on the words, preternaturally aware of the women coming closer.

Why hello, Lady Montpress, is it not? She practiced what she would say, running the words through her mind. *Let us put the past where it belongs.*

"I think the plays are over here, Alice. Do you fancy them at all?"

Meg looked up.

Goodness, you look lovely today, she would say—

Their eyes met. Lady Montpress stopped in her tracks. Her sky-blue eyes went wide.

Meg's heart beat once.

"No, I do not," Lady Montpress said, and she turned away, standing with her side toward Meg and her voice pitched just enough to carry. "I can't abide the theatres, such filthy places. You never know what kind of diseases one will end up accidentally bringing home."

The lump in Meg's throat swelled large enough to block her breathing, her knuckles curling tight around the little book in her hand. Tears—of surprise, of anger, of humiliation—pricked sharp in the corners of her eyes, but she would not, could not let them fall.

Neither could she run past the ladies, bolt for the door and the fresh air of freedom. Not while they were heading for the stairs themselves, not when they would see her so upset.

She waited, instead, pressed her finger against the divot under her nose to stop the tears from coming, stared out the window into the bright sun to account for any watering that might remain.

Meg hadn't cried when her brother left or when her mother died. The only tears she shed were held for the stage. She was not about to start crying for real now.

The shop cat jumped up to the windowsill and walked back and forth along it, trailing his tail along Meg's arm. "She's not *that* pretty, anyway. Those simpering big eyes and white dress—all she needs is a bell around her neck and she'll look like a cow," Meg told the cat firmly.

He head-butted her, as if to say *I know you're lying, but it will be all right.*

"Thank you," she told him, buried her fingers in his soft fur, and waited to believe it.

Chapter Twelve

James approached the door to the shop with some mild trepidation on Thursday morning. Would Tibbert still be furious? Would James now have to make good on his threats to strike out on his own?

The bell above the door rang out cheerfully when James entered, and a moment later, Tibbert's sour old face appeared in the curtained door to the back rooms. He looked James up and down with pursed lips, then slowly vanished behind the curtain once more.

If that's how he wants it, I'm not going to disagree.

It made for a far more peaceful day.

Friday dawned fair and clear, the ideal day for an outing. Cecily was at the breakfast table, dressed in a pale-blue muslin that he was quite sure had been recently retrimmed. Or had it always borne white flowers around the neck like that? She looked happy, regardless, and that was always a blessing.

He kissed the top of her head as he took his seat at the table, and she beamed up at him. "Please tell me we are still going picnicking, James. Master Tibbert has not called for you today?"

"He has not," James promised, and the stab of guilt poked at him again. "Have I been so dreadfully neglectful these days?" He covered her slim little hand with his, and she curled her fingers around his in what felt like forgiveness.

"Only a little." Cecily squeezed his hand one more time then let go, reaching for a roll and some butter to spread upon it. "But today you shall redeem yourself. Miss Ceniza is still coming, yes? And what of Miss Armand?" The look she gave him was an attempt at shrewdness, softened by her youth and innocence. "I suppose the question I should be asking is what of *either* of them. Which *one* are you courting, James? And don't dissemble," she said bossily, spreading her napkin on her lap. "I know when you're up to something."

James brought his teacup to his lips to hide his flash of surprise. "You know far more than you should, dear girl, and far less than you think." Leaning back in his hair made him look nonchalant. There was no way she could discern the truth, as unspoiled as his baby sister was by thoughts of the world and of men. "The women are particular friends, and it would be unseemly for me to be out with either of them unchaperoned. I happen to enjoy their company. And that is all." He cut into a sausage and ate it defiantly.

"And I'm Princess Augusta."

"You're acting like a spoiled princess. Perhaps I shan't take you after all, if you're going to ask impertinent questions."

"Oh, James, no!" Cecily's feigned superiority fell away and returned her to the girl he adored. She grabbed for his hand again, almost knocking over his cup in her haste, sending tea splashing to the tablecloth. "I shall be ever so polite and circumspect. I must see Miss Ceniza again, and you with her, and Miss Armand as well."

He laughed, partly in surprise, and partly from the whip-crack-quick turnaround of her mood. She balled up her napkin and flung it at him in annoyance. "You're beastly."

"I adore you, and I am greatly anticipating a lovely day out together," James corrected her, and it was so much like meals they'd shared long ago that he half expected their parents to sweep through the door and take their places, the two empty seats at the breakfast table filled once more. "As for the other—"

He hesitated. She did not need to know anything of adults' private arrangements. Yet she surely deserved some kind of answer.

"I admire Miss Ceniza greatly," he admitted.

"I knew it!" Cecily squeaked.

"And Miss Armand has always had a place in my affections."

"Are you keeping them both dangling after you?" Cecily asked with a sudden burst of shrewdness, giving him a look that would peel paint from a wall.

"Not in the slightest. I have been honest with both about my divided feelings, and I have every expectation that we shall be able to resolve things to everyone's satisfaction." So there.

Cecily's look of skeptical disbelief was a masterpiece that he was determined to ignore. "Miss Ceniza is unlikely to accept anyone's suit, especially one from an untitled man," he explained gently. "She has other demands made on her. Miss Armand..." He trailed off, Sophie's hot-and-cold behavior on Wednesday's walk home nagging at the back of his mind. "We shall see," he finished lamely. "Now, finish your meal. I'll be at the shop this morning, but will return at noon. Make sure that you'll be ready to go."

Her eyes stayed on him as he ostentatiously bent his head to his breakfast and ignored her.

Sunshine, flowers in bloom and the basketful of clever little pasties made by their cook went part of the way toward soothing James's disappointment when Meg was the only one to meet them at the park. Why had Sophie sent a letter only to Meg and not to them both? Did she somehow imagine he'd be angry at her, when he already knew what being in service entailed?

Still, Meg was bright and cheerful, her flowered gown as soft as rose petals. She knew what a pretty picture she made, curled on a cushion, twirling her parasol slowly above her. The sunlight filtered down through the leaves, dappling the three of them with ripples of sun and shadow, birdsong providing accompaniment for their leisure. Dark circles seemed to linger under her eyes, her conversation a little more brittle than natural, but she ignored him when he tried to ask, and so he let the matter drop.

Cecily was listening to Meg's chatter with rapt attention, her own laughter as sweet and carefree as the birdsong.

"But his new bride was a very good cook," Meg carried on with her story, beaming a smile at James when he reached over to refill her glass of wine. "So there we are in the final act, and Mr. Wallace is supposed to be dueling the wicked count for my honor. He reaches for his sword on his hip, and—" She gestured at her side with her fingers. "You could hear the seams popping on his coat from the first balcony! He did his best to recover, and Bexley was very clever and pretended to slice at his side during the fight, so that it looked intentional. But honestly, we giggled about it for simply *days*."

"Sounds as though the gentlemen could use some stays in order to keep themselves in fighting trim." James chuckled, though in his heart of hearts he felt both a mixture of pity and envy for the poor bastard.

"There, a new clientele for your skills, sir." Meg set her parasol behind her and leaned forward precariously, selecting an almond from the small dish of them set on the blanket. Her bosom swelled forward, peaches and pink—

His *sister* was there beside him as well, and James deliberately looked away.

"I think you should have a difficult time convincing most men into such things, James," Cecily replied, not seeming to notice his momentary distraction. "In my experience, men are loathe to make themselves uncomfortable in any way."

"In your experience, kitten?" James laughed in surprise. "And how is it that you have experience with what gentlemen do and do not enjoy?"

"Living with you, of course," Cecily replied smartly, and were she ten years younger, he would have fully expected her to stick out her tongue. "Unless you would argue that you're no gentleman, or that you would yourself wear a pair of stays!"

"I should not have the aptitude for moving gracefully in them, though there are some dandies about the town who cut quite a figure in their narrow waists." He pretended to ponder. "What say you, Miss Ceniza? Shall we try and encourage this new fashion? We shall soon have men in stays and women in breeches, and not be able to tell the one apart from the other."

"There are some women who look very well in trousers, I dare say," Meg replied smartly and with such insistence that he wondered for a moment if it came from experience. "Else breeches roles would never be as widely used as they are."

"I should like to try on a pair of breeches," Cecily declared, but from the glint in her eye he'd guess that she was joking, simply to rile him up. "I think they look comfortable, and they'd be ever so useful for riding astride."

She had better be joking.

"Since when has that been a desire of yours, Cece? You complain every time we don't hire a coach."

Cecily's eyes narrowed—had he pushed that little bit too far? "Ugh! Don't tease, James, not in front of Miss Ceniza! You're terrible." And she rose to her feet with a huff. "I'm going to the riverside to pick some greenery for our table tonight. I won't be back until you're a decent human being again."

"Don't go too far," James called after her. "Stay in sight, if you please." She marched off without replying, but she kept to the path and didn't go charging off into the nearby copse of trees, so that was a good sign.

"She's a sweet girl," Meg said with a playful smile. "She reminds me a little bit of me."

Heaven forbid. There'd be no keeping her home and safe if that were the case.

"The world only has room for one of you in it," he said instead, wiser now than when he was younger. At least about some things. "Cecily's young yet, but I do hope she keeps that passion for life as she grows."

"She's never known anything but love." Meg stared over his shoulder, her smile growing wistful and tinged with a sadness that he hoped never again to see on her face off-stage. "Why should she lose her joy?"

"Why indeed?" *She'll never again have a mother to guide her, for one. And while I'm doing the best I can, I still don't think it's enough.*

He was veering into melancholy territory with those thoughts. Better to retrench and turn the conversation to something more pleasant and more fitting to the gloriously sunny day. "On the subject of joy," he began, rummaging at the bottom of the basket for something he had slipped in there earlier.

"Oh?" Meg prompted eagerly, before he had the chance to find it and continue speaking.

He drew out a slim packet, wrapped in a scrap of silk the same walnut-brown as her eyes. "I hope this will bring you some, and keep thoughts of me as close to your heart as it rests."

The anticipatory delight that lit up those same brown eyes was worth every stolen moment, nicked fingertip and late night candle-end. Meg tugged one tail of the delicate ribbon and opened her gift, the carved busk catching the sun and almost glowing with the reflected light.

"Oh," she gasped, and "oh!" again. "It's beautiful!" She traced the carved flowers across the smooth-sanded whalebone, then turned the busk over to note his maker's mark on the back. "You carved this? For me?"

"It's tradition among sailing men to decorate whalebone busks for their sweethearts," James explained, his own smile a mirror of hers. "I've seen many in the course of my work and thought I would try my hand at it. I've made one for Miss Armand as well," he added with a grin, "so you'll not have to beat or chide me for unequal giving. Unless such things amuse you, of course."

"Naughty boy." Meg laughed. "Perhaps we shall try that one day. But for now, you're forgiven. Only I hope hers isn't quite as beautiful as mine." She was teasing, her whole body light, and he laughed in return.

"Now, will you try it later on?" he asked, dropping his voice low, heat and anticipation trickling up from the base of his spine. "I would be most pleased to assist you out of those stays. And back into them. Eventually."

She returned his gaze with a look just as heated, moistening her lower lip in a gesture that had to be deliberate. It worked. "Perhaps I'll test it now," Meg

227

suggested, her coy smile doing things to him that shouldn't be allowed in public.

"What, here?"

Meg tossed her head, setting her few loose curls to bouncing. "On the picnic blanket right in front of you? I rather think not. No, I'll switch busks over there, behind a tree, and make sure you've gotten my sizing right." She clasped the whalebone busk to that selfsame rising, golden bosom. James's trousers became uncomfortable, pressing against his slowly filling cock in an urgent reminder not to get carried away.

"I'm a staymaker, dearest one"—James laughed— "and I work with actresses half the time. There's little I haven't seen when it comes to bodies."

"Some things have to remain a mystery, darling."

And with that she rose to her feet, smooth as any cat. She sashayed toward the trees and out of view.

Cecily stopped her walk back across the green, a bundle of ferns draped over her arm, and watched her go. James could all but count the besotted stars in her eyes.

"Isn't she magnificent?" Cecily breathed out, running back to the picnic blanket. "Oh James, if you and she were to be married, then she would be my sister forever. Wouldn't that be marvelous? She could take us to the theatre all the time, then."

James settled back on his heels, one eye on capricious, glamorous Meg, ducking behind a tree. Any moment now she'd begin to unpin her bodice, untie the ribbon at the front of her stays, slide out the whalebone piece that divided her breasts and held them high...

He forced his mind and eyes away. "What, and have the two of you lost backstage for weeks on end? What is the point of having family if you never see them? No, I should forbid her from taking you to the shows completely. Most of them are not suitable for your age, regardless."

"When I'm an actress like Miss Ceniza, you won't be able to stop me." Cecily tossed her head smartly, her curls bouncing under the brim of her bonnet.

"When you're a *what*?" James recoiled at the very idea. Cecily on stage, his little sister being gawked at by men like a side of beef, expected to take patrons to support herself? "No, absolutely not. That is out of the question and beyond the pale even for you, Cecily Glover."

"Whyever for?" Cecily stood staunchly, hands on her hips. "Miss Ceniza is an actress and she's admired by everyone! Mrs. Edwin has the Duchess of York as her own particular patron, Miss Ceniza told me so herself! And duchesses are always in the best of taste!" She stamped one slipper-clad foot imperiously.

"Sit down, Cecily," James implored. There was no one about but Meg to overhear them, but even so! She couldn't be encouraged in public temper tantrums, even in empty parks. He rose up to stand when she would not sit. "Next year, when you're older, I'll make sure you're introduced to every duchess in Town, if that will please you. But be an actress? No. Acting is a perilous existence, full of uncertainty.

"When I promised Mother and Father that I would look out for you, they meant me to find you a good match, with a kind man, so you might live your days in comfort." He rested his hands on her upper arms. "I want better for you than life on the stage. You are meant for so much more."

Meg came back around the tree.

"So much more?" she echoed, and her dark eyes were black and unreadable. Her knuckles clenched white around her old busk, plain and yellowed with age. "Better than me?" Her voice caught, her breasts heaving with her rapid breath. "You're ashamed of what I do? How *dare* you? You who waited and watched and drooled after me like any other conniving rake!"

She flung the piece of whalebone at him, but light as it was, it fell to the picnic blanket, harmless. "I thought you held me in higher esteem than that. That you might have learned by now that I am more than the sum of my bosom and my ankles—"

"That's not what I meant!" James protested hotly.

Meg didn't listen. "But it's what you feel—you can't deny it. You wouldn't want your sister to end up being *like me*." She whipped her head around to address Cecily, whose face had gone pale. Bright pink spots flared on Meg's cheeks, her fury hot. "Oh, he'll bed me, but he'll never respect me." Then back to James, with a spat-out, "Marriage was never even on offer with you, was it?"

"James!" Cecily stared at him, wide-eyed and horrified.

"But you hate marriage!" James spluttered, caught more off guard than he had ever been in his life. His mind pinwheeled and spun in circles. How had this had gone so terribly wrong, so quickly? Meg's temper burned hot—was there any hope of escape? "The first time we met, you called it 'a farce, meant to ensnare women with false promises'! I remember your exact words, and—"

The tears now sparkling in Meg's eyes weren't false, he would bet his life on that. "That doesn't mean I don't want to be *loved*!"

She stormed off, her skirts a tumble of muslin around her legs. He started to chase after her, his feet tangling in the picnic blanket and tripping him up. He stumbled and fell to his knees, pain shooting up his thighs from the impact. It didn't come close to the pain in his heart as he watched her storm away toward the path.

"James Glover," Cecily breathed out, her ferns forgotten and her eyes dark. "What have you *done*?"

"I'm not entirely sure," he replied grimly. "But help me pack, Cecily, make haste! I'll take you home. And then, somehow, I'm going to fix my mistakes."

The midafternoon street was all a-bustle as Sarah hurried back to the townhouse, bottles clinking softly in her covered basket. She was hardly the only lady's maid out running errands this afternoon, but she was perhaps one of the few who were desperately wishing that she too were taking in the sweet spring breezes in St. James's park. This hadn't been an urgent errand, but after Wednesday night's revelations, it was more important than ever to be seen to be doing her utmost.

As preferred as the "natural" complexion seemed to be these days, there were still things that could be of assistance, even to a lady of a certain age. "'Adhering firmly to the face, giving a light and delicate tint that cannot be distinguished from nature',' Sarah read off of the paper bill in the store window as she passed. She carried a bottle of the same in her basket. "'Almost unparalleled in the annals of personal improvement.' For five shillings a go, it had better be."

Attempts at distracting herself aside, however, there was no way she could miss the pink-and-cream bundle of gauze and ribbons that was heading her way down the busy street. Sarah stopped, the townhouse in sight, before Meg could carry her away like a whirlwind. "What on God's green earth is the matter with you?" Sarah scolded between clenched teeth, when Meg clutched at her arm. "I told you in my letter, I can't be—"

She took a closer look. Meg's face was streaked with tears, her eyes red-rimmed. "What has happened?" Sarah demanded instead. "Who has hurt you?"

"No one." Meg shook her head. "Not like that. But oh, Sa—*Sophie*, I need to talk to you. Come for tea, please, you must!"

Lord, she was in one of her strops again, and what Sarah needed or wanted didn't matter. "I cannot. I'm expected back in the house within minutes, Meg. I cannot simply drop everything and be at your beck and call. If James said something to upset you, just ignore him. I'm sure he'll come apologizing soon."

"You're as bad as he is." Meg dashed a tear from her cheek with the back of her hand. "Neither of you think that I have any feelings at all. Oh, there's silly little Meg. Never mind anything she says, she's just here to be *pretty*."

"Now you're being ridiculous." Sarah shifted her basket from one arm to the other and racked her brain for something to say. "Meg, come on now. You're putting words to my lips that I never said." She wasn't going to get anywhere until Meg had had a moment to speak her piece, was she? "What happened?"

"James doesn't care about me," Meg got out, her chest heaving as she struggled to keep her emotions under control. "He said things about me, being just an *actress*, as though it were something to be ashamed of! I know there is unkind gossip about actresses, but Sarah, I have worked so very hard to be more than what I am—so have you! Why won't he understand?"

The answer was as simple as it was hurtful. "Because he hasn't ever had to."

"Miss Ceniza—" James. He jogged quickly toward them, crossing the road in front of a cart and ignoring the driver shaking his fist at them all. "Miss Ceniza, please, wait."

Meg drew herself up tall, her chin lifting stubbornly. "How did you find me?"

"Where else would you go?"

And this was about to become a drama that would rival anything Meg had played out on stage. Except this time, it was taking place four yards from Sarah's front door. "Not here, please," she asked, her stern and low voice garnering shocked looks from the quarreling lovers.

"Then where?" James asked, casting about as though looking for a doorway to duck into. "For we must have this resolved. I'll not leave you still thinking so badly of me over a simple misunderstanding."

"This way." Sarah led them around the corner to a small garden patch with a single bench. It was not private, as such, but it was out of view of the front door of the townhouse, and out of the way of the passersby, any one of whom might know Lady Horlock and be curious enough to gossip.

"It was more than a misunderstanding," Meg protested, her eyes betraying the depth to which she'd been wounded. "You insulted me, James, and everything I've done with my life."

"But you cannot look at me and tell me that it's the life you would choose above all others." James took Meg's hand and she pulled it back. "Even if you could choose from any existence? Would you not rather have a tidy house of your own, conduct salons from your parlor, attend the theatre as a fine lady in a box, instead of playing the stories for pennies a day and audiences who would rather gossip among themselves?"

He looked at Sarah helplessly. "Sophie, surely you can understand. I want Cecily to be happy, to be secure and to be loved. She used to speak of marrying well, having an estate to manage, children playing at her feet. Is that not the dream of most girls? Even your life of service is better than putting yourself out to managers, waiting for one of them to find you worthy for a week or two, and then to scrape and chase patrons for support."

"Oh no." Sarah's temper flared. He meant well, most likely, but he would not understand, *could* not understand how things were for others. "A life of service? Mending a lady's clothes, mixing her perfumes, listening to her complain about the dreadful lack of shrimp at the evening's soiree, when I am lucky to see fish once a week? I am very well settled in my employment, sir, do not mistake me, but it is no better, and certainly in many aspects far worse, than being an actress. And as you well know, our moral failings are precisely the same: actress, lady's maid or staymaker."

"I do not elevate myself above you." James grew insistent, reaching out a hand to each. "If I could marry both of you, bring you home to live with me, provide you as much comfort as I could, for God's sake, I would do it in an instant! Marguerite, Sophie—"

"And is that the sort of life you would want for Miss Glover? Marriage to a man who only sees her as a soft pet to be protected?" Meg argued. "Until he wants her wild in the bedchamber, that is."

"I want her to have a life of dignity." He gestured to Sarah as though using her for an example. "Is that so wrong?"

Sarah was utterly and completely done. "Enough, both of you." They fell silent, two pairs of eyes, one dark, one fair, staring at her soundlessly. None of it made any sense, and the minutes were ticking by too fast. "Miss Glover has more options than either of us have ever known, Meg. Why is this even under discussion? Encouraging her to the theatre unless her talent is exceptional would be folly.

"But as for you, and your blanket condemnation—" This she addressed to James, and come hell or high water, she would say it now, and in her own voice—false accent be damned. "You will eat your crow here and now. 'Sophie Armand' is a role, and I am as much an actress as Meg, though you deride her for it and elevate me above all rational sense."

Meg bit her lip, watching wide-eyed as Sarah bared her soul.

"Sophie is nothing but a piece of French furniture to decorate my employers' homes. My name is Sarah Harlow. My father could be any one of twenty, forty, fifty different men, and until her death, my mother was a common whore."

James recoiled as she knew he would, with no sugar in her words or in her tone to make the horrid truth easier to consume. "Oh yes. Do not speak to me of dignity and choices, *sir*, I have made harder ones by far than you shall ever know!" She swallowed hard around the lump in her throat, made up of stuck goodbyes. "And neither Meg nor I need rescuing."

"My God," James breathed out. "All this time, you—"

"But *Sarah*," Meg broke in. He jerked his head to look at her in something like disbelief. "Sarah, look at me—I am serious."

Sarah was engaged now and could not break off her attack for anything. The dam had burst, and she was drowning in a decade's worth of words she had never said. "You haven't been serious a day in your life, Meg. For ten years I've been pulling you out of scrapes and listening to you deny responsibility for your actions, aiding and abetting your fond fancies—why? Because I love you. Well, no more." She cut her hand across the air between them. "This mess is entirely one of your own devising."

Sarah shook the tears from her eyes and changed her direction. "*James*. I adored you, and you courted me, wooed me, all but won me, all the while your body yearned for *her*. Meg, you were greedy, wanted to have us both dangling for you, and look what a mess this has all become! No, I haven't time nor strength. Leave me be, both of you. I have my own self to protect. The world is not a kind place to those who transgress its laws, natural or otherwise."

The torrent slowed to a trickle, the rush to a searing pain. She held her head high so that the tears would not fall, and she left the garden the way she had come.

Meg called her name. She didn't turn around.

Sarah walked away, and Meg's heart broke again. It shattered, like a crystal goblet dropped upon the floor, and nothing in the world could put it back together.

"Meg—" James's voice was beseeching, his look of confusion so real, so honest, that she almost gave in to the urge to pet him and explain. But his foolishness had been the start of all this, and the ending his fault too!

"Don't touch me!" Meg pulled her arm away from his outstretched hand. "Go home to your sister and look up ducal heirs for her in that book of aristocratic snoots. I don't want to talk to you right now."

Sarah had walked away, and so could she! She was trained for this, to control emotion and show only what she wanted the audience to see. She could be Hippolyta, Amazon Queen, and leave dratted Theseus behind to *rot,* for all she cared!

She made it to the corner again before she hovered, indecisive. She could chase Sarah, but that wouldn't go as she wished, not until Sarah's temper had time to cool. Sarah would be easier to talk to when she was feeling less fearsome and put-upon.

Home, then, and her own bed, her pillows piled about her.

No, James could find her there too easily, if he wished, and she was firm on one point. She needed time to think. Whether either of them believed her capable of it or not! And oh, that stung—Sarah's words rang in her head just as loudly as James's had. Never serious, low-class, not fit to be a role model for anyone, even dear Miss Glover who had been so kind. Meg was the worst kind of flibbertigibbet, apparently, a pet to be teased and petted and never once taken for the adult that she was.

Grace. She would go to Grace's rooms and find solace there. Grace would let Meg curl up by her fire, and she always had a bottle of sherry stowed somewhere convenient. Her shoulders were broad, and could hold up the world.

Decision made, Meg turned down a different avenue than her normal path, and blended unnoticed into the crowd.

Chapter Thirteen

Cecily paced back and forth in front of the parlor window, her eyes fixed on the street outside. James had been true to his word, delivering her back home and then running off again like a hero from the storybooks still on the shelf in her old nursery. He didn't have a horse in the city to gallop away on, which would have been better, but minor obstacles like that could not stand in the path of true love.

She felt a bit sorry for Miss Armand, of course. She was terribly clever, and funny, and much calmer than Miss Ceniza, though just as pretty. But it was the latter, not the former, who had inspired her brother to such wild frenzies of feeling, and so that appeared to be that, as they say. She was not going to think too hard about how her brother had apparently *ruined* Miss Ceniza as well, whatever secret intimacies *that* meant. That simply couldn't be the case. There had to be another explanation.

Lord, what it must feel like to be so passionately in love! She twisted a curl around her finger, catching a glimpse of herself in her reflection in the window. It wouldn't be long now before she was truly grown and old enough to receive suitors of her own. Assuming that James would ever decide that she was an adult and not in braids anymore.

The front door slammed open, and Cecily jumped in surprise. James barged in, his hat screwed up in his hands and his cravat all askew. She ran to him, but he put up a hand and shook his head at her, his face set in the most horrible of expressions. "Not now, Cecily."

"Whatever can have happened?" She reached out to lay her hand on his shoulder, but he only patted it once, twice, then moved away from her. "Will Miss Ceniza not forgive you? You only meant the best, James—surely she can see that it was a simple mistake."

James began to climb the stairs, pausing only to answer her question. His head hung, hair flopping over his eyes, and he seemed to simmer with some awful feelings that were eating him from the inside. "I think it unlikely," he said, his words clipped. "I think it highly unlikely that we shall see much of Miss Ceniza, or Miss Armand, from now on. Comport yourself accordingly."

And with that, he stomped up the stairs. She heard his bedroom door open, the little creak singing in the hinge, then close immediately behind him.

She bubbled over with questions—*what did you say? What did* she *say? Why is Miss Armand angry with you, and how did she become involved? Did you bed her too, James? Is that why both of them are angry with you now?*—none of which she dared to voice.

Problem: her brother was unhappy, desperately unhappy.

Answer: find the things he was missing and couldn't be happy without. That meant Miss Ceniza and Miss Armand. They could not be angry with *her*, and if she went to speak to them, then surely they would give her a few minutes. And then she could explain for him.

I'm terribly sorry for my brother. He tries very hard to come across as a gentleman, but really he's a big oaf prone to blunders of the worst sort. Only say you'll forgive him, and all will be well, I promise.

Yes, that was an excellent speech! Cecily took up her pelisse and buttoned it over her bodice, seating her bonnet neatly on her head. She only had a few moments to sneak out before the household stopped fussing about James and started taking notice of her again—she had to move quickly. She stopped long enough to dig James's appointment book out from his writing desk and tear out the page with Miss Ceniza's address written upon it.

She had a mission all her own now. James would see that she wasn't too young to be trusted.

Lady Horlock had either not noticed or chosen not to comment on Sarah's withdrawn mood and red-rimmed eyes when she had returned from her errands. And why should she be bothered? Why, in fact, should *Sarah* be bothered? She had been the one to sever connections, to finally scream out all her frustrations and fears. James and Meg were complications that she didn't need, random factors in a life that was already random and trying enough as it was.

Horlock himself was nowhere to be found—and unsurprisingly, neither was Ellen. Not in the stillroom, nor the servants' hall. And Mrs. Colby wouldn't be venturing out from the kitchens so close to the dinner hour. It meant that Sarah was free, for a moment, to sit herself down at the little stillroom table and set her head in her hands without worry of discovery.

Why should she be upset? Why did the hollow ache inside her chest swell with every breath, growing and burning until it tangled around her lungs and settled like a cannonball in her belly? She wasn't wrong! James was a selfish lout and Meg a foolish girl, neither of them with the sense of a newborn puppy. How could this entertainment of theirs have ended in anything but disaster and heartache?

Sarah would have done well to follow her doubts in the first place and ended things before they began. She had worried about losing James if she said no, and now she had lost them both by saying yes.

Tears welled up in her eyes and she dashed them away, leaving wet trails sparkling on the back of her hand. It was *fine*. She would be *fine*. She was used to doing things herself, after all.

People came and went in a life, some becoming friends, some lovers, but always, always, they went away again after serving their purpose. Every person who passed through had something to teach her.

And now she was wiser again. James and Meg had taught her about carefree lust and desire, about friendship taking flight and how a heart could throb and burn in time with *two* others at once.

I don't want to be any wiser than this. Please God, when will I have finally learned enough?

The door to the stillroom locked, the rushlight burning silently in the corner, Sarah slid to the ground, held her knees close to her chest, buried her face in her arms and wept.

Thank goodness Grace had been home! Meg's mind had been racing so fast, pinwheeling in all different directions; she never would have been able to settle on somewhere else to go and have her cry. Only now, curled at Grace's feet and wrapped in a rug to cut the chill from the floor, Meg started to feel a little foolish about the entire disastrous day.

"He doesn't care one whit about my heart or my mind," she sighed. Grace's toe nudged her in the hip, and she let her head fall back into Grace's lap. "So I'm pretty. I *know* that. I thought..." She trailed off.

"That this one would be different," Grace finished her sentence, her voice as dry as the desert. "Men and women are not the same creatures, Meglet. They are bred for taking, and we are condemned to give and give, until we are all used up."

Meg wrinkled her nose, pondering the notion. It couldn't be as simple and as hopeless as that, could it? It was easier to focus on that question than other problems of the day, anyway. "I don't see why it has to be that way. We're all made of the same stuff, after all. Only somehow, they get to have ambitions and we are supposed to be content with a pot on a fire and a baby on the breast." She wrinkled her nose. "I don't even like babies. Smelly, screeching things."

Grace ruffled Meg's hair, the familiar and comforting touch of her hand a reminder of when Meg had once felt safe, so long ago. "You may feel differently about that one day," Grace said, and there was mockery in her voice.

"Hardly. Unless they were your babies, or Sarah's. Then I could give them back when their nappies were soiled. Oh, *Grace*." Meg flopped over onto the rug, arm descending gracefully over her head. She settled like that, as though posing for an elegant portrait. *Lady in repose.*

"It's just all so…so complicated. Why couldn't you have been born a man?" She plucked at the knee band of Grace's breeches. "Or to the love of ladies? Then you could keep me in the manner to which I should very much like to become accustomed, and all would be well."

"I would keep you in stale bread and cheap wine, my dear." Grace rose and stepped over Meg, not paying any attention to her dramatics. "And a new gown once a year, if we were lucky." She busied herself with filling the kettle from the jug of water on the table and set it over the low-banked fire to boil. "What do you feel for him?" she asked, with her usual bluntness. "None of your memorized speeches, Meglet. Truth."

Meg tucked her thumbnail between her teeth and considered. For James, the man? What *did* she feel?

He was beautiful, in that way that the best of men were, all rippling muscle and taut lines. His hair shone like burnished gold in the sunlight, tumbling over his forehead in silken waves. His eyes glowed when he looked at her, focused on her, like she was something special and magical.

244

Like if he took his eyes off her, even for a moment, she might disappear.

But it went deeper than that, deeper than the primal stirrings at the sight of his firm, muscled forearms, at the way his breeches snugged tight against the rounded shape of his buttocks, honed by walking and riding. More vital than the burning hardness of his cock, encircled by Sarah's fingers, glistening with his desperation and his need.

He loved his family. His adoration of his sister was evident in every kind word he passed to her, every smooth set of his hand beneath her elbow if she ever seemed unsteady, the instinctive way he held chairs, fluffed pillows, filled her glass when it was half drained, without even seeming to notice what he was doing.

When he smiled with delight at some ridiculous thing Meg said or did, it only made her try to remember it, so that she might do it often and win that glorious sunny and approving warmth once more. His arms around her felt safe. Secure. Like home. Or like she imagined a memory of "home" to be.

He was an artist. She had snuck a peek at some of his drawings, the windswept lines of a muslin gown, the carefully planned lines of stays and whalebone, hips and breasts. He saw a world filled with beauty and had ambition to fill it further.

She had set out to seduce him based on nothing more than the prettiness of his face and the contents of his pockets. Somehow, James had become so much more than that.

But in his eyes, she had not changed at all.

"I think I could have fallen for him utterly," she said softly, "if he but showed one inkling, one sign that someday he could respect me."

"'Could have' is not enough, sweeting." Grace fussed about, accompanied by the clinking sounds of jars opening and closing, and pouring water. "He's shown his true mind now. Forget about him and move on."

Meg pushed herself up on one arm, her hair tumbling across her shoulder. "Do you think?" she asked dubiously. *Move on?* Would that mean letting Sarah go as well? She was angry, but she had been angry with Meg before, and it had always worked itself out. Somehow.

Grace shook her head, those dark eyes glinting with amusement. Her hair was loose today, puffed around her ears like a rich black storm cloud, and the simplest and plainest of plain gold beads glinted in her ears. Why did she not have a patron or a lover? Surely she was pretty enough to find one, if she chose. "There are a great many men in the world. A reasonable number of them even live in London. One of them, surely, will see beneath all those curls of yours and find the soft-hearted, clever lady hidden inside."

She slid her hand into those curls and waggled Meg's head back and forth until Meg broke out into giggles. The mug Grace pressed into her hands was warm and smelled of things like cinnamon and cloves, and she cupped it in her palms gratefully.

"How is it you always know what to say to make the world better?" Meg asked in all seriousness.

Grace snorted with derision. "Because those are the only parts you ever hear."

"You're awful."

"So leave." Grace sat again, setting her own mug aside and taking up her script once more.

Meg leaned against Grace's knee once more, wreathed in the clove-sweet steam that somehow smelled like home. "Never."

"Then run lines with me and make yourself useful as something other than decoration." Grace nudged Meg until she reached for the marked-over script and turned to the beginning of the scene. *The Skirts of the Camp*, another foolish comedy. Lord love a duck, was there never to be a good drama for either of them? "From 'it's charming,' if you please, in the part of Susan, the chambermaid."

"'It's charming, however, that he has found us out—'" Meg dutifully read, skimming ahead with her eyes to catch the sense of the character.

Grace stood and arranged herself, and her *self* fell away, to be replaced by Clara, dutiful daughter bound to be married to a man she could never love. The change was subtle, telling, and drew Meg along with it until she could feel the air drift and surge around them. "'He expresses strong alarms that my father will persist in marrying me to a distant relative, who, in consequence of bearing our family name, will possess a principle part of its property. I had the misfortune to be too captivating to this more remote branch of kindred.'"

"'Ah, ma'am! It's neither in your power nor mine to help being pretty!'" It was a silly character to play, but there was truth in every scene, when one looked for it.

"'But that my fate should be ruled by the combination of half-a-dozen letters!—a name!'"

And there it was, the truth that was the hook, the moment when written lines became a woman's life. And right now, Meg wanted to be anyone, have any life, other than her own.

Once again, James found himself pacing circles in his room, lost in thought. Was this to be his pattern now? Bursts of frantic emotion followed by long hours of restless regret? It was hardly the promise he had made to the girls, and to himself, when their grand experiment had begun. But that promise had been made without all the information.

How was he supposed to make sense of any of it?

First of all, and most disarming, Sophie—no, *Sarah*— was not French. Not only was she not a French émigré, she was also of the lowest possible birth. Not only illegitimate, but so beyond legitimacy that nothing could ever redeem it. But despite that, she had escaped, denied the heavy weight of her origins, and made something respectable and worthy of herself. In the face of depravity she had grown a heart that was generous, loyal and true. That spoke of a nobility of self that went beyond parentage or social rank. And not only that, but she had protected and cared for Meg for more than ten years, while both of them had been orphaned and alone.

That must have been beyond difficult. How must her young heart have cried out, in loneliness and in pain. Had she cried in Meg's arms at night, or had they clung to each other as Meg wept for all the things they both had lost?

He had been preoccupied mourning his own parents and never once considered what might have become of hers.

So then what had Meg's full story been, to put her in Sarah's path? She had never pretended to *be* Spanish, despite her stage name. Why had he never thought to ask her more?

Would she have told him the truth if he *had* asked?

In the long run, did any of it matter?

He had begun the year with the idea of finding a wife, of convincing Sophie—*Sarah*—to stand beside him through the best and worst of times. To laugh with her, walk and talk with her, to read to her by the fire on long winter evenings while she worked on embroidery draped softly in her lap. Someone to hold at night, to kiss deeply and fuel the passion of her body; someone who would love him with her whole heart in return.

And then by some miracle, he had found Meg as well. Two women so different and yet in some ways so very much alike, each promising something new, and who looked at each other with the same kind of love he could feel blossoming in his breast.

Usually, when a man loved two women, he had to lie and deceive at least one of them in order to have them both. This honest way of living was something no horrid novel or ribald tavern conversation had ever prepared him for.

A knock at the door brought him out of his reverie. It would be Cecily, surely, come to tell him off for his uncouth behavior earlier. He sighed, contrite, and called out for her to come in. But when the door opened, it was not his sister standing impatiently in the hall.

"Mrs. Lambert?"

His housekeeper entered with a tray, an older woman of middling height and stoutness with a mass of brown curls that a dozen hairpins and a cap could barely keep in check. She had been a nursery maid under his mother, taken the position as housekeeper when old Mrs. Pruett had gone to live with her daughter in Yorkshire. And now she studied James with a frown that put lines about her pursed lips as she set his meal down on his dressing table. "Mr. Glover. Are you quite all right?"

"Yes, yes, I'm fine." He tried to smile, had the feeling that it was coming out more as a rigid grimace, especially from Mrs. Lambert's reaction.

She bustled over, dusting her hands on her apron, and pressed her hand against his forehead before he had the chance to say anything else. "You've not got a fever," she fussed, the same way she had when he'd been a boy of ten. "But your color's up, and you've not been yourself at all these past few weeks."

"Honestly, Mrs. Lambert, I'm well," he protested again, holding up his hands to fend her off. "Only distracted."

"Anyone with half a mind and one good eye can see that." She pulled out the chair and pointed at it imperiously. "Sit. Eat something. And then once you have some strength back, you can tell me what's been gnawing at you."

It was ridiculous, and impossible not to laugh. "Aren't I your employer, Mrs. Lambert? I rather think I should be the one giving commands around here."

"If I hadn't been the one changing your clouts and washing your linens when you were still in swaddling clothes, I'd more than likely agree. Now sit down and unburden yourself, Mr. Glover. You're useless to everyone, including yourself, when you're pacing circles that the maids can hear from downstairs." She stayed, one hand on her hip and the other on the back of the chair, until he gave in and sat down.

The soup smelled marvelous, and he was hit with a wave of hunger that he hadn't anticipated. He picked up the spoon and waggled it in the air to show her that he was obeying, and only then did Mrs. Lambert take the other chair opposite him, fold her work-reddened hands tidily in her white-aproned lap and wait him out.

Charing Cross was an area Cecily did not know, except for seeing some of the streets in a blur en route to and from the handful of concerts James had permitted her to attend. Seen from the road, the alleyways had seemed charming. From where she now stood at the intersection, casting about to find the streets that would lead her to Miss Ceniza, that charming realness turned to squalor. Alleyways piled with rubbish loomed, dark and pungent, and every once in a while she thought she saw a glimpse of a dirty face peering out at her from a window, a tattered dress, the shadows of children who scattered when she turned to get a better look.

Men in laborers' clothing stared at her, making no attempt to disguise the way they dragged their eyes up and down her body. If only she could hide, wrap her arms around her chest, or had enough forethought to take a shawl that would conceal her from that scrutiny! She felt unaccountably filthy.

A doorway loomed before her, the wooden door cracked and painted over in red, then green, the flaking color showing other layers underneath. This was not it. It had to be the building beside, with wooden stairs that ran up the side of the wall to a nicer door above.

The door next to her swung open, and Cecily squeaked with surprise. There was no louche young man with black mustache or wicked vicar lingering there to trap her, though, just an old lady with a shawl around her shoulders, jewels in her ears and a gold tooth that winked in her mouth when she smiled.

"What is all this, then?" The lady leaned upon her stick, her red lips curling up in a smile. "An angel, I do declare. Are you lost, little one? Come, let me help you."

"Oh, how kind!" Cecily's fear began to ebb—who was she to be so critical of an older woman's looks, when she was so kind? Did not the pastor say "judge not" only last week? "Yes, yes, I am. I'm searching for someone who lives near here, but I think I have lost my way."

"Then come inside, please, and have tea. Your family must be worried, with you out on the streets." The old lady stepped away to give Cecily room to pass, the rooms behind her only half lit and smelling sickly sweet.

"There is only my brother, and he does not know I am out—" Cecily hesitated, the strangeness of the moment

252

catching up with her. The crone's hand shot out to grab her about the forearm, her clutching grasp far stronger than it had any right to be. Cecily yelped, and heard footsteps running behind her.

"Begone, hell-hag!" A man's cane swished down and tapped the old lady on the arm. She dropped her hand and snarled a curse at Cecily's savior. She retreated into her apartments, the door swinging only partway closed. Cecily was alone in the alleyway with the gentleman.

She turned, getting a good look at him for the first time.

He was terribly handsome, in a dark red coat that cleaved snugly to his arms and shoulders in a way that seemed somehow distressing. How, though, Cecily could not name. He had dark hair, combed and tidy like James never managed to accomplish with his own, and he held himself with strength and power. Despite that, Cecily still did not feel safe.

"You must be more careful, child," he said, and his voice was like a low purr from a jungle cat. "Agatha is a procuress of the vilest sort. Once you enter her den, you would never leave…intact."

Cecily swallowed hard against her fear, her heart thumping. "Then I must thank you, sir, for your excellent timing, and ask you to render me one more favor." She lifted her chin in the imperious way that Miss Ceniza sometimes did, when she wanted to get her way. "I am looking for the apartments of an actress, Miss Marguerite Ceniza, but I have lost my way. Do you know if I am on the correct street?"

The interest in his eyes seemed to flare brighter at the name, though why that should be, she could not fathom. He

253

smiled again, and there was something of the wolf in that dark look. Cecily backed away a step, her nerves sparking warnings once again.

"You are," he said, and nodded to someone behind. "Miss Glover, you have most certainly come to the correct street."

"How do you know my name?" Alarm set in now, fast and thick, panic surging in her throat and blocking her breath.

A footstep shuffled behind her, she turned to see who it was, and a white-hot flash of pain blinded her to all else. She fell, fell forever, and as the darkness rose up around her, she heard his voice one last time. "Bring her. This is better than I had planned."

Chapter Fourteen

An hour or so was all it took for Grace's soothing company, the warm drink and a little peace and quiet to smooth out the last few jagged edges of Meg's nerves. By the time the dregs in her cup were cool and Grace all but done reading the script pages she was leafing through, Meg had sorted out her plan of action. It would be a good one.

"Where are you off to now?" Grace handed Meg her spencer, helped her to shrug into the snug little jacket that went so well with the ribbons on her reticule.

"Bond Street," Meg said firmly. "There is a very pretty painted inkstand in the window of a stationer's there. I will have it for my Sarah as a present, then she will forgive me for being impertinent, and all will be well once more."

Grace frowned, the look forming a crease between her dark brows that made her look much more serious than even her normal affectation. "Are you sure that impertinence is your current sin?" But she shrugged when Meg could not come up with a quick answer and took her own man's coat down from the hook on which it hung. Her hair she bundled into a cap, brought her collar up to meet the brim at the back of her neck, until she looked for all the world like a boy five years or so Meg's younger.

"Are you to be my escort?" Meg asked, unable to hide her delight.

"I'll come along. I have errands to run of my own, and you have the world's most distressing propensity for finding trouble when left to your own devices."

"Oh, pooh. You have no taste for excitement, that's all."

Oddly enough, Grace only smiled, followed Meg out of the room and locked the door.

The sun had almost set outside by the time they emerged, the streets still filled with life and energy as day labor turned to evening pleasures. It was not yet dark enough for the boys to be out with their lanterns, but the light that spilled from the shop windows cast long spills of amber and gold across the ground.

"So tell me more about this play," Meg began, her hand tucked in Grace's elbow. "Who is the leading man? Do you think it will open well?" They made an easy picture, she could see in their reflection in the windows. But Grace was not tall enough, nor was she golden-blonde with the glint of sunlight in her eyes, the way James looked when he smiled. Nor was she ever like to tilt her head in and whisper something bright and scathing, the way Sarah would when they crossed paths with those worth mocking. If the world were a kinder place—

No. If Meg had been less selfish, realized from the start that something had been eating Sarah's heart from the inside, been less concerned about James's slip of the tongue or been willing to accept his apology for what it was.

(She was still a little angry at James, but that would ebb away eventually. She wasn't wrong, hadn't *been* wrong to be upset, but what good was it to hold on to old frustrations? It wouldn't get her what she wanted, which was James—and Sarah—back in her arms.)

Lord have mercy, she was utterly done in.

"Well enough," Grace was saying, when they turned a corner and all but bumped into a familiar shawl-wrapped shape. "Beg pardon," Grace began, but the woman she'd narrowly avoided didn't pay her any mind.

"Good evening, Miss Ceniza," Agatha said, lifting her head high enough for the shawl to slide back down to her shoulders. Age had lined her face and turned her hair to silver, but her red lips and the fierce gleam in her eye showed there was still power there not to be trifled with. "It is a good thing we meet like this—I have some information you will want."

"Me?" Meg frowned.

"She has no business with you, you old baud." Grace shifted her weight so she was angled between the two of them, sizing up Agatha's cane as though imagining its use as a weapon. An old woman's walking stick!

"Be polite," Meg chided her. Agatha grinned wide, her gold tooth catching the light.

"Were it you, Amazing Grace, I would say nothing at all," Agatha replied, "and leave you to the Baron's devices." Grace curled her lip, but glanced at Meg and said nothing.

The Baron... The image of his untouched letter flashed into Meg's mind, a blink of memory that spread a sourness in her gut and made her heart beat faster with nerves. "What of him?"

"He's been lurking about," Agatha reported, settling her cane in front of her, both gnarled and wrinkled hands crossed atop it and her shoulders hunched. "Himself, or some of his boys, taking their turns on watch. Best you not go home, child."

"Not go home?" Meg recoiled. "I've nowhere else to lay my head, madam, and I'll not let some overgrown toad of a bullcock—"

"You'll stay with me." Grace's voice was as insistent as it was calm, and as the hand on Meg's arm was firm. "And not get yourself in trouble."

"As for the sweet little visitor you had..." Agatha trailed off, and a slow, confident smile spread across her face. "Well. That more will cost you."

"Cost her? You nasty baggage, I ought to—"

"You ought to *nothing*!" Agatha thundered at Grace, her head up. For an instant she was the image of what she had once been: powerful, wealthy, the most sought-after procuress in London, with the most beautiful girls at her command. And with them, the secrets of the mighty, whispered across embroidered pillows and silken sheets. All of London's great men had needed and hated her in turn.

And now she bought and sold street-corner gossip for pennies.

"The choice is for Miss Ceniza," Agatha continued, the thunder-strike of contempt passed and gone. "If she would like to know more, I require my fee. A sovereign, no less. We all must make our way in the world somehow."

There were coins in her reticule; the choice was easy. *Sweet little visitor* and *Baron John Thomas* ran together in Meg's mind with images of the red-sealed letter on her table, the tough grabbing her arm in the alley, the confrontation she had forced Sarah to have out in the street, until all she could see, think, hear was Sarah, in trouble, Sarah, needing her help. Sarah, being hurt in terrible ways, while Meg sat and *took tea* with Grace for hours on end. What was a painted inkwell to *that*?

Meg's fingers trembled as she drew out the coins and counted them into Agatha's steady hand.

"There." She lifted her chin and stared Agatha in the eyes, red-rimmed and rheumy. "You have your price, now tell me what I need to know."

"The Baron was lying in wait," Agatha began, settling in on her stick once more, her voice going into a kind of singsong cadence. "As he will, for he desires you in his stable of mares."

"What business have you had with that pimple?" Grace's brow furrowed in consternation, even as Meg shook her head.

"Nothing, and therein lies the problem. He'll not have me," Meg said firmly. Agatha's eyebrow went up, and then down. "Pray, madam, continue."

"And I was sitting by my window with my tea, as I am wont to do in an afternoon—" She lingered lovingly over every slowly drawn out word. Meg's heart twisted painfully in her chest, her fingers tapping impatiently. "When I hear a commotion, aye. I look out and who do I see, but a sweet golden angel, a girl no more than seventeen, unless I miss my guess, and in a gown of stuff too fine to be anything less than a merchant's girl-child."

"What happened?" Meg could only imagine one person that could be, but why, oh why had Cecily been there? "If she's been hurt in any way, Agatha, if you've done something…"

"What, and come to tell you straight away so that you could bring down the magistrates?" Agatha delivered a look of such scorn that it could peel whitewash from the walls. "The Baron took her, in lieu of yourself, Miss High-and-Mighty. What he's done with her since, of course, I have no way of knowing." But her pressed smile, her lips tight, suggested that she had some very good ideas as to what Cecily's fate had been. "Miss Glover, he called her. She had come looking for you."

"For me? But why—" Meg broke off with the sudden realization. They had fought. James had no doubt returned home, his mood foul, and then when his beloved sister had begged to be of help and succor—he must have told her all. And then she had come…for Meg. So in many ways, this entire thing was Meg's own fault.

"She's in jeopardy because of me," she said softly.

"Perhaps." Agatha sniffed. "Or perhaps she is, by now, out of jeopardy forever and no longer your concern. Be well and by God, ladies, and have a pleasant evening."

Sarah, she needed to go to Sarah and get her to help, because she would know what to do, and—no.

This mess is one of your own devising.

She could not go to Sarah again.

Stunned by the revelations and by her swirling thoughts, Meg said nothing as Agatha took her leave. Grace made a swift half-step forward, as though to rush the old lady, but Agatha neither blinked nor flinched, and Grace did nothing further.

"You need to take some of that hoard of your savings and move to a safer neighborhood," Grace said firmly. Then, with more kindness in her eyes, she ducked her head, adjusted her hat, and her dark brown eyes searched Meg's face for something. "What are you considering?"

She wanted to cry, the burning wave of grief and frustrated anger rising up inside, blocking her throat tight and sparking pain and dampness in the corners of her eyes. *No.* She would not cry, even as the first tears began to trickle down her cheeks. Meg dashed them away with the cuff of her sleeve, and sucked in a trembling breath that didn't do enough to settle the queasy grief clenching tight in the middle of her chest.

"I am going," she said, her voice shaking, "to clean up my own messes."

Grace's look at her was one of pity, and that stung worse than anything beyond the knowledge of Cecily's fate. She must be terrified, that petted, sheltered girl, in the hands of men whose knowledge of depravity far outstripped anything that the worst of horrid novelists could ever begin to imagine.

"What are you going to do?" Grace asked again.

Another breath, another, and Meg had her fear back under control. One more, and her tears dried, hopefully never to be revisited. "I," Meg began, and this time her voice did not shake, "am going to get her back. It is my fault she was there, my disdain for the Baron that kept him coming around, and so it is my guilt alone that they ever crossed paths. So I shall go fix it."

Grace took her arm, before Meg could start walking at all haste toward the main street. "Wait, Meglet. Do you have any kind of plan? He surrounds himself with leather-headed bullies. His rat hole of a home is armed and guarded like a garrison. You'll never get in, never mind find your friend and escape again. Not alone."

"But I won't be alone, will I?" Meg seized Grace's hand and stared into her eyes, trying to impress upon her everything that she was feeling and could not find to put into words. "An innocent girl is in danger, Grace, through no fault of her own. You and I are the only ones who can do anything about it. Tell me I have your allegiance."

It didn't take Grace long to nod, though her shoulders rose and fell silently in what looked for all the world like a sigh of resignation. "Yes, of course you do. But that doesn't change the fact," she said as she began walking, "that we also need a plan."

How would Moll Cutpurse deal with such an event? Or Lady Macbeth? Meg was no Ophelia, to wither away and drown. Let she and Grace be Anne Bonny and Mary Read, then, gentlewoman pirates bent on revenge for women's griefs.

"To the King's Theatre," she said aloud. "The Baron's bordello is not ten minutes from there, and the propmaster's shop has a broken latch."

Grace took long strides in her breeches and leather boots, so that Meg had to take three to every two of her steps. "This isn't a play, Meg, nor a game of pretend."

"No. It's something so much more important than that." The crushing horror in Meg's chest was slowly lifting away, replaced by something even newer—a surge of power and a drive forward that dwarfed any fear. "Which is why we'll need a little extra help."

James had only intended to describe the picnic, the harsh things he'd said, without going into further detail. A brief word about a courtship gone wrong and she would be satisfied, surely. Something intent about the way she listened, though, and her eyebrow quirking up with skepticism when he glossed over a point—he kept talking despite himself. He unfolded the bulk of the story to her as he ate, naturally omitting some of the parts that would lead to a chamber pot—or worse—being dumped over his head.

And when he had finished saying all that he was going to say, about actresses and lady's maids and sisters, Mrs. Lambert's brow was deeply furrowed. She set her elbows on the table, her chin upon her hands, and she sighed.

"I speak as someone who's known you since the day you were born, James Glover. And you haven't got a mother anymore to tell you when you're being a cow-headed fool."

"Should I be concerned, Mrs. Lambert?"

She snorted. "I should say so. For you're being a cow-headed fool."

"Excellent," he sighed, more glibly than he felt inside. "I'm glad we have that covered."

She pinned him down with a gimlet stare, that same look which had made him confess every stolen sweetmeat and pulled pigtail as a child. "You're angry because both women hid truth from you. But how well do you truly know them, if you never once suspected something was amiss? Surely over the course of the years you've known Miss Armand you've asked after her parents or shared childhood stories?" She knew the answers to her question—she had to—but she sat and watched him anyway.

"No," James admitted, and felt even more the fool for saying it aloud. "Our conversations were always of the moment, or the future." Pretty flirtations that made him feel bold, handsome and potent at the time, but ultimately had no other meaning.

"Then what of Miss Ceniza, who disdains marriage but appears the most lovely and alive when she enacts stories of desperate and enduring love upon the stage? I presume you asked her about her dreams for the future, her ambitions? Or did you assume her memorized speeches, designed to attract a protector, to be truth?"

"It's unfair to throw my own words back at me this way," he pointed out. Mrs. Lambert only set her cheek in her hand and waited.

"No," he admitted again, the weight of the single word falling like a stone into water. Unlike the rippling water, though, he saw his own faults reflected clearly. And in the way of dreadful nightmares, now that he had, it was far too late. "I've been a fool and a cad, haven't I? I've taken them both for granted most horribly."

"Mmm." Mrs. Lambert made a soft sound of agreement, and she patted his hand gently. "He can be taught."

Silence fell for a moment, and he asked the question that weighed most heavily on his mind. "Is it possible, do you think, for someone to truly love two people at once?" His voice came out more raw than he'd intended.

Mrs. Lambert didn't answer right away, surprise flashing in her soft brown eyes. She thought for a moment, frowned deeply, then squeezed James's hand. "Some people find love twice in their lives or more, else no one would ever remarry after widowhood." *True enough.* She seemed to be thinking things through as she spoke, as though she'd never considered the question before. *When would she ever have had cause to?* "Is it so impossible that you were simply unlucky—or lucky—enough to find both of your own intended loves at the same time?"

It was a pleasant thought, if one that hardly uncomplicated matters. "What is there to be done about it?

"That, I cannot begin to answer." Mrs. Lambert stood, beginning to tidy up the remnants of his simple meal. "You have a dilemma, dear boy, and one that only you and the women in question can resolve."

She took up his tray and headed for the door, but the rapid, fluttering knock came before she could get there. There, *that* would be Cecily, and James was in a much better mood to see her now. "Come in," he called, and Mrs. Lambert stood aside to grant the new visitor passage.

Once more, it was not his sister. Sally, the maid, wrung her hands in her skirts, her face pale as the white linen of her cap. "Begging your pardon, Mr. Glover, sir, Mrs.

Lambert, but there's a problem, and you both ought to know."

Was she sweating? James's first impulse was to stand, to gesture her in. "Whatever it is, it can't be that dire. Sit down, catch your breath," he encouraged, but the girl just shook her head.

"Oh sir, no sir. Only you must say that you won't be angry, because it was not our fault."

"Out with it, girl," Mrs. Lambert requested crossly, impatience making lines in her forehead.

She nodded, gulping. "It's only that no one can find Miss Glover, sir. She's not in her room, nor the parlor, nor anywhere else in the house. And Nicholas thought he heard the door open again right after you came home, sir, but he can't swear to it."

That got him moving, across the room and into the hallway, Cecily's bedroom door standing open, her room obviously empty. "She's gone out without a chaperone?"

"No one saw her leave, sir."

What was that foolish girl doing? Seemly or unseemly were beside the point—it was coming on to night, the shadows lengthening as twilight sank the world outside into shades of blue and purple-gray. It was no time at all for a girl of sixteen to be wandering the streets alone. Even if she managed to avoid the unwelcome attentions of men, there were still carriages and thieves to be avoided, alleyways dark enough for any cutpurse to hide himself away.

"Damnation!" he exploded, turning around in the hall as though he would see her coming out of the upstairs parlor, her sewing in her hand. The maid—Sally—flinched. "Where would she have gone?"

James didn't wait for an answer; the servants wouldn't have been able to give him one, regardless. He hurtled down the stairs to the front hall, casting about for something—anything—that would give him an indication of his sister's intentions.

There, on the table where the salver for visiting cards usually sat. His daybook, not where he normally left it. Nothing else seemed out of place, no cards suggesting visitors that he hadn't seen or flowers from an unknown suitor. The book sat heavy in his hands, heavier than its size accounted for, and he flipped the pages with his thumb.

One was missing, the torn edge ragged.

What had he written there?

The page before bore clients' names, the page following a note about the gala at the Olympic Pavilion. Miss Ceniza's address, then—that was the page that had been torn from the book, and was probably, even as he stood there in the half-lit hallway, in Cecily's reticule or pocket.

God help them both, his baby sister was on her way, on foot, at night, to Charing Cross. There was nothing for it but to go retrieve her and pray that she had made it to Meg's lodgings without incident. She would have to learn about the darkness that lay in people's hearts someday. His plan had always been to keep her from that knowledge for as long as was humanly possible.

Driven by impulse, and a thick, sour sense of foreboding that seeped up through the pit of his stomach, James mounted the stairs again, two at a time. Mrs. Lambert had already sent Sally off about her business, and he didn't stop to speak with her before ducking into his room again. There, the long lacquered case with its walnut inlays that sat upon his dresser, the latch and hinges gleaming brass in the soft, waning light. He took it down and its smaller cousin, laid them both upon his bed, dark stains against the pale blue bedclothes.

The wood was smooth beneath his fingers, polished and varnished to a high sheen, and the lock opened easily at his touch. His sword lay inside, not a fancy gentleman's weapon but a sporting blade, the point still sharp enough to do damage. The revolver in the other case was less common. The seven-shot pepperbox flintlock was a French weapon, one he'd acquired only a few years ago. It was patently unsuitable for dueling or for hunting, good for the novelty of the hand-turned six-barrel design and an owner who enjoyed the intricate workings of such things.

And now, if necessary, for his sister's protection.

The revolver, now loaded, went to his coat pocket, heavy and reassuring. He buckled on his sword belt without fumbling, though it had been more than a year, perhaps two, since he had last taken up arms, even in practice. But the hilt still fit well in his hand as he slid the blade home, and when he left the house again, hat on his head and sword on his hip, the fierceness of his demeanor was enough to make the boys scatter from the stoops where they were playing.

His luck was holding. He swung up into a hackney coach lingering at the stand and gave the address to the unimpressed driver. The coachman's breath smelled of cheap ale, the coach of horse and hay, but it was faster by far than walking on his own two feet. There was no telling what Cecily had gotten into in the hour or two that she'd been gone.

With any kind of grace, she would be sipping tea with Meg and sharing complaints about him. Yes, that was the outcome he should expect. He would barge in and Cecily would rise from the chair by the window and stamp her foot. Meg would…throw something at his head, most likely. And he'd be grateful for it.

Chapter Fifteen

James was not as lucky as he had hoped. The coach drew up to the right corner, he paid the man and disembarked—and there was no light flickering in the window of Meg's apartments. He crossed the street and mounted the stairs two at a time, his heart sitting high in his throat. Had he been wrong? Had Cecily not come here after all? If she had come and the women had left together—how would he ever find them tonight?

The door wasn't latched, and it swung open at his first touch. The room beyond lay in semidarkness. Even the fireplace was cold, no coals glowing low to welcome a weary traveler home. Meg's lodgings had never been neat, but the disarray that met him could be nothing but a deliberate and violent attack.

Clothes lay scattered on the floor and bed, her trunk open and rifled through. Books lay askew where they had fallen, and white feathers littered every surface, her pillows slashed and pulled apart.

Either someone had been looking for something—looking and not found it—or someone was violently furious with her. So much so that they had vented their rage upon the girl's home, when the girl herself was not to be found.

He ran into the middle of the room, his heart beating wildly. He picked up the cloak hanging from the end of the bed; there was nothing and no one beneath it. Again, a dress that had fallen to the floor. No bodies lay hidden below.

There was no blood. Whatever else there was in the mess, there was no blood at all.

The wave of relief that broke over him could not be described in words. James pulled the delicate silk of Meg's dress to his chest, dipped his head to press his nose into the ephemeral, delicate layers. The fabric smelled like her, lilacs and roses, and a fist clenched painfully around his heart.

They had not been here at the time of the attack.

With haste, now, because there could be no doubt that some kind of foul business was afoot. What else was out of place, or missing? The times he'd been a guest here, he had not been paying close enough attention to the surroundings, too intent on the women in his arms, against his lips, their mouths and bodies wet and slick along his cock.

A folded letter lay on the table, the wax seal still intact. Something Meg intended to send? Or something she had received and not read? He shouldn't trifle with it; the chance that it had anything to do with this business was remote.

But then, if it did not, why did the burglar not open it as well? Perhaps because he knew it held no new information?

Before he could talk himself out of it, James ran his finger beneath the wax and broke the seal. The strong masculine hand was utterly unfamiliar to him, but the bold lines across the page left him with no doubt about the kind of person he was looking for.

Margaret,

You have defied me for the last time. I tender this final offer, and then no more. Come to me of your own free will or I will be forced to find other methods of persuasion. I imagine Miss Armand of Bruton Place would make a lovely addition to my staff. Or what of that golden rose of Chelsea? You see, I know of your attachments. And I have clientele who know of you. If you please me, and them, they will shower you with jewels and riches beyond that which a Cheapside girl could ever dream. If you refuse, you will be taken anyway.

Come to my halls, come alone, and your particular friends will remain, in my adventurous circles, entirely and eternally unknown.

You know where to find me.

Baron Thomas

The blood drained out of his face as he read the letter over once more, to be sure he had made it out correctly. Some brazen cock-pimp wanted to add Meg to his list of ladies of convenience, and she had refused him. More than once, if the letter was to be believed. And now, having failed to win her, he had resorted to threatening her friends. And Cecily among them.

Fine. Next order of business, find this baron and make him bleed, bleed until he disclosed whether or not he knew anything about the location of James's sister, and of Meg. Because he could not, would not—not for a moment!— allow himself to believe that they had been hurt or killed. If they had, if one finger had been laid on either of them, his vengeance would be brutal and swift.

But still, James hesitated at the door, hand on the hilt of his sword.

It was all well and good to go storming off down the street, but how was he supposed to find the man? Meg knew where to find him, but Meg wasn't here.

Sarah. Sarah would know what to do. She had grown to adulthood in the worst areas of London, if all she had said was true. She would know the bauds and whores, the secret ways in and out of the houses and alleyways that supplied the flesh trade.

If only she didn't hate him. If only he had done everything so differently, paid more attention to her fears and worries. Was it possible to be enough for two women? Could *any* one man be enough to satisfy both? Or was it enough to be one of three lines in a triangle, supporting and being supported in turn?

That was a new thought, one that deserved a lot more examination at a future date. For now, though, it was all an entirely moot point unless Sarah could be convinced to speak with him. Perhaps she wouldn't for his sake alone, but she might for Cecily and Meg.

His blood burned in his veins, fire in his heart. It was time to set all mistakes aside, and all his meaningless concerns about what a gentleman should or should not do. Ladies that he loved were in danger—there was no more room for reflection, or for questions.

Now was the time to *act*.

Her fit of self-flagellation only lasted a short while—Sarah still had duties to attend, and the household would not freeze in time while a single lady's maid broke into pieces over a love affair gone wrong. Sarah had washed and dried her face and sat down in the servants' hall with her ladyship's mending, the house buzzing around her as they closed in toward mealtime. Soon Lady Horlock would summon her to dress for dinner, Sarah would go, and everything would fall into the same old rhythm as it ever had.

The door opening came as a shock, Sarah's head jerking up and eyes refocusing from the tiny stitches she was making across the torn gusset in the countess's white linen shift.

Mrs. Colby, broad-beamed as any sailing vessel, Teutonic and mighty, her apron tucked securely over her dress to protect it from the stains of boiling sauces, gestured to Sarah from the doorway. What else could she do but set aside her plainwork and go?

"Mr. Glover's to see you," Mrs. Colby reproved her, but there was a questioning look in her eyes. "This is becoming something of a pattern, my dear child. Is there something you want to discuss?"

"Not now, Mrs. Colby, please," Sarah begged, twisting her hands in her apron despite herself. "Did he say why he's come?"

"No, only that he's worked himself into such a state of panic I've half a mind to send him away until he can be calm. But he insists."

"I'll be there momentarily." Sarah untied her apron, half pulled it off, then smoothed it back down again. No, she had no intention of fluttering her lashes at him. Why should she change anything about her appearance when he was the one who had barged in when the house was preparing for dinner? Uncouth man! He would get her as she was, and with not a moment's effort more.

Sarah retied her apron strings with a firm yank and her jaw set. Then, patting her cap to ensure that her hair was tucked up beneath it, she followed Mrs. Colby back through the door and into the kitchen proper.

The cook went back about her work, and Sarah ducked out of the way of scampering scullery maids and hallboys as they whirled around preparing for the evening meal.

James was waiting for her in the back hallway. He had his hat in his hand, but from the frantic measures of his pacing, he had not come to grovel, nor to court. He crushed the brim of his fine top hat in his hands even as she watched, not seeming to notice the destruction.

"Mr. Glover," Sarah said firmly, though the sight of him sent pain shooting through her once more. He was in agonies himself, his hair a tumbled mess that called for her to comb it out, his usually soft blue eyes hard and fierce. He burned, his every step so tight and powerfully controlled that he was a floppy-haired puppy no longer, but a potent and powerful predator. The cub had become the lion.

"Miss Armand," he breathed out, and his eyes locked on her. "Thank you for agreeing to see me," he began, then shook his head and seemed to change his mind. "I know you are wroth with me, and you have a right to be. But I need you to set all that aside for the next while."

In that instant when his eyes stared into her soul, the vein throbbing with his clenched jaw, tight over the things he wasn't saying—she would have given him the world, if only it would ease his suffering. If only she could take him in her arms, smooth his brow, save him from the anger or the grief that seemed to have overtaken him entirely.

How had she fallen so far, so fast?

And how can I redeem myself again from this captivity?

"I don't hear a request for forgiveness in that speech," she fired back without considering her words. "Nor an apology, so no, sir, I 'need' to do nothing at all along those lines. And if you continue to speak to me that way, I will have you escorted out!"

There. That should be the blow to sever any threads that remained.

And yet, he didn't go. James set his hat down behind himself without looking at the table, reaching for her hand. "There is no time for this," he insisted, and only once his coat moved could she see that he had a sword hanging from his belt, like a naval officer or a gentleman of rank. "*Sarah.* I need your help. Meg needs your help."

Of course she does— The words died on Sarah's lips when he took her hand in his, the panic and passion that suffused his frame passing through her like a wave. "What's gone wrong?" she said instead, her lips stumbling on the words.

"It's my sister and Meg. They've gone missing." And there, that was the reason for his stark fear and the anger burning in his eyes.

"When?"

"Not two hours gone now. Cecily was home when I returned, but left immediately following. I believe she went to Meg's, but *her* apartments are turned inside out. And I found this."

He pulled a folded paper from his pocket, his coat still hanging heavy on that side. The handwriting on the letter was not familiar, but the signature was, and Sarah's throat closed over, her blood freezing to ice when she read the name.

"Do you know," he asked insistently, "who this lord is, and where he can be found?"

Memories, some distant, some more recent, flooded Sarah's mind at the question. Did she know him? Who did not, who had spent any time in the *demimonde*? John Thomas's girls were not the polished and high-class ladies who accompanied dukes and counts to the operas and musicales. They were as interchangeable as the urchins who begged in the street, always young, very young, always beautiful to begin with, and broken when he abandoned them. If they were ever seen again. Too many young women had passed through Mother Lilah's front room with bruises forming on their arms and legs, purple and blue shading into green; too many with sad and broken eyes, remnants of once-fine dresses the last shredded memories of their dignity.

Lilah did what she could with salves and with potions, but while some girls vanished and some escaped, there were always a few who returned to him. And always, always there was new flesh coming to Town to seek husbands or fortunes, only to be sold to feed the endless appetites of the rich.

And in the middle of it all, Thomas himself in his fine wools, his silks and velvets, his ebony cane, a fat and deadly spider in the middle of his poisoned web.

"I know him, and he's no aristocrat. He's a whoremonger with a house in Covent Garden. And if he has Meg and Miss Glover..." She looked up at him, her eyes wide and, judging by the surprise on his face, some fearsome expression on her own. "Then there is no time at all to be lost. He is not gentle, nor does he have, I think, any understanding of human feeling. Someone in the district should be able to tell you where his house is, if you go quickly."

"You must come with me. You know the people, do you not? They will be more likely to give answers to you. If he's taken them anywhere, or—"

He didn't say the rest. He didn't need to.

A bell sounded in the hall, one, twice, shrill and insistent. "I cannot," Sarah pleaded. How could she run off? She was needed here, though Lady Horlock's evening maintenance was so much less important than Meg or little Cecily. "If I leave, I'll be sacked. Her ladyship needs me now, and I cannot get away. I could meet you somewhere, once they've sat for the meal—it could be an hour, no more."

"And by then, God alone knows what could have happened." He took her elbow, firm but not hard, his heat and strength flowing into her as though she was the dying sapling and he the summer rain. "I'll go alone if I must, but your help could make all the difference."

The bell rang again, louder and for longer, and she *must* go with him, find Meg and Cecily and bring them home, and yet—and yet she had no choice but to stay. "I know, believe me, I *know*—"

"Armand!"

That voice was never heard in the back hall, and all commotion in the kitchen ceased when Lady Horlock's command rang out. Sarah's false name echoed in the narrow space and she froze at the sound.

"Armand, what are you doing there? Why do you not come when called?"

And there, the demon whispering in her ear. Ellen strode confidently behind Lady Horlock, a gleam of satisfaction in her eyes. "There, your ladyship. I would not believe it either unless I had seen it for myself. She brings her paramour into your house to make love to him under your very nose."

"That is not the case," James said firmly, stepping forward to put himself between Sarah and Lady Horlock, his hand resting as though for security on the hilt of his sword. "Your ladyship, I apologize for the disturbance to your household, but I had an urgent message that had to be conveyed."

Lady Horlock glared at them both through her pince-nez, a stare so cold that it would shrivel the sun to ice. "Come away from there, Armand. Messages or not, you are a servant in my employ and so you shall come when I call! Since last summer, you have been unreliable and scatterbrained. I tell you now, my affairs are the only ones that you should be concerning yourself with."

The flush of heat that immediately thawed her limbs was born of anger and frustration, not of fear. Lives were in danger, lives and sanctity of body, and here came this avenging demon, fierce and proud, to demand that Sarah come and help her do what? To dress. To rouge her face and set her curls and pretend that the most important thing in this lifetime was how her ladyship appeared before her uncaring husband at the dinner table.

"My deepest apologies, my lady," Sarah began, and in front of her, James's shoulders tensed beneath his dark wool coat. "But this time, I cannot obey." Her heart seized tight in her chest at what she was about to do, fear crawling up her throat. But that had to be like nothing compared to what the others were living through even as they stood there. "There is an emergency, a family matter, and I must go. Allow me an hour, perhaps two, and I will return to my duties with a joyful heart."

"Family?" Lady Horlock snorted. "You have no family beyond us."

"They go to revel in sin, your ladyship—he is her lover. I've seen them pressing lips when they thought they were alone." Ellen smirked, and Lady Horlock seemed to grow sharper, blade-straight in her stance at the information.

"Go, girl, and you will not come back." And that, without question, was to be the lady's final position.

"If I stay," Sarah said, "I will lose two of the only people worthy of being called *family* to me." The words sprang off her tongue as though she hadn't considered them before she heard herself saying them. But it was true, so true. James's breath came out in a huff and she couldn't see his face, nothing but the working of his jaw and the power of his broad shoulders, but she knew. She knew and he knew and it would be all right, in the end.

The choice was simple.

"I am dreadfully sorry, my lady, more than words can say. But I must go."

"Go, and you will not be welcome back in this house!" Lady Horlock thundered. "And you will have no reference from me! Treacherous girl!"

Sarah took her shawl from the hook behind the door and swung it over her shoulders. But she could not leave yet, not while there was still a snake in Lady Horlock's bosom. The old bat was no friend of Sarah's and a petty tyrant over her household, but she was, at the end of all things, a woman like any other.

"If you wish to know treachery, my lady, look to Ellen. She is the one who darkens the door of your husband's chamber. Mine is not the only sin in this house, but at least my transgressions have been born of love."

There, it was said, but ambiguously enough that James could imagine she meant Meg, or the girls in general, or the kind of affectionate love that lingered between friends.

"Come," James said, and she took his hand. Right there, in front of a terrified-eyed Ellen and a furious Countess of Horlock. Her die was cast. Oddly enough, at the moment, she had no regrets. "We haven't a moment to lose."

Chapter Sixteen

The last few strands of red lit the darkening sky as Meg and Grace slipped through the alleyways and back streets of Covent Garden. Their outward appearances had not changed overmuch since their stop at the King's Theatre. Only the sword belt on Grace's hips, the bag on her shoulder and the extra weight that Meg carried about her person suggested that they had paused for supplies at all. The Lover's Legs lay beyond the alleyway where they paused, a ramshackle construction that had once been a grand house. Now the stones crumbled at the corners, a sickly strand of ivy attempting to climb up the single corner toward a dilapidated balcony that ran along the far side. Paint peeled on the wooden doorframe, and only the light spilling from a handful of windows suggested that there was life within.

A bullyboy lingered on the stoop, idly cleaning his nails with a small knife, his eyes darting back and forth along the road.

"One watchman," Grace murmured, sliding back in beside Meg, who hadn't noticed her move at all. Between her brown skin, her dark clothes and her dancer's sublime ease, she became a shadow in the deepening night. "If I had to hazard a guess, I'd say that he'd keep the girls up above. They would have to go through his men to get to the door should they try to flee."

And since Miss Glover wasn't expecting any sort of rescue, there was no way to signal her or hope that she could signal them. Meg turned to whisper in Grace's direction, "We'll have to get inside to find her." A carriage trundled past and Meg pressed herself back against the wall, hoping beyond hope that her dark cloak was enough to keep her mostly concealed. Pale-green dresses were a poor choice for wearing when sneaking about.

"What's your plan?" Grace's voice came softly, and Meg hesitated. The idea had been for *Grace* to come up with a plan—wasn't that how it worked? Meg got people into situations, and they were smart enough to get her out of them again.

Except not this time.

Think!

The door was on the ground floor. Cecily was probably on the second. "There's no way to get in without being seen," Meg thought aloud, and Grace made a disappointed noise. "So we'll have to count on at least one of us *being* seen."

"That seems like a bad idea."

"No, but look," Meg insisted, the threads of her idea beginning to weave themselves into some more tangible image behind her eyes. "If someone were to go inside the house next door—"

"It's a bakery, already closed for the day."

"Go in there and get up to that balcony, then climb over the railing, it would be simple enough to cross between the two houses—from there open the door and go inside."

"But without knowing where Miss Glover is, it would be a fool's errand."

"So we need to find out where she is, and then get her out by the balcony."

"What do you have in mind?"

"You can climb." Meg turned and grasped Grace's hand, so close, small and warm. "You've the strength in arms and shoulders to pull yourself over, darling dancer, where I would only fall."

"You're stronger than you think," Grace said with a rueful twist to her mouth. She took her hand back and shook it out, as though Meg's hopeful squeeze had been too tight. "All right, supposing we perform this madness. I go up and in. Where will you be?"

"Down here," Meg replied stoutly. "Being seen. The Baron is expecting me, he must be. He'll know that old Agatha would pass on his news. So I'll go in and announce that I'll bend to his will. I will whore for him, but only on the condition that he release Miss Glover. While he gloats, you go across and in through the window. Either they'll release Cecily and I'll signal you so that you can get to me, or I'll signal you so that you can come in and create a diversion for both of us to get away."

It made sense when listed out like that; why, it was practically the Merry Wives of Windsor! All they would need would be James carried out in a laundry basket to complete the scenario. "Don't you see? It will have to work!"

Grace shook her head, her lips pressed thin. That wasn't how she was supposed to react, the first time Meg had taken charge of anything important on her own. "There are many, many problems with this plan, Meglet."

Meg set her fists to her hips and glared at Grace from under the dark wool hood. "Have you got a better idea?"

Grace stared back, her jaw working. Then, slowly, she relaxed and shook her head. "...not at the moment, no."

"Then," Meg proclaimed grandly, "let us proceed." She peeked around the corner, but the guard was still watching the other way, down towards the main road and the carousing passersby. Was it wrong for her pulse to be racing, her blood pounding hard through her veins? Never in her life had her heart beat so loud, her toes and fingers tingling and her stomach tied up in a tangle. If someone weren't in danger, this would be terribly exciting.

Grace girded her sword on tighter and knelt to adjust the knives she had tucked into her boots. "Are you armed?" she asked, and there was a tremble in her voice for a moment that she did her best to hide.

"I am." Meg patted her thigh, and the daggers she had tied there with her stocking garters. He would find those if he touched her. They probably made for funny shapes under her slim gown, but at least while she had the cloak on, they were mostly hidden away. The dagger that she had managed to squeeze into the front pocket of her stays was a little safer. At least in the short-term.

"Good luck," Grace said, and pressed a kiss to Meg's cheek. "Miss Glover is very lucky to count you as her friend," she added gently, "and so am I. But just so we're clear—if I die doing this, I will come back and haunt you for the rest of your days."

Meg shook her head, but the sentiment refused to be chased away. "We will all be having tea in Miss Glover's parlor before the clocks chime ten," she said, with a great deal more confidence than she felt.

Some noise thumped down near them, followed by shouting. The guard wandered away from his post toward the noise, and Grace, her hand unaccountably cold, squeezed Meg's arm tightly. Then she was gone, darting silently across the road to vanish again between the buildings on the other side.

Meg swept her hands down the front of her skirt, adjusted the cloak on her shoulders, held her head high and stepped into the street.

It was getting dark outside. The fireplace in the little room was cold, and there was no sign of anyone coming to light it or a candle for her. Cecily curled her knees up against her chest, wrapped her arms around them and shivered.

At least it was spring, and not winter. At least the only place she'd been hurt was the back of her head. At least she was alone, and the guard on her room was keeping his smelly self outside in the hall.

Something small and furry scuttled over her toes and she bit back a shriek, muffling it with her fist against her mouth. *Mouse. It was a mouse, only a mouse!* The grimy mattress that she sat on was lumpy, ends of straw sticking out of the ticking every which way and poking into her skin. That and the sheet carelessly thrown over it were the only things of note in the room, other than a nightstand and a jug, and an empty chamber pot in the corner.

What *was* this place?

She'd woken up as she was being carried up the stairs in this house, wherever it was, thrown over some brute's shoulder like an undignified sack of potatoes. She'd tried to yell, but the noise hurt her head, and she'd kicked him, and all she'd gotten for her troubles was a very sore toe. And as of yet, no one had come in except once, when the guard looked in to make sure she was awake. But even he'd closed the door on her without a word, only a leer and a slow regard up and down her body that made her feel dirty. Even her dress and stays and petticoats weren't enough to protect her from the crawling filth of that stare. She was going to insist on a hot bath when she got home. A hot bath and a lot of soap.

Her bonnet had gone missing somewhere along the way, and her hair started to slide out of its carefully set pins. She reached up to untwist them, a bright sting of pain on the back of her head going along with the movement. Her fingers were sticky when she brought them down, sticky and dotted with something dark. That was her blood she was staring at, already clotting and set. So the injury couldn't be that bad, could it?

She'd banged her head open once before, when she was very little, chasing James across the wooden footbridge that spanned the brook next to their house. Her toe had caught, she'd fallen; he'd cradled her in his strong arms that day, caught her up and carried her home, where Mother had laved her head with cool water until it ran clear and the cut stopped burning. There was only a tiny scar there now, just under her eyebrow, where you had to squint and look close to see it.

This one would be larger.

Water—was there water? A jug on the nightstand was half full, and she tore a small strip off the hem of her dress to soak and dab away the blood. It stung, but nowhere nearly as bad as the first time.

James. Think of her brother and let the memory of safety try to tamp down the nausea and the terror. James would realize she was gone, and he would be looking for her.

How would he know where to begin? She had made sure not to tell anyone, and surely he would never imagine to ask that old woman.

And who else other than her captors even knew what had happened?

Still, James had carried her home before. He would come for her again. All she had to do was wait, be calm and not give in. She would be brave. She had no other choice.

Sarah kept her head high until they had sped their way down Bruton Street and away. Only once they were out of sight of the door did her step slow. She pulled her shawl closer around herself and stared, hollow-eyed and distant, at the ground ahead of them.

It wasn't difficult to guess what she must be thinking.

James stopped as well, pulled her into his arms without a moment's pause. She resisted, put her hands against his chest to push him away, but he held her steady, the pulse in her wrist thrumming hard against his thumb. "I have you," he murmured softly, and that was when she faltered. She laid her head on his shoulder, stopped pushing back and away from his embrace, and let him fold her into his arms.

She smelled sweet, honey and wine, and she allowed the intimacy, laying her palm against his chest and her forehead against his shoulder. He held her like that, his arms about her, and Sarah curled in against him, winsome and so very small.

A minute passed like that, perhaps a little more, her rapid breathing slowing to match his steady in-and-out. He dared to touch the hollow of her back, flatten his hand against the gentle curve of her spine. Sarah breathed down into his hand, sucked in air in a long, shuddering, single breath.

Then she let it out, raised her head and nodded. "I am well," she said, though it was obviously untrue. Her armor was sliding back into place, walling off the vulnerability and pain in her eyes. "There are other paths for me. Right now we have more important things to attend to."

He could argue, fight for the chance to see that softer side once more, but she was right. "We will revisit this conversation." When things were not quite so immediately dire. "Now, where does the Baron hide himself?"

Sarah shook her head, and his heart fell. "He moves from place to place. When he grows too bold or offends the wrong lord and the magistrates close one of his houses, he moves to another to continue his blighted business unmolested."

"You mean to say that you *don't* know how to find him?" James asked, appalled.

"I didn't say that," Sarah snapped. "I don't know where he currently holds his girls, but I know how to find out. Follow me. And for the love of God and all the saints, keep your mouth shut. You'll look like a client no matter what we do, and that will still tongues. Don't make it worse by sounding like you're in league with the law." And she set off toward New Bond Street at a rapid pace.

He caught up to her in a few long strides, Sarah's face flushed and everything about her in a fluster. "Don't tell me what I may or may not do! This is my *sister* and possibly Meg in trouble as well. I have as much right-"

"To browbeat people you despise into giving you the information you need?" she replied, with a bitterness he had never seen in her before.

No, that was a lie. He had seen it once, earlier that afternoon.

"We go among whores and bauds, *Mr. Glover*, and the wretched refuse of the city. You may wish to turn back now, for the sake of your refined sensibilities."

"Unfair!" He let the word out with an explosive shout, and some shopkeepers and passersby turned to watch them go. "When have I ever acted with such ill designs? Ever shown myself to be less than compassionate?" He seized Sarah's elbow and wheeled her around, using her own momentum to spin her to face him. "Be angry at me for invading your home, for contributing to your dismissal, for causing trouble between you and Meg, yes, fine. I accept the blame for all of those, though my intentions—flawed, obviously enough—were good. But while I have been insensitive in my words and clumsy in my designs, I have never, not once, been cruel."

Her chest heaved, fury and some other glut of emotion warring it out in her eyes, but she said nothing.

"Hate me all you must," he said, more softly now, "but know that I am sorry. I care nothing for your past, Sarah Harlow, nor your childhood, except in my desire to make up for everything you have ever lacked. I only care about the woman you are now and the future yet to be written."

Her eyes locked with his, then slowly, moments crawling by, she unclenched her jaw and the fierce, desperate anger faded from her eyes. She pulled her elbow from his hand, and he let it go.

"And Meg," she said, apropos of nothing.

"I'm sorry?"

"You care for Meg as well?"

What had that to do with anything? "Yes, of course I do."

"Then remember that speech," Sarah said, ducking her head and rearranging her shawl to lie neatly over her shoulders. "She'll need to hear it as well. Once we find her and your sister."

And that, he supposed, was as close to a concession as he was going to receive any time soon.

Chapter Seventeen

True to her word, Sarah led him through the city streets and down through a series of alleys, each more filled with trash and grime than the last. The buildings pressed closer together as they wove their way along the streets, James stretching to step over puddles of some unknown substance and Sarah folding her shawl more carefully to conceal the bare skin below her collarbone.

The air smelled danker down here, combinations of cooking smells and other, fouler things warring for his attention. The buildings leaned closer together, wooden stairs, hastily constructed, teetering beside boarded-over windows and signs with their paint peeling. There was a butcher with a grocer's beside hardly worthy of being called by that name, with a barrel of old apples out the front door that had by all appearances sat there all winter long.

"Have you money with you?" Sarah asked, pausing in her stride. She tipped her head up and looked at him expectantly, chestnut curls peeking from beneath the edge of her cap.

"A little, yes. Are you in need of something to eat?" He frowned. "Surely there are better places than this."

"Not I, and we are close to our first destination. Only give me enough for a few sausages and a little milk." She paused, then looked up at him through her long, dark lashes, all hints of anger fading. "Please?"

"What can I say to that?" James gave up trying to understand her and pressed a coin into her hand. It could hardly cost a fortune, and if she had something specific in mind, well. He had made up his mind to trust her.

Sarah was out of the shop again in moments, a packet and a bottle beneath her arm. A group of soldiers in uniform wandered by, arms about each other and bottles in their hands, howling some ribald drinking song. Sarah drew her shawl up over her head and ignored them, despite their calls to her. James stepped between them, swinging his coat back to show the sword he wore on his hip, and the leader raised his hands, backing away.

She led him up a steep and narrow staircase, knocking perfunctorily on the weathered wooden door at the top. "Who goes?" a reedy, rasping voice answered from within.

"It's Sarah, auntie." She pushed the door open.

The smell assailed him first, not of waste but of the sickroom: camphor and brandy, and the overwhelming, acrid stench of cinnamon and cloves.

He knew those smells, the thick pungent odors that had swathed around his father, then his mother, as they succumbed to the fevers that sapped their strength, their minds and then their lives, one after the other.

James's knees buckled under the weight of memory, slammed back into his mind at such speed that he could neither dismiss it nor bury it deep where it belonged. He grabbed for the doorframe to steady himself and took in the rest of the tiny room.

It was clean, surprisingly enough, as clean as one could expect given the surroundings. A mattress lay in the far corner, a mound of blankets piled around the gaunt and aged figure of a woman. She reached up with shaking hands to take Sarah's, and Sarah bent to kiss her on both cheeks without a moment's hesitation. She was small, withered with age though she had likely never been tall, her skin a rich brown like the men who hauled cargo at the dockyards, or paintings of Mughal princesses from Delhi. Her hair was white as sun-bleached linen, the long braid down her back heavy and thick.

He took a step forward, Sarah pressing her hand against the old woman's forehead and then her wrist. "You're not eating," she scolded, then turned. "James, this is Mrs. Lilah Patel, who raised me as best she could after my mother died. Mother Lilah, this is Mr. Glover. A…friend."

"Welcome," Lilah creaked out, and offered him a gummy, toothless smile. "And it's good to see someone else is looking after Old Lilah's little squirrel. Very good, very good."

"We need your help, Auntie," Sarah said, and she stood, busying herself amidst the scattered collection of cooking utensils set upon the hearth. "James, would you be so good as to check the pot there?"

Putting himself to work was better than standing about looking like a proper tit, so the task was simple enough. By the time he had the pot moved back on the hob and the handful of coals stoked up into something more properly

294

resembling a cooking fire, Sarah had the sausages finely chopped and ready to tip into the gruel.

"You're good to an old lady." Lilah slowly unfolded herself from her blanket nest, reaching for the walking stick that sat against the wall within her reach. James had himself beside her before she could fall over on herself, supporting her elbow even as the smell of cloves and brandy tried to choke him from the inside out. There was more substance to her than first appeared, thankfully, strength in the muscles beneath her paper-thin skin.

"Only a fraction of what I have left to repay your kindness." Sarah paused halfway through her turn, stopping midsentence as she watched James lead Lilah in her desperately slow progression toward the rickety old table and its single chair. "But I need your help again, Auntie, and Meg needs your help."

"Oh dear, oh dear. What's that silly mouse gotten herself mixed up in now?" Lilah squinted blearily at both of them. "If it's ridding herself of a situation she needs, you'll want Dottie at the King's Oak. She's still in the trade, or she was."

"Nothing like that." Sarah answered without batting an eye, James stunned into silence.

As easy as that? No questions, no whispered confidences, only "go to and have it done"? There was so much he still had yet to understand. Looking around the room brought only a few smaller hints of what Sarah's life must have been like.

Two sampler cushions sat in pride of place against the wall, childish stitches blocking out letters and animals prancing about the squares. An ancient school bench lay beneath the window, piled high now with fabrics and debris, but if he squinted in the dim light, let the shadows from the flickering rushlight play with his senses, perhaps he could see it: Meg and Sarah curled together on the bench, samplers in hand. Lilah fussing about at the fireplace, stirring some heavy pottage that filled the air with warmth.

"She's been mixed up with the Baron, she and a young friend of ours. Where is he living now?"

Lilah looked at him again with a gimlet eye, slowly shaking her head. "That one's danger, squirrel, hadn't I always been telling you that? You two were always testing trouble, running about and getting in over your heads. Needed real mothers and fathers, you did. Ah, but I did the best I could."

Sarah knelt, and James headed for the fireplace to stir the pot before the contents could burn. The mixture bubbled, soft and fragrant, the meat adding richness to a gruel that even the weakest of invalids could stomach easily.

"You were everything to us both," Sarah said firmly. "And now we need you to be fearless again. Where is the Baron?"

"Holed up in his manor, no doubt, no doubt." Lilah tipped her head one side to the other, her braid sliding on her aged shoulders as she moved. "He likes them young; his clients like them younger. It's no place for a little mouse, or a mouse's friend."

"Where, Auntie?" Sarah squeezed her hands, an edge of desperation creeping into her voice. A search of the boxes and canisters by the fire revealed a small length of cheesecloth tied around a handful of raisins, and with a burst of momentary inspiration, James added a few to the mixture before he ladled it into a chipped bowl, the glaze long-cracked.

"Only a few streets from here." Lilah perked up when James set the bowl before her, placing a spoon beside it. His handkerchief made a napkin for her lap, giving the old lady a modicum of dignity as she ate.

The look he received from Sarah—a bewildered expression that turned to something magical and approving shining from her eyes—was thanks enough for such a tiny act.

"The Baron roosts in the green house on the corner," Lilah continued, "with the cockerel on the sign. The men come to him there, all hours, all kinds, all kinds. Rich men and poor, but the rich men he likes better."

"Who doesn't?" James replied dryly, and old Lilah burst into a shaky, crackling laugh that made Sarah smile again.

"Be well, Auntie." Sarah stood and kissed Lilah on the top of her head. "I'll return tomorrow once all is settled and bring some cheese and fruit, if you feel well enough."

"Be gone with you." Lilah settled herself, ruffling up like an old dowager hen. "I've enough to take care of myself—who do you think took care of you all these years? Off with you, off."

"We've been dismissed from the royal presence," Sarah murmured to James as she passed, a smile darting about on her lips.

James moved to follow, but Lilah caught him by the hand before he could leave. She tugged him down, until he was eye-to-eye with her. She had lost her jovial smile and she spoke softly, as though her command was meant for him, and him alone. "Bring my little mouse home."

"I will." He swore the promise devoutly, quietly, even as Sarah waited for him at the door. Lilah squeezed his fingers one last time and let him go.

It wasn't until they left the room again, trotting down the stairs that he realized. At some point during the visit, he had stopped noticing the medicinal smell of cloves.

It was getting harder to be brave when the commotion erupted outside the room. It wasn't right outside, but other than that it was impossible to tell where. There were raised voices, mostly men, and a big door opening and closing somewhere. Cecily pressed herself back against the wall by the window, tying her hair out of her face with the rest of the strip of fabric she had torn, turning it into a long queue down her back. It wasn't tidy, but it was a lot simpler than trying to find and replace all her pins in the mostly dark.

The voices grew nearer, a woman's voice among them, and footfalls creaking loudly, thunderously, up the stairs outside. Cecily grabbed the jug with her water and ran for the door. Any minute now they would open it and—

The door swung open, and voices carried from beyond.

"Take that little girl out of there and teach her to do a threepenny upright—"

"You'll not touch her. The marquess prefers virgin flesh, and virgins he will have."

She raised the jug high as she could and brought it crashing down—on the guard's upper arm. He cursed strenuously from his unreachable height at least a foot and a half above her head and shoved someone else inside. His arm caught Cecily on the backswing and she stumbled into the wall, tripping over her dress hem and falling onto her hip. It stung, would bruise later, but that didn't matter nearly as much as the furious, venom-spitting face of the other girl now in the room.

"My freedom for hers, Thomas, that was the deal!"

"Miss Ceniza!" Cecily blurted out in surprise and in shock.

"And so the deal has changed." The man from the alley smiled his awful, toothy smile again and set the candle he was carrying down on the nightstand. "My best client likes the sound of this one."

He reached down and cupped Cecily's chin in his meaty hand. She squeaked and scrabbled backward, away from him, and he let her go with a dark chuckle. "And so why should I give up a fat purse for a girl who will only try to fly the first time I let her off the jesses?" He tapped his nose and smirked. "I am not as foolish as you seem to imagine I am, *Marguerite*." He said her name with a sneer, like it was somehow funny. "Behave yourselves. I will be back for Miss Glover shortly."

Miss Ceniza lunged at him like she was about to try and bite him for lack of a better weapon, but he left the room quickly and closed the door fast behind him.

At least he had left the candle, this time.

"Miss Ceniza!" Cecily pushed herself to her feet and went to her, not caring that her dress was torn, her head sore and her face dirty. The questions bubbled out of her, a rushing torrent of desperate need and fear. "Are you all right? What are you doing here? Did you come for me? Is James here? How are we going to get out? Does anyone else know?"

Miss Ceniza pulled Cecily into her arms, and they clung to each other for a moment. And for that moment, the world felt solid and safe again. "Are *you* all right?" she asked, letting Cecily go long enough to look her over with a critical eye. "That's blood, isn't it? Did they hurt you?"

"Only my head," Cecily said truthfully. "And even then I think it looks worse than it is. My brain isn't even a little bit rattled."

Everything about Miss Ceniza seemed to relax, then, like there had been something else she'd been desperately worried about, most likely that same distantly horrible "something" that led the marquess to prefer virgins.

"That's good," was all she said, though, and looked around. "We're not close to the balcony, are we?" she said, like that was important, and she frowned.

"No, but there is a window, and I think it opens. But I haven't tried yet." Cecily pointed, but when they swung the shutters back, there were small glass panes beyond and a latch that wouldn't budge.

"No matter," Miss Ceniza muttered, though a crease formed between her eyebrows as she frowned.

"What can I do?"

"Get the candle, there, and set it in the window."

There was something fierce about her now, something wild and powerful, and Cecily eagerly obeyed. The stub went on the windowsill, flickering and guttering in the air as she moved it, carefully cupping her hand to protect the little flame. The tiny light reflected off the dozens of diamond-shaped panes, and outside, she could have sworn she saw a black shape, moving on the roof next door.

"Now," her would-be savior said, taking Cecily's hands in hers, "tell me all you can remember, from the moment the Baron approached you. Don't leave out a thing."

There were no streetlights in this section of town like the kind that lit the intersections in St James or Mayfair with their soft yellow gas-glow. The street outside was dark, nothing but the stars and full moon shining overhead, and the squares of light that filtered through windows of houses, flickering with rushlights or candles.

"What did she say to you?" Sarah asked.

"She made me swear to make an honest woman of you," he teased, and Sarah stepped on his foot, hard.

The green house on the corner had lanterns outside, hung on hooks that the linkboys would have to raise and lower at the beginning and end of each day. The eerie glow illuminated the sign, a rooster in half-crow, his head tipped back in some obscene parody of life. A thickset man stood at the door, hand on a sword at his waist. He scanned the street first one way, then the next, and James tugged Sarah back into the doorway in which they hid, to keep her from his line of sight.

"What is the plan?" Sarah asked quietly.

James frowned. There was a balcony, some windows on the second floor, probably a similar design on the building's rear. One door that he could see, guarded by one man. And somewhere inside, if the stars aligned properly, Cecily and Meg.

If they were not there, then…then he would have to deal with that as it happened.

He straightened up, tugged his sleeves down with a snap and checked once more for the reassuring weight of the revolver in his pocket, the sword on his hip. "We go in the front door," he said simply, and Sarah gestured as though to say "you must be joking."

"You can't imagine that they'll let you in and simply hand the girls over—"

"No, perhaps not," James agreed, watching the guard pick his teeth with his boot knife. "But it's dark, my suit is well-cut, I've never met this friend at the door before and the Baron's clientele are men with some money. I'll get inside."

"And from there, then what? Wave your sword around and demand their return?"

"Find the Baron, run him through and liberate my ladies, yes." It sounded so easily done, when phrased that way.

And from the way Sarah stared at him again, as though seeing something for the first time, weighing and measuring it carefully against her expectations…perhaps it might just be that simple.

"You must be joking," Sarah said, and made his life complete.

"The longer I wait, the more chance the Baron has to do something to Meg or Cecily."

She took a breath, one that seemed to go right down to her toes. "Come, Sarah," he coaxed. "You should go around the back and see if there are alternate entrances, or wait here until I bring them back. But I go, whether you approve or not. Someone has to do the right thing, and I have the means to go about it."

"If you think you're going in without me," Sarah said tartly, wrapping her shawl around her head and laying the corners over her shoulders, covering that distinctive chestnut braid, "then I know you've lost your mind. Call me your concubine or mistress for the night if you will, to make your story stronger, but I am coming with you."

And now it was his turn to hesitate, to imagine the terrible things that could so easily happen if he brought a woman into a fight, in a house where women were already subject to the whims of cruel men—

"Give me your knife," she said, and held out her hand. He stared into her eyes, those gray eyes that snapped with fire and the purest of will, and something inside him changed. Something inside *her* had changed—no longer willing to duck her head and hide, Sarah stood, proud and chin high, and she held out her hand for a weapon.

"Careful with that," he took the chance to tease her, half his attention still on the man at the door. The guard shifted from foot to foot as James slid the knife from his belt and handed it to Sarah. "It's sharp."

She wrapped it in a kerchief and slid it down between her breasts without a moment's hesitation, and James blinked.

Right. Do not underestimate that woman again.

The door guard shifted from foot to foot, looked around as though to ensure himself the coast was clear, then trotted down the stairs and around the side of the building. "Here's our chance." James urged Sarah onward, and they started out into the street. There was barely enough light to see what he was doing, but the sound of the man relieving himself against the wall was enough to make James uninterested in learning more.

They were to the door, James's heart pounding in his chest, by the time the guard noticed them. "Ho there!"

James turned the handle, pushed the door open and entered, Sarah pressing close by his side.

The room beyond was better lit than the street outside, but not by a vast margin. Candles burned in front of mirrored sconces, sending flickering reflections of light dancing throughout the room. Five men sat around a wooden table, gaming dice scattered across the nicked and badly scuffed surface, two with girls in their laps in different states of undress. The smell of festering wine and hard liquors permeated the space, as though bottles had been left to fall and drip their dregs out onto the stained rug that sat beneath the table and chairs. A staircase ran up the side of the room to the floor above, the railing picked out by another pair of small sconces and stubs of candles flickering in their place.

"Who have we here?" a jeering voice rang out over the calls of the men at their dicing, and the women draped across them, bosoms bare. "If it isn't the staymaker. You'll find that my girls do better out of their stays, sirrah. We have no need of your services here."

The speaker was a long, lean, dark-haired man, lounging with his feet on the table, and his arms across the rests of the finest chair in the room. The purple velvet cushions and the lush red-lined cloak draped over the back did little to hide the sharpness of his gaze or dim the crawling sensation up the back of James's neck. The man from the theatre. He had been hunting Meg this whole time.

"Baron John Thomas, I take it?" James advanced, swinging his coat back to display the sword at his hip, and the chatter at the table died. One of the girls, a buxom blonde in little but shift and stockings, a bruise darkening to green on her cheek, slipped from the lap she'd been perched upon and faded into the back corner. "I believe you have something of mine."

The Baron pushed himself back from the table, rocking it and knocking over two of the cups. Port wine spilled across the surface, dampening the edges of the cards before his "guests" scrambled to pick them up.

"And what if I do?" He stood, a snake coiling to strike. "It's a poor guardian indeed who allows a jewel like that out unescorted. I think I'll do a better job of protecting her. Helping her to find her true calling. Isn't that right, Miss Armand? Miss Margaret fits in here very well indeed."

"He's trying to provoke," Sarah murmured, her teeth gritted. "Don't give him the satisfaction."

But trying or not, his insults were not something that could go unanswered. "Marguerite Ceniza is mine," James said firmly.

The Baron only laughed. "I can give you another with better tone in her privy parts, and consider it a fair trade."

How *dare* he! Anger burned through James's heart, blanked his mind to nothing but shades of red. He felt fingers in the palm of his free hand, Sarah squeezing him tightly before letting go.

I am with you.

"Produce Miss Glover and Miss Ceniza now"—James drew his sword with a *shing* of metal and a swish of steel— "or face the consequences. And if either of them have had a finger laid upon them, by you or anyone else-"

"You'll *what*?" the Baron scoffed. Footsteps scuffed behind James and he caught a glimpse of burly men moving into position behind him, drawing daggers and swords of their own. "You're outnumbered and outclassed here, staymaker. Go back to your needles and thread."

"Stand aside or fight!" The ticking clock on the mantel sounded a chime as ringing and deep as the bells of hell itself. Every moment was one that Cecily and Meg might be traveling farther away from him, or fallen under the hands of some cruel bastard, recipient of God alone knew what kinds of tortures.

The Baron kicked aside the chair in front of him, and his friends cheered drunkenly. Two passed coins back and forth as the Baron took a sword from one of his guards, a nobleman's fancy blade with swirls of metal forming the elaborate knuckle guard. He swished it through the air in a pattern more evocative than effective.

"Come on then, *boy*. Let us have our sport."

"*En garde.*" James paid cursory respect to the guard position, but slid into a fast parry as the Baron struck first and fast. His tip whipped past James's cheek and James slammed it away with the bottom of his blade, the metal ringing on metal too loud and too close for comfort.

He raised his sword, the French smallsword's simple hilt sitting easily in his hand even after the months of little time for practice. *My kingdom for a larger bell to guard my hands!*

The Baron lunged again, and again James dodged and parried. The next time the Baron tried for his snake-swift strike, James was ready.

"Leave off, you *brute*!" A shout came from behind him at the same instant, Sarah's foot coming down in the instep of a guard standing beside her.

"I never touched her!" the guard yelled. The Baron glanced over, and in the moment of distraction lost his solid grip on his sword.

James reached in, caught the point of the baron's blade on the *forte* of his own and spun his wrist to the outside. The Baron's sword flipped from his grasp and clattered into the corner of the room. James stepped forward and pressed the tip of his sword against the Baron's throat, and the Baron raised his hands in surrender.

His eyes flickered back over James's shoulder just long enough to mean a problem. James shoved his elbow back and caught the bully's stomach. He folded with a grunt, but the moment was just long enough for the Baron to slip free of James's sword point and back away.

"Almost, but not nearly good enough," he jeered, retrieving his blade from the corner where it had landed.

In a movement swifter than the thought generated to provoke it, James tossed his sword to Sarah. Would she be there to catch it? Unaccountably, wonderfully, with a new and brilliant rush of clarity, he had faith.

She caught it, flicked her wrist as though to check the weight and took a stance that was a reasonable imitation of the one he had held a moment before. *Good girl.*

The pepperbox revolver came to his hand with no effort at all, as though it had been waiting for this fight, this very moment.

Whatever he had been or done before, whoever James Glover had once wanted to become, the power surged through him now. It all came down to this, to the men surrounding him with murder on their minds and the women in captivity somewhere here.

James drew the gun out of his pocket and aimed at the Baron's forehead. "Bring them to me," he said firmly, "or you die."

Chapter Eighteen

Without a clock there was no way to know how much time had passed while Meg and Cecily were locked together in the small, dirty room. Enough time for Meg to have explored every inch, even pulling the mattress aside to see if there were any trap doors or other such useful conveyances hidden beneath. Or perhaps a convenient rust-free patch on the lock that would reveal a hidden latch.

The room remained obstinately inescapable, except for the stubborn window latch to which she next turned her attention. Cecily sat on the mattress, her knees pulled up to her chest, and watched sadly as Meg made her methodical explorations. "I imagined James would have come for me by now."

"I don't think he'd know where to find you." Meg hiked up her dress to slide one of her daggers from its sheath, and Cecily's eyes went wide. The dratted sash latch wouldn't move an inch, though, even with the added leverage from the dagger. It was so rusted over that it must have been stuck in the locked position for a hundred years, and without an act of God, Meg wasn't going to be able to budge it.

"But you did. You're more my sister than he's ever been a brother." Cecily sank her chin in her hand and dashed away a tear that threatened in the corner of her eye.

"Don't reject him just for this, sweetness. He's given a great deal to care for you." Meg had never let a thing like a little rust stop her before. She turned the dagger and started to chip away at the layers of corrosion holding the latch in place.

Cecily sat up straight. "He's heartless, and he hurt you!"

"He's not the only one at fault." Meg ran her fingers around the edges of the latch and came away with only dirty fingers for her troubles. This would make for a terrible thrilling novel—there were always extra keys and secret panels hidden somewhere in books like that.

"You like him," Cecily said after a moment, a vague sort of *something* off in her voice. "Even though he did something to make you angry with him, you still like him. Don't you?" There was a pause as Meg searched for an answer that wouldn't betray too much, then, "It's more than that, isn't it? Do you love him?"

"That's twice someone's asked me that tonight," Meg said, keeping her voice as light as she could when her heart was trying to escape through her throat. "Do I look like that much of a silly calf around him?" It wasn't an answer, but it was a reply.

Cecily paused a while before answering, and she hardly sounded certain about it when she did. "Maybe…not?"

"I had a brother, once," Meg said, to move the conversation back onto different subjects and keep Cecily's spirits up.

"Had?"

"Mm-hm. My father was awfully cruel to him; he'd fly into rages and say terrible things. My brother ran away one night and never came home again. James would never do that to you."

Cecily perked up with interest, and whether it was nosiness or real sympathy, Meg's story seemed to be taking her mind off of their predicament. "That's dreadful! Is that after you came to the city?"

"Oh no, it was before. Mother and I left not long after. To come to London, and try to find him." A little more at the hinge, and perhaps— "Father never followed or looked for us, not that I knew, and Mother got ill not long after. She died here, and I stayed."

"Is that when you met Miss Armand?" Cecily frowned thoughtfully.

"That's right. She and her guardian took me in, gave me shelter, companionship, love. All those things," Meg said pointedly, "that you have from James without ever questioning."

Cecily looked away, not meeting Meg's eyes. A moment passed, while Meg wrestled with the stuck window frame. Then, "Did you ever find your brother again? Are you close?"

"I did." Meg wrenched the latch again, and it seemed to shift. Maybe it was her imagination, maybe not, but it certainly *felt* like it had! "I saw him playing once—he's a musician. I stood at the back. He had a fine suit on and played the most beautiful music. I couldn't spoil his happiness by bringing the news about Mother into his life."

A soft hand covered Meg's. Cecily took hold of the lever alongside Meg and threw her weight into trying to force it open. "So you just left? Without ever telling him you were there?"

"He wouldn't know me now to see me." It was a melancholy truth, but they couldn't all be happy stories. And he had looked so very lovely, his eyes closed and the violin tucked under his chin. He'd played the kinds of music Father would never have approved of, all lilting and strangely angelic. The music of the spheres.

"I was only a little girl when he ran away. But I know that he's found something to love, something that makes him happier than all the world. You could see it in his face when he played."

"Ow!" Cecily let go and stuck her finger in her mouth. Meg rapped the hilt of her dagger firmly against the latch and this time, oh, it moved this time, she saw it go! Only a little more, and then the window was theirs. "You do that too, you know."

Meg blinked, leaning on the latch. "I do what?"

"Look so very happy, like you've found what you've been searching for. I see it when you're on stage—and I see it when you're with my brother. And with Miss Armand. The three of you belong with each other, I think, though I can't imagine exactly how. Perhaps if you and my brother were to marry, Miss Armand could keep house for you?"

The latch moved and Meg lurched forward with it, forgetting to let go. It sprang free, the window creaked when she smashed her shoulder into it, and shouting erupted from somewhere downstairs, shouting and the clanging of metal like something important was happening.

A length of rope tumbled down from somewhere above. A moment later, Grace's head appeared, though upside down, her legs entangled in the rope like a fakir or an acrobat. She gestured frantically at Meg, but the glass muffled whatever she was trying to say.

"Get the window," Meg urged, all else forgotten. She grabbed the sash and pushed it up with all her might. It budged, but only barely. It didn't move, not until Cecily got beneath it as well and pulled, her face flushing pink with the effort. The window flew up with a crack and a groan.

"Are you ready?" Grace asked, her hat long gone somewhere, one hand reaching out to take Cecily's. "Time to make our escape."

"I can't go up like that!" Cecily squeaked, the excited flush gone and her hands shaking at the very idea. "I'll fall!"

"Bring the rope in and we can tie her around the waist, like a boy on the catwalk," Grace instructed. Meg reached out to take Grace's hand and draw her in through the window, where she would be safer. "If you climb up and pull her, I can stay below and hold the line. Then drop the rope back down for me."

Grace's foot had barely touched the floor, the rope still wound about her arms, when running footsteps sounded outside.

There was a crash, a shout of "*Bring them!*"

Grace grabbed for Cecily. Meg whirled to face the door. It flew open, one of the Baron's guards nothing but a black shape framed by the light from the hallway. Grace and Cecily were nowhere near close enough to the window to get away before they were grabbed or shot. Caught!

Meg hiked her skirt as the huge beast of a man advanced. She pulled out her second knife. One in each hand, she stopped dead between Grace and Cecily and the brute who had come to take them.

"Do you know how to use those?" Grace hissed. She unwrapped the rope from her arms and kept hold to one end, pushing Cecily back between her and the wall.

No, Meg wanted to cry. *No, I've never. I've never hurt another human being on purpose and I don't want to do it now! I'm a child in a great big world and I don't want to know these things at* all!

Instead, she summoned up the spirits of them all, of Viola and Gallathea, Moll, Medea and Joan, every woman she had ever read and every part she had ever played or dreamed of playing. They coursed within her, a hundred furies singing in her blood.

Meg smiled, and the guard before her took a step back, surprise written large across his thick, dumb face. "I played Mercutio once," Meg said, as bold and brave as she could be. "I think I'll do just fine."

The guard lunged for her, a wickedly sharp knife in his meaty hand. Her head high and her friends at her back, Meg raised her own and prepared to fight.

Bring them to me, or you die.

Something had changed in James. If pressed, Sarah would not be able to name it, but he was as far removed now from the man squabbling with Meg this afternoon as Sarah was from a chicken leg. His hand with the gun was steady, his back straight and tall, and he radiated such power and confidence that in that instant, had she been a soldier and he her commander, she would have followed him to the depths of hell itself at a single word.

The Baron saw it too, his bravado flickering for a moment. He looked from James to Sarah, the unfamiliar sword trembling slightly in her clammy hand, then back to James and his steady aim. Then he relaxed, nodded and said, "Have it your way, then."

Sarah barely had time to register the scrape of footsteps behind her before her instincts took over. She ducked as the man whose foot she'd stepped on lunged for her, arms outstretched. She stabbed blindly with the rapier as she slid beneath his tree-trunk-like forearm, a yelp of either pain or outrage following the impact.

Opening her eyes, she only saw the large man in shirtsleeves and breeches turn around, his hammer-like fist swinging for her head. Her hand slid on the sword hilt, fear making her palms sweat. She swung it anyway, closing her eyes at the moment of impact.

This is going to make such a mess.

The rapier bounced off the goon's side with a whip-crack sound and he yelped with pain. No blood seeped out from under his shirt, and the surprise stopped her cold.

"Pointy tip," James called out, his arm in a lock-grip from an attacker of his own. "Dull sides! Stab it like a needle!"

If that was some kind of joke at a time like this, she was going to run *him* through with his stupid needle-sword once they got out of there.

If they got out of there.

The goon grabbed Sarah's wrist and wrenched it with such force that her hand opened despite herself. The sword clattered to the floor. With strength born of desperation and a rage swelling up deep inside, she grabbed at her skirts to haul them up and kicked her booted foot high between his legs.

It made an intensely satisfying *thud* sort of sound.

He folded over, as men do, his face going purple and hands clutching at his privy parts. She fell when he let her go, landing hard on her right shoulder. A burst of pain spat through her arm, but she could move her fingers still when she sat up. Nothing broken, thank God.

Shouting and chaos filled the room, everything coming in flashes and pieces.

James grappling with the man who had grabbed his arm.

The gun held up high and pointing at the ceiling.

The two men at the card table laughing and jeering.

The Baron moving fast toward James and his opponent.

The girls were gone. Where?

What now? Retrieve the sword, first. She scrabbled at the floor, not taking her eyes off the scene unfolding in front of her. She grabbed it, pushed herself to her feet. James shot his elbow backward and struck his assailant in the stomach. The gun went off, a burst of sound in the small parlor that sent her ears ringing hopelessly.

"James!" she screamed, and couldn't hear herself screaming. He still stood, though, the revolver in his hand. His attacker had let him go but wasn't bleeding. A hole in the wall plaster explained where the bullet had gone.

The Baron was right behind him, and still James didn't turn. He stared, stunned, at the revolver in his hand as though the shot had come as much of a surprise to him as to everyone else. The men at the card table scrambled for the door.

"James!" Sarah screamed again, but her ears rang— and if hers did, his must doubly so. He didn't turn.

Baron John Thomas grabbed James's shoulder, spun him around and hit him, square in the jaw. James staggered from the impact, and the Baron seized the gun.

Knife fights in real life weren't at all like practiced routines for the stage.

Meg had managed to avoid the first strike by jumping away, but there was no way she could get close enough to hit back. Not when the guard's arms were twice as long as hers and he actually knew how to use his weapon. He swung at her a second time and she jumped back again. The blade caught her across the stomach, sliced through her cotton dress, wicked sharp and gleaming steel that was sure, any moment, to pierce her flesh and end her life.

Meg shrieked.

The knife glanced off the stiff whalebone of her new busk like an arrow off knight's armor.

It gave her a second, only a second, to move. Meg dropped straight down as he lunged for her, scrambling between his legs to push herself through and *out* and *away*.

"Hey, ugly!" Grace's voice rang out. The guard wheeled around, furious, and Grace was there, the candle in her hand. She flung it, the melted tallow splashing his face and neck. He let out a yell, his hands flying up to protect his eyes. Grace pushed Cecily toward the door, and Meg reached for the guard's knife from the floor before following.

A sound like a gunshot cracked out below, unbelievably loud and sudden. It was followed by screaming, but she couldn't make out what was being said.

Meg's pause was a second of hesitation too long. Grace and Cecily were already in the hall, but the guard grabbed Meg's hair, twisting his hand in her tumbled curls. Pain ripped through her scalp and neck, hot and sharp, as the guard jerked her back. She stumbled, falling to her knees.

The rest happened in slow motion, each moment pausing so long that it felt as though Sarah wasn't moving at all.

She started to run. James reeled from the punch. The Baron leveled the gun at James. Sarah reached the Baron's

318

side. The Baron saw her a moment too late. She brought the sword down on his head, hilt-first. He stumbled, but didn't fall.

The vibrations from the impact ran up the sword hilt and set Sarah's injured shoulder on fire with a white-hot jolt of pain. She dropped the sword and time sped up once more. The only thing near to hand was a heavy pewter jug sitting on the table. It was half full of something dark, probably terrible wine. She didn't stop to think any more about it, but grabbed the handle and pulled the jug into her hands.

The Baron started to straighten.

Lifting the jug with both hands, the liquid inside sloshing around, she cracked it down over his head.

The impact rang out, the wine erupting from the jug as the heavy metal base slammed across the back of John Thomas's thick skull, drenching both of them in cheap red wine.

He reeled, dropped to his knees, his head, shoulders and suit sodden and dripping red—with wine or with blood, Sarah couldn't tell. But he didn't fall. Her ears must have been clearing, for she heard the crush and snap, the ringing of the jug as it fell from her hands to roll across the floor.

Something else fell with a crash. "Go!" she shouted at James, and this time, he heard her. He didn't stop to scoop up the gun, just grabbed her by the waist, his sword in his other hand, and bolted for the stairs to the second floor.

"Go, go, go," he urged her, pressing her up the stairs before him. Voices rang out from above, women's voices, and more than one.

"After them!" John Thomas howled, rage thick in his voice. Of his men, though, only one moved toward the stairs. The others had fled, but for one who still curled, cringing on the floor. Flames licked up from the rug where one of the sconces had fallen during the scuffle, the still-lit tallow candles sending up pungent curls of smoke.

Meg was no fighter, and trying had only brought her closer to ruin. The guard pulled her up to her feet and he didn't look happy at all, the skin on his jaw and the side of his neck beginning to redden where Grace had splashed him. "Come here, trollop," he snarled. "And none of your tricks this time."

If Grace was smart, she'd be getting Cecily out of the house and as far away from it as possible.

The guard was much bigger than she was, and he could probably snap her neck as easily as she could bite into a ratafia cake. Joan of Arc couldn't help her now.

Meg would have to do it her way.

She went limp, sighing as dramatically as she could, her body slithering down, down, down until he was forced to lay her none so gently on the ground.

"Hey." He shook her roughly, and she forced her body to stay loose. "Get up!" She held her breath. "Ohhh, hell."

A shuffling meant that he was down on his knee; she didn't dare open her eyes.

"Wake up, damn girl!" He was right beside her now, and when she cracked her eyes, she saw his hand under her nose, checking her breath.

Meg sucked in a lungful, and let out the loudest, piercing, most blood-curdling scream she had ever screamed, from lungs practiced at projecting to the back of a theatre a thousand seats strong. It rang loud enough to rattle the window in its frame, or so she imagined, and the guard reared back from her, hands clapping over his ears like he'd been stung.

She rolled, her dress tangled around her legs, her hair tangled around her shoulders, her scalp sore and her hands worse. Once out of reach she scrambled to her feet and bolted, out the cell door and to freedom.

Grace and Cecily waited on the other side. As soon as Meg had cleared the door they slammed it shut, and Grace threw home the bolt that kept the door secure from the outside. The pounding of the guard's fists on the door terrified another startled squeak out of Cecily, but the bolt held firm.

"We're all right," Meg soothed, grabbing Cecily and folding her into a hug. Grace tugged gently at one of Meg's curls, and otherwise let them be. "Now to find the door."

But more booted feet thudded rapidly up the wooden stairs. There was no time to run, only a handful of doors behind them, all bolted in the same way. There was no access to outside there. And the stairs to the next level, with the balcony, were beyond the flight that led down.

They were trapped, with no way out.

Meg drew her last knife, warm from being tucked into her stays, her breathing so rapid that black spots swam before her eyes. Grace paused, slid out the sword that she had liberated from the theatre's storage. She stepped in front of Cecily, who had gone white with terror and seemed about to collapse entirely.

"Places, Meglet," Grace said softly. "It's time to fight for real."

James hit the stairs running, ears still ringing from the accidental shot he'd fired. A bone-chilling shriek of agony ripped through the air. Sarah was right behind him, her hand locked in his, so that could mean only one thing—*Cecily! Meg!*

If either of them had been hurt, or worse—he couldn't bear to consider worse. They'd be no use to the Baron dead, so they must still be alive! And where life existed, healing was possible. Anything else could be repaired, the seams restitched, the rents patched. If only they were still alive.

He didn't know what to expect when he hit the landing, his heel skidding on the gaudy blue-and-orange carpet runner, but the trio of women facing him with blades forward was not it.

"Cecily!" he shouted, and his sister turned. Meg was with her, and a handsome dark-skinned woman who had been on stage with Meg in some of her plays.

"James!" Cecily bolted toward him, hurtling into his arms. She was smudged with dirt and her tear-stained face and red-rimmed eyes showed that she'd been upset, but otherwise—

"Are you hurt, sweetheart?" He patted down her arms, held her out at arm's length to scan her critically.

"Only my head, and Miss Ceniza—oops." She giggled. "*Meg* kept me safe after she got there. She and Grace, and oh, James, you should have seen it, they were magnificent!"

Someone hammered on a door in the hallway, a man's voice cursing a blue streak.

"Sarah! You're all bloody!" Meg shrieked in dismay.

"Meg!" Sarah ran to Meg's side. "It's only wine, I promise. I'm well—as well as can be. What of you?" She seemed to know the other girl, for there was quick conversation between the three that spoke of easy familiarity. The rush of desperate relief all but drowned him.

He couldn't stay back, not even with a witness and Cecily on his arm. James closed the distance between them and cupped Meg's face in his hands. She beamed up at him, exhausted and pale, but despite that and her torn dress, the tumbling tangle of her unbound hair, she had never looked more beautiful and *alive* than in that moment.

"We knew you'd come," Meg said smugly, squeezing Sarah's hand and turning her cheek in to James's palm.

"Always," he murmured. Her lips parted softly, so lush, so nearly something he had lost forever. Uncaring for the company around them, he kissed her, his fingers sinking into her dark curls, her body melting into his with soft abandon.

"Oh *my*," Cecily squeaked, sounding both pleased and utterly scandalized together.

"Look alive." Grace said sharply. More footsteps, and two of the Baron's men burst onto the landing, swords in hand.

"Behind me," James ordered, and he advanced, sword at the ready. The one in front—the one that Sarah had kicked before—scowled darkly and sank into fighting stance, his rapier drawn and off-hand spread.

And then, something new. Smoke filtered up around them, filling James's lungs with acrid-tasting fumes. The second goon, taller, slim and brown-haired, looked down the stairs, face contorting with fear. "Fire's spreading," he said, and edged away. "Dammit, man, the fire's spreading down there. It's not worth *this.*"

"That bitch *maimed* me," his friend snarled, lunging. James parried easily, steel ringing loudly as their swords collided. "I'll take my revenge piece by bloody piece."

"You'll take your bollocks home in a kerchief, if you lay one finger on me," Sarah fired back.

"Do what you want," the taller goon said, shaking his head. "I'm getting my arse out of here." And with that he backed away, slid his sword back into his belt and headed down the stairs at a rapid pace.

"Get yourselves out of here!" James didn't dare take his eyes off his opponent long enough to look back over his shoulder. "I'll keep him busy long enough for you to escape!"

"Oh, is that right?" The guard attacked, pressed his advantage, his sword clanging off every one of James's parries, forcing him back first one step, and then another. "You'll die first, staymaker, and then the whores, one at a time, after serving me any way I order them to."

James twisted his arm, caught the guard's blade with his and pulled, flung it the same way he'd disarmed the baron downstairs. *If it works once—*

The guard didn't let go. The smoke in the air was getting thicker with every passing second, and still he had to clear their way to freedom. James ducked, stepped aside to avoid a strike, then rushed the guard and—luck on his side—forced him back against the wall, James's arm and sword against his throat while he kicked and writhed.

"I can only hold him for a minute!" he shouted. "Go!"

Grace and Cecily ran, coughing, covering their noses and mouths with their arms or—in Cecily's case, the top layer of her skirt—to keep out the smoke. The air was hot, sweat beading on James's face and on the forehead of the man he held captive. The guard spat at him, his eyes black with fury.

Meg and Sarah remained behind.

"What are you waiting for?" James shouted.

Sarah ran down the hall, throwing open the bolts on the locked rooms. Most were empty, but a guard staggered out from one, his skin red and blistering as though the fire had already gotten to him. Meg held a knife that James had never seen before, raising her arms against the guard as though she knew how to defend herself. She backed away, keeping herself between the furious man and the others.

"Now we can go!" Sarah lifted her skirts and ran toward him, and James let go of his prisoner with a grunt and a warning squeeze against his throat.

"Count to five before following, or you'll die by my hand."

Sarah grabbed James's arm. The guard dropped to one knee and wheezed for breath while his fellow cursed them all. James, Meg and Sarah, together once more, bolted toward the stairs.

The stairs held, though they creaked alarmingly. Meg clung to James's arm, Sarah forging on ahead. The fire had spread across the room, consuming books and furniture as though they were nothing but annoyances. The front door stood open, and they had only a few steps to make it out, and to safety.

A shape rose from the fire, black and flame-bitten. His clothes smoked, the sodden mess of wine on his clothes preventing them from catching.

Baron John Thomas stepped out of the flames and pointed the gun at James. "You will die, staymaker, and I will *piss* upon your grave!"

James pushed Meg toward the door, the only action he had time for. The Baron squeezed the trigger.

The revolver didn't fire.

He snarled, spun the soldered barrels and aimed at them again.

He pulled the trigger.

The pepperpot's six remaining chambers fired at once, the bullets jammed into the malfunctioning mechanism. The revolver exploded in a searing burst of white-hot flame, the powder igniting all at once from the terrible misfire.

The Baron dropped it, or it fell, for there was something badly wrong with the shape of his fingers in the firelight. He screamed, dropping to his knees and clutching his hand. James didn't stay to watch the rest.

The fresh air outside washed over him, clear and clean by comparison, and he fell to the ground, gasping for breath. A bucket brigade had formed, neighbors and locals hauling water to put out the fire before it could threaten their own homes and businesses. As for the women—

They stood in a cluster. Cecily talking earnestly with the woman she had called Grace. Grace looked over at him and nodded. She turned to leave.

"Wait!" Cecily called out, and Grace paused. Cecily ran to her and embraced her with carefree exuberance. Grace hesitated for a moment, then put her arms about the girl and hugged her in return. "Thank you," Cecily said once she stepped back, her lower lip quivering. "If it hadn't been for you, you and Meg, and I'm a stranger to you—"

"Not any longer." Grace nodded to James, her expression fading back to seriousness, her walls going back up. "*You* be more careful." She poked Meg in the arm. Meg responded by folding herself into Grace's arms. Grace's eyes flashed wide in surprise for a moment. They murmured quietly to one another for a moment, then Grace pried Meg off of her, ducked her head, replaced her cap on her head and slipped away.

"Will she not stay?" James asked. Cecily immediately wound her arms around his elbow and hung on tightly.

"Not and be seen here." Meg shook her head.

"We should be vanishing as well." Sarah unwrapped her shawl and tucked it around Cecily, covering the tears in her dress and the soot and ash on her face and hair. "There will be questions, and I don't feel like being the one to answer them."

Meg looked from one of them to the other, then at Cecily, and an awkward silence fell. Of course it would. The last time they had all been in the same space had been this afternoon (had it only been half a day? How was that possible?) when everything had turned so upside down.

"You'll both come back with us," James said firmly. "I need to get Cecily home, and I'll not let either of you wander the streets cold, hurt and exhausted. I have a cook, a bathtub and spare rooms with fine beds and soft linens. I'll brook no argument." That last was to Sarah, who had set her jaw in that way he'd learned meant she was preparing to dig in her heels. "Not this time."

"Come on," Meg sighed, tucking her hand through Sarah's arm. Sarah hesitated, but didn't pull away. "That sounds like heaven. And frankly, the way I feel right now, anything else can wait."

Chapter Nineteen

It might have struck Sarah as odd that, after knowing James for at least three years, she had never once seen his house, nor even known where it stood. The events of the past few hours had left her numb, though, the world whirling around her until details blurred and nothing at all seemed surprising anymore. To come to Chelsea, then, and a fine townhouse in the heart of a district known for musicians and artists, its taverns and dining rooms nestled in behind the parks and pleasure gardens of the south city— it was as different from either Mayfair or Charing Cross as those two locales were from each other. And she was just as out of place.

She rubbed at her arms, chill now that the excitement had passed and her blood had stopped pounding loudly in her ears. Her shawl was put to better use with Miss Glover, who needed it more than she did at the moment. Coming up the white staircase, though, instead of the servants' door, a liveried butler opening the door for them all as though they were fancy folk and not a motley collection of ragamuffins, she wanted her shawl back. Or a long cloak to hide under, lest the servants see her and recognize her for the pretender she was.

James didn't seem to care, though, waving the housekeeper down, his arm firmly around Miss Glover's shoulders. Meg dropped Sarah's arm and straightened her back. Even with her hair down and flowing, her gown ripped and stained with soot, her beauty shone out like the sun.

"Good heavens, Master James, Miss Glover, what on God's green earth have you been doing?" The housekeeper, for so she must be, bustled over to the group and tutted critically at the bedraggled sight before her. She wore no cap, her tightly curling brown hair held in place with what must be a truly astronomical number of pins, only a handful of gray streaks betraying her age. Her apron was starched and neat, her chatelaine jingling with keys amid the little silver scissors and needle cases. "Never mind, I can see for myself. You've been up to your necks in trouble, no doubt."

"At ease, Mrs. Lambert," James soothed her, never taking his arm from Cecily, who remained wide-eyed and said little. "There's no permanent damage done. Only we've had rather a trying evening. Have the guest bedroom turned out for Miss Ceniza and Miss Armand; they'll be staying with us tonight."

Sarah moved to object—that hadn't been the agreement at all!—but then closed her mouth again before she said anything. Where else *could* she go? The Horlocks' house was closed to her; she would be lucky to gain permission to retrieve her few personal belongings come the morning. Meg's lodgings were impossible as well—the

Baron's men would no doubt be sitting there and waiting for her return.

She was entirely at the mercy of whatever hospitality James might choose to extend.

"Have hot baths prepared and supper trays sent up," James instructed, and Sarah's last ounces of strength to resist vanished in a puff of selfishness. "And a pot of tea," he added, almost as an afterthought.

"A trying evening indeed, by the sounds of it," Mrs. Lambert snorted, though she looked the women over with kindly, if curious, eyes. "There's little to be done about that bodice, my dear," she said to Meg, "but we can find you something to tide you over." She gathered Cecily up under her wing like a redoubtable mother hen and bustled her up the stairs.

Cecily went without complaint, still holding Sarah's shawl close about her shoulders.

"James, we can't—" Sarah began, the tightness in her gut and the treacherous prickling behind her eyes not allowing her to go that quietly, not without some last stab at protecting her pride.

"We most certainly can," Meg interrupted. "I thought when I saw you together that you two had made up? I simply can't believe that you haven't. And Sarah, darling, I know you *must* have forgiven me for my foolishness, because you came for me." She gripped Sarah's hands tightly and would have leaned in closer, but for Sarah's pull away.

A wounded expression flitted across Meg's face. "Upstairs," Sarah murmured. "We should not be having these conversations here."

James laid his hand on Sarah's arm, and everything about his touch was as warm and tender as Meg's hands in hers. She wanted to lean in, wanted to let him hold her, wanted to take Meg into her arms and promise they would be together forever—

She did nothing of the kind. Not here.

"We should not be having these conversations at all," James said firmly. "Not until everyone has eaten and had a chance to bathe and change into clean clothes. Important things should not be decided on empty stomachs." He smiled without any happiness touching his eyes, something sad and hopeful and tentative wavering at the edges of that generous mouth.

Sarah ducked her head, and took her hands back, but some similar sort of hope nibbled at the edges of the overwhelming sense of relief. The two of them might be hopelessly optimistic fools, but they were *her* fools, and she could not hold on to the anger much longer.

Not after seeing Meg in the hallway, her hands bloodied, her gown torn. Not after charging through the streets at James's side, her pulse pounding and her blood up.

Assuming either one of them would take her back, now that she had excoriated them so cruelly. Forgiveness and friendship were one kind of emotion; trusting her with their hearts again was quite another.

"Your house, sir," she said finally, and Meg cheered. "Your decision."

James's face seemed to lighten, as though some strange weight had fallen from him, and when he chuckled, the warmth was back in his voice. "If you could only convince Cecily of that, then my life would be much simpler."

"No man in the annals of history has ever been able to kindly convince a woman to do something she has set her heart against," Meg declared airily. "I don't see that beginning now. And *we*, unless I misunderstood, have been promised hot baths."

"Upstairs, my good ladies." James gestured, and Sarah let go of any semblance of control over the scenario. Numbness and acquiescence seemed the most reasonable solutions at the moment. At least until she had the opportunity to think. "Let me show you to your chamber."

He was home, in the place where he should be most at ease, and still James could not shake the frantic buzzing in his ears. He wanted to run, to fight, to punch the air and cry for victory—none of which he could get away with in his upstairs hallway.

"'Scuse me, sir." Sally came by with hot water steaming from her urn, and he stepped quickly aside. She bobbed carefully and headed into the guest room, the barely opening door revealing nothing of what or whom lay behind.

He had promised them baths and rest; they would hardly be standing about waiting to talk to him. Not after the sort of day they'd all had.

James crossed the hall and closed his own door behind him. The fire burned in the grate, the bedclothes were neatly turned down, and still the room felt cold. Cold and empty.

The burgundy drapes hung tidy and neat, the dark wood of his bed frame and dressing table polished. Save for a bowl of garden flowers Cecily had insisted upon arranging, there was no sign at all to suggest that any woman had ever belonged there.

Could that now be changed?

When it came right down to brass tacks, if he forced them to decide, there was no doubt as to their answer. Sarah and Meg would choose each other. They had been loving friends for more than a decade—what was his recent interference compared to that?

There was one thing he could offer that would make him stand out, one thing (well, *two* if one were to be technical) that was his prerogative to provide. Perhaps, with that as an inducement, he could make himself into a more attractive option.

This wooden box wasn't sitting on his dressing table. He had to dig through his trunk to find it, carefully wrapped in linen and stowed away beneath his winter wardrobe. A flash of white caught his eye and he pulled the small mahogany case from the trunk with reverence. The linen fell away at his touch, the box gleaming dully in the light. And inside, on a bed of cream-colored velvet, his mother's jewels.

The pearls and silver were for Cecily, for whatever coming-out he could provide for her next year. They were not gentry—she would not have a Season—but she could at least answer invitations and attend dinners without looking out of place.

He would sit with her and design her gowns over the fall; that much, at least, he could do.

The pieces he had been looking for were nestled down beneath a fold. Two rose-gold rings, both slim and made for a woman's gentle hand. The posey ring—his mother's wedding band—simple and without jewel. He held it to the light, the flowered engraving around the outside catching the glow of the lamp. It shone with its own dawn-tinted fire, pink and gold, solid and pure. Inside, the promise, in letters that curled and looped as gracefully as the flowers. *For She Whom I Love.*

And then there was the other, also rose gold, but this one set with gems that blazed and gleamed when they caught the light. *L*apis, *O*pal, *V*ermeil, *E*merald. His mother's favorite hoop ring, the one she had worn nested in against the wedding band like sleeping lovers.

His mother had worn them both together on one finger.

Who would wear them for him?

Could he dare—? What would be the answer?

He set the rings back in the box, placed the box on the table so that he could see them winking at him wherever he moved. He stripped off his smoke-ruined clothes, washed in the cool water from the ceramic pitcher on the nightstand and carefully shaved his face.

When something was this important, it paid to look the part. This time, he would do *everything* right.

Glorious. Heavenly. Other words Meg couldn't think of at the moment. She closed her eyes and sank as far down in the tub as she could without sending water all over the bedroom floor. The warm water rose over her skin, soothing and releasing the tightness in her cramped muscles.

It had been hotter at first, of course, but she'd sent Sarah in to wash first with a stamp of her foot and a pointed finger.

Sarah hadn't argued at all, just *gone* without complaining, and that was worrisome. And even then she'd only taken a few minutes. It was entirely possible that she'd barely stepped in the water at all, only washed and gotten out, lost entirely in her own head.

The water stirred around Meg's hair and she swished her head back and forth to feel the way it tugged at her long, wet curls. A hot bath was a luxury unheard of these days, even one that Sarah had been in before her.

The fire crackled merrily in the hearth, sending her shadow flickering on the screen pulled around the tub for drafts. She fluttered her hands in the light impishly, making a butterfly, then a bird.

Sarah moved around in the room beyond, her skirt rustling as she changed, then the steady shush-shush as she brushed out her hair. It was a lovely set of sounds, familiar and warm, even more so because they meant Sarah was nearby. There was peace in that, security and love, an all-consuming adoration that made Meg's heart swell and heat rush through her body, hotter even than the warm water she sat in.

My passion, my love, the better part of me.

James would be so happy with Sarah by his side, and Sarah would make a marvelous Mrs. Glover. She would be mistress of this house, taking to the management like a duck to water, setting Cecily up the way a girl should be. Despite only being a year older than Meg, Sarah had always been the one to care for them both. And heaven knew wonderful, fumble-tongued James needed someone with sense to look after him.

Sarah hadn't been wrong about that. She had been cleaning up after Meg for a long time, and this evening was only the latest in a long string of disasters that Meg had almost caused and Sarah had narrowly averted. But more than that. Sarah had been born into her life. Meg had chosen it, in a way, or her mother had accidentally chosen it for her. Either way, she could have changed her fate—could have gone home—to a father who despised the world, but would at least have given her room and board. Mother Lilah would have had an easier time of it with only Sarah and her other occasional strays to look after.

But for love of Sarah, and fear of losing her forever, Meg had stayed.

And love was why Meg would have to give her up now.

James could only keep one of them. No matter how much the dear man tried to make them both happy, he would eventually have to choose. Wives didn't like having mistresses about—no one knew that better than she. God above, she would miss him! His easy smile, his laughter and his jokes, the heat of his hands and his mouth on her skin, his thick, gorgeous cock and the way it filled her up so completely. Everyone else was so inconsequential as to be entirely forgotten. Everyone except James and Sarah.

She had been so angry at him, and it all seemed so foolish now. He and Sarah had come for her, like princes of old or heroes in a play—come for her with pistol and sword, fought through swaths of enemies to reach her and carry her away. Her *and* Cecily.

James had been ready to lay his life down for them both. Because above all, more than anything, he was loyal. And because he loved his family.

There would never be another man like him. Not for her. And he would take her Sarah away as well, away to a country manor somewhere, and they would live their lives together, never thinking of the girl they'd left behind.

Meg ignored any wetness that might be on her cheeks, and she took a breath. She let it out slowly as she sank below the rippling surface of the bath, blowing it out in a tiny stream of bubbles as the warm water closed over her shut eyes.

Let her enjoy her bath first. And maybe a night in that gloriously soft bed. Then she would go and leave the only people she would ever love to be happy, together.

Meg splashed away behind the folding screen, and while it was good to have a few moments alone—almost alone—to think, Sarah's ears rang with the near-silence that filled the bedroom.

She had been furious with them both, but James had called, and she had gone. If she had truly been finished with them completely, she never would have made that choice. James had been magnificent in his righteous anger, St. George in the flesh. He hadn't hesitated but strode forward to take on all comers, and that glow of life he carried with him had transfigured into an all-encompassing flame.

And Meg—Sarah couldn't help but feel guilty about that, at least a little. She had told Meg off for causing problems, and so she had taken it upon herself to solve this one alone.

She could have been killed, so easily. She, Grace and Cecily all.

Honestly, Meg was the sort of woman who would fall into a privy and come up with a fistful of diamonds. Somehow, things always seem to work out in her favor.

Including where they had landed themselves now, in James's fine house. If it had not been for Meg's foolishness, it was probable that Sarah would never have seen this place at all.

The room itself allowed no reason for complaint. The furniture and paint were neat and cared for, of solid make if not the latest fashion. The sun would shine in the high, arching window in the morning, and she could, if she chose, step out on the small, extended balcony to greet it. Curtains hung around the bed to keep in warmth in the winters, but they would hardly need their enfolding security and heat tonight. Sarah ran her hand across the bedclothes, the fine white sheets and coverlet stitched by a delicate feminine hand.

Not Cecily, surely. Perhaps their mother, in some year long past?

She could almost envision it, if she closed her eyes. A woman, tall and with the same sweet and simple grace as Cecily, with James's laughing blue eyes. She would have sat in the window of a morning, brushing her hair out as Sarah had done, her girl binding it up into curls and dressing it with winding ribbons, flowers or pearls. Her children would have run in, James and Cecily, and she would laugh and pull her little ones up on her knee.

Or it was Sarah sitting there, her own children coming in to wish her good morning, a little girl with golden curls and a boy with hair turning to auburn as he grew.

Meg made a sound like a sigh and the water splashed.

Sarah shook her head and the vision disappeared, back to the mists of her overactive and entirely unhelpful imagination. What she needed to be doing was making a decision about her current situation, not muddying the waters with foolish dreaming.

The room was untidy, Meg's clothes scattered hither and yon. Sarah rose and, for lack of anything else to keep her hands busy, started to put it to rights. Mrs. Lambert had been right about the dress. Sarah shook it out and held it up with a critical eye. There was a rip—no, not a rip, a *cut*. Someone had *cut* at Meg, and it was only by the grace of God that there was no sign of blood on the delicate fabric.

There—her stays lay on the floor, long-bodied ones that came down to sit upon the tops of her hips. There was a split in the fabric there as well, clean edges not yet frayed. Sarah ran her fingertips along the slashed coutil, only the first layer damaged. The fabric had been too thick, the curls of cording too tightly sewn on, to allow her attacker to succeed.

Thank goodness for well-sewn garments!

The slash cut across the front of Meg's stays from seam to busk pocket. James would have to replace the entire top layer on that side in order to make them usable again. Sarah's fingers moved by habit, untying the delicate ribbon that held Meg's busk in place. The whalebone would need to come out in order for the stays to be repaired.

Except that the busk she slid out of the tightly-stitched stays pocket wasn't the old smooth piece that Meg had always worn before, the one she always said was most perfectly suited to creating an ideal figure. This one was new, carved by a skilled hand with exuberantly blooming flowers and vines.

And on the back, the initials she expected. *JG*.

Her thumb slipped across the intricately carved surface, every edge smoothed by sanding, every curve and curlicue shaped in perfect arcs.

Love had gone into this, love and care, time and dedication. James had given *her* a handful of apple blossoms.

James had kissed *Meg* in front of Cecily, and not Sarah.

He could hardly publicly declare for them both.

And now, standing in this perfectly appointed room, Meg's dress draped over her arm and her stays in Sarah's hands, Meg splashing away in the bathtub before the fire, Sarah wearing Cecily's cast-off morning gown…it was all so very familiar. Sarah's place in this arrangement was obvious, even if the other two didn't understand it yet. Sarah had the proof of where James's heart truly lay.

So be it. She had survived alone before—she could do so again. James and Meg were so much the same, both lighting up the world around them. Each of them glowed, drawing in others with their charm, wit and beauty. If anyone could overcome Meg's fear of marriage, her reluctance to bind herself to any man, it would be James— slow to anger, careful in his touch, devoted to his partners' pleasure and nothing at all like Meg's father.

Their children would be utterly devastating, and Meg, Sarah's lost little country mouse, would at last be tucked away somewhere truly safe.

Meg didn't need her anymore. James would look out for her, and Sarah would move on.

Somehow that thought, simple and obvious an answer as it was, stabbed through her heart more painfully than any blade ever could.

James paced the length of his study once, twice, then back to the fireplace again. The invitation to join him had gone up to the ladies' room more than five minutes ago, and still he was alone. He seized the poker in a fit of restlessness and stoked the fire far more than it needed. The flames spat and jumped, sending sparks flying up the flue. The rings weighted down his waistcoat pocket, heavier and heavier by the minute.

The clock ticked, irritatingly unaware of the way every noise made his heart jump.

Still, why shouldn't he be nervous? This was his future on the line, after all. And how cruel it would be, now that he knew exactly what he wanted, if he had waited and dithered too long. He had made mistakes, certainly, been proud and insensitive, not shown the depths of his feelings enough, early enough. He had been carried away by the notion of two women at once and never once given the proper thought or attention to their feelings or their needs.

That would all change now. If he could only get this chance to make everything right.

Voices echoed softly in the hall, beyond the open door. James hastily put the poker back in its stand and set his hands behind his back. His hair curled down around his collar, his jacket tossed over the back of the chair by the window, his shirtsleeves rolled up to expose his forearms. It was a casual thing, intimate without being sexual, but when the women—both Meg and Sarah, as he had asked—entered the room, he was struck with the sensation of being entirely too exposed.

Mrs. Lambert had found them clothes, organza confections in pale blue and green. Meg had left her hair loose, her black curls falling down her back like a curtain, while Sarah's auburn hair was tied back in a simple, perfect, elegant braid. They took his breath from him, leaving his lungs aching and empty. It was all he could manage to bow deeply, hands clasped behind him.

The walk from the fireplace to the door to turn the key in the lock gave him the moments he needed to collect himself. When he turned back to them, he could form words again, though they were still as beautiful, as differently glorious, as before.

Meg reclined lazily across the *chaise longue*, though her eyes tracked him wherever he moved, while Sarah curled her feet up beneath her on the end of the chesterfield and folded her hands carefully on her knee. "This all seems very dramatic," she began, and Meg stifled a nervous giggle.

"I thought," James began, "that we could use a moment to ourselves to talk." He took his own seat on the other end of the couch, placing himself equidistant between the girls, and able to look them both in the eyes. His pulse raced, his heart beating so loud that surely the ladies could hear it, see right through him, and how much he had riding on this moment. "First, I owe you both apologies. I let my pride speak for me, and I underestimated your strength, both of body and of will. I have felt my failures so keenly these past few hours. Can either of you find it in your hearts to forgive me?"

Meg ducked her head and the curls fell in front of her face. Surprisingly, Sarah was the first of them to speak. She wrapped her arms around her knees and lifted her chin in that gesture that seemed to mean so many things. "If anyone here is guilty of pride, it's me. I held my counsel to myself so long and said unforgivable things once the dam burst." Her cheeks flushed pink, but she held his eyes, then Meg's, without flinching.

"I don't know what you two are on about, but I haven't done *anything* wrong." Meg tossed her hair and sank down so that she was lying on her side, one arm cushioning her head on the raised back of the lounge.

Sarah frowned, her brow creasing, but when James looked at Meg, truly looked at her, the grief in her dark brown eyes seemed enough to drown them all entirely. "Except being unbearably silly. So I understand, and you don't need to worry about me," Meg said quietly, as though she were part of a conversation James wasn't privy to. "I'll be just fine. I can, after all, take care of myself."

"No," Sarah insisted, shaking her head. "Don't be ridiculous. You should stay here, Meg. There's no telling what the Baron's compatriots would try to do if you went home. If there's anyone out of place here—"

"It's none of us," James said firmly, cutting in before what had started as a good discussion could fully devolve into one more of those roundabout conversations where everyone spoke a lot and nothing was actually said. "That is what I wanted to say, to both of you, here and now. While we are all able and willing to set aside our anger and pride to listen."

He had their attention, and God help him if he did something to spoil the moment now! "We make a very good team, the three of us."

Meg tsked. "The three of us and Grace—"

"And Grace, yes. I am very much in her debt."

Sarah made a sound that half sounded like a snicker or an aborted chuckle. "Are you suggesting we go into business together? As what, bawdy-house arsonists?"

"I imagine the market for that would be slim," Meg scoffed.

"But the benefit in heaven would be outstanding."

Their faces were lightening, smiles growing, but James had to keep things on track or he'd end up hopelessly outvoted. Perhaps a pleasure he could one day take for granted. "Tomorrow I'll go to the law, find out the aftermath of the fire. Bring the Baron up on charges, if it turns out he did survive. He'll cause us no more trouble, one way or another—I swear it. But in the meantime, Sarah, what have you planned for yourself next?"

Meg looked confused. "What does he mean, darling?"

Sarah flushed again, the pink only having just receded from her cheeks, and looked past them both, not meeting their eyes. "To rescue you—let us say only that I turned in my notice rather precipitously."

"Your employment, oh darling—" Meg gasped, her hand coming to her mouth in a natural way.

"Let me propose a solution." James leaned forward, elbows on his knees and his heart thumping rapidly. "One that does not come from any attempt to rescue you, since I think we have all learned that neither of you need any rescuing, at all." Not quite true, but worth it to hear the laugh tumble from Sarah's perfect pink lips and Meg's dramatic sigh.

"Perhaps there are times when it is good to have help, however embarrassing it might become," Sarah offered as consolation.

James nodded, but could not be dissuaded from the speech he had been turning over in his head a dozen times since Sarah's hand had found his in the parlor at the Baron's bawdy house. He reached for her hand again, and she let him take it. "I would be forever bereft and a much poorer man, Sarah Harlow, if I were to allow you to leave my life instead of cleaving you forever to my side. You were magnificent today, are magnificent *always*, and I can think of only one other person in the world I would wish beside me just as much."

Meg sat up, her knuckles going white on the edge of the pillow, and Sarah frowned at the hand James held in his. "What are you asking?" As though she didn't know.

"A proposal," he said immediately. Meg sucked in air, and he looked her way with a hopeful smile. "Trust me, just for a moment. I only need you to trust me," he asked, not begging, but with a strength that swelled up from deep inside. Meg looked at him with skepticism written all over her delicate features, but released her death grip on the pillow.

Right. Try this again.

"Marry me, Sarah," James said. "Marry me and be my helpmeet as I will be yours. My house, my servants, my life, all these I give to you, pledging forever, if you will only say yes and be my wife."

Sarah looked at Meg. Meg shrugged helplessly and looked back at her, and a hundred conversations passed back and forth between their eyes.

Now or never.

This would be the part where he would find himself slapped soundly from both sides, if he misstepped. A silent prayer, for guidance and luck, and then he spoke again.

"Before you answer, consider this as well—Meg." He reached out with his other hand and offered it to Meg. She frowned, her brow furrowing in an echo of Sarah's, but she placed the tips of her fingers in his open palm, and she listened. "Margaret," he said deeply, fondly, putting all the love and desire in his body out toward her. "Marguerite the untamed. Tell me honestly. I know that I hurt you with my foolish assumptions, but would you ever be happy as a wife,

347

a mother of children, bound to others by the chains of the law? Even with me?"

Meg dropped her eyes, her dark lashes making sweeping shadows across her high cheekbones. "No," she said finally. "You know I could not."

"Then be free, but freely with *us*. I have the money to be your patron—that is, if Sarah will accept me, *we* have the money to be your patrons and give you fine apartments all your own. I, at least, would be yours as well, for as long as the arrangement suits us all. Sarah should make up her own mind on the matter."

It was the most unconventional arrangement he could imagine. Since when did a man ask his hopeful bride to approve his choice of mistress?

Especially since she was Sarah's before she was ever mine.

What an odd thought, for an entirely new and bizarre arrangement. And yet, for them, it seemed to fit.

"Wait, wait a moment." Sarah laughed sharply, but did not take back her hand. "Do you mean to say that you are proposing to us *both*?"

Meg's eyes snapped wide, as though she hadn't quite made the connections yet on her own. James nodded, and her ruby lips made a little O of shock that he needed to kiss away. "In a sense, yes," he said instead. "I want a family, a home and you, Sarah, as my wife. For I am in love with you, and I daresay I have been for a very long time. I was too much of a fool to understand.

"And I find myself in the odd and enviable position of also being rather madly in love...with my future wife's mistress."

"I've not said yes yet—" Sarah said warningly.

"But will you say no?" James stood, drawing them up to him by their hands, pulling them to stand side by side with each other and with him, a perfect and complementary triangle. "Let the three of us come together as surely God has intended for us."

"Just like that?" Meg asked, her tone so wistful and unsure.

James hazarded an answer. "Why not?"

A dozen gears slowly turned behind Sarah's eyes, until finally, inevitably, she smiled, slow and careful, a rose blooming in the first sunrise of the world. "Why not, indeed?"

Meg stuck out her lower lip and elbowed James. "You have to say it properly, you know. Sarah likes things done properly."

He laughed, and the glint in Sarah's eyes meant the sort of trouble he was gleefully binding himself to, forever and ever, amen. James straightened his back and sank to one knee. Sarah extended her hand, carefully, tentatively, and he took it full and held her tight.

"Sarah Harlow, will you be my wedded wife, to have and to hold, for the rest of our lives?"

And then he turned, taking Meg's hand once more in his. "Margaret—" He stumbled, suddenly unsure. Ceniza was her stage name, but what was her real one?

"Ashbrook," Meg said, and it suited her well.

"Margaret Ashbrook, will you be our mistress and ours alone, as long as we all shall love?"

"Yes!" Meg exclaimed, giddy, turning her head to look at Sarah.

She took a moment longer to answer, but not too long. Just enough to set every single one of his teeth on edge. "Yes."

The posey ring in his pocket came to his hand, and it was the right choice. He slipped that one on Sarah's hand, over the calluses from hard work, and the soft, delicate skin in the crook of her fingers. It sat there on her finger as though it had been made for her hand, and he pressed his lips to it reverently.

Then the hoop ring, sparkling and gleaming in the light. It would send rainbows dancing across the ceiling if the candle was held just so, a jeweled band for a princess among women. He slipped it onto Meg's hand, the right one which she held out to him, and it nestled between her fingers like he had between her thighs.

He stood, brushed off his knees, and when he looked up, Meg and Sarah were already entwined, their lips moving warm and freely against each other. He coughed into his hand, the giddy grin spreading wide across his face. They broke apart, turned to him, and first Meg rose up on her toes to claim his mouth, seeking, diving deep and tasting of sugar and butter. Then Sarah, tentative and careful but no less loving, her slender body fitting flush against his side as if to show that she had been formed precisely for him.

He brushed his lips against Sarah's gently and she kissed him back, one of her arms and one of his still snug about Meg's waist. Sarah's tongue danced across his lips, her round, firm breasts pressed tight against his side. He groaned softly, arousal thickening in his blood and coiling low in his stomach.

"We'll marry as soon as we're able," he said, swallowing hard and trying to catch his breath. "Meg and Cecily shall be your bridesmaids, if that pleases you all. Tomorrow, we'll be off to Bond Street to buy you a trousseau, and Meg gowns fit for a jewel of the first water."

"And you?" Sarah asked, cocking her head.

"I may consent to escort you. If I think you'll look well enough on my arms."

"Oh!" Meg ran her devilish fingers up his side, tickling him in the armpit and his waist together. "You're rotten! Sarah, help me!"

She did, the traitor, pushing him abruptly on the shoulders until he toppled backward, his knees catching on the edge of the chesterfield. He fell onto it, grabbing for Meg's hands and pulling both girls down along with him. They collapsed in a heap of muslin and petticoats, James losing himself somewhere beneath.

One pair of lips met his, then the other, hot, slick and sweet. He found Sarah's full breast and cupped it in his palm, while Meg's curls fell across his brow and she pressed kisses to his mouth. Neither woman had yet said they loved him, but that hardly mattered in the moment, for they were showing him with their lips and hands and bodies just how much he was a part of them both—

"Oh my God." Cecily's voice interrupted the moment from somewhere in the room, laced thick with shock and dismay.

All movement ceased. James pulled back his hands from the wonderful soft and warm places he'd lodged them, and sat up. Sarah and Meg popped up after him, one and then the other, frantically tugging hair and bodices back into place.

Cecily darted out from behind the long curtains, one hand over her mouth and the other wrapped around her waist. Her hair was wet and braided, her wrapper pulled close around her over her pale pink morning dress. "Oh James, what would Mother and Father say? How could you—and in the *parlor*?" As though that were the worst of it all.

And this was not the way he had intended to broach the subject, if indeed he ever had to. She was too curious for her own good. "Would the kitchen have been better?" James snapped back, nettled and ruffled, trying to catch his equilibrium again even as it kept slipping out from under him.

"Being a gentleman would be better." Cecily hovered near the windows, uncertainty written all over her face. "How does this…" She trailed off, looking back and forth from Sarah to Meg, and then once more to James. "What would Father think about any of this?" she asked, her brow furrowed as though she contemplated an exceedingly tricky math problem.

James stood, raking his hands back through his rumpled hair, to keep it out of his eyes—and give himself a moment to think. "I would hope," he said after a moment, "that he would be happy for us, for finding happiness."

Her clothing rearranged to be decent and her curls patted back into place, Meg rose from the couch and held

352

out her hands. Cecily stepped forward and put one of her hands in Meg's. Sarah shifted where she sat to watch them, her eyes shadowed.

"There are many truths about adulthood that hurt as we learn them," Meg began, gentler than James could have managed. "And one of them is that many men—not all, but many—will never be satisfied by their wives. They pay girls to satisfy their desires for more than one woman, or to give them things they imagine they could not find at home."

Was she painting him as some kind of whoremonger, after everything they'd just been through? "That's hardly fair," James began to object, but Meg quelled him with a fiery glare.

"And some," Meg continued, as sweet as could be, "fall in love with two women at the same time, and use the same methods to have both at once—lying to everyone, including themselves. What James has done is remarkable, Cecily. He has found a way to share his heart with two women at once—and still remain a truly honest man."

Cecily chewed on her bottom lip for a moment, lost in thought. He should go over to her, try to make her promise not to reveal any of this to anyone, but he stood, rooted to the floor, waiting for her reaction.

"And you don't mind?" Cecily asked, looking between Meg and Sarah, still sitting demurely on the couch. "Sharing him, I mean?"

Meg laughed softly, a merry sound that soothed all ills. "That is the beautiful thing about Sarah being my own beloved friend. I have half of her, and half of him, and together that makes one whole person for each of us."

"I don't think it works that way—" Sarah objected, but Cecily seemed to take it in stride. At least, she nodded, and wrapped her fingers tightly around Meg's.

"Only you, James," Cecily said, letting go and crossing the floor toward him, Meg following suit. "Only you could find a way to give me *two* sisters at once." She wrapped her arms about James, and nestled in under his chin.

"Er," James said, resting his chin on the top of her still-damp head. "Cecily, dearest little sister…how long were you standing there?"

"Since before. I snuck in while you were moping about in your room, because I knew you would never tell me anything on your own. This is not what I expected to learn," she confessed, letting him go. "But I am very glad that you're going to marry James." She said that to Sarah, kneeling before her on the floor in a spill of delicate skirts. "Is that Mummy's ring? How lovely!"

She was warming up to them now, and that was a very good sign, but when Cecily turned her head to look up at him, danger was written there. "Cecily," James warned, but there was no stopping the hurricane once she had begun.

Cecily's eyes narrowed at him. "I do hope Meg has a ring as well, *James*. And more than just one or two new dresses, too. She isn't getting a church wedding, but she should still have a proper trousseau."

"All is well, sweetheart," Meg moved to soothe her, but James's tolerance levels for his little sister were just about at their limit. That had nothing to do with the slow return of blood to his brain from other regions, or the curdled ache of thwarted desire. Nothing at all.

"If your curiosity has been satisfied," he prompted, "perhaps it's time to retire for the night."

"Why?" she asked impertinently. "Are you going to make more plans for this family without me?"

"Cecily, *out.*"

"Don't let him boss you."

"You're not helping, Meg."

"Sarah, darling, relax! Smile! This is a joyous moment."

James flopped down on the couch beside Sarah, pinched the bridge of his nose and groaned inwardly. "I have made a terrible mistake."

"I think you're all adorable." Cecily sat back on her heels and cupped her chin in her hands. "And I shall be the kindest, most helpful bridesmaid there has ever been. As long as I can come shopping with you tomorrow. James promised to take me for ices."

All of them together in Gunter's sounded wonderful and dangerous at the same time. "Cecily," he began warningly. "Remember that, for everyone's sake, certain things must be kept discreet. I'll not have anyone's honor threatened, or reputation damaged—"

"Don't be ridiculous," Cecily snorted. "I can keep a secret as well as anyone."

Sarah, who had been sitting and touching her new ring with gentle fingers, started to laugh. It began as a chuckle, low in her breast, and became a peal of wondrous laughter, richer, warmer than Meg's silvered bells, but just as lovely. "I think ices would be lovely," she managed after a moment, then leaned in and carefully, so tentatively, laid her head on James's shoulder.

James slipped his arm around her and drew her close. "We shall be a jolly company tomorrow, make no mistake." Meg curled against James's other side, with a quick, cautious look at Cecily. She melted into James nevertheless, and he curled his other arm snug about her slim waist.

He made eye contact with Cecily, for the first time that evening, and saw the still slightly bewildered acceptance and love in her smile. "Will this do, dear sister? Is this family enough to fill our home with laughter once more?"

She nodded, her eyes bright.

Sarah brushed her hand against her face, as though to wipe something away, but she smiled up at him when he turned to look. "This is the strangest family I think I have ever heard tell of," she said, her mouth crooking up at the corners.

"Strange, perhaps," Meg replied, "but perfect. In every possible way."

Chapter Twenty

It took another half hour at least to get Cecily packed off to her own room, with promises to stay in there for the remainder of the night.

Not that Sarah believed her, not after that performance in James's study, but at least she was giving lip service to the request.

It would do Cecily little good to go looking for them in the guest room, mind you, since the three of them ended up alone after all, this time in James's master suite. The room positively reeked of moneyed masculinity, all dark woods and somber colors, save for a splash of brilliant pinks and blues from a bowl of flowers set near the window.

James seemed to follow her gaze to the flowers, and he laughed softly. "Cecily will persist in trying to civilize me."

Meg turned from where she had been examining her new ring in the firelight. "Are you suggesting that you're not easily tamed, Mr. Glover?"

They flirted and teased, and Sarah sank down into the chair by the writing desk. The rose-gold ring with its beautifully etched flowers felt new and strange on her finger, as though if she moved her hand too fast, it would fly off and vanish. It hardly seemed real, any of it—from the moment James had come to the door and she had thrown her lot in with him, the entire night seemed to blur and run together.

Was she engaged to be married? It hardly seemed possible. Only this afternoon she had cast both her lovers out of her life, with the notion that it would be forever.

(Mother Lilah should be the one to give her away. She would be glad of a new dress, and a chance to see her "little mice" well settled at last.)

Perhaps it was all a dream, and she would wake with the sunrise, back in her attic room at the townhouse on Bruton Place.

The rough and callused hand that brushed gently along her cheek didn't feel like a dream. And when James sank down on his knees before her, he was as real and solid as the chair she sat in. His hair tumbled down over his brow again and she brushed it away from his eyes, golden-brown waves that would never be easily tamed. The waves fell like silk between her fingers, and a few made it back behind his ear. She trailed her fingers back down the strong line of his jaw, so soft and smooth that he must have only just shaved. His eyes searched her face, framed by lashes that were a little ridiculous on a man, but only added to his firm, powerful beauty.

"How are you?" he asked, not "are you well" or "do you feel all right" or any other general question that she could shrug off with a one-word lie.

"Dizzy," Sarah confessed, and Meg's hands slipped down over her shoulders from behind. Meg tightened her arms in a gentle hug around Sarah's shoulders, pressure that lifted a good hundred pounds of weight from Sarah's mind. "I find it hard to believe that any of this has just happened."

"It has," James promised, and he took her hands in his. She didn't resist, his palms so broad and strong that he could clasp both her hands in one of his, if he tried. "All of it."

Sarah tipped her head back and let Meg nuzzle the top of her head for a moment, her touch soft and so familiar. "Then you want to marry me," she said, her voice catching and trembling, despite her best efforts. A rush of heat flushed her cheeks, but neither Meg nor James showed that they had noticed.

James nodded. He caressed the backs of her hands with his thumbs, moving in tender, gentle circles that sent an odd ache growing in the core of her body. "I want to marry you. I love you, and would have you for my wife." He hesitated, seemed to be searching her face for something, then kept talking. "If you're having second thoughts, then know this. I will wait. If you say not now, we'll hold off until you're certain. If you say you're not sure, I'll court you, make love to you, dance upon your every whim and remind you how our bodies can burn together. We were made for each other, the three of us, and I won't lose you again. Not even for an afternoon."

The truth was written upon his face, in his eyes, in the curve of his lip and the heat of his hands around hers.

"No second thoughts," Sarah said. "Perhaps not even first ones." She laughed wryly at her own silliness, and he chuckled along with her. Meg nuzzled in, still standing behind the chair, her face tucked in to Sarah's neck and her arms about Sarah's shoulders. Some potent energy flowed between them, brightening when James reached out a finger and linked it easily through one of Meg's. A circle, unbroken, like the bands they now wore.

There was only one thing left to say.

"I will marry you," Sarah said again. "But not because I have no other choices. I'll marry you," and she took a breath that settled low inside her gut, "because I love you. And I want to be with you."

The world, despite her fears, did not screech to a halt, nor shatter. James brought the hand he still held to his lips, and pressed reverent kisses to her knuckles, the tips of her fingers, and then when he turned her hand over, her open palm. Her skin flushed hot where his lips pressed, all that heat gathering in the hollows of her thighs and stomach. Nothing before had ever felt so right; she could never give this feeling up again.

Meg made a soft noise against Sarah's throat.

"And you, silly goose." Sarah laughed. "Of course I do."

And when James stood and drew her up after him, pulling Sarah close against himself, she went gladly. Meg followed, moving around the chair. Sarah melded against James's body, the long, lean muscles of his thighs firm against hers, her hands moving slowly across the broad expanse of his chest. He had no cravat on, the divot of his throat visible in the open neck of his shirt. Sarah pressed her lips to it, breathed in the hint of soap and fresh water lingering on his skin.

He didn't let her linger there long. James slipped two fingers beneath her chin and tilted her face up toward his.

He crushed his lips down on hers in a passionate kiss, fierce and uncompromising. He cupped her jaw and held her in place, his other hand sliding around her waist and pulling her hips into his.

James's cock pressed against Sarah's lower belly, hard and thick enough that she could feel him through their layers of clothing. His tongue traced her bottom lip, his teeth scraping gently against it, just enough to encourage her to part her lips and allow him inside. Her breath caught, her hands pressed against his chest.

Every inch of her skin burned for him, on fire with the need to get closer, to be rid of the layers of fabric that divided them. Meg seemed to hear her thoughts, hands tugging urgently at the back of Sarah's borrowed dress.

Sarah slid her hands into James's hair, holding him in place so she could kiss him back as fervently as he had kissed her, her lips bruising under the pressure. She only let go when Meg pushed the sleeves of her gown down her arms, freeing her from the bodice's snug confines.

Meg made short work of Sarah's stay laces, trailing her hot lips down the back of Sarah's neck even as her clever, wicked hands reached around to stroke Sarah's breasts through the soft cotton.

James dropped his hands and sank to his knees in front of her. Air escaped in a rush from Sarah's lungs when he stroked his hands up her legs beneath her skirt. She couldn't see what he was doing, the delicate fabric bunching over his forearms as feather-light touches trailed around the tops of her ribbon-gartered stockings, across the sensitive skin at the backs of her knees. A giggle bubbled up from deep inside her chest.

Meg tugged Sarah's loosened shortstays down low enough to free her breasts entirely. She stroked her thumbs across Sarah's nipples and they tightened at the touch, pleasure rolling down through her body to pool in her lower belly. She gasped and James laughed, pulling her skirt up high enough to expose her naked thighs.

The heat of his mouth on her skin made her feel tight and needy everywhere, not just at that burning spot where his teeth and tongue played across her thigh. He nudged her legs apart, hands still holding her skirts up at her hips, his fingers sinking into the flesh there to hold her solidly in place.

Meg stood behind her, her bosom pushing into Sarah's half-naked back, her wicked fingers pinching and toying with Sarah's nipples, leaving then coming back wet from Meg's mouth to tease and stroke once more.

But how could she focus on that when James's mouth moved higher, leaving butterfly kisses and tender little nipping bites along the gentle swell of her belly, then down again?

He closed his mouth over her clitoris and Sarah's back arched, her legs spreading wider of their own accord. Give him room, give him access, the only things that mattered in the world were the heat and pressure on her cunny, the movement of his tongue down and back, the circles he drew with the tip and the burning fire of his mouth.

Pleasure below, Sarah's hands digging into James's hair to hold him in place so that he couldn't move, couldn't leave her until she was satisfied. Pleasure above, Meg's body twined with hers, full round breasts pressing against her skin, the tiny rushes of pleasure-pain from Meg's teeth pressing on her throat, her shoulder, the tingling length of her spine. Pleasure everywhere, Meg's fingers teasing and toying with her nipples, then her hands cupping Sarah's breasts and squeezing them tight, her thumbs and fingers moving, always moving.

James let go of one of her hips and slipped his hand between Sarah's thighs, her skirt folds falling down to cover the side of his face. He suckled and teased at the core of her pleasure, the little nub of nerves firing and flaring with every puff of breath and flick of clever tongue.

Something pressed firm at her entrance and she opened to take his two fingers in. He filled her up just like that, clever fingers delving deep, crooking and pressing in, sliding out and pressing against some glorious spot inside.

Meg was beside her now, still holding Sarah up even as her knees buckled, her mouth on Sarah's nipples to match James's mouth on her cunny.

He plunged inside her, sucked hard at her folds, pressed the flat of his tongue up and over, over again. Hands, nipples, mouths and sweat, stinging and spinning out of control—

Sarah arched and cried out, digging her fingers into James's hair. He sucked harder and Meg drew half Sarah's breast into her mouth.

Lightning struck, the world went white. Her body shook with her ecstasy, a dam inside her mind shattering to let the rush of ecstasy flood her senses. Sarah came; she came again, again, and *again*—once for each of them and once more for their love eternal.

Shaking and trembling, her knees unable to hold her, Sarah let James and Meg maneuver her towards the unrumpled bed. Her brain could barely function, coated in a thick and glorious haze, but even so she could remember enough to shed the rest of her clothes, only her stockings staying on.

James's cock had to be painful to him, so hard and erect that it pushed out against the fallfront of his trousers in a gorgeous thick ridge. Sarah sprawled on her knees on the bed, her skin hot and her face flushed, prickles of sweat stinging behind her knees. She stripped him down, popped the buttons and let his trousers fall open, his prick freed for their examination.

The hunger rippling through her body was new in its power, the freedom glorious. James groaned, ran his hand over her jaw again, scrubbing the pad of his thumb across her bottom lip. Sarah nipped at it and he shuddered, his prick jerking against the flat of his lower stomach. He paused to shrug off his shirt and waistcoat, and as he pulled them over his head, Sarah leaned in and sank her mouth down around the gleaming red tip of his erection. It was a lewd trick, an old one she had learned from girls who were hardly good society, but it was one he seemed to appreciate deeply nevertheless.

James cried out, muffled by the fabric over his head, and Meg laughed. His clothes hit the far wall when he flung them, diving onto the bed to roll atop of Sarah, his prick high and hard between her thighs.

"Minx." He laughed, even as Meg seized his face and tipped it up so she could kiss him as well.

Sprawled on her back beneath him, James's arms holding him up over her, Sarah could see everything as James and Meg kissed. Meg's high, firm breasts, the soft swell of her round hips, the way James bucked against the air as though searching for something, the nest of black curls over Meg's mound that begged to be touched.

James groaned, a sound of desperation that deepened when Sarah took his prick in her hand and stroked it, once, twice. He thrust into her hand, the head of his cock vanishing in the tight circle of her fingers, then reappearing, only stoking Sarah's hunger higher.

Meg rose up on her knees, her perfect pear-shaped body glorious in the flickering candlelight. Sarah ached, empty, and there was only one way to finish this that would leave her satisfied.

"James," she urged. "I need you inside me." She tugged at his prick and he needed no further invitation. He rose up on his knees as well, a mirror of Meg in his glorious, beautiful, perfect masculinity. He scooped Sarah's stockinged legs up over his arms, his hips pressed up between her thighs. He thrust and rocked against her, his prick sliding up between her slick folds, rubbing and pressing against her clitoris until she bucked to get closer, needed to get closer still.

Sarah reached for Meg, pulled her leg across so that Meg was straddling her shoulders. She smelled of sex, of lust and need, glistening and as needy as Sarah.

"Please," Sarah urged, and with one long, slow move, James positioned himself and pressed his prick inside.

Meg shifted forward and leaned in to against Sarah's mouth. Sarah tasted her, the musk and desire there, and Meg started to shake apart above her.

James pushed in, hard and fierce, lifting her legs higher, coming in deeper, thick and hard, filling her up, soothing that burning, desperate, empty ache inside.

Sarah suckled at Meg's clitoris, tasted her skin, ran the tip of her tongue around in circles as James had done for her. Meg cupped her own breasts and held them high, pinched her nipples and played with them, her breath coming fast in trembling gasps.

They moved together, all three, until Meg's hips trembled in Sarah's hands, until the thick growing heat in Sarah's belly could no longer be denied, until James groaned, raw and raspy, his hands trembling where he clung to Sarah's thighs, his cock pushing into her with desperate speed.

"My loves," he groaned. "My girls."

Meg cried out, grinding down against Sarah's mouth to take her pleasure, her body shaking apart.

Sarah closed her eyes, enveloped in the heady scent of lust, the sensations of her body, Meg's sex like ripe fruit upon her tongue, the building, rising swell inside that threatened, like the ocean waves, to dash her apart upon the rocks.

Someone's thumb skated over her clitoris and Sarah exploded, shaking and tight, muffling her scream of pleasure in the plump softness of Meg's glorious thigh.

James started to laugh, a warm, rich, glorious sound, and he grabbed on to Sarah's hips, pulled himself in tight one more time, so deep that she would die, filling up every empty space within her body and her soul. He held still, his muscles trembling and pulsing, and he came inside her.

They collapsed in a tumbled heap of skin and limbs and sweat, Sarah's head ending up pillowed on James's strong chest, the soft ends of the blond hairs there tickling her cheek. Meg sprawled on top of both of them, burrowing in the sticky warmth of their bodies and settling between them with a soft sigh of contentment.

Someone's hand was on Sarah's hip, someone's shoulder warm against her lips. She would have to open her eyes to figure out whose was where, and honestly, at this stage, none of that mattered.

"I love you," Meg's voice murmured soft in her ear. "And I love you," she added, followed by the sound of a kiss.

"I love you both, so much," came James's muzzy, exhausted reply. "Never go away."

"Never," Sarah promised, surrounded by warmth, the last of all pieces falling softly into place. "Never again."

And we shall all live happily ever after.

Epilogue

A pretty, good-natured spring swiftly turned to summer, and Sarah went back to the house on Bruton Place only once. Mrs. Colby had a trunk ready for her, and with James's and his man's help, all Sarah's worldly possessions were installed at the Chelsea house, in the sunlit room where she had imagined herself on that first, eventful night. Meg had her apartments. Not in Mayfair—out of reach of James's pocket, as lovely as that would have been—but on an adjoining street in Chelsea, a little suite of her own where the sun dappled across the wooden floor in late afternoon, and she could strew her laundry anywhere she pleased.

That made this glorious, sunny June afternoon the first time the newly minted Mrs. Glover had seen Lady Horlock since the night of the abduction. The countess was impeccably turned out, her hair dressed under a bonnet in the latest high fashion. A new abigail had been quickly found to take Sarah's place, obviously enough. That should have stung, but it didn't. The shopping basket over Sarah's arm and the tidy dress she wore marked her as a married woman out of service as thoroughly as the ring shining on her finger, and that was more than enough to help her hold her head high.

And then, the oddest thing—instead of cutting her as they came toward each other on the street, Lady Horlock dipped her head in greeting and *smiled*. Perhaps the dapper middle-aged gentleman at her side had something to do with it. He glanced at the countess and took his cue from her, nodding at Sarah politely.

Sarah found her voice. "Lady Horlock. It is a pleasure to see you again. You look very well." What else did one say to one's former employer? Especially when her secrets and confidences had for years been Sarah's to keep, but things had ended so poorly.

"And you, Mrs. Glover." So she had been keeping up with the news. "I would venture to say that married life suits you well." Lady Horlock glanced at the man beside her, a good ten or fifteen years her junior, if Sarah had to guess, and dressed with impeccable taste. "Lord Whitney, Mrs. Glover, only just married this spring." She didn't return the introduction, but that was all right. Lord Whitney didn't seem the sort to care very much about staymaker's wives.

"Congratulations," he offered politely.

Lady Horlock took charge of the conversation again. "The news of Master Tibbert's retirement has been a blow to the ladies of the *ton*. I was, however, gratified to hear that your husband will be continuing to serve the shop's clientele."

And with that, all concern and worry about the conversation evaporated like so much steam in the air. "He is as dedicated to his craft as ever he was, your ladyship,"

Sarah said, back on firm footing. "I think you will notice no difference at all in the craftsmanship."

"Indeed, one might even go so far as to say it has improved." Was that a little amused sort of smile playing over Lady Horlock's lips? Good heavens.

Sarah bobbed a curtsey. "I will be sure to tell him so."

"I have heard that you have a play opening at the Olympic Pavilion on Thursday next."

Now the old lady was starting to confuse her. Since when had Lady Horlock been interested in plays? "I do," Sarah answered, regardless. "My friend Miss Marguerite Ceniza is to play the lead. You may have seen her once or twice before, if you attend at the Pavilion, and of course you are familiar already with one draft of the script." The impertinence slipped out, but Lady Horlock only looked amused.

How far you've come, my girl, mouthing off to a countess on the high street.

"Indeed. I shall have to ensure a clear calendar and come see how the final version has improved."

She couldn't quite hide her surprise. "To the theatre, your ladyship?"

The smile on Lady Horlock's face turned wistful, and for a moment she looked almost soft, and young. "I used to be quite fond of it, you know. His Lordship preferred cards." And then she perked up, a glint coming back into her eye. "Now that he has removed himself to the countryside, I find that I have a freer social calendar."

And all Sarah could do was blink. Blink, understand, and then smile. "Your ladyship?"

Lady Horlock met her eyes, and the flash of something approaching understanding and sympathy was there, if only for a moment. "Indeed," was all she said. That, and "Good day to you, Mrs. Glover."

"And to you, your ladyship. Sir."

Then they were gone, moving gracefully along the busy street toward the park.

Had Lady Horlock's eyes ever sparkled so before? Perhaps once, but not in the years Sarah had known her. The smile on her face and lightness in her step made her look almost ten years younger, a match indeed for her handsome young escort.

Good for her.

And now Sarah herself had to hurry back to the shop, so that James could focus on his sewing and not on the traffic in and out, then tonight to the theatre for rehearsals of *My Mistress's Son.* If she wasn't there on time Meg was like to explode from fretting.

There were hardly enough hours in the day to get everything done, between running her own household properly, mounting a play, learning to manage the business end of the shop and keeping Cecily out of trouble. But the sun was shining down on them, the world was wide and filled with endless possibilities for adventure, and she would never have to face anything alone again.

Perhaps her next play would be about an older lady. One whose troubles didn't end when she won her "good match", but who kept her head high and her hopes of love alive regardless.

Her jaunty velvet hat perched on her pinned and curled hair, the exquisitely carved busk from James tucked securely in her stays and her new green walking gown cut with a little extra room in the front to grow with her as she needed it, Sarah Glover moved through the busy London streets, humming softly to herself as she went.

About the Author

Tess has been a fan of historical fiction since learning the Greek and Roman myths at her mother's knee. Now let loose on a computer, she's spinning her own tales of romance and passion in a slightly more modern setting. Years of obsession with the early modern era have provided the basis for her current novels, most especially with the performing arts communities of Georgian London. She has a Masters degree in History, which has proven very useful for things that would utterly dismay her professors.

Tess lives in the Canadian Maritimes with her partner of fifteen years and two cats who should have been named Writer's Block and Get Off the Keyboard, Dammit.

Learn more about Tess and her projects at her website, http://tessbowery.com, or on social media at @tessbowery on Twitter, and http://tessbowery.tumblr.com.

ALSO BY TESS BOWERY

Rite of Summer

Treading the Boards Book #1

ISBN: 978-1-7753003-0-4 (digital)

ISBN: 978-0-9866184-9-9 (print)

-

Love is a terror worse than stage fright.

Violinist Stephen Ashbrook is passionate about three things—his music, the excitement of life in London, and his lover, Evander Cade. It's too bad that Evander only loves himself. A house party at their patron's beautiful country estate seems like a chance for Stephen to remember who he is, when he's not trying to live up to someone else's harsh expectations.

Joshua Beaufort, a painter whose works are very much in demand among the right sort of people, has no expectations about this party at all. Until, that is, he finds out who else is on the guest list. Joshua swore off love long ago, but has been infatuated with Stephen since seeing his brilliant performance at Vauxhall. Now he has the chance to meet the object of his lust face to face—and more.

But changing an open relationship to a triad is a lot more complicated than it seems, and while Evander's trying to climb the social ladder, Stephen's trying to climb Joshua. When the dust settles, only two will remain standing...

That Potent Alchemy

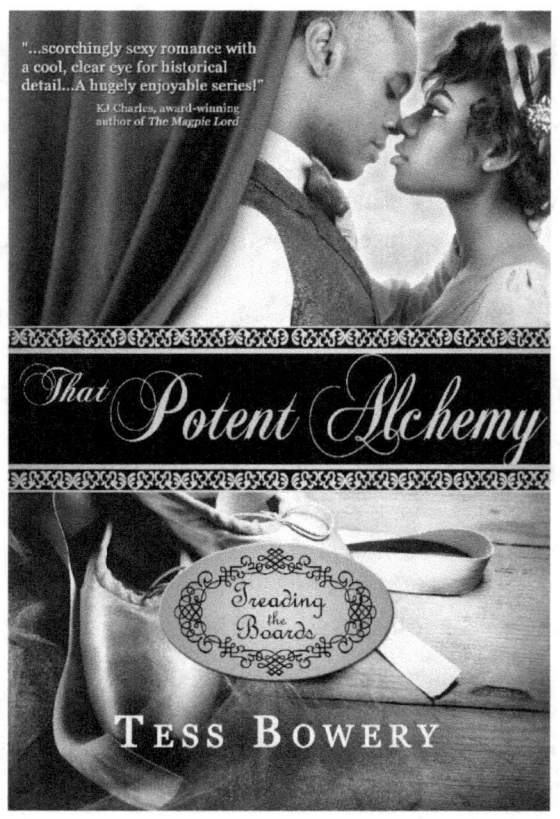

"...scorchingly sexy romance with a cool, clear eye for historical detail...A hugely enjoyable series!"
KJ Charles, award-winning author of *The Magpie Lord*

That *Potent Alchemy*

Treading the Boards

TESS BOWERY

Treading the Boards Book #3

ISBN: 978-09866184-7-5 (digital)

ISBN: 978-1-7753003-3-5 (print)

Love can be the hardest leap of faith.

Child prodigy Grace Owens left dancing behind years ago. Gossip said she cracked under pressure, but the truth was harder to explain. Four years later she's made a fresh start in London, where she doesn't have to play the perfect femme. The other actors don't ask questions about her fondness for breeches, or why she's never married, or whether this is truly what she imagined her life would be.

Isaac Caird is a stage machinist and special-effects man, a showman invisible, the hand behind the wheel that makes the world. He's seen a lot of actresses come and go on the Surrey's stage, but no-one has ever caught his eye quite like Grace. He wants her on his stage, in his workshop... and in his bed.

Grace wouldn't give a smooth-talker like Isaac the time of day under normal circumstances, except nothing about the summer of 1811 is *normal*. The Prince Regent has taken the throne, the aristocrats are restless, and the Surrey playhouse's very future could depend on the two of them pulling off the greatest spectacle London has ever seen.

But can Isaac and Grace survive the curse of the Scottish play... and each other?